NEVER LOVE A STRANGER

HAROLD ROBBINS

The searing story of a handsome, ruthless man who worked—and killed—his way to the top of the New York rackets.

King of an illicit empire, he was surrounded by criminals who wanted his fortune and his life . . . and adored by a beautiful woman who wanted his love, and made an impossible bargain to get it!

Books by Harold Robbins

The Adventurers
The Betsy
The Carpetbaggers
The Dream Merchants
Dreams Die First
Goodbye, Janette
The Inheritors
The Lonely Lady
Memories of Another Day
Never Love a Stranger
The Pirate
79 Park Avenue
Spellbinder
A Stone for Danny Fisher
Where Love Has Gone

Published by POCKET BOOKS

HAROLD ROBBINS
NEVER LOVE A STRANGER

PUBLISHED BY POCKET BOOKS NEW YORK

POCKET BOOKS, a division of Simon & Schuster, Inc.
1230 Avenue of the Americas, New York, N.Y. 10020

Copyright 1948 by Harold Robbins

Published by arrangement with Simon and Schuster

ISBN: 0-671-44596-0

First Pocket Books printing January, 1962

65   64   63   62   61

POCKET and colophon are registered trademarks
of Simon & Schuster, Inc.

Printed in the U.S.A.

Call no man foe, but never love a stranger.
Build up no plan, nor any star pursue.
Go forth with crowds; in loneliness is danger.
Thus nothing God can send,
And nothing God can do .
Shall pierce your peace, my friend.

From the poem *To The Unborn,* by Stella Benson
as published in *Twenty*

BY PERMISSION OF THE MACMILLAN COMPANY, PUBLISHERS

ACKNOWLEDGMENT

THE AUTHOR WISHES TO EXPRESS HIS GRATITUDE
TO *MR. ROBERT L. SCOTTINO,*
FOR HIS KIND WORDS AND CONSIDERATE EN-
COURAGEMENT DURING THE LONG YEARS
IT TOOK TO WRITE THIS BOOK.

What Came Before

MRS. COZZOLINA tasted the soup. It was rich and thick, tomatoey, and with just the right touch of garlic. She smacked her lips—it was good. With a sigh she turned back to the table where she had been stuffing ravioli with shredded chicken. It had been a long, hot June day but now it was beginning to grow damp. The sky outside had grown darker and she had had to turn on the light in the kitchen.

"These American girls," she was thinking as her pudgy fingers lightly shaped the dough and poked bits of chicken into them, the sweat damp on her forehead and just over her lips where the slight, dark shadow of a mustache was visible. "Planning babies so they don't have to carry them in the summer! Who ever heard of such a thing? Why in the old country," she smiled thinking of when she was young, "they just had them. You didn't plan children there." She had a right to think the American girls were foolish. She was a midwife and business had been bad all summer, and she had seven children of her own to feed since her husband had died.

Somewhere in the darkness of the house the doorbell rang. She picked her head up at the sound and cocked it to one side as she tried to think who it might be. None of her customers was due until next month, and she came to the conclusion it was a peddler. "Maria," she shouted, her voice echoing through the dim hallways, "go and see who's at the door." Her voice was harsh from many years of shouting at her children and at the peddlers on the street from whom she bought most of her foodstuffs.

There was no reply. Again the doorbell rang, this time it had a harsh, strident, demanding tone. Reluctantly she wiped her hands on her apron and went through the long narrow corridor to the front door. Through the colored panes of glass in the window she could make out a dim shape. She opened the door.

A girl was standing there, a small suitcase on the steps near her. Her face was thin and drawn but her eyes glowed with a warm, frightened luminosity, much like an animal's in the dark. She was obviously pregnant, and to Mrs. Cozzolina's experienced eye was in her last month. "Are you the midwife?" The voice was soft but somehow afraid.

"Yes, madam," said Mrs. Cozzolina. She knew a lady when she saw one. There was something about them that stood out even when they had fallen upon hard times.

"I'm sorry to bother you but I'm new in New York and I—" The girl stopped a minute as a tremor seemed to run through her body. When she spoke again an urgent quality had come into her voice. "My time has come," she said simply, "and I have no place to go."

Mrs. Cozzolina was silent for a few seconds. If she took the girl in that meant Maria would have to be turned out of her room and Maria wouldn't like that. She didn't like to sleep with her sisters. And maybe the girl didn't have any money; maybe she wasn't even married. Automatically her glance went to the girl's hand. There was a small gold ring on her finger.

"I—I have some money," the girl ventured, reading Mrs. Cozzolina's mind.

"But I have no room," Mrs. Cozzolina said.

"You must have," the girl insisted. "I haven't time to go anywhere else. And I saw your sign, 'Midwife.' "

Mrs. Cozzolina gave in. Maria would have to sleep with her sisters whether she liked it or not. "Come in," she said to the girl and took her bag.

The girl followed Mrs. Cozzolina through the dim hallway and up a flight of steps to Maria's room. It was light there and she could look out and see a row of three-story brownstone tenements and a boy cutting pigeons from his flock with a long pole from a near-by roof.

"Take off your jacket," Mrs. Cozzolina said, "and become

comfortable." She helped the girl undress and lie down on the bed. "How long ago did the pains start to come?" she asked.

"About an hour ago," the girl said. "I knew I couldn't go any further. I had to stop."

Mrs. Cozzolina examined her. The girl felt a little nervous. This wasn't how she had planned to have her baby. It was supposed to be in a hospital with George somewhere near by, somehow always hovering in the background to reassure her that things would turn out all right; or home where you could sense the presence of people who loved you and were near you, where you could draw courage from them. This was so different. She was a little afraid.

Mrs. Cozzolina straightened up. The girl was small—she was built small; she would have a hard time. The passageway was too narrow for the baby to come down easily. Anyway, she had about six or seven hours to go; maybe she would dilate more than you could expect. That was always a wonderful thing to see: how a girl turned into a woman capable of bringing forth a child under your eyes. But this looked as if it would be difficult. Mrs. Cozzolina had a feeling about it, but nothing of what she thought showed in her face. "You have some time to wait." She smiled at the girl. "But don't worry, it will be all right. I know; I have seven myself."

The girl smiled back tremulously. "Thank you, thank you very much."

"Now you try to get some sleep," Mrs. Cozzolina said, moving toward the door. "I'll come up in a few hours and see how you are feeling. A little sleep before is always a good thing." She went out and down the stairs. It wasn't until she had almost finished cooking supper that she remembered she hadn't asked the girl's name. "Well," she thought, "I'll do it when I go back upstairs," and turned to finish her cooking.

The girl had shut her eyes and had tried to sleep, but she wasn't sleeping. Thoughts kept trailing through her mind slowly, like distant scenes through a train window—home and George. Those were the two important things her mind always came back to: home and George. "I wonder what they think of me now? And George, where did he go?" She was supposed to meet him that day. It was a long time ago.

It had been raining and she had left the apartment to meet him on the corner near the restaurant. The wind had been blowing and she was chilled and had waited two hours before she went home again. She had called his office in the morning and they told her he left last night at his regular time but he hadn't come in as yet. And he disappeared. She hadn't heard from him since, hadn't seen him, and she couldn't understand it. This wasn't like him. He wasn't that kind of a man. Something terrible must have happened to him.

She looked out the window and wondered what time it was. It had become dark, and occasionally she heard thunder rolling in the distance and could see flashes of lightning, but it hadn't started to rain. The air hung heavy and oppressive around her, and she could hear the clink of dishes and subdued voices coming up from the kitchen, and smell the thick, heavy odor of cooking that came in through the partly open window, for the kitchen was directly below the room she was in.

When the children began to come in for supper, Mrs. Cozzolina had shushed them, telling them to be quiet for there was someone upstairs. Maria had made a fuss over her room but by now she had subsided because her mother promised her something when this case was over. They finished eating and Mrs. Cozzolina looked up at the clock on the icebox. It was eight o'clock. She jumped to her feet. The poor thing had been lying alone upstairs for almost four hours and they hadn't heard a cry from her. The girl had courage, Mrs. Cozzolina thought, thinking of the women whose giving birth was three quarters vocal and one quarter effort on their part.

Telling the girls to do the dishes, she went upstairs to the girl's room. "How you feeling?" she asked the girl.

"All right," answered the girl quietly, "I guess."

"How often are the pains coming?" asked Mrs. Cozzolina, bending forward to examine her again.

"It seems like about every half-hour," said the girl.

"That's good," said Mrs. Cozzolina as she straightened up. But it wasn't—there was no dilation at all. She went downstairs and ordered the girls to keep hot water and clean towels ready.

It was near midnight when the storm broke loose over the city. It was near midnight that the baby started to come. The girl just lay there quietly, her mouth grimly shut, holding the towel tied around the bedpost and writhing in pain. Her face was white and her eyes were wide, black pools of fear.

It was near two o'clock in the morning when Mrs. Cozzolina

sent her oldest son to get Doctor Buonaventa from the corner. And on the way back, she added, it wouldn't hurt to stop by the parish house and get a priest.

She watched the doctor cut the girl open and take the blue, squirming child from her belly. She slapped the life into it and heard his angry protest at leaving his warm and comfortable shelter. She watched the doctor work frantically to save the girl's life. And she knew he had lost when he motioned for the priest to take over. And as the priest stood over the girl she knelt by the side of the bed and prayed.

Because the girl was so young and so brave.

Because she had lost her own husband and knew that this girl too had lost.

The girl turned to her and smiled a little. There was a question in her eyes. Mrs. Cozzolina held the crying baby to her and put it down beside her. The girl looked down at it and rested her head against his little head and began to close her eyes.

Then Mrs. Cozzolina remembered she hadn't asked the girl's name. She leaned toward the girl. "Your name?" she asked, her voice filled with fear of having the child go through life without a name.

Slowly the girl opened her eyes. She looked as if she had come back a long way "Frances Cain," her voice barely carried to Mrs. Cozzolina's straining ear. She shut her eyes, and then suddenly they opened and were blank. Her jaw hung loosely toward the pillow.

Mrs. Cozzolina took the child and stood up. She watched the doctor cover the girl with the sheet. The doctor took out a slip of paper from his bag. He said in Italian: "We'll fill out the birth certificate first, eh?"

Mrs. Cozzolina nodded. First, the living.

"What's his name?"

"Francis Kane," answered Mrs. Cozzolina. It was only right —a name he could always be proud of, a name he could carry. His life would be hard enough; let him have this, which was his mother's.

PART ONE

Chapter One

ACROSS the street, high in the steeple of St. Therese, the bells were ringing for the eight-o'clock Mass. The kids were all lined up waiting to go to their classes and the sisters had just come into the yard. A second before, all had been confusion as we milled around, playing games, calling to one another, but now all was quiet. We formed double rows and marched into the school and up the winding staircase to our classrooms. We seated ourselves with a rustle of books from the boys' side of the room and a rustle of starched middy blouses and skirts from the girls' side of the room.

"We will begin our day with a prayer, children," Sister Anne said. We folded our hands on the desk and bent our heads.

I took the opportunity to shoot a spitball at Jerry Cowan. It hit him on the back of the neck and stuck there. It looked so funny I almost began to laugh in the middle of the prayer, but I stopped myself in time. When the prayer was over Jerry looked around to see who did it but I pretended to be occupied with my books.

Sister Anne spoke to me: "Francis."

I stood up guiltily. For a second I thought she had seen me shoot the spitball at Jerry, but no, all she wanted me to do was write the day and date on the blackboard. I went to the front of the room and taking a large piece of chalk from the box wrote in big letters on the board: "Friday, June 5th, 1925."

I stood there and looked at the teacher. "That's all, Francis. You may sit down," she said. I returned to my seat.

The morning passed by lazily. The air was warm and sultry and school would be out in a few weeks and I wasn't interested in school anyhow. I was thirteen and big for my age, and as soon as school was over Jimmy Keough would let me run his errands and pick up his bets for him from the bookies that worked in the near-by garages—the half-dollar and quarter bets he didn't have the time to bother with himself. And I would make a pile of dough—maybe even ten bucks a week. And I didn't give a damn for school.

At lunch time, while the other kids ran home for lunch, I would go over to the dormitory building in the back of the school, and we orphans would eat in the dining room there. For lunch we had a glass of milk and a sandwich and a cupcake. We probably ate better than most of the kids in the neighborhood who went home. Then back to school we would go for the afternoon. In the afternoon I felt like going on the hook. Jeeze, it was hot! I could go swimming off the docks down at Fifty-fourth Street and the Hudson. But I remembered what had happened the last time I had gone on the hook.

I think I set the world's record for hookey playing. I played hookey for six straight weeks in a row. And if you think that's something, remember, I lived in the school and returned there to sleep every night. I used to swipe the letters that would be sent from the sisters to Brother Bernhard, who was in charge of our dormitory, complaining about my absence. I would forge replies to them, saying that I was sick and signing them "Bernhard." This went on till one of the sisters came to visit me and they found out. I got in that night after a strenuous day in the movies. I saw four pictures. Brother Bernhard and Sister Anne were waiting for me in the hall.

"There he is, the rascal!" Brother Bernhard cried, "I'll teach him, the sick he is!" He came toward me. "And what have you been doing wi' yoursel'? Where ha'e ye been bummin'?" As he grew excited the Welsh accent in his speech, which ordinarily made it soft and beautiful, would come out until you could hardly understand a word he was saying.

"I was workin'," I said.

"Workin' ye were," he said. " 'Tis lyin' ye are." He hit me in the face. I put my hand to my cheek.

Sister Anne looked at me. "Francis, Francis, how could you

do it?" she said softly, almost sorrowfully. "You know I had the most hopes of you."

I didn't answer her. Brother Bernhard slapped me again. "Answer the taycher."

Angrily I faced them and the words tumbled from my mouth.

"I'm sick of it—sick of the school, sick of the orphanage. I'm nothing but a prisoner here. People in jail have as much freedom as me. And I didn't do nothin' to deserve it—nothin' to be put in jail for—nothin' to be locked away at night for. It says in the Bible the truth shall make you free. You teach to love the Lord because he has given us so much. You start my day with prayers of thanks—thanks for being born into a prison without freedom." I was half crying. My breath came fast.

There were tears in the corners of Sister Anne's eyes, and even Brother Bernhard was silent. Sister Anne came over to me and put her arms around me and drew me close to her. "Poor, poor Francis, can't you see we're trying to help you?" She kept talking quietly. "What you did was wrong—very wrong." I stirred in her arms. I tried to bring my hands up and wipe my eyes, but they became tangled in her gown and somehow came up against her breasts. I kept my hands there, holding my breath and innocently opening my fingers. Her back was to Brother Bernhard and he couldn't see what I was doing. She was growing confused. I looked up innocently into her face. "You must promise never to do that again," she said.

I wondered what she meant—playing hookey or—? "I promise," I said.

She turned to Brother Bernhard. Her face was white and there were beads of sweat standing across her forehead. "He has been punished enough, Brother. He will be good from now on. He has promised. I will go now and pray for the good of his soul." She turned from Brother Bernhard and walked toward the door.

I turned to Brother Bernhard. For a moment he looked at me. "Come and get your supper," he said, and led the way into the dining room.

I was thirteen and very large for my age and very wise in the way of the streets. And I wouldn't play hookey this afternoon, no matter how good the swimming would be, for I was going to be good and go back to class and plague my teacher Sister Anne. Because she looked at me, I knew that she thought of the hallway and of the way I had felt her breasts and of the way I had found out that sisters were women. And I was thirteen.

The lines hadn't formed yet when I reached the schoolyard. Near the gate a ball game was going on and everyone was hollering. I got interested in the game and the next thing I knew I was on my back on the sidewalk. Jerry Cowan and another boy had one-a-catted me. I looked up at Jerry; he was laughing.

"What's so goddam funny?" I almost snarled.

"You, ya dope! That's for the spitball. Thought I didn't know." He laughed.

I got to my feet. "O.K." I said. "Even Steven."

Together we sat at the edge of the curb and watched the game till school started, Jerry Cowan and I—the son of the Mayor of New York, and a bastard from the orphanage of St. Therese, who by the grace of God attended the same parochial school and were pretty close friends.

Chapter Two

I HAD lived at the orphanage ever since I could remember. It wasn't as bad a life as most people seem to think it. I was well fed, properly clothed and carefully schooled. If I hadn't received my share of family love and interest I wasn't particularly concerned about it. I had been endowed with, among other things, a certain amount of self-sufficiency and independence that others do not generally acquire until much older.

I had always worked at one job or another and very often had loaned nickels and dimes to other children in school who were supposed to be more fortunate than I. I knew the days the different fellows would get their allowance, and the devil help them if they didn't pay me back! About two weeks earlier I had loaned Peter Sanpero twenty cents. The week after that he had ducked out before I could catch him and when I did see him later he was broke, but this week I meant to get my dough.

After school that afternoon I stopped him in the yard. He was walking with a couple of his pals.

"Hey, Pete," I said, "how's about my twenty cents?"

Peter fancied himself a tough guy. He knew the answers. He was a little shorter than I but much broader and heavier. "What about it?" he asked.

"I want it," I said. "I loaned you the dough. I didn't give it to ya."

"Screw you and your twenty cents too!" he said in a nasal, singsong voice. And then he turned to his pals. "That's the trouble with those bastards from the orphanage. We pay tuition and donate to the school for their care, and they act as if they were the owners of the place. You'll get it when I'm damn good and ready to give it to yuh."

I got sore. I didn't mind being called a bastard. I'd been called it often enough. It didn't bother me. I wasn't like the McCrary kid Brother Bernhard had told to stick a "Junior" after his name so people would know not to call him bastard. Besides, I had heard Brother Bernhard often say: "You children are the luckiest. We're all God's children. But you are most like our Lord because you have only our Lord for parents." No, being called bastard didn't bother me, but no one was going to welch on me and get away with it.

I threw myself at him. He stepped to one side and clouted me on the jaw. Down I went. "You wop louse!" I said. He threw himself on top of me, his fist hitting my face. I could feel my nose bleed. I drew my leg up and kicked him in the crotch. His face got white and he began to roll off me. I worked one hand free and punched him in the neck just under the chin. He fell sideways off me and lay face down on the sidewalk, his knees drawn up under his belly, one hand clutching his crotch, the other holding his side. He was moaning but only squeaks came from his throat.

I got to my feet and bent over him. My nose dripped blood onto his clothes. I reached into his pocket and took out a handful of small change. Carefully I counted out twenty cents. I showed it to his friends. "All I want is my twenty cents, see?" I said, "and none of you try nothin' or you'll get what he did."

They watched me walk away, wiping my nose on my arm, and then they bent over their friend.

I walked into Jimmy Keough's poolroom. Jimmy Keough

was sitting behind the cigar stand, his green shade over his eyes. "What happened to you, kid?" he laughed.

"Nothin' much, Mr. Keough," I said proudly. "Some guy thought he could welch on me. But he didn't."

"That's a good boy, Frankie," Mr. Keough said. "Never let a guy welch. The minute you do you're licked. Now go in the back and wash up and then sweep out the place." I could hear him say to one of the men there as I walked away: "That kid'll be all right someday. He's only thirteen, but he kin figure out my pay-offs on parlays and 'if' bets better than I kin myself."

The washroom smelled of stale tobacco smoke and urine. I climbed up on the bowl and opened the window near the ceiling. I washed my hands and face and dried them on the tail of my shirt. Then I went into the poolroom to start my afternoon's work.

My afternoons at Keough's were the high spot of my day. I would start by sweeping out the place. There were eight pool tables in the place and I would sweep under each and down the length of the store. Then I would brush off the tables very softly so's not to spoil the felt, and after that I would wipe off the wood on the tables. My next job would be to ice down the cold soda and beer. This was during prohibition and the beer was kept downstairs in the cellar. Whenever someone wanted a beer or a shot of whisky he would ask Jimmy Keough, and if Jimmy Keough was busy he would send me downstairs after it. Sometimes he would keep a couple of bottles under the counter.

About four o'clock the phone would start ringing and the race results would start coming in. Then I would mark them on a blackboard at the back of the store in a kind of corner where no one could see it unless he walked back there. I would rack the balls and run errands for the men there. Sometimes I would go across the street and get them sandwiches. I kept my shine box there and if any of them wanted a shine I would give it to him.

I used to get three bucks a week for this and whatever else I could pick up there. The job was good for an average of six to eight dollars a week. When school closed Jimmy was going to send me out to the garages to pick up the small bets. He said I'd make ten to fifteen bucks a week at it. At six thirty Mr. Keough would give me all his slips of paper to figure up. The day's bets were on them and I used to figure them for him. At seven o'clock I would leave and run back to the orphanage for supper. After supper I would come out for a couple hours, but Mr. Keough would never let me hang around the place at night. I don't know why.

Peter Sanpero didn't come to school the next day, but his mother did. She stood there in the classroom and glowered at me as she spoke to Sister Anne. Sister Anne sent her to the Sister Superior. A little while later a girl came with a message for Sister Anne.

"Mary Peters will read the lesson while I'm out," Sister Anne said. "Francis, come with me."

I followed her down the hall to the Sister Superior's office. We went in. Brother Bernhard, the Sister Superior, and Mrs. Sanpero were there. Mrs. Sanpero was talking. "Unless you can control such little ruffians or send them where they belong to be . . ." She stopped when she saw me come into the room.

The Sister Superior spoke. "Come here, Francis."

I went over to her.

"What is this I hear? You've been fighting with Peter and hurt him severely. Why?" she asked in a slow, kindly manner.

"He owed me twenty cents and wouldn't pay me," I said, "and he called me bastard." I knew that would gain their sympathy.

"Francis, you'll have to learn to control your temper. Names will never hurt you and Jesus commands you to turn the other cheek. I want you to apologize to Mrs. Sanpero and tell her you're sorry."

An apology would cost me nothing so I apologized to her. I went over in front of her and said: "I'm sorry, Mrs. Sanpero. I didn't mean to fight with Peter." She didn't answer.

I went back to the Sister Superior. "And now, Francis, as punishment for fighting, I've told Brother Bernhard to keep you on the grounds after school for the next two weeks," she said.

"Two weeks," I said. "You can't do that—you can't."

"Faith!" boomed Brother Bernhard, "and why can't we?"

"Because," I said, "someone else will get my job at Jimmy Keough's."

"Ye've a job now?" he said, nodding his head. "And pray tell me what it is ye do there?"

"I sweep and clean and run the errands," I replied.

"Oh, ye sweep and clean, do ye? I'll gi'e ye enough sweepin' and cleanin' tae keep ye," he said.

"You may go back to class now, Francis," the Sister Superior said.

"Come along, Francis," said Sister Anne. Silently I followed her out into the hall. On the stairway down to the classroom she stopped and turned toward me and took my hand. She was two steps below me and her face was even with mine.

"Don't feel blue, Francis," she said, her eyes looking into mine. "Everything will be all right."

Before I knew what I was doing I kissed her hand. "I love you," I said. "You're the only one that's fair, that understands. I love you."

She held my hand tightly and leaned toward me, her eyes swimming in tears. "You poor kid," she said and kissed my lips. In that second she knew I wasn't a child—that I had left my childhood far behind me. She straightened up with a gasp. Our eyes locked just for a moment, and then she turned away, head bowed, and silently we continued back to the classroom.

Chapter Three

THE problem of avoiding Brother Bernhard was a simple one and after the first day or two worked like a charm. I would simply report to him in the dorm and then skin out the window and down the pole and be on my way. In the evening I would return in the same manner I left, and no one was the wiser.

It was on one of those days I met Silk Fennelli.

Silk Fennelli was the big man in our neighborhood. He ran everything: booze, gambling and the pay-off rackets. He was the most respected and feared man in that section. I use to see him once in a while when he stopped by at Keough's on business. He always had his boys with him. He was tough, hard and smart. He wasn't afraid of anything or anybody. He was my hero.

Sometimes when I was through at Keough's early, I would take my shine box and go out for a while and pick up some extra change. This afternoon I walked into the speak at the corner of Broadway and Sixty-fifth. The best dough was in the speaks.

I went from one customer at the bar to the other. "Shine, mister?" I would ask. "Shine?"

The fat barkeep, beads of sweat showing on his bald head, swore at me. "G'wan! Get to hell out of here! How many times do I have to tell you kids not to bother the customers in here? Now get out before I kick you in the can!"

I didn't answer but turned and started back toward the door. As I walked toward it some wise guy at the bar stuck his foot out and I fell over it. Down I went on my hands and knees, the shine box falling from my shoulder. The bottles of liquid paste smashed on the tile floor and ran over it in an odd mixture of black and brown. I was bewildered for a minute and sat there, haunches on knees, as the paste ran in all directions over the clean tile.

Suddenly I was yanked to my feet by a fat hamlike hand that grabbed me by the neck. It was the barkeep. He was raging. "Come on. You're on your way out before I . . ." He was so mad he stuttered as he dragged me toward the door.

Almost at the door I snapped out of my daze. I tore myself loose from his grasp. "Gimme my shine box," I shouted, "I want my shine box."

"Go on! Get out! It'll teach you not to come in here anymore. Beat it!"

"I won't go wit'out my shine box," I shouted. I dodged around him, ran back into the saloon, and started stuffing the brushes, rags, and cans back into the box.

The barkeep caught me just as I started to get up. He slapped me on the side of the head. My ears rang. "I'll teach you little bastards to stay out of here," he snarled. He hit me again and grabbed me by the neck so I couldn't move. I squirmed trying to escape his grip but he held too tight. I tried to kick him but he had too good a grip on me.

"Let him go, Tony, I want a shine," said a quiet, well-modulated voice from one of the booths against the sidewall.

The barkeep and I both turned around. The barkeep still held one hand in the air as if it were stuck there, and the other hand still held onto me. I don't know which of us was the more surprised. I saw a slim good-looking man of about thirty-five or forty sitting in one of the booths with one hand lying half clenched on the table, the other toying with a pocketknife attached to a chain running through his vest. He wore a dark-gray suit, a well-shaped black hat, and shiny black shoes. His gray eyes were half closed and a thin mustache showed over his well-shaped lips. White, gleaming teeth shining out of darkly aquiline features completed the picture. It was Silk Fennelli. He watched us steadily.

The barkeep cleared his throat. "All right, Mr. Fennelli." He let me go and went behind the bar.

I wiped my face on my sleeve and walked over to the booth. I dragged the box along with me. There were two other people in the booth with him: a young, well-dressed man and a good-looking dame.

"I can't give you a shine, mister," I said.

"Why?" Fenelli asked.

"I spilled the black polish all on the floor," I replied.

He reached into his pocket. He took out a wallet, removed a five-dollar bill from it, and held it out toward me. "Go get some," he said.

I looked at it and then at Fennelli and without saying a word started toward the door. A porter had started to mop the floor where the polish had spilled. As I went out I heard the other guy say: "Fifty will get you a hundred he won't be back, Silk."

Silk Fennelli laughed. "You're on."

"I don't think he ever saw that much money in his whole life," the dame said.

"You're probably right at that," said Silk. "I didn't either when I was his age."

I didn't hear what they said to that because I was out the door by that time. When I got back they were eating. I placed the change on the table and said: "I didn't mean to keep ya waiting, but the store man didn't have change of a fiver and I had to run all over the block to get it."

I knelt down on the floor and began to shine his shoes.

The other man took out his wallet and peeled off some dough and gave it to Fennelli. Silk put it in his pocket without counting it. "This ought to teach you, you can't beat the expert."

I was through with one shoe and I tapped his foot. He put the other foot on the box. "What's your name, son?" he asked.

"Francis Kane," I said. "But you call me Frankie. All my friends call me Frankie."

"Oh, so I'm your friend, am I? Better be careful, son; friendship is not a thing to so lightly bestow. Don't be careless with it," he said.

"I dunno what you're talkin' about," I said, growing confused. "You're O.K. with me." I finished the shine and got up.

The other man and woman stood up. "Well, we have to be going, Silk. See you later."

Silk got to his feet. "So long," he said to them.

When they had left I asked him: "Did you collect, Mr. Fennelli?"

"What do you mean?"

"I mean the bet. I heard it. Did he pay off?"

Silk Fennelli laughed. "You heard it."

"Yeah," I said, "I'm no sap. I know what the score is."

Fennelli laughed again. "Sit down," he said, "and have a sandwich. Where do you come from?"

"St. Therese Orphanage," I said.

"Okay, so you know the score," he said to me as if I were an equal. "You look familiar to me. Where'd I see you before? At one of the playshops?"

He referred to the stores he had converted into little playgrounds in our section. Everybody said it was a great thing he was doing for the children of the neighborhood, keeping them off the streets. I heard Keough say it was more than that; it was Fennelli's way to educate his customers. In them were all kinds of games that kids played for free—games of skill and chance that outside cost from a nickel to a quarter to play. After the kids were a certain age they were not allowed in the playshops and would go elsewhere to play the games and pay for them. Oh yes, Fennelli was a big shot, he even sent his customers to school. But as most people would say, someone has to be in that business and he really deserves the breaks for he's a regular guy.

"Nope," I answered. "I work over at Jimmy Keough's."

The waiter came up at a signal from Fennelli. I ordered a roast-beef sandwich and a glass of beer.

"You're too young to be drinking beer," Fennelli said. He changed the order to cream soda.

He watched me eat. I ate quickly and in a few minutes I was through. Then I got up. "Thanks, Mr. Fennelli."

He smiled at me. "It's O. K., kid, I shined shoes once, same as you." He reached in his pocket and came out with a few bills folded over in his hand. "Here," he said, "take this and beat it."

"Yes, sir," I said, and when I saw it was five bills, "Thanks again." These guys liked you to voice your thanks. It made them feel good, it didn't cost you anything, and I knew this guy was worth the effort of being nice to. So, just for luck I thanked him once more and walked out of the saloon.

Ray Callahan was standing on the corner, his shine box at his feet. I walked up to him. Ray was a nice kid. His old man was a rummy; they were on home relief. Ray used to turn his dough over to the old lady, who would spend it on the bottle as often as the old man.

"Hi, Frankie," he called.

"Hi," I replied. "How ya doin'?"

"Not too good," he muttered. "Only forty cents all afternoon."

I flashed my five bucks at him. His eyes bugged out. "Jeeze!" he gasped, and then said in a low whisper: "Where'd ya clip it?"

I laughed. "Ya gotta know the right people." Then I told him the whole thing.

"Boy," he said, "you're lucky!"

We walked down the street together. It began to get dark. I could see the occasional window lights flicker on.

"How about comin' upstairs with me?" he asked. "If you got nothing else to do."

I knew he wanted me to go along so's he wouldn't get hit for not getting many shines. "O.K."

We heard his father and mother shouting and hollering at each other as soon as we got into the hallway.

"Christ!" he said, turning to me, "they never stop. I guess I'm gonna get it."

I didn't answer and we started up the stairs. At the first landing a man came out of a doorway and, brushing past us, hurried down the stairs. He left the door a little open behind him, and a woman's voice called out through the door: "That you, Ray?"

Ray stopped. "Yeah." He turned to me, "That's Mary Cassidy—I run to the store for her."

She came to the door. "Will you run down to the delicatessen and get me a few bottles of beer?"

"Sure, Mary," Ray said. He put his shine box on the floor

and, taking some change from her outstretched hand and telling me to wait here for him, he ran off downstairs.

Miss Cassidy said to me: "You don't have to wait in the hall. Bring the boxes in here and wait."

Silently I picked up the boxes and took them into the room. She shut the door. "You can sit down here till Ray gets back." She indicated a chair.

I sat. She went into the next room and then came back with a can like an enema can, which she filled with water at the sink and then went back into the other room. A few minutes later she came out.

"He's not back yet?" she asked.

"No, ma'am," I said. This time I got a good look at her. She didn't look bad standing there, kinda pretty, her face and mouth painted. She had light blond hair slightly frizzed. I watched her so intently she kinda flushed. There were small beads of sweat gathered on her forehead. She had dark bluish-green eyes and was kinda tall. I wondered if Ray knew she was a whore. She'd make a good lay, I thought. I wondered how to ask her if she would—for me. I had never. But I had five bucks in cash in my pocket and that made me feel brave.

"I got a couple a bucks," I said to her.

"So what!" She eyed me curiously. There seemed to be a faint brogue in her voice.

I didn't know just what to say then but I looked her straight in the eyes. We stood there a few seconds without a sound. Then she said: "You're kind of young, ain't you?"

"I'm fifteen," I said. It was getting easier to lie all the time. Besides, I almost had convinced myself I was fifteen.

"Did you ever before?" she asked. Her breasts looked awful big and juicy to me.

"Sure," I said, "lots of times!" I was getting nervous.

"O.K.," she said, "come on." She led the way into the bedroom. I followed her. At the edge of the bed she turned around and faced me. "Give me the money."

I took two dollars out of my pocket and gave it to her. My hand was trembling. She took the money and put it under the pillow. Then she slipped her dress off over her head and lay down on the bed. "Come on," she said.

I opened my pants and let them down. My knees were shaking. I got into the bed and lay down beside her. I tried but it wouldn't work—I was too scared, too nervous.

She was getting impatient. "Hurry up. I ain't got all day. Ray might be back any minute."

No use—I was too jumpy. It just wouldn't work. She tried to help me but it wouldn't work. Finally she got out of bed. I lay there for a minute watching her. When her back was turned I stuck my hands under the pillow and took my two bucks; I wasn't going to pay for nothing. She didn't see me. I stuck the money in my shirt pocket.

A few seconds later she came back to the edge of the bed and threw the towel at me without saying a word. She slipped on her dress.

I got out of bed and pulled on my pants while she watched me. Together we walked into the front room.

She laughed at me. "Better come back when you grow up, sonny. I always say: 'You can't set a boy to do a man's work.'"

I looked at her. I could feel the blood run out of my face, leaving it white like when I was mad. I felt like hitting her with my shine box. She must have sensed it because her eyes kinda widened and she took a step back. I could feel something tying my stomach into knots. I glared at her.

"You don't have to get—" she started to say when the door opened.

It was Ray. He held a bag in his hand. "I got the beer, Mary," he said.

I looked once more at her. She couldn't take her eyes off me. I hoisted my shine box and went out into the hall.

I heard Ray ask her something and I heard her laugh. Then they came to the door. At the door she gave Ray a dime for running the errand. She started to close the door. Then, as if she forgot something, she said to Ray: "Here's a dime for your friend for waiting for you," and she tossed it at me and shut the door.

I caught the dime and flung it back at the closed door. "Yuh cheap, goddam whore!" I shouted, and without looking at Ray, ran down the steps and out of the house.

Chapter Four

FIFTEEN days more and school would be over. I couldn't wait for it to come so's I could go to work for Keough and make some real dough.

I left the school with Jerry that afternoon. He seemed to be surprised when I walked out the gate with him.

"I thought you were confined to school, Frankie," he said.

"Yesterday was the last day," I answered.

"Doing anything special this afternoon?" he asked me.

"Why?"

"Nuthin'," he said, "I was just curious."

We walked along for a few minutes without saying a word. Then Jerry said: "Frankie, how would you like to come out to the country with me this summer?"

"Quit your kiddin'," I said.

"I'm not kidding. I mean it." His blue eyes were earnest. "I asked Papa, and he said to bring you over to the house for dinner some day this week and we'd talk about it."

"Nuts!" I said, "they probably wouldn't let me go anyway."

"They would if my dad asked them to let you go. You know who he is?" Jerry said.

Yes, I knew his father; everyone did—big Jerry Cowan, New York's smiling Mayor. You saw pictures of him in the papers every day—carnation in his buttonhole, white teeth gleaming, shaking hands with the representative of the latest corn-growers' association or some other crummy outfit. Yeah, his old man could get almost anything he wanted. He was Mayor of New York.

We were at the door of the poolroom. I stopped. I looked into the poolroom. It was dim inside and I could hardly see into it. I thought of spending the summer in there with the smell of needled beer and urine from the toilet. I thought of spending the summer in the country with Jerry. He probably had a swell joint with servants and everything. There'd probably be fishing and swimming and all kinds of stuff. A picture of me diving into a lake flashed in my mind. I had never swum in a lake. It must be swell. Some fellows told me it was. I had gone to Coney a couple times but mostly did my swimming off the dock at Fifty-fourth Street. Golly, a summer in the country would be swell. I turned to Jerry. "Naah, Jerry," I said. "Thanks anyway. They—I mean—I got a job here. I gotta work this summer. I can't be broke. I gotta make a little dough. And hell, I hate the country anyway! I always get the heebies there."

Jerry looked at me and then laughed. Jerry was no dunce. He knew what was on my mind. Jerry was a strange friend. He wasn't an easy one to make friends with; neither was he stuck-up. He was just—particular. I don't know why he liked me, but if I could see far enough ahead, if I could only have known what Jerry and I—but we'll get to it when we get to it. It's bad enough we can look back and remember; it would be a lot worse if we knew what was coming.

"O. K.," he said, "if that's what you want. But come over to my house for dinner one evening anyway." I noticed he said "dinner" not "supper" the way I did.

"I will." I stood awkwardly on one foot. I didn't know whether to thank him again or not. Then I thought: "To hell with it! I thanked him before." Aloud I said: "I gotta go in to work." I stood there watching him walk down the street and turn the corner.

I turned and looked into the poolroom. The clock on the back wall said three-fifteen. I was early. I didn't have to be there until four, and I didn't feel much like working right then. I looked for Jimmy. He was talking to some geezer and didn't see me; so I ducked and scooted up the block and sat down in the sun on the steps of an old tenement, waiting until it was four o'clock before going back to Keough's. I thought about going to the country with Jerry.

I lit a cigarette and was waiting for the time to pass when I heard some yelling going on over the other side of the street. A couple of kids I knew had cornered a Jewish boy and were giving him the works. I looked on with idle interest. I felt too lazy to go over and join in the fun. They stood around him in a half circle and tormented him.

"How does it feel to be a half-man?"

"Christ killer!"

"Muff diver!"

The boy stood there tensely, his face white but calm. His eyes proudly flashed hate at them. They edged toward him threateningly. He dropped the book he was carrying and pressed his back closer to the wall. He started to raise his fists. He seemed to be a little shorter than I. He was blond, blue-eyed and thin-featured. Finally he spoke.

"I can lick any one of you in a fair fight." His voice betrayed no fear.

They gave him the horselaugh and moved closer toward him. "You can't lick our boots!" one of them said.

I got to my feet and walked across the street. This was going to be good.

"Hi, Frankie," one of the boys said.

"Hello, Willie," I replied.

"Let's get the little Jew son-of-a-bitch!" cried one of the gang.

"Nix," I said. "You heard him. He said he can lick any one of us. You're not going to let him get away with that. One of us is goin' to fight him."

The crowd looked at me doubtfully.

"Well," I said, "who's goin' to do it?"

There was no answer.

"O. K.," I said, "I'll do it."

The circle broke and I walked through. The boy looked at me. I knew he was sizing me up.

I put up my fists. He stepped forward and swung at me wildly. I dodged it easily and stepped back. He didn't know anything about fighting. He followed me and threw several punches that I blocked easily.

The crowd began to holler.

"Sock him, Frankie!"

"Kick him in the nuts!"

I fell back till I was near the edge of the curb when I realized I still had the cigarette in my mouth. I kept it there to show them that I knew I could handle him. He swung again and missed. He was beginning to breathe heavily. "Golly!" I thought, "he knows I can lick him. Why in hell don't he run for it?" I pretended to slip on the curbstone, and the cigarette fell from my mouth. When I looked up he was still there waiting for me. I stepped toward him, hit him a ripper in the guts, and followed it with a right cross to the jaw. Down he went on his back. The boys began to jump up and down. "Kick him!" they kept hollering. The boy tried to get up but couldn't quite make it. Finally he just lay there watching me with his eyes. I put my hands down. Willie yelled: "Let's roll him in the gutter." The boys started to move on him. I stepped across him and stood in front of him.

"I licked him," I said. "Leave him alone."

They looked at me a moment and saw I meant it. They didn't know what to do; they looked at one another.

"O. K.," I said, "you've had your fun. Now beat it."

They began to walk off. I watched them go around the corner. When they had gone from sight I sat down on the curbstone next to where the boy was lying. I took a package of cigarettes from my pocket and offered him one. He shook his head in refusal. I took one myself and lit it. We were silent for a few seconds. Then he sat up slowly.

"Thanks," he said.

"For a sock in the kisser?" I said and laughed.

"For letting me off easy," he said. "That gang—"

"Aw, they're all right," I said. "They just wanted to have a little fun. They didn't mean nothin'."

"Some fun!" he said dryly and got up and picked up his book. He looked a little shaky.

I looked up at him from the curbstone. "You ought to learn how to fight if you're goin' to hang out in this neighborhood."

He didn't say anything to that, but if the set of his mouth meant anything I could see he was going to learn.

Just then Father Quinn came down the street and I jumped to my feet.

"Hello, Francis," he said to me.

"Hello, Father," I said, touching my hand to my forehead in a half salute.

"You haven't been fighting with this boy have you, Francis?" he asked quizzically.

Before I could answer, the boy spoke up. "Oh, no, sir, we weren't fighting. Francis was giving me a boxing lesson."

Father Quinn looked at him. "Well," he said to the boy, "don't let him get too enthusiastic over the lessons. He sometimes forgets himself." Then in another tone of voice, the kind he used when you don't show up for Mass, he asked: "What's your name, son? I don't remember seeing you in church."

"I'm Jewish," the boy said quietly. "My name's Martin Cabell."

"Oh," said Father Quinn, "you must be Joe Cabell's boy."

"Yes, sir."

"I know your father. He's a good man. Will you give him my regards?"

"I will, sir."

"Well, boys, I must be going now. Remember what I said: no fighting." He turned to walk off and then stopped. "Francis," he called back to me, "you'd better take that cigarette out of your pocket before you burn a hole in your trousers," and walked on.

I took the cigarette out of my pocket. I didn't think he saw me stash it when he came up. Martin and I looked at each other and laughed.

"He seems like a regular guy," Martin said.

"He's O. K.," I answered.

We walked down the street together.

"Live around here?" I asked.

"Yes," he answered, "my father owns the drugstore down at Fifty-ninth and Broadway. We live on Central Park West."

We reached the corner of Ninth Avenue. I looked in a jeweler's window and saw it was after four.

"I gotta beat it," I said. "I gotta go to work."

"When you're through come over to my father's store and have a soda on me," Martin said.

"I will," I said. "See ya around." And left him. A few feet later I broke into a run. I didn't want to be too late or Keough would be sore.

Chapter Five

KEOUGH'S was empty when I got there. It looked like business was dead that afternoon. I quickly cleaned up the joint and grabbed his books and made up his figures as the results came in.

About five-thirty a few customers came in to square up, and I was sent downstairs after some cold bottles of beer. When I came up, Silk Fennelli was there talking to Keough. He glanced at me and then said slowly: "Hello, Frankie."

"Hello, Mr. Fennelli," I answered, proud to be noticed by the big shot.

He went on talking to Keough and when he was through he came over to me. "How about one of those special shines, boy?" he asked.

"Right away, sir," I said and ran to the closet and got out the shine box.

I gave him a really good shine. I rubbed till I could almost see my face in the leather.

He was pleased. I could see that. He gave me a half a buck and asked me if I had been thrown out of any saloons lately.

I laughed my reply. Keough came over and Fennelli told him what had happened. They both laughed.

I put the shine box away and started in again on the figures. Keough and Fennelli came and looked over my shoulder.

"Docs he do your figuring?" Fennelli asked Keough.

"Yeah," said Jimmy, "and damn good too. He knows his stuff."

Fennelli smiled at me. "Keep up the good work, boy. You'll be a big man in the business some day."

He waved good-by and went out. I saw him step into his car and ride off.

"Big man in the business some day!" I thought, his words ringing in my ears. "That's right, the biggest gambler in town— that's what I'll be. Only I won't be gambling. I'll run the business like Silk Fennelli does. The flunkies will do the dirty work and I'll rake in the gravy. And I'll have a bigger car than Fennelli's—"

And so with my dreams the afternoon passed and before I knew it it was time to go home.

It had started to rain when I got outside. I didn't feel like reporting back for supper; so I walked over toward Broadway. When I got to Cabell's drugstore I was pretty wet. I went in. Martin came up to me.

"I'm glad you came," he said. "How about that soda?" he led me over to the fountain.

I had chocolate. When we were finished we sat there talking. He was a year younger than me but in the same class at public school. After we had been talking a few minutes a girl came over and spoke to him.

"We'd better hurry, Marty, or we'll be late for supper." I thought she must be his sister and I was right.

He introduced us: "Frankie, this is my sister, Ruth."

"Hello," I said.

She smiled at me. "Glad to meet you," she said. She was about fifteen and really lovely—blond hair combed in a semi-boyish crinkly cut and blue eyes like Martin's. And like Martin she had a way of looking straight at you when she spoke. She had a neat, trim figure and was in the sixth term high. I was about half a head taller than she, and when Marty asked me how old I was, I told him I was almost sixteen, hoping to make an impression on her.

Martin told her what had happened that afternoon, and she looked at me rather strangely and then walked away. I wondered what was eating her but said nothing to Martin.

Marty looked at me and said: "Women are funny. About what you said this afternoon about fighting—I got a pair of boxing gloves home; how about your coming over and giving me a lesson?"

"Tonight?" I asked.

"Sure," he said, "after supper. Why don't you go home to eat and then come over to my house and we can box?"

"I don't think I can," I said. "I live in the orphanage. If I go over for supper I don't think I'll be able to get out."

"Oh," he said. He frowned for a minute and then brightened up. "I got an idea. Wait here a minute." He ran into the back of the store. I could see him talking to his father through the glass partition. He pointed toward me. Then his father said something, and he came out and back to me.

"I fixed it," he said. "You're going to come home to supper with us. Then we can have our lesson."

At first I didn't want to go but I gave in.

His father and mother had gone out that night. The three of us, Marty, Ruth and me, were given supper by the maid, a young woman of about twenty-two named Julie. She was a French-Canadian and spoke with a funny little accent. She sat down to eat with us. The meal was a simple one and we were through quickly. Afterward we went into the parlor. They had a new radio and we were able to get some music on it. It was the third time I had ever heard a radio and it was very interesting. An hour after supper Martin suggested we go to the den and box.

It was O. K. with me. Ruth stayed in the parlor. She said she was going to read.

The den was a nice room with books lining the walls and a couch and some chairs scattered around. We pushed the chairs to one side and laced on the gloves.

"Put your dukes up," I said. "Lead with your left. Keep your right back here near your chin—like this." I fell into the fighting pose. He copied me. I stepped back and looked at him. I moved his left out a little and his right elbow down a little closer to his side. "O. K.," I said, "now all you've got to do is hit me."

"I don't want to hurt you," he said.

"Don't worry," I said, "you won't."

He dropped his left and swung with his right. I blocked it and stepped in close.

"Nix," I said, "that's not it. You left yourself wide open. When you drop your left I can step in and hit you like this, see?" I faked a punch. "Jab with your left. It keeps the other guy away from you."

"I see," he said. For a few seconds he remembered and then he forgot. I let him swing a couple times and miss; then I stopped.

"Don't forget to keep your left up," I said.

We had begun to box again when the door opened. Automatically I looked over his shoulder. Ruth came in. I watched her and he hit me on the shoulder. Without thinking, I crossed with my right and popped him in the eye. Down he went.

Ruth ran over to him. He sat there on the floor. She looked up at me. "You filthy beast! Why can't you pick on a guy your size?" she snarled at me.

I was so dumbfounded I couldn't speak.

"It's not his fault, Ruth," Marty said, "I asked him to teach me how to fight."

"But your eye," she wailed. "Look at it. It's turning all colors."

Sure enough, tomorrow it would be a beautiful shiner. I found my tongue. "Jeeze, Marty, I'm sorry. I didn't mean to hit you so hard." I helped him to his feet.

"It couldn't be helped," he said and laughed.

Julie, hearing the noise, came into the room. "You'd better put a cold towel on it," she said, "or it'll swell up."

He shook off his gloves. "O. K.," he said, "we'll have another lesson soon." At the door he turned to me and said: "Wait here, I'll be back in a few minutes."

They left the room and a few seconds later I heard the water running in the bathroom.

I still had my gloves on. Julie picked up the gloves Marty had dropped on the floor. "Can I try them on?" she asked.

"Go ahead. They're not mine," I answered.

She put them on. "They're very clumsy," she said.

"You get used to them," I said.

"My father said I should've been a boy," she said. "I was always a tomboy."

I didn't answer.

"Show me how to box, Frankie," she asked. "Not really—I mean just an idea."

"O. K.," I said.

"But don't hit me," she said quickly. "I am so afraid of getting hurt—especially here." She put her hands under her breasts and pushed them up.

I looked and then gulped out an answer. "All right, just swing at me a few times and then we'll quit."

She held her arms out funny-like and took a couple of swings at me. They missed, and then she stepped in close and swung. I blocked them and then stepped in and clinched. She caught my arms under her elbows and locked them against her sides. I could feel her close to me. This fighting with a girl had a bad effect on me. It was too exciting—the wrong way.

"You're very strong," she said, pressing herself against me.

I looked up at her. She was a little taller than I—black hair and wide, full mouth. Her eyes looked funny-like. We stood there a second and suddenly became aware that Ruth was in the doorway looking at us. We broke loose immediately.

I flushed. "She wanted me to show her how to box too," I said lamely. I could feel my ears burning.

"A regular Gene Tunney, aren't you?" Ruth said bitingly. "Martin wants you."

I took off the gloves and gave them to Julie, then followed Ruth into Martin's room. He was stretched out in bed with a cold towel on his eye.

"I'm sorry this happened, Frankie. But meet me over at my father's store tomorrow and we'll get together again."

"O. K., Marty," I said, "I'm sorry I hurt you. See you tomorrow." I turned and left.

Ruth followed me to the door. She held it open for me and I stepped out. "Good night, Ruth," I said.

"Good night," she said and started to close the door behind me. Halfway she stopped. "Would you like to do me a favor?" she asked.

"Sure," I said.

"Then stay away from my brother. You're cheap and filthy and rotten, and you'll only spoil him." She clipped the words out savagely and shut the door in my face.

I started to walk slowly down the hallway.

"Psst," I heard someone call out. I looked up. It was Julie standing in another doorway in front of me.

I looked back at the door I had just come out of, and wondered what she was doing in the other doorway.

"Come here," she whispered fiercely. She motioned with her arm. I followed her through the door. It led into the kitchen of Martin's apartment and then through the kitchen into a small room on the far side of it away from the rest of the apartment. She closed the door behind us.

"This is my room," she whispered. "Be quiet."

She was telling me to be quiet. Hell, I was so excited I couldn't speak—only look at her. She flicked out the light and walked toward me. She put her arms around me and kissed me. I could feel her tongue flicker in and out against my lips, her hands against my body. I could feel my hands running over her, and she fell back on the small bed.

"You're so strong," she said. "You mustn't hurt me. Please don't hurt me." And after a while she said: "Hurt me, please hurt me. . . ."

It was midnight when I left her. Walking through the streets, wet and muggy, I felt now I was a man. But I was a fool. I was not yet fourteen and big for my age and too big for my breeches.

Chapter Six

IT WAS Saturday morning and Keough left me in the store all alone. He was taking his wife and kid down to the station to put them on the train for the country where they were going to stay all summer.

I had all the tables set, the beer iced in the cellar, and the place swept clean. I had cleaned out the toilets, polished the glass showcase in which he kept the cigars, and was now washing down the windows. They were half covered with black paint so no one could see in, and just had the words on each window, "Billiards" in small, black letters. I had wet the windows with a brush and then wiped them down with a squeegee on a long mop handle.

While I was working, Jerry and Ray came down the street. They stopped to watch me.

"Jeeze!" said Ray, "you're as good as a regular window washer."

"It's a trick," I said proudly. "Ya gotta know how to work the squeegee, see?" With a final wipe and flourish I finished. I picked up the pail and brush and walked into the store. "Come on in," I said to them. "Keough's out."

They came into the store. It was the first time any of them had been in the place. Kids weren't allowed.

"How's about lettin' us shoot some pool, Frankie?" Ray asked.

"Can't. Ya gotta be an adult. Minors can't play. See the sign?" I pointed to a sign over the cash register that read, "Minors not permitted." "We can get closed up if you play."

"How about comin' swimmin' with us this afternoon?" Jerry asked.

"I'd like to," I said. "Maybe if you'll drop by this afternoon and we're not busy, Jimmy'll let me off."

"O. K.," said Jerry. "We'll stop by on the way to the docks."

The afternoon was hot and Keough had come back from the station in a good mood and whistling: "My Wife's Gone to the Country, Hooray, Hooray!" We weren't busy and he let me off for a couple hours.

The three of us walked down the street toward the Fifty-fourth-Street dock. I saw Marty on the other side of the street. I called: "Hey, Marty!"

He came over to us, and I introduced him all around and asked him to come swimming with us.

"I'd like to," he said. "That is if the other fellows don't mind."

"Hell, no!" I said. "The more the merrier."

The dock was crowded when we got there. I saw some fellows I knew. Pete Sanpero was there with his gang, but he didn't say anything to me so I didn't pay any attention to him. We swung ourselves under the dock and got out of our clothes. Then we jumped into the water. It was warm and dirty near the dock because a sewer emptied there, but when you swam out a little ways it was nice and fresh. We splashed around a little and then I said to the others: "I wish we could fly back to the docks from here so we wouldn't have to get that slime over us when we go back."

Jerry called back to me: "If you'd come up to the country like I asked you, you could swim in a real lake."

An airplane roared overhead. We all turned and yelled. Then Ray said: "I wonder if that was Rickenbacker."

"Hell!" I said, "if it was, it was an angel. Rickenbacker's dead."

"No he isn't," Marty yelled. "He's alive. He shot down the ace of the German flying circus, von Richthofen."

"Anyway America has the best goddam airplanes in the world. And American fliers are best," Ray said.

We floated on our back awhile and watched the ferries and the Hudson River boats go by. Then we got out of the water and stretched out on the docks in the sun. We were stark naked and too far from the streets for anyone to see us. We lay there quietly awhile. The sun was hot and I covered my face with my shirt.

A shadow fell over me and I heard a voice say: "Who let this goddam Jew down here on our dock?"

I thought it was someone talking about Martin so I lay there quietly waiting to see what would come of it.

"Hey, fellers," the voice cried. "Come over here and look at what makes a Jew."

I heard a couple of feet come over and stop not far from me. "Jeeze!" one of them said, "funny lookin', ain't it?" They all laughed.

"Come on, Jew," said the original voice. "Let's see what the rest of you looks like." There was a minute's silence. Then a foot prodded me roughly and the voice said: "I mean you. Don't you know when you're spoken to?"

I took the shirt from my face slowly and sat up. Jerry, Ray, and Marty were sitting near me, looking at me. I saw Marty had put his trousers on so they must have meant me. I had been circumcised when I was a kid. I got to my feet and faced my tormentor. He was a guy I didn't know. "The name's Kane," I said slowly. "Francis Kane. And I'm not a Jew. Want to make anything of it?"

"That's right," one of the boys called. "He's from St. Therese."

I took a step toward the other fellow. "All right," he said, "I'm sorry. But I don't like Jews. I'd like to see one here. I'd kick him off the dock."

Before I could answer, Marty stepped up in front of me. "I'm a Jew," he said quietly. "Let's see you kick me off the dock."

The boy was a little taller than Marty. Marty's back was toward the water. Suddenly the fellow made a rush toward him, intending to push Marty into the water. Nimbly Marty side-stepped and the fellow, not being able to stop his rush, plunged over the side of the dock into the water with a big splash. I burst out laughing and the others followed.

I leaned over the edge of the dock and yelled to the guy splashing in the water: "The Jew was too smart for ya, huh?"

He cursed back at us and tried to clamber back; but he was so mad he missed and fell back into the water. We laughed again. Just then a yell went up: "A dame's comin' down the dock!" All of us who didn't have any clothes on jumped into the water.

Later when the woman had gone we clambered back on the dock and got dressed. "I gotta get back to work," I said, and we walked back to Tenth Avenue in silence.

At the door of the poolroom Jerry said: "Don't forget: after church tomorrow you're coming over to my house to meet my father."

I went into the store and Keough was there, hot and perspiring and busy. When he saw me he hollered: "Bring up some beer from the cellar. It's a hot day and the boys are all thirsty."

Chapter Seven

KEOUGH was closed on Sunday. I had to stay at church through all the Masses because I was an altar boy. After the last Mass, near twelve o'clock, I would generally go back to the orphanage, have dinner, and then go out for the rest of the day. Sometimes I would go to a movie or up to the Polo Grounds and sneak into the ball game. This Sunday I had promised Jerry I would go home with him to see his father.

Jerry's father was the Mayor of New York—the great democrat, the people's man, a regular, friendly man with a big hello and a glad handshake and baby-kissing lips. I didn't like him. It dated from a long way back—long before I knew Jerry Cowan. It was when Mr. Cowan was alderman from our district and he made a speech at the orphanage's Thanksgiving dinner. He made a nice speech that none of the kids could understand, but then we didn't care. We were too full of turkey. I was about nine at the time. He sent me into the superintendent's office to fetch some cigars from his overcoat. When I gave them to him he held out a big shiny quarter to me and said: "This is for being a good boy."

"Thank you," I murmured, taking the quarter. Then I remembered what the teacher had taught us and I went over and put the money in the church box.

Mr. Cowan saw it. "That's a real fine young man," he said and called me over. "What's your name, young feller?" he asked.

"Francis Kane, sir," I said.

"Well, Francis, here's five dollars more for the church, but before you put it in the box tell me, what do you want more than anything else for Christmas?"

"An electric train, sir," I said.

"An electric train you shall have, my boy. I have a son just about your age at home and that's what he wants too. You both shall have it." He smiled at me as I put the five-dollar bill in the church box.

I counted the days till Christmas. Christmas morning, when I went down to the big tree in the dining-room, I expected to find the electric train, but it wasn't there. Maybe it didn't come yet. I couldn't imagine he would forget. The day passed and no electric train came.

I didn't really give up hope until I had gone to bed. Then quietly I began to cry into my pillow.

Brother Bernhard, who had been walking in the hall, heard me and came into the dormitory. "What is the matter, Francis?" he asked in that warm, friendly voice of his. Sobbing, I sat up in bed and told him about the electric train.

He listened quietly and then said: "Francis, do not weep for a small thing like that. 'Tis not very much for a man to cry for. 'Tis better you cry for the love of your friends and for us who cannot give thee half the love thee needs. And besides"— Brother Bernhard was a practical as well as a sentimental man—"Alderman Cowan has been in Florida for the past month, and no doubt he was too busy wi'e his other affairs to think of ye."

He stood up at the side of my bed. "Now go to sleep, lad. Ye'll be needing ye're strength for tomorrow. I'm after taking ye to Central Park for sleigh riding. For 'tis snowing, which ye can see if ye'd but put your head to the window."

And I put my head to the window and sure enough the snow was coming down in great big flakes. Dry-eyed, I lay back in bed. I heard Brother Bernhard go back into the hall. He met someone there and I could hear him saying: "I don't mind the politicians breaking their promises to their voters, but I wish the scoundrels wouldna try to break the hearts of little boys as well."

Then the light in the hall flickered and went out, and I began to hate Alderman Cowan with all the fury of a small boy's soul.

When I first met Jerry, just before his father was elected Mayor, I didn't quite know what to do about him. He was a likable, friendly boy who never understood that the real reason for taking him out of a private school and transferring him to St. Therese was political. I liked him but I didn't know whether to carry my grudge against his father to him.

So I took the shortest way of finding out. I offered to lick him. Halfway through our fight—we weren't getting anywhere, we were too evenly matched—I put down my hands and said to him: "The hell with it!—I like you."

He never knew why I did that—maybe he thought I was a little cracked—but in that nice, friendly manner of his he offered me his hand and said: "I'm glad. I like you too."

And we became fast friends. That was the year before. We had chummed together all through the school year just passed, and now he wanted me to meet his old man so's he could get me to go to the country with him. I had never told him why I didn't like his father, or, as a matter of fact, that I didn't like his father. I kind of hoped Jerry would forget about his suggestion, but no dice; right after the last Mass he showed up.

"Ready, Frankie?" he asked with a smile.

"Yeah," I grunted.

"O. K. then, what are we waiting for? Let's go!"

A butler let us into his house. "Hello, Master Jerry," he said.

"Robert, where's Dad?" he asked.

"In the library. He's expecting you," replied the butler.

I followed Jerry into the library. His mother and father were there. His father still had the same ready smile and crinkly eyes. I was struck by the way Jerry looked like him when he smiled. But Jerry had the quiet, sensitive mouth of his mother, and her gentleness.

"So there you are, son!" his father exclaimed. "We have been waiting luncheon for you."

"Thanks, Dad," Jerry said, and indicating me, "This is my friend Frankie, I have been telling you about."

His father and mother turned and looked at me. Suddenly I was very conscious of the patched shirt and trousers I was wearing.

"Glad to know you, boy," said his father, coming over and shaking hands with me.

I don't remember what I said, but the butler came in and announced luncheon and we all went into the dining-room.

The table was a big, square thing and in the center of it was a big bowl of flowers. If you wanted to say anything, you would have to look up over it, around the side of it, or under it. There were more knives, forks and spoons than I knew what to do with, but I watched Jerry and got along all right. We had ice cream for dessert. Then we went back to the library.

"Jerry told me he wants you to come to the country with him," Mr. Cowan said to me.

"Yes, sir," I replied. "I'm very thankful to you but I can't go."

"You can't?" asked Mr. Cowan. "Is it against the rules of the uh—orphanage?"

"Oh no, sir, but I've got a job for the summer and I can't leave it."

"But the country's much better for you than working in the hot city all summer," said Mrs. Cowan.

"Yes, ma'am, I know, ma'am." I didn't want to hurt her feelings. I liked her. "But I need things. And I'm going to high school in September and some dough—I mean—money would come in handy. You know what I mean. I want to be . . . a little like the others—not taking charity all the time. I'm sorry ma'am. I don't mean to be rude."

She came over to me and took my hand. "I don't think you're rude, Frankie; I think you're a very fine boy."

I didn't know what to say to her. A few minutes later Mr. and Mrs. Cowan left. They had an appointment somewhere, and we went up to Jerry's room.

We idled around a little while. Then Jerry said: "How about coming up to the attic. It's all fixed up as a playroom. We can have some fun."

The first think I knew when we got into the room I saw a big electric-train set. It was terrific: bridges and tunnels and switches and three locomotives. "Oh, boy!" I said, "that's some-thin'!"

"Yes," said Jerry, "Dad bought it for me three years ago before we went to Florida. Want to play with it?"

I looked at it quietly for a minute, feasting my eyes on it. Almost instinctively I moved toward it. Suddenly something stopped me. A thought flashed through my mind. At least he didn't forget his own son's present.

"No," I said aloud, my voice trembling foolishly. "It's too hot here. Let's go swimming."

Chapter Eight

I WAS going to start high school the next term. Jerry was going up to George Washington High on the Heights, and I decided to go there too. Marty also planned to go there. I didn't think very much about what I wanted to take up because I regarded school as a necessary evil. I would leave as soon as I was seventeen and legally permitted. My only ambition was to be a gambler and a bookie—and rich.

Graduation at St. Therese was a simple, quiet affair. We were all assembled in a great hall with parents and friends and teachers, and were given three speeches and a diploma.

My name was called. I went up to the platform and took my diploma from the Monsignor who had come especially for the presentation. Then I went back and sat down with the rest of my class. After the ceremony I stood around watching the kids and their parents, laughing and proud.

I guess I felt kind of funny at being left so alone. I saw Jerry and his folks. There was a crowd around them, and Jerry couldn't see past them or he would have called me over. After a while I started to ease toward the doorway. It looked as if no one was coming to see me anyway, and I'd feel better outside. Someone tapped me on the shoulder. I turned around. It was Brother Bernhard. Father Quinn was with him, and both were smiling.

"Congratulations!" boomed the good brother.

Father Quinn, still smiling, echoed him.

I smiled suddenly, just beginning to feel the salt stinging my eyelids. I couldn't speak for a moment.

Brother Bernhard looked at me shrewdly; there were times when I thought he could read my mind. "Thought we weren't coming, eh?"

He didn't give me time to answer before he continued: "We

wouldn't be after missing the graduation of one of our boys, would we, Father?"

"That we wouldn't," answered Father Quinn. "We're very proud of you, Francis."

I found my voice at last—not the same voice I usually used, but a voice. "Thank you," I said, "thank you."

Brother Bernhard put his hand on my shoulder as we walked toward the door. I began to feel pretty good again. Once we were outside, Father Quinn shook hands with me and wished me luck again and walked off toward the church while Brother Bernhard and I walked toward the orphanage.

We entered the courtyard silently. Suddenly he stopped me. "Francis," he blurted gruffly, "I've a present for ye." He held out his hand.

I was so surprised that for a moment I stared stupidly at the package in his hand.

"It's for ye," he said, thrusting it at me. "Take it."

I took the package and opened it. It was a wrist watch. I gulped and held it up. The sun shone on it, and it was beautiful. I strapped it on my wrist with trembling fingers.

"D'ye like it?" he asked.

"Like it!" I said, my voice suddenly light and gay. "I like it better'n anything in my whole life."

He smiled and took my hand, and together we walked into the big gray building.

Chapter Nine

THAT summer was the first I had ever spent so much time with people. I learned how to get along with them—how to joke and laugh, how not to get sore at every insult. I learned lots of things that summer, and Julie taught me most of them.

The day after I graduated, Marty had invited me to his house for supper again. His parents were out that evening.

I got there early. He met me at the door and greeted me.

"How about a little boxing now," he said, "and after supper we'll loaf around?"

"O. K.," I replied.

We had been boxing almost an hour when Julie stuck her head in the door. "Supper's ready," she said.

We took off our gloves. I washed my hands. Marty wanted to take a shower so I went into the kitchen to wait for him.

"Where's Marty?" Julie asked.

"He's taking a shower," I replied. "He'll be right out."

She was wearing a smock tied at the side. It was tightly fit and she looked almost like a kid except for the way she would walk. "How are the boxing lessons coming along?" she asked, coming over and taking my hands.

"All right. He's O. K.," I said.

"How about your other lessons?" she asked with a slow smile.

"What other lessons?" I asked stupidly.

"These," she said, pulling my arms around her.

I held her close. She was warm and she felt good close to me. It seemed that her warmth reached out toward me. I kissed her on the lips. She closed her eyes. When she opened them they were soft and swimmy.

She tilted her head to one side. "Kiss me here." She indicated her throat.

"Why?" I asked.

"Because I like it, silly," she said. "You'll like it too. Don't you love me?"

"That's kid stuff," I said awkwardly.

"Kid stuff?" She looked at me in pretended amazement. "And how old do you think you are, Mr. Rip Van Winkle?"

"I'm almost sixteen."

"Well, I'm almost four years older than you are, and I don't think it's kid stuff. Kiss me." I kissed her on the throat. At first it seemed funny but then it felt good. She guided one hand of mine toward her breast. It felt soft and warm and I could feel her nipple growing in my palm. She whispered in my ear. It was almost as if she were talking to herself. "There's something about you, Frankie. I can't understand it. Kids don't usually make me feel that way. But you—you're different. You're like a man, hard and selfish and calculating, and like a kid, soft at the tiny corners of your mouth. You're strong, and when you hold me you're as gentle as a baby. Say you love me."

I shook my head, still kissing her throat. I held her tight.

"Say it!" she commanded. "Say 'Julie, I love you.' "

I moved my lips up to hers and didn't say anything. We heard Marty whistling as he came out of the bathroom. We fell apart. I looked at her. She was beautiful. Her eyes were sparkling and her mouth was still puckered a little with my kiss.

"I'll make you say it—later," she whispered fiercely before Marty came into the room.

I laughed happily. Just then Marty came in. "What's funny?" he asked.

"Nothing," I said, feeling like a dope.

We sat down to eat. About ten minutes later Ruth came in. "I'm sorry I'm late for dinner, Julie, I was stuck at the club. We're electing a new president, you know." She sat down at the table and looked at me. "You here?" she said.

"Yes," I said, feeling that nothing could bother me now. "Do ya mind?"

Julie brought over Ruth's plate and sat down at the table. She looked at Ruth and me as if she could see the antagonism flowing between us.

I looked at Julie and it seemed to me that she was laughing down deep in her eyes where I couldn't get to see it.

After supper we went into the parlor for a while. At 8:30 I said good night. Ruth again walked me to the door. "I see you didn't take my advice," she said.

"Why don't you mind your own goddam business?" I replied nastily. I think the language shocked her a little because I heard her gasp. At the door when I turned and looked at her, I saw there were tears in her eyes. Instinctively I reached for her hand. "I'm sorry," I said.

She shook my hand loose. "Don't touch me!" she said coldly. "I hate everything about you. You're not like other boys of your age. There's something old and mean and hard about you; something basically vicious; something that makes me think you'll spoil everything you touch—even my brother."

I tried to speak but couldn't. I stepped outside and closed the door behind me.

Julie was waiting at the other door. "What took you so long? I thought you would never come out."

"Nothing," I said, following her into her room. I turned her around and kissed her—first on her lips and then on her throat where she had wanted me to kiss her before. I untied her smock and put my hands inside; her skin was cool and smooth. I pushed her toward the bed.

She stopped me. "Say 'I love you' first."

I held her tight and rubbed my hand along her thighs, up and down. Her knees seemed to sag and all her weight was against me. I moved her toward the bed.

She stiffened her body against me. "No," she said, "Say 'I love you' first."

I held her. She felt straight and hard. I looked at her mouth; it was not soft but firm, determined.

"I love you, Julie," I said hoarsely, pulling her closer to me.

Chapter Ten

"IT'S easy," Jimmy Keough was saying to me. "You've got the whole territory from here to Sixty-fourth Street. I told the boys you'd be around. All you've got to do is take their bets, write them down, and bring 'em here to me before the races are run. If you can't get here on time call me and tell me what you have. We'll run your book on a split. As long as you're ahead we'll split fifty-fifty on the take. When you're in the hole you have to make up your deficit before we split again."

I nodded my head. We had gone over this many times before. I was anxious to get started. I had a pad and a couple of pencils and two racing forms in my pockets. I started for the door.

Jimmy called after me. "Now remember, don't take any markers except those I okay. And don't forget to call if you can't get back on time."

"All right, Jimmy," I said and stepped out the door. The street was bright and hot. It was nearly eleven o'clock and it was going to be a scorcher. I looked at the address book Jimmy had given me. The first stop was a garage on Tenth Avenue and Sixty-third Street. I walked there. I was supposed to ask for a guy named Christy.

I walked in past a couple of cars and it was cool in there. A big Negro was washing a car. "Where's Christy?" I asked him.

"Ahm Christy," he answered. "Whadda yuh want?"

"I'm from Jimmy Keough," I said.

He put down the hose. "Got the dope sheet?" he asked.

"Sure," I replied and gave it to him.

He took it and called: "Hey, Joe, the book is here."

I felt good; he called me the book. At last I was getting somewhere. From out of the darkness somewhere in the back of the garage another man appeared. He looked at me curiously for a moment then went over to Christy. Together they studied the sheet. I leaned against a car while they made up their minds. Finally Christy called me over. I walked over, sat down on the running board of the car, and took out the pencil and paper.

He spoke to Joe. "Partners on everything today, hunh?"

"Un-hunh," Joe said.

Christy turned to me. "Okay, boy. Heah is ouah bets. Tomorrow youah boss is broke."

I laughed. "Go ahead and break him. He can afford it."

They laughed at that.

"Gimme fifty cents on Docket and Red Rose for the daily double," Christy said, "and fifty cents win and place on Garageman. That's a hunch," he explained to me.

"Sounds good to me," I said professionally.

"Yeanh, it ought to pay a good price too. Ran out of the money the past three times. And fifty cents place on Red Rose." He stopped.

"That all?" I asked.

"Thass all for today." He laughed. "But you bring aroun' a barr'lful a dough tomorrow and we'll go you hot and heavy." He handed the sheet back to me.

"Well, if I need any help in toting it over, I can always call you up and you'll come for it in a truck," I said.

"Anytime, boy, anytime!" He laughed and handed me two dollars. I stuck them in my pocket carefully.

"See you tomorrow, fellas," I said and walked out.

My next stop was at the delivery entrance of a loft building on Sixty-second Street. There was a big landing platform raised about three feet off the ground. Two trucks were backed up against it. Several men were sitting around eating sandwiches and smoking. I walked over to one of them. He was eating a big dill pickle.

"D' ya know Al Andrews?" I asked him.

"That's him over there against the elevator door," he said, pointing with his pickle to a tall man.

"Thanks," I said, walking over to Andrews.

"Al Andrews?" I asked.

The man nodded his head.

"I'm from Jimmy Keough," I said.

"Come in here," he said. "I don't want the boss to see me."

I followed him into the corridor, then into the men's room. I gave him the sheet. He took it and, unbuttoning his pants, went into one of the stalls and sat down.

After a few minutes he spoke. "Jesus, I don't like nothin' today!"

I laughed. "There's a winner in every race."

"But not for me," he said. "Every dog I played the last week is still running."

"Maybe you're due for a change in luck today," I said hopefully.

"Maybe," he said, doubtfully, looking at the sheet. Another few minutes passed. Then he said: "Tell you what. Gimme a dollar place on Smoothie in the second race, if two to win on Short Stop."

I wrote it down. "Anything else?" I asked.

He looked at the sheet for a few minutes more as if it were a crystal ball. He shook his head and handed back the sheet. I took it. He reached down and pulled his trousers part way up and fished for his money. He couldn't find it. He stood up and holding his pants with one hand, he felt with the other and found the dollar. Letting his pants drop to the floor he gave it to me. I put it in my pocket and started out.

"See you tomorrow," I said. He didn't reply. He was looking around behind him for a roll of toilet paper.

A drugstore just down the street was the next stop. I picked up three dollars there. Then a restaurant where some fellows who ate there played about seven bucks. A beauty parlor, a candy store, a few more garages and repair shops, a shoe store, another restaurant, and I had only one more stop to make. It was a furnished-room house. I rang the bell. The door was opened by a colored girl.

I looked at my paper. "Miss Neal in?" I asked.

"Sho," she said. "But you kinda young to be askin' foh her."
She led the way up to the second floor. "Miss Neal?" she asked
through a closed door.

"Come in," a voice answered.

I went in. There were a few women sitting in there in kimonos and house frocks.

"I'm Neal," said a big, dark-haired woman standing up.
"What do you want?"

"Keough sent me," I said looking around the room. I guessed
correctly—I was in a whorehouse.

"Oh," she said. "Got the sheet?"

I gave it to her. Another woman took the other one. I stood
around while they looked at it. I shifted from one foot to
another. Finally one of them told me to sit down. I sat in a
chair and looked out the window into the street. I got nineteen
bucks in bets there. I looked at the wrist watch Brother
Bernhard gave me. It was nearly two o'clock. I had to hurry
back to Keough's or I'd be late. I ran all the way back to the
store.

"How'd it go, kid?" Keough greeted me.

"Pretty good," I said, taking out the betting slips and putting
them on the counter. We totaled up the slips. I had $51.50 in
bets. I gave him the money and got busy cleaning up the place.
The afternoon went by quickly. When I finished figuring
Keough's slips I figured mine. There was $22.50 profit in my
book. Split with Keough and my share was $11.25.

"Eleven dollars and twenty-five cents for one day's work," I
thought to myself as I went back to the orphanage for the
night. It was more than I had ever made in one week before. It
was more money than I had ever had at one time before. This
beat going to the country for the summer.

Chapter Eleven

AT THE end of my first week on the route I had made fifty-one dollars. That and the six dollars I got for cleaning up Keough's place brought my earnings to a total of fifty-seven dollars, which was more than most families earned in my neighborhood. I don't suppose I really knew the value of money. I gorged myself on franks and hamburgers and cokes. For the first time I always had money in my pocket. The kids in the neighborhood all had something at my expense. I couldn't resist showing my roll or spending it treating them. I was a real big shot.

I had a date to go swimming with Julie after church Sunday. When I met her she was carrying a small bag. "Where's your bathing suit?" she asked when we sat down on the train.

"I got it on," I told her.

She laughed. "How will you get back?" she asked. "Your suit will be wet."

I looked dismayed. "I didn't think of that."

"Well, silly, I'll let you put it in my bag." We sat back. The train was at Times Square, and the crowd piled in—all heading for the island to escape the heat. We took lockers at a small bathhouse near Steeplechase. I almost forgot my money but remembered just in time to take it with me. On the way out I bought a white belt that fitted around the outside of the bathing suit and had a pocket in it to keep the money. I was on the beach before her. I waited a few minutes till she came out. She had a red bathing suit on, and it looked swell. Without her high-heeled shoes on she was a little shorter than I was. She looked like a kid about my age instead of older, and I felt good about it.

The water was swell. We swam around awhile and then lay on the sand. The sun was hot. Her body was mostly white and she was getting a little sunburned. I was brown from swimming off the docks.

"How's your job doing?" she asked.

I rolled over on my stomach beside her. "Pretty good," I said, "I made fifty-one bucks last week."

"Fifty-one dollars?" she cried incredulously.

"Yeah," I said. "Wanna see?" I took out my roll from the money belt.

"Put it away," she said, "I believe you."

I put the money back.

"What are you going to do with it?" she asked.

"I don't know," I answered. "Get some clothes I guess and some things I always wanted. I'm tired of always wearing hand-me-downs and charity clothes. I'd like to pick out something myself—something I really like and would be mine." I took out a package of cigarettes and offered them to her. She took one and I took one. I lit them, cupping my hand against the wind.

She drew a deep drag of her cigarette. "You ought to open up a savings account," she said. "Some day that money will come in real handy—when you go to college, I mean."

"Who the hell cares about college?" I answered. "I'm going to be a bookie and make some real dough. And you're going to be my girl."

"Do you really want me to be your girl?" she asked softly.

"Sure!" I said. She looked so pretty then I wanted to kiss her but there were too many people around.

The day before Jerry went to the country, he came over to Keough's to see me. "I wish you were going with me, Frankie," he said.

"I can't," I said. "This job here . . ."

"I know," he said, "but if you change your mind you write me and I'll get Dad to fix it up."

"I will," I said. "Have a nice summer, Jerry."

"You too," he said, looking around him doubtfully.

"See you in September."

We shook hands self-consciously and he left. I watched him go. I envied him more at that moment than I ever had before. It must be swell to get everything you want by just asking, I thought. Then I went back to cleaning out the toilet. When I finished that I was going out to see my customers. I had taken Julie's advice and started a bank account over at the Corn

Exchange on Broadway and Sixty-third. It was nearly the end of my second week as a runner and I had almost seventy dollars in the bank. My book had been hit for eighty dollars yesterday, and I would have to make up the deficit before I split any more profits. But I wasn't worried. I had learned that an occasional hit was good for the bookie as well as the player. They always played it back. They felt lucky and would bet heavier, and in no time at all they would be back in the hole again.

Walking across town, I met Marty and Ray. They were going over to the docks swimming. They asked me to go with them but I told them I couldn't, I had to work. Marty asked me to come over to his house and see him, and I told him I'd try to make it tonight but that I might be busy. A couple of other fellows called them and they left me to join them. Near the garage that was my first stop a bunch of kids were playing stickball in the street. I stopped for a few minutes to watch them. I shagged one fly ball and threw it back. One of them that knew me called: "Want a game, Frankie?"

"No, thanks," I answered and walked away. I went into the garage. "Hey, Christy!" I called. "Where are you?"

He came out from under a car. "Hello, Frankie," he said with a big grin on his face.

"Well, you did it," I said smiling. "You win twenty-one bucks." I paid him. His partner Joe came out and I handed them the sheet. They played six dollars in place of their usual two.

Somehow the day did not have its usual satisfaction for me. Due to the winnings, I got the biggest day's play I had ever got, but I didn't feel too good about it. On the way back to Keough's I passed the dock at Fifty-fourth Street where the kids were swimming. I leaned against a pole and watched them, diving and splashing and swimming and hollering. I felt like going over there and joining them, but I had to get back with the bets.

A voice behind me said: "I bet you'd like to go with them, Frankie."

I turned around. It was Silk Fennelli. "Why no, sir . . . I mean . . . that is . . ."

He smiled, "That's all right, kid, I understand. I know how you feel. You'd like to be with them—swimming, playing ball, or shooting craps on the corners. But you can't. You got a responsibility—yourself. Those kids don't think any further ahead than the next minute, but you're different. You want to get ahead. You want to amount to something. You're going to be big time, and you're learning now that for everything you get you got to give up something else—something maybe that you want or would like to do. And you have to make up your mind which it's going to be. I was like you once."

"That's it, Mr. Fennelli," I said. "I don't feel like those kids any more."

"That's the good boy," he said placing his hand on my shoulder, friendly-like. "Where are you going now?"

"Back to Keough's," I said.

"Hop in my car. I was just going there myself. Besides, then you can give me one of your special shines."

I followed him into his car. I felt pretty good when we stopped in front of Keough's and I got out with the big shot. He had asked me how I was doing and I told him. He thought it was fine.

Once in Keough's, I gave Jimmy the slips and the money. Then I got out my shine box and gave Mr. Fennelli a shine.

"The kid's all right," said Fennelli to Jimmy.

"Smart boy!" said Jimmy, looking proud as if he were my old man.

When Fennelli wanted to pay me for the shine, I didn't want to take the money. It was half a buck.

"Go ahead, kid, take it," he said.

I saw he was going to insist. "Toss you for it," I said to him. "Double or nothing."

"O.K.," he said, tossing the coin into the air, "you cry."

I watched it spin end over end. When it almost hit the ground I called: "Tails."

Tails it was. He picked up the half and gave me a dollar, which I put in my pocket. "You'll get along, Frankie." He smiled.

"Yes, sir," I said. "Thank you."

Keough laughed. "Get us a couple bottles of beer, Frankie."

I brought two cold ones up from the cellar and opened them. They drank quickly. When they were finished, Fennelli said to Jimmy: "Ready to square up for last week?"

"Sure thing, Silk!" Keough said. "You know me—always pay up on time." He took out a roll of bills, counted out six hundred dollars, and handed it over to Fennelli. Fennelli stuck it in his pocket without counting it.

I left them and got out the mop and pail and began to wash

the tile floor in front of the store near the counter. It was hot, so I took off my shirt and threw it in a corner. The sweat ran down my face and I wiped it off on my arm. When Fennelli passed me on his way out he waved to me. I waved back to him, giving him a half salute, just like I did for Father Quinn.

Chapter Twelve

THE summer wore on. It was just like any other summer in New York: hot, muggy, tiring; people returning from work with tiredness painted over their faces like masks; kids shouting in the streets; crowded parks and beaches; paper headlines shouting the weather; no school; noise coming in through the open windows.

Just another summer in New York. But not for me. I liked it. For the first time in my life I felt free and not beholden to anyone. It was late in August. I had seven hundred dollars in the bank. I had a girl. I had two new suits. I ate in restaurants. I had money in my pockets. I could go where I wanted and do what I wanted. People and the kids looked up to me. I was somebody. I was living high. I began to think about having to go back to school. I didn't want to go. I was making too much money. Yet I knew I couldn't get out of it. I wasn't old enough to quit. I tried to plan how I would continue to make book while in school. I would ask for the morning session up at high school and then I would be out in time to get the bets. Things were looking up. I thought patronizingly of the other kids in the orphanage and in the neighborhood. I was really going places.

It was late afternoon, Saturday, August 22nd. I had just squared up with Keough for the week and had another eighty-four dollars in my pocket. The poolroom was crowded with fellows, cursing, swearing and shouting. In a few minutes most of them would start drifting home to spruce up for their Saturday-night dates and parties and dances. We were out of beer and cold drinks. Keough looked over the counter at me and said: "I'm tired. I think we'll close early tonight and I'll catch a train and go up to see the wife."

"Should I pass the word?" I asked him.

He nodded.

I walked around the table calling out: "Closing time. Closing time."

In a few minutes the place was empty. Keough counted up the cash and stuck it in his pocket. "Let's go!" he said.

While Keough was locking the door, Fennelli's car drove up and stopped in front of the place. Silk got out and walked up to us. "Closing early, Jimmy?" He smiled.

"Yeah," answered Keough. "Goin' up to see my wife."

"That's good," said Fennelli. "Got anything for me?"

"Sure thing, Silk," said Keough. "You know me—always ready!" He stuck his hand in his pocket and came out with his roll. There was a big, thick rubber band around it. They stood in the doorway of the place, and I stepped out to make room for them, my back to the street.

I heard the whirr of a motor in the street behind me. Suddenly Silk and Keough looked up. They seemed to be staring at something behind me. I felt nothing unusual. Keough got white and his money fell from his hands to the stoop.

I bent down to pick it up saying: "You shouldn't be so careless with your . . ." I heard the sharp reports of a gun. I looked up suddenly. Keough had his hands on his belly and was sliding down against the door. I stared at Fennelli. His hands were against his chest. He began to slump forward, his hands slowly coming away from his coat. Blood started to spatter against me. It was then I began to move. I didn't think. I just ran, first scrambling on all fours and then running like hell. I didn't look back. I dodged down one block, then up another until I didn't know where I was going. I only knew that I was running.

Instinctively I stopped in front of Marty's apartment house. I ducked inside the door and ran up the stairs to his apartment. I went to the back door where I knew that Julie would answer, and rang the bell. It was then I began to realize how frightened I was. Before that I just had been running by reaction. My heart was pounding and I could hardly breathe.

Julie opened the door. I brushed past her and slammed it shut.

"Why, Frankie!" she said. Then seeing my shirt covered with blood: "What's the matter? What happened?"

I didn't answer. I walked into her little room just off the kitchen and threw myself across the bed, where I lay, my breath rasping through my throat.

She followed me into the room and shut the door behind her. "What happened, Frankie? Are you hurt?" Her eyes were large with fear.

I sat up. "No," I answered. "They just shot my boss and Fennelli."

"They?" she asked. "Who?"

"I dunno. I just ran." I stood up. Suddenly I realized I held something in my hand. It was Keough's roll. I must have grabbed it instinctively. I stuck it in my pocket and went over to the window and looked out. "I wonder if thcy followed me here?" I asked almost of myself.

Julie stood beside me. "You poor kid!" she said. "You're frightened to death." She drew me close to her.

"I'm not frightened," I lied. I buried my head against her breasts. It seemed so warm, so safe there. I didn't want to move. A tremor shook me: first one, then another. I tried to fight them but couldn't. In a few seconds I was shivering and my shirt was covered with sweat. I just stood in the circle of her arms, shivering, my teeth chattering like a baby. . . .

A little while later I was sitting in the small armchair in the corner of her room. I began to think. "No one saw me come here. I guess they were after Fennelli. They didn't want me. They had to get Keough 'cause he saw them. I didn't see them. They didn't want me. The cops may want me for questions. But I didn't see nothing. I'm safe as long as I keep my mouth shut. I won't be bothered." Julie went into the other room to get me a drink. "What'll I do with the dough?" I took it out and counted it. There was 653 bucks there. I put it back in my pocket. Julie came back with a cup of coffee.

"Here, drink this," she said, "you'll feel better."

I smiled at her. "I feel better already," I said, drinking the coffee gratefully, "but I can't leave here with this shirt on. It's covered with blood." I took it off and gave it to her. "Here, throw this down the incinerator and give me one of Marty's."

She didn't answer. She took the shirt and left the room. I heard the door of the kitchen open, then the slam of the incinerator. Then she came back into the apartment and went to

Marty's room. A few seconds later she came into the room with one of his shirts over her arm.

I put it on. It was a little tight fitting but not bad. "I better get out of here," I thought.

"Thanks, Julie," I said. "I'd better get out of here before the family comes in."

"You don't have to rush," said Julie. "They all went to the country for the weekend except Mr. Cabell. And he won't be home until one o'clock in the morning when the store closes."

I had supper there and left about nine o'clock and went to the orphanage. I sneaked in the delivery door and up to the dorm. The kids were all asleep. I undressed and tumbled into bed gratefully. I was tired. I fell asleep almost at once.

In the morning I ran downstairs before anyone else and grabbed a look at the papers. The *Daily News* had given it the front-page spread. A big headline shouted: "Fennelli Shot," and the story was on page two. I turned the page. There was a picture of Silk Fennelli in the right hand corner. Underneath was the story:

Gang War Again Breaks Out In New York
Silk Fennelli, famous gambler and racketeer, was shot and seriously wounded, and James (Jimmy) Keough was shot and killed today, by an unknown gangster. Keough was shot twice through the heart, and Fennelli was shot once in the chest and once in the groin, yesterday afternoon in front of a pool parlor that was run by Keough. Police are looking for a boy known to work at Keough's who may possibly be a witness to the crime. Fennelli's condition, it was stated at the Roosevelt Hospital today by the doctors, was serious but not critical. Fennelli true to the code of gangland would not make a statement. "I don't know who would want to shoot me as I'm a guy who minds my own business," he said. The police are working on the case and expect new developments to arise shortly.

I put the paper down. I thought I could recognize a warning to me from Fennelli in the paper—a warning for me to mind my own business. I went on into the dining room for breakfast and then went over to the church to serve altar. I didn't have a thing to worry about.

Chapter Thirteen

AFTER a week had gone by and I hadn't been troubled by anyone, I began again to feel safe. Again I could walk on the streets without being afraid. I had seen in the papers that Fennelli was getting better and would be discharged from the hospital in about three weeks. Keough's was closed and my job was gone, but somehow that didn't bother me. I put the money into another account, and as far as money went I didn't worry about it. I had seen Julie a few times during the week and we said nothing about what had happened.

One morning Brother Bernhard stuck his head in the dormitory door and said to me: "Francis, will ye step into my office and see me after breakfast?"

"Yes, sir," I said.

Later when I went down to his office I saw several people there: the Sister Superior who had charge of the lower grades of the school, Father Quinn and a stranger. He looked like a cop.

I was worried but tried not to show it. I walked over to Brother Bernhard and said to him: "You wanted me, sir?"

"Yes, Francis," he said. "This is Investigator Buchalter of the child welfare commission." To Mr. Buchalter he said: "This is the boy we were talking about."

I waited for them to speak. For a few moments there was a strained silence in the room.

Finally the Sister Superior said: "Francis, you've been a good boy in school. I've known you and watched you since you were a baby. And now I have something to tell you. Something I don't like to tell you but I must. Francis, have you ever thought of being anything else besides a good Catholic boy?"

"No, ma'am," I answered cautiously.

Father Quinn smiled. "See?" he burst out, "just what I told you." He fell silent again.

The Sister Superior continued slowly: "If someone were to come and tell you that you were of another faith, how would you feel, Francis?"

I let an inaudible sigh of relief escape my lips. This wasn't about the shooting. "I wouldn't believe it, ma'am," I answered.

There were smiles all around the room then—proud smiles, smiles saying better than words, "This is a good Catholic boy."

She continued, more at ease than before: "Francis, don't you remember anything about your parents at all?"

It seemed like a foolish question to me. She knew as well as I that I had been here ever since I could remember. I answered politely: "No, ma'am."

"Well," she said, "Mr. Buchalter investigates the parents of all the children here. From time to time he reviews their history in an effort to learn more about them and help them. And he has something to tell you." She looked at him.

He looked very uncomfortable. "You see, Francis, it all started a little while ago. Your case came up for review again when you graduated from St. Therese." His tone of voice was almost apologetic. "When a child enters high school, we again go over the child's history—in this case, yours—to see if there are any more things we can learn before approval is granted—if any relatives can be found. Well to make a long story short we found a relative of yours still alive: an uncle, your mother's brother. Some time ago he wrote us telling of his sister who had come to New York at the time you were born. She died at the time we found you. He identified her by a ring that she had worn and we had kept in the case files to give to you when you came of age. It wasn't a valuable ring, but an unusual one. His description of the design matched with your mother's ring. And now, legally, he wants you to come and live with him. We have determined that he is a good man and responsible man. He has two children of his own. He will give you a good home and take good care of you." Mr. Buchalter stopped.

Father Quinn spoke quickly. "But, Francis, he's different than we are. He does not believe as we do, Francis," his voice was deadly quiet and serious, "he's not of the faith."

I looked at Father Quinn questioningly. "Not of the faith?" I repeated after him, wondering just what that might mean.

"Yes, Francis," Father Quinn said heavily. "He's not Catholic."

I didn't even know what the hell he was talking about.

"In all probability, Francis," Brother Bernhard said, "you will go to live with him in a little while after certain details are worked out. But don't forget all the things you've learned here, Francis. Never forget the Church that has sheltered you and brought you up. Always be a good Catholic no matter what people say."

"Yes, Brother Bernhard," I said, more bewildered than before.

"Your uncle is outside, Francis. Would you like to meet him?" the Sister Superior asked gently.

"Yes, ma'am," I answered automatically. My mind was whirling. I had a family. I wasn't a bastard. I had a family.

Mr. Buchalter went to the door. "Will you come in, Mr. Kane?"

A man stepped into the doorway. He was tall—almost six feet—slightly bald, broad-shouldered and ruddy-faced. He had soft brown eyes and there seemed to be a mist over them. As I looked at him I remembered vaguely hearing somewhere that all non-Catholics went to hell. Somehow I didn't care. I would never mind going to hell if someone would only look at me like that—someone with love and kindness and worry wrinkles in the corners of his eyes as if he were afraid that I wouldn't like him. He smiled and the room lit up. He held out his hand to me. I took it. It was warm and friendly and full of secret understandings that seemed to flow between us like live electric currents.

"So you're Frankie!" he said. His voice was a great deal like him; it was deep and richly warm and trembled just a little.

"Yes, sir," I said, and my voice was shaking too. And there were tears in my eyes too. And there was love in my heart too. For I knew no matter what else in this world, I was kin to this man. I was of his blood and family. I knew it. I felt it.

And it wasn't until a while later that I knew he spelled his name "Cain."

And it wasn't until a few days later that I knew I was a Jew.

Chapter Fourteen

I HEARD somewhere that news has a mysterious way of traveling. Before I had been back in the dorm for more than a few hours, it was all over the place that I had been adopted. The other kids asked me questions and I answered them as best I could. In all truth, I didn't know very much to tell them. I couldn't wait until the afternoon was over so that I could go and tell Julie the news.

I phoned her first to find if the coast was clear, and then went up.

She opened the kitchen door and let me in. She seemed rather tired, but I didn't pay any attention to that and launched into the tale of what happened that day. She was sitting in the chair at the foot of her bed and I was sitting on the edge of the bed as we spoke.

When I had finished she said: "I'm very happy that things are working out for you the way they are. You deserve a break." She spoke without enthusiasm. Her tone of voice was tired and dead sounding.

I looked at her. "You don't sound happy about it."

She stood up and walked over to the window. Her back was toward me. For a minute she didn't speak. When she did speak, her tone of voice was brittle and hard, as I had never heard her voice before. "I'm going home, Frankie."

"Why?" I asked. And then before she could answer: "You don't have to do that. I'll still be around to see you no matter what happens."

She turned and looked at me. "For a free lay?"

I shook my head, "No, because I like you. You ought to know that; you made me say it often enough."

"You don't like me," she said a little coolly, "any more than you'd like any girl who'd let you do it." She turned to the window again. "We'll never see each other again."

I stared at her back for a minute before I spoke. "I still want to know why, Julie?"

Again she looked at me. "If you want to know, you shall. There's nothing in it for me laying for a kid like you. You can't do anything for me. You couldn't even marry me if I should get knocked up. So what's in it for me, outside of being your instructor?

"No, Frankie, summer school's over, so beat it like a good little boy! You've had your fun—now beat it!"

I went over to her and took her arm. She shook it free roughly.

"But Julie—"

"Get out, Frankie!"

A funny lump came into my throat, and I walked to the door. "Good-by, Julie."

She didn't answer me. I opened the door and went out. Outside her door I took a cigarette from my pocket and lit it. I heard the faint creak of her bed, and then I could hear her crying. I walked away from the door and let myself out of the apartment.

I went out into the street. It was a bright, sunny afternoon but I didn't feel it. I felt chilly, almost cold. I walked into the park and threw myself on the grass. I looked up into the sky with unseeing eyes. Thoughts kept running through my mind—Julie, Julie, Julie.

I wrote to Jerry and told him I had been adopted. He sent me a letter saying he was very glad for me. The week flew by and at last it was the day I was to leave. That afternoon my uncle would come to take me away. I had packed my things in a couple of cardboard boxes and had taken them downstairs to the superintendent's office.

I didn't feel like going back to my room. I heard some noises from the gym down in the basement. I thought I'd go down there and see what was doing.

As I started down the steps I heard the lunch bell ring. I went back upstairs to the dining-room. I seated myself at the table and bowed my head while Brother Bernhard said grace. It was then I began to get the strangest feeling—a feeling that I had never been there before. The faces around me seemed strange, indifferent. The white marble table top felt cold and new. I put my fingers on it and felt where I had scratched my name into its surface with a key. It felt rough there, and I wondered how long ago I had done it. It was many years ago—I couldn't remember when. I wasn't hungry. I began to wonder how my aunt would like me, if my cousins would like me. Then I thought that I didn't want to leave here.

Halfway through the meal I asked Brother Bernhard's permission to leave the table. He seemed to understand how I felt and said it would be all right.

I went out into the yard. This was where I had played ball and stood in line to go up to school. It was empty now and deserted, but suddenly I could hear the voices of the kids waiting for the school bell to ring. I could see them running about playing tag and ball, leaving their books in the line to hold their places. I looked up at the steeple of St. Therese half expecting to hear its chimes.

A shadow fell across my path. I looked up. It was Brother Bernhard.

"You're feeling strange, Francis?" He made the statement rather than asked a question.

I nodded.

"I know how you feel, Francis," he said. "I've watched you grow for many years, from when you were a little baby. I remember the first steps you took, the funny way you'd look when you fell and then tried to get up again. You'd never cry. You'd set your mouth in a funny little line and try again. I watched you when you were sick. I tried to help you understand the ways of people. I watched you grow into a fine, strong lad and I was proud of you. I tried to be both a mother and father to you—to cushion your disappointments, to hold your head high when you would fall into despair. I knew you better than any one—better than you yourself did. I knew when you were happy and when you were sad. There were some things I couldn't tell you—things you would have to learn for yourself. I watched you learn them. I watched them form hard lines about your mouth, throw shadows behind your eyes. But there was nothing I could do about it—just hope that you would be all right, that it wouldn't hurt you too much. But always there is the feeling that it wasn't enough."

I looked at him and said: "Oh, no, Brother Bernhard! You were wonderful! I couldn't ever thank you enough for what you did."

He smiled. "'Tis not I that ye should thank, Francis. It's the

Church. And yet the feeling persists in me. I know there are many good things we teach here. But outside these walls, Francis, is where you learn more than anywhere else." He gestured with his hand toward the street. "We who live here live sheltered, quiet lives, free from the struggle, and we lose touch with it. When you're within these confines we can watch you and guide you. But when you're outside. . . . Who is there that can be of help? Who is there to give you shelter and defend you against the thoughtlessness of others? No, Francis, I am afraid there is much more to do—things we never think about. We must learn to walk outside with our boys." He took out his handkerchief and blew his nose. "Enough sentiment, Francis! Did ye say good-by to Father Quinn, the Sister Superior, and all your teachers. We'll miss you."

"I'll miss them too, sir," I said, "I told them good-by this morning."

"Good boy!" he said, walking toward the building with me. "I'll see ye again before ye go." He started into the building.

"Brother Bernhard," I called him back.

He turned toward me. "What is it, son?"

"Is it a mortal sin to be a Jew?" I blurted out.

His face softened as he stood there looking at me. When he finally spoke, he spoke very slowly and quietly: "No, son, it isn't. It couldn't be. You see a lot of us are prone to forget Jesus Christ was a Jew."

"But, Brother, if I'm a Jew and I live with my folks, I could not come here to church. And I would not attend confession and be absolved of my sins. Then when I die I would surely burn in hell."

He came back to me and took my arm. "Francis," his voice was very low, "as much as we like to think it is, heaven is not a private preserve of us Catholics. It is a place where all good people are welcome. I like to believe that it is open to all mankind regardless of the manner in which they worship our Lord, as long as they do believe in Him and live according to His lights. Be a good lad, Francis, and love your people. Do what is right and ye'll have naught to fear." He smiled. "Do ye understand me, son?"

"Yes, sir," I answered, "I think I do."

"Good!" he said. "And now I must go. Luncheon must be almost over." He mussed my hair half affectionately and went inside.

The kids were coming out from lunch. They poured into the yard from all the doorways. I went into the building through the gymnasium entrance.

I stood on the steps of the gym looking around me. There were a couple of kids playing with the basketball on the other side of the room. Peter Sanpero was among them. I decided to walk over and say good-by and to tell him to forget all the arguments we had had.

The group fell silent as I approached. They watched me walk toward them. I could feel something was wrong. The back of my spine tingled, and yet I could not understand why. I had learned a long time ago not to show that I felt anything was wrong. So I continued to walk toward them. I stopped in front of Pete and stuck out my hand.

"Will yuh forget what happened, Pete?" I asked.

He looked at me, ignoring my hand. Then he took a step toward me. "Sure I'll forget," he said, and hit me in the chin. I went head over heels on my back over a boy who knelt down behind me. Several pairs of hands held me down. I couldn't move. At first I was too surprised even to try. Pete stood over me.

"Yuh Jew son-of-a-bitch," he snarled at me, "sneaking into our school and never telling anybody!" He kicked me in the side. I could feel the pain running across me. He bent down and hit me in the face. I managed to pull one hand loose and grabbed his shirt. He pulled back at the same time hitting my face. I hung onto his shirt and he pulled me up with him. My other hand came free and I fastened them around his throat and neck. He was back against the wall and the other boys were swarming against me, hitting me in the back and in the neck. I paid no attention to them. For the first time in my life I fought without thinking. I was crazy with hate for him. I squeezed his neck. Then methodically I began to butt his head against the wall behind him. His hands kept punching me in the stomach. Blood was running down my face from my nose and mouth. Then the other boys jumped on me, and we were all rolling around on the floor, over and over. I felt my jacket tearing away. But I didn't care. All I wanted to do was kill Pete. I wanted to kill him—kill him! I banged his head against the cement floor. Suddenly strong hands grabbed my shoulders, lifting me up, pulling me away from Pete. Suddenly everything was quiet. Brother Bernhard was holding me and I couldn't move. Peter was still lying on the floor.

His face was stern, his eyes blazing mad. "Who started this?" he asked us.

One of the younger kids piped up before he realized what he was saying: "Peter. He said it was about time somebody taught that dirty Jew a lesson." And just as quickly he fell silent.

Without relaxing his grip on my shoulder, Brother Bernhard said to them: "Go to your dormitories." And to Peter he said: "Go home and never come into this gym again. It's only for those who live here."

He held onto me as they went out. When the last one had left the room he let go of my shoulder. He looked at me, his face softening. "Bear them no grudge," he said. "They still have to learn."

I looked at him, my breath coming fast, blood running down my nose, and pain running through my side. I said nothing.

"You'd better wash up," he said more gently. "Your uncle is waiting and you can't change for everything is packed."

I walked into the lavatory and washed my face. Brother Bernhard stood silently behind me and handed me paper towels to dry myself with. Silently we walked upstairs and into the superintendent's office.

My uncle was there. There was a woman with him, who I supposed was my aunt. I guess I made a rather frightening picture as I stood there, my jacket and shirt hanging in shreds around my back covered with blood. Her face grew white. I started across the room. Pain began running down my side and across my chest. There was a roaring in my ears. I felt as if I were falling down into a circle and faces were whirling around me—Brother Bernhard, my uncle, my aunt, Peter, Marty, Raymond, Jerry, Jerry's father, Ruth, Sister Anne, Father Quinn, Jimmy Keough, Fennelli, Julie.

I tried to open my eyes. I could hardly move them. They seemed to be swimming in tears. At last, after hours of trying, I opened them. I was in a white room. My aunt and uncle and Brother Bernhard were bending over me. Out of the corner of my eye I saw a nurse leave the room. Vaguely I wondered what a nurse was doing in my room. I tried to speak.

Brother Bernhard put his finger against my lips. "Hush, lad, don't try to talk. Ye are in Roosevelt Hospital. Ye've three broken ribs. Lie still."

I let my head roll back on the pillow. A calendar on the wall with but a single page on it said in big letters "September 1, 1925."

It was my last day at the orphanage of St. Therese.

Interlude

MARTY

MARTIN stood at the door listening to the tinkle of the chimes coming from within the apartment. He took off his cap. The light from the big overhead fixture turned his thinning blond hair to an almost dull gold matching the oak leaves he wore on the shoulders of his uniform. Half idly he wondered to himself what they would be like. Four years—it was a long time.

People changed in four years. They change a lot. He laughed wryly to himself. He ought to know. For four years he had been watching boys turn into men—old men, tired men. He had watched them walking back to first aid with virginal looks of disappointment and horror imprinted deeply on their faces. Their disbelief in the realities of pain and horror that had surrounded them would leave its mark on them—inside—deep inside.

That had been his job—to remove from inside them those hidden, invisible scars that had been engraved in their souls. The marks on their bodies were comparatively simple to handle. You took a knife and cut and prayed. And after awhile you stopped praying but kept on cutting with an inner feeling of despair. They either survived or didn't. It was as simple as that.

His job wasn't that simple. The things he did to them were not tangible things. They didn't live or die by what he had to do. And yet it made as much difference as if they had lived or died. Only you couldn't see it if you didn't know where to look for it. Sometimes you would suddenly notice a mouth stop its almost imperceptible trembling, or a new light come into an

eye, or the tiniest shake disappear from the hand; or sometimes
it was just in the way a man held his head or the way he walked.
And you would realize you had won. An intangible, viscerous
triumph that would almost slip by you if you hadn't looked up
at the right moment.

Janet opened the door. A moment passed while they looked
at each other. "She hasn't changed much," he thought wildly,
"the same small face, blue eyes, and blond hair, the ends flying
around her face making her look childlike and gaminish."

"Marty," she said in a sweet, pleasing voice.

He felt the soft press of her lips against his cheek and mouth.
The light, tender kiss of friendship, of welcome.

"It's been—" she started to say as he let her go.

"Four years," he said with a smile. "I had just been thinking—"

"So were we," she broke in. "It's a long time. We wondered if
you had changed."

"Funny, I was wondering the same thing about you and
Jerry." She took his arm and drew him toward the living room.
He continued to speak while allowing himself to be drawn
along with her. "For a few lonely seconds I felt like a stranger
standing in the hall waiting for you to open the door."

She took his cap from him and gave it to a maid, who seemed
to appear from nowhere and disappeared as quickly as she had
come. Jerry came running into the room.

The two men clasped hands looking at each other, each
reluctant to let go. They spoke, almost together, the foolish
things that grown men say to each other when deeply moved.

"Marty, you old sawbones!"

"Jerry, you old ambulance chaser!"

Janet came up with some drinks. They raised their glasses.

"To reunion!" toasted Jerry with a smile, inclining his glass
toward Martin.

"To you two!" Martin returned.

"No, wait a minute," interrupted Janet.

The two men looked at her.

She looked back at them proudly, smiling. "To friendship,"
she said, holding her glass high. "The durable kind."

They drained their glasses.

Dinner was one of those things that Martin had dreamed
about for a long time—a rich, white tablecloth, sparkling sil-

ver, impeccably clean china, candles on the table. And these were his friends—the friends of his childhood, with whom he could retrace the steps of time and live again those very young, exciting days when all the world was new and every day was different and every tomorrow had hope.

It was inevitable they should talk about Francis. They always did sooner or later. This time Janet started it and Martin picked up the thread. Memories flooded into his mind and spilled over to his tongue—Francis, the first days they had met and spent together. It was as if it had happened yesterday.

"I remember the first time I saw him," he heard himself saying. "We were only kids then. I was about thirteen and a bunch of boys ganged up on me as I was coming from school. He gave me a licking and then chased the others away.

"It was strange. I never could understand why he liked me, but, as far as I felt, he was wonderful." He laughed a little. "He did the things that all boys wanted to do and did them well. At that time I had been interested in boxing but I wasn't too good at it. He was good. I knew that as soon as I tried to hit him.

"But there were other things about him that drew me to him: an instinctive, almost reluctant, sense of fair play, of feeling for the other fellow; a certain quiet competence and surety in himself and in what he did. Older people didn't faze him. He spoke to them as he did to me, as an equal, as if he were one of them.

"It was from him I drew a sense of equality. Before that I was always aware of the fact that I was a Jew. I had been reminded by obscenities scrawled on walls, by beatings in the streets, by sly sniggering remarks, and by being tripped up and having my books knocked out of my hand. I was in a fair way toward becoming twisted and bigoted myself, attributing every little incident that had happened to that fact. But he cured me in the way he took me into his little group without question, the way he had me meet his friends without explanation.

"He accepted me and so did his friends. Maybe it was because of him that they did. Maybe not. I don't know. But I like to think that he helped.

"I remember many years later when I was going to med school that I thought of him and realized that it was as much due to him as anyone else that I was doing as I did. He once said something to me about a fellow I didn't care very much for. 'Oh, he's all right. You just gotta understand him, that's all.'

"And in those words I found an answer to almost everything that had been festering in the back of my mind. If you understand a man, if you know why he does things, you don't have to be afraid of him, you don't have to let your fear lead you to dislike him, you don't have to let your dislike lead you to destroy him. I don't know whether I thought it all out when I was young or when I was in school, but in some way I associate the two as if they happened together.

"It was in Germany in 1935 that I again thought of him. I was attending the university there, taking specialized courses. One day coming from lectures, I walked along the street reading a book I was very interested in at the time. I had to concentrate even more than usual because German was a tough language for me, and I bumped into a man. Without looking up I apologized and proceeded on my way.

"Then it happened. For a moment I was confused and a kid again back on Fifty-ninth Street being tormented by a group of ignorant kids. Then I heard the word '*Jude*' used in that evil, nasty manner. I looked up and saw the man in a uniform which I recognized as a storm trooper's. He struck at me, and I beat the living daylights out of him.

"Then I turned and went back to school and asked the professor, who incidentally wasn't Jewish, why they permitted that to happen? 'You don't understand, my boy,' he said, wagging his very gray head, 'the people are sick and unhealthy and afraid and of their fear is born a hate. . . .'

"That moment I thought of Frankie and what he said. 'Why don't you people who do understand explain it to them?' I asked.

" 'We are only a few and they won't listen to us,' was his answer.

"I left Germany the next day without finishing the semester. I had something to tell the folks back home, but they didn't understand what I was saying. Only a few did—you both, and Ruth, and others that I could count on the fingers of my hands. The rest just didn't believe—or didn't care.

"Many were the times when I was tired and discouraged with the progress I had been making with a patient that I felt like saying to him, 'Oh, the hell with it! Get out of here. I can't do anything for you,' and I'd remember what Frankie said and I'd say to myself: 'It's not the patient's fault, it's mine. I don't understand, don't know what's wrong. And if I don't know, how can I help?"

"I would have another whack at it. Sometimes it would work—maybe more times than less. I know there were some cases I couldn't do anything for, but it wasn't for the lack of trying. It was because I didn't understand them, was too stupid to see what was wrong. It was my ignorance that was to blame, not theirs."

He laughed a little and raised a glass of wine to his lips. "There speaks Martin Cabell, the greatest psychiatrist in the world, explaining his failures in the light of reason. Or maybe it's because I have a feeling of inferiority myself."

He took another sip of the wine and looked at them. As he spoke, his face had lost its intensity, had relaxed and grown soft, younger. Suddenly he smiled. It was the same old smile— warm and fresh and young. "Old friends," he thought contentedly. "The same as before. They haven't changed. You can still talk and they will listen." The world seemed right again, and for the first time since he had come back, he felt at home.

PART TWO

Chapter One

DURING the days that followed at the hospital I learned a great deal about my uncle and his family. He had a job as a salesman for a dress house downtown, and they had been living in New York for the past ten years. They had a fairly comfortable five-room apartment on Washington Heights.

His wife was a quiet, gentle woman whom I worshipped almost on sight. She would never by word or action ever show herself to be thinking unkindly of me. She would come to the hospital every day bearing a little gift of fruit or cookies or a book to while away the time. She would stay as long as she could and then leave. Sometimes she would bring my cousins with her. They were two little girls about eight and ten years old.

At first the girls were prone to regard me with awe and a certain mixture of friendliness and shyness. Later as they became more accustomed to me, they would kiss my cheek as they came in and left.

Morris and Bertha Cain and their children, Esther and Irene, were the first real family I had ever had, and if I felt strange to them or they to me, it was easily understandable. Family relationships that seemed normal to most people were only strangely intricate to me. I could never figure out the problem of who was whose cousin, and second and first cousins had me completely licked. But we got along.

I left the hospital near the end of September and stepped

right into a new world. Uncle Morris had a small Buick car and he drove me home. He had called for me alone. Upon arriving in the apartment, I found out they were planning a little party for me. Aunt Bertha had baked a cake, and I met lots of other relatives of ours. When they had all gone I was shown to the room that would be mine. It used to be Irene's room (she was the older of the two) but she now shared a room with Esther or Essie, as they called the younger. My clothes were already hung in the closet and the place seemed very warm and friendly to me.

I remember Uncle Morris saying: "This is your room, Frankie." And opening the door, he motioned to me and I crossed the threshold, he and Aunt Bertha following me. The children had already been put to bed. I looked around it. The first thing I noticed was a small framed picture of a young woman on the dresser.

Aunt Bertha saw me looking at it. "That's your mother, Frankie. It's the only picture we have of her and I thought you would like to have it."

I went over to look at it. She was about nineteen when the picture was taken. Her hair was combed down with a bun tied in back as was the fashion in the days when the picture was taken. Her lips were half smiling and a reflection of hidden laughter seemed to dance in her eyes. Her chin was firm, rounded but strong—too strong perhaps for eyes and lips like hers. I looked at it for a few minutes.

Uncle Morris said: "You look very much like her, Frankie. Your eyes are the same color, and the shape of your mouth is so much like hers it almost isn't a boy's mouth at all." He went over to it, picked it up, looked at it, and then put it down. "Would you like to hear about her?" he asked.

I nodded.

"Supposing you undress," he said, "and we'll talk while you're changing."

Aunt Bertha came into the room and, opening one of the drawers in the dresser, took out a new pair of pajamas and gave them to me. "We thought you could use some new things," she said and smiled.

"Thank you," I said, taking them from her, feeling strangely about it. I had yet to learn how to accept a gift. I began to unbutton my shirt.

"You need never feel ashamed of your mother, Frankie," my

uncle began. "She was an unusual girl. You see, a long time ago
we all lived in Chicago. That's where we came from. Your
mother was the pride of the family. When she was twenty she
had already graduated from college and was going to work.
That was about when that picture was taken, a few months
after she had graduated. Fran was a high-strung girl, an active
one. She used to be a suffragette and always spoke about equal
rights. The family took an odd pride in her. At that time
women didn't have the right to vote they have today, and she
was always going about and making speeches about it. She was
a very good bookkeeper, and once at Marshall Field's (that's a
big department store in Chicago where she used to work) she
was the only one that could find a mistake in the inventory that
they used to take every month. About that time I came to New
York. A little while after that she fell in love with a man who
used to work down there. She wanted to marry him but my
mother and father would not consent. You see, he wasn't
Jewish and our family was very strict. To make the story short,
she ran away with him. I got a letter from her saying she was
going to look me up in New York as soon as she got here. That
was the last anyone ever heard from her. We tried to find her
but couldn't. There wasn't a trace of her anywhere. Shortly
after that my mother died and my father came to New York to
live with us. He always used to say to me: 'If we hadn't been
such fools and tried to make Faigele do what we wanted, we all
still would be together.' He died soon after my mother. He was
never very happy when she had gone."

He picked up the picture again and held it in his hand.

"But that was what happened yesterday," Aunt Bertha said.
"Today is what matters most. I feel somehow they all know
that you are with us and they are happy—just as happy as we
are to have you here. We want you to love us as we love you,
Frankie." She took the picture from my uncle's hand and put it
back on the dresser.

"Yes, ma'am," I said putting on the bottom part of my
pajamas and laying my pants on the chair. I sat down on the
edge of the bed, took off my shoes and stockings, and slid
between the sheets.

"Good night," they said. Aunt Bertha bent over me and
kissed my cheek.

"Good night," I said.

They went out the door. Aunt Bertha paused with her hand

on the light switch before she turned it out. "Frankie," she said.
"Yes, ma'am?" I answered.

"Don't say 'Yes, ma'am' to me. Call me Aunt Bertha." She
flicked the light and went out.

"Yes—Aunt Bertha," I half whispered to myself, putting my
hand on my cheek. It was still warm where she kissed me. I fell
asleep with the moonlight on my mother's picture, and it
seemed to me in the dark that she was smiling.

Chapter Two

I AWOKE early the next morning. The apartment was quiet
and everyone seemed to be still asleep. I got out of bed and
walked over to the dresser and looked at my watch. It was half
past six. I walked over to the window and looked out.

The morning was still grayish; the sun hadn't come up yet.
My room faced a courtyard and around it were two other
houses. Through the open windows came an occasional ring of
an alarm clock and the smell of early-morning coffee. The sides
of the buildings facing the courtyard were painted white to
better reflect the light. I turned back from the window and
slipped on my underwear and trousers and walked quietly to
the bathroom to wash.

When I had finished washing I went back to my room and sat
down. I had to get used to this. It was strange not to be sleeping
in a room with a bunch of boys in it, and I missed the morning
horseplay and jokes. I heard someone walking in the hall outside my door. I walked over and opened it. It was my aunt.

"Good morning, Frankie. You're up early." She smiled.

"Yes'm," I said, "I'm used to it."

"Did you wash already?" she asked.

"Un-hunh." I replied, "I'm all dressed."

"Then would you mind running down to the baker for some
rolls?" she asked. "It will save me the trouble."

"I'll be glad to, Aunt Bertha," I answered.

She gave me some change, told me what store she wanted me to go to, and I left the house.

It was near seven and people were beginning to go to work. I picked up the stuff she sent me for, and bought a *News* on the way back.

Once in the house, I put the stuff on the kitchen table and sat down to read the paper. A few minutes later my aunt came in and put on the coffee. About ten minutes later my uncle came in, sat down at the table and said: "Good morning, Frankie. Did you sleep all right?"

"Fine, Uncle Morris," I said.

"I see you have the paper," he said. "Anything new in it?"

"Nothing much," I answered and held it toward him. "You want to see it?"

"Thanks," he said and took it from me.

Aunt Bertha came over with the plate of toast and put a glass of orange juice in front of us. Without looking at it, my uncle reached over his paper and picked it up. I drank mine slowly.

Then we had some eggs and then coffee and some pieces of Danish pastry that I had brought up from the store. About the time we finished, the kids came in and sat down.

"Good morning," they said in unison, and going to each side of their father, they kissed him on the cheek. He gave them each a squeeze and went back to reading his paper and drinking a second cup of coffee. Then they went over to Aunt Bertha and kissed her. She bent to kiss them and whispered something.

They came over to me and kissed me. I laughed. They pulled up chairs to the table and sat down.

Uncle Morris looked at his watch. "Time for me to go," he said. "Are you going up to school today, Frankie?" he asked.

"I guess so," I said.

"Well," he said, "let me know tonight how you make out." He kissed his wife and went out.

"What school are you going to, Frankie?" asked Essie, the younger.

"George Washington High," I answered.

"I go to P. S. 181," she said.

"That's nice," I said. We were quiet for awhile. I didn't know what else we could talk about.

Aunt Bertha gave the kids their breakfast and then sat down. She smiled at me. "Did you like your breakfast?"

"It was swell, Aunt Bertha."

"I'm glad," she said.

"I think it's time you got started," she said. "You don't want to be late the first day you go there."

"No," I said, "I don't." I went into my room and put on my tie and jacket—then back into the kitchen. "So long," I said.

Aunt Bertha got up from the table and walked to the door with me. In the foyer she gave me some money. "This is your allowance for the week," she said, "for lunches and things. If you need any more, let me know."

It was three dollars. "No," I said. "It's enough. I don't think I'll need any more. Thanks."

"Good luck," she said, and I closed the door behind me. I felt funny. I didn't know why. Everything seemed so different. Maybe it was because I didn't have to attend Mass before I went to school.

George Washington High School was at 191st Street and Audubon Avenue. It stood on the top of a hill overlooking the Heights and across the East River to the Bronx. It was a new red brick building with a dome on it.

I was sent to the superintendent's office. I gave the clerk my name and waited while she looked up my card. She found it and told me to go to Room 608 when the nine-o'clock bell rang.

When the bell rang, the halls were full of kids running back and forth to their rooms. I found the room without too much trouble. I went in and gave my card to the teacher in charge. He directed me to a seat in the back of the room. I looked around me. The class seemed mixed—about twenty colored boys and girls, and twenty white. The boy sitting next to me was colored.

"New here?" he asked with a big smile. "My name's Sam Cornell."

"Mine's Kane," I said. "Francis Kane."

Things certainly were different here.

It was at the end of the first week in school that we first got around to talking about religion. I had often wondered why Jews were as they were; now I thought I understood. They didn't go to church during the week—not even on Saturday, which was their Sunday. I supposed I missed the routine of attending Mass every morning.

It wasn't that I was particularly religious. Most of the time I went only because I had to, and many were the times I had

ducked Mass if I possibly could. But it left a void in the routine
I had been used to ever since I was a kid.

I was sitting around the house. I had read all the papers and
was getting restless. Uncle Morris was down at the office Saturday mornings squaring up his accounts for the week. Just Aunt
Bertha and I were in the house; the kids were out playing.
Finally I put the papers down and got up. "Aunt Bertha," I
asked, "is it O. K. for me to run downtown for a while?"

She looked up at me shrewdly. "Sure it is, Frankie—you
don't have to ask."

I went into the other room to get my coat, and came back
into the parlor. She was watching me curiously, sort of embar-
rassed-like. I could see she was too polite to ask me where I was
going, and I didn't know just what to say to her. I didn't know
whether I could tell her I was going to see Brother Bernhard
and maybe afterwards drop into church. But she was smarter
than me. As I went near the door, she spoke.

"Will you be gone long, Frankie?" she asked.

I stopped. "I don't know," I answered. "I thought I'd kinda
look around and see some friends."

"Oh!" she said. "Your uncle and I had planned for you to go
over to the synagogue today with us. I thought you might like
to go now if you've nothing better you'd rather do."

I stood there quietly a moment while I turned the idea over
in my mind. My aunt was smart all right. Maybe she was even
a little bit of a mind reader. Then I answered: "Do you think it
would be all right for me to go? I've never been to one before."

She smiled slowly, her voice very soft: "Of course it's all
right. We'd be very happy if you would come."

"O. K," I said, "if you say so."

"Wait a minute," she said. "I'll get my coat and go with
you."

As we walked to the synagogue she was very quiet. We came
to a gray brick building. "This is the synagogue," she told me.

I looked at the building. It wasn't very impressive: just a flat
one-story affair, no statues of saints over the door, not even a
Jewish star—just a plain building with a plain door. It didn't
look like a holy place where people came to worship. I felt
vaguely disappointed.

I was even more disappointed when we went inside. The
door was a few steps below street level and you had to walk

down to it. Once inside the door we were in a small room that had very plain gray painted walls. I started to take off my hat.

My aunt stopped me. "In synagogue, Frankie, you keep your hat on. You must always cover your head."

I looked at her for a minute, not understanding. Everything was backwards here.

She led me through the door on the opposite side of the room, and we were in the church. There were a few people in there. This room too was very plain. There were plain mahogany-stained benches on the floor, most of them needing a new coat of paint. The wall too needed a new coat of paint and some plastering because it was badly cracked in some places.

At the far end of the room there was a raised platform with four posters, over which was hung a faded red velvet canopy. Under the canopy there was a sort of a closet; and a man stood in front of the closet. He was reading aloud in Jewish from a scroll that was held in front of him by two other men.

We started down the aisle and entered one of the rows of benches near the front. I started to kneel, but my aunt put her hand under my arm and shook her head slightly. I sat down beside her.

"A Jew," she whispered, "does not kneel to his God. His humility must be of the spirit, not the body."

I looked at her, my eyes wide. This wasn't very much like church at all. You didn't have to behave very differently here than anywhere else except you had to keep your hat on.

"Where is the rabbi?" I asked her. The only men I saw on the platform were all dressed in plain suits.

"He's the man reading from the Torah."

I guessed she meant the man that was reading from the scroll. Maybe I expected someone dressed in elaborate robes; but if I did, I wasn't to see one.

My aunt picked up a small book from the bench beside her, opened it, and gave it to me. Half the page was printed in Jewish, the other half in English. "This is what he is reading," she said, her finger pointing to a line. "He reads the Hebrew but you can read the English."

The man had paused for a moment while the scroll was turned. Then he began again. His voice had a monotonously soothing, sing-song tone about it.

"Boruch atto adonoi, elohenu melech ho'olom. . . ."

I looked down at the book. My aunt's finger pointed to a line in English. I read it.

"Blessed art Thou, O Lord our God. . . ."

This was something I could understand. I shut my eyes and I could see a picture of Father Quinn, kneeling in front of the altar, the soft light of the candles turning to gold the white of his robe. I could hear the soft voices of the choir rising. I could smell the resin and the incense and the warmth of the church. My lips moved involuntarily: "Hail Mary, Mother of God."

My aunt touched my shoulder, I opened my eyes startled for a moment. She was smiling softly but I could see the tears sparkling in the corner of her eyes.

"It's the same God, Frankie."

I could feel the tension flow out of me. Suddenly I smiled at her.

She was right: the Word meant God in no matter what language you spoke it—English, Latin or . . . Hebrew.

When we got home Uncle Morris was there, and my aunt told him where we had been. He looked over at me. "What do you think of it?" he asked.

"I don't know," I answered, "It's pretty strange."

"Would you like to go to a Hebrew school to learn more about it?" he asked.

I hesitated before I answered, and my aunt spoke for me: "I think we had better let him make up his own mind on that question, Morris. He's old enough now to decide what he wants. Let him think about it and if he wants to go, he can tell us."

I was very grateful to her for that. At the moment I didn't know whether I wanted to go or not. But Aunt Bertha had told me the same thing Brother Bernhard had, and if that was true, I couldn't see what difference it made whether I went or not.

"But," Uncle Morris protested, "He should prepare for his *bar mitzvah*."

Again my aunt answered, with an understanding smile toward me, "It doesn't really make much difference now. *Bar mitzvah* won't make him any more of a man than he is already, and if he feels the need of a faith, I don't think he'll have any trouble finding it. He's already doubly blessed."

Those were the last words they ever spoke to me on religion. I was left free to make up my own mind on the subject, and I

never gave it more than a passing thought after that. I never
went to Hebrew school or to a church or synagogue afterward,
but then I never gave much thought to God either. I felt con-
fident that I would be able to deal with Him when the time
came for me to have to—just as I would deal with everything
else in my life, when the time came and not before.

Chapter Three

YOU can never bring back old times; that was something I
learned then. Though Jerry and Marty and I would still pal
around together, we couldn't recapture the closeness that had
existed between us before I moved uptown. It wasn't because of
less camaraderie between us, it was rather that I was in process
of normalizing. I was no longer on the outside looking in; I had
a family of my own and I liked it that way. I began to learn
things about care and consideration for others which I had
never known before. But that feeling was directed solely
toward my family, and to others outside my family I still kept
my original attitude. It was like being two different people—
almost. It would have been hard to tell where one set of feelings
would leave off and the other would begin. But I didn't think
about it, and, what's more, I didn't even know about it at the
time—so I didn't care.

Things moved along. I was a fair student, no better or worse
than any of the others. Not too greatly to my surprise, I drifted
into a position of leadership among the other boys. I took this
as being quite in order; I always had been a leader. I was more
aggressive than most, more forward than the others. I wasn't
troubled by the vague adolescent speculations about sex, and
would look amusedly at their attitudes and conversations. I
already had passed that stage. Then too, I was a more than
capable athlete. I made the basketball team and the swimming
team my first year in school. I played basketball the only way I
knew—that was to win. To hell with rules of so-called sports-

manship and fair play! They were only for the dumbbells who weren't fast enough or smart enough to get away with breaking them. Besides, I hated to lose.

And yet, despite my attitude toward others, my closeness to my family grew as bit by bit they chipped the raw, sore edges from my nature. Little by little the slightly defensive air I carried within myself like a mental chip on my shoulder began to disappear, and soon left nothing but a forward-looking aggressiveness, which in turn became better concealed as I learned to use the social amenities to bend others to my way of thinking.

The Friday night before the Christmas holiday we had a basketball game between James Monroe High and ourselves, and a dance was to follow the game. I had heard there was some talk about me running for class president, and though I played dumb about it, I was aware of the talk and knew that a great deal would depend on how I showed up in the game tonight whether they would ask me to run or not.

I went out on the court determined to show to the good. I played a hell of a game—rough borderline playing that I learned so well down on Tenth Avenue. I played to the grandstand to the point of taking the play away from the rest of my team. When the final score came on, we had won and I was the undoubted star of the game.

I knew some of the boys were a little sore because of what I had heard them say in the showers. I laughed to myself. Let the clucks grumble! If they made too much noise, I'd shut them up. I got dressed and went out to the dance and stood on the edge of the floor watching the crowd for a moment until I caught sight of Marty and Jerry in earnest conversation with the faculty adviser to the G.O. council. I knew that his permission had to be obtained before I could run for class office. Still playing dumb, I walked toward the door, pretending to be on my way out, but making sure I passed them and came into their line of vision.

"Hey, Frankie!" Marty cried, "Where do you think you're goin'!"

"Home," I said smiling. "I promised my aunt I would—"

"You can't go," he interrupted, "You're the big moment of the evening. The kids want to see you. Besides, you're expected at the dance."

"By who?" I asked.

"By the folks," he said. "It would be a hell of a thing if you walked out on them now. There's talk of running you for class president next month, and how would it look if you didn't show up?"

I laughed inwardly. Just then Jerry came up.

"Hey, Jerry," Marty said grabbing him by the arm, "Frankie's going home."

"What for?" Jerry asked, turning to see me. "You sick or something?"

"No," I replied, "I'm tired. What the hell! I ran around all evening."

"Nuts to that!" Jerry said, "You're going to the dance. You're going to be the new class president."

"Look here, guys," I said to them, "How about telling me the score? About this business of being president—who started it?"

Marty and Jerry looked at each other. Marty spoke. "You see it's like this: we thought that it would be a good idea. You are the best-known guy in the class. Everyone likes you and you'd be a cinch for the job."

"What would I have to do?" I asked.

"Not much," Jerry said. "You'd be on the student-teachers advisory committee and would be a big help to the class. Besides, you get certain privileges too. You come to the dance, and later I'll tell you more about it."

"O. K.," I said. "But first I'd better call home."

I did and then went back into the gym. A six-piece band was playing off in the corner and a bunch of kids were dancing. There was a table set up and some kids were getting punch and soft drinks there. Marty came up to me. A girl was with him; I recognized her. She was a nice kid from my biology class. I didn't remember her name, though.

"You know each other," Marty said to me. "She's going to run for vice-president with you." And he walked off and left us.

We looked at each other. She smiled. It was a very nice smile. It transformed her face into something alive and gay. "Don't you want to dance, Frankie?" she asked.

"Oh," I said awkwardly, "of course! But I'm not so good at it."

"That's all right," she said. "I'll help you." She came into my arms. For a few moments I was stiff, and once I stepped on her foot. But she smiled and said: "Take it easy! Relax!"

I did. And it wasn't too bad. At last the music stopped. "That wasn't too difficult, was it?" she smiled.

"No." I grinned. "But you're too good for me."

She laughed pleasantly. "You'll catch on. All you need is a little practice."

"Would you like some punch?" I asked.

We walked over to the refreshment table. We said hello to many kids on the way over, but no one called her name and I didn't find it out then. We danced most of the dances together. Several times I was stopped and congratulated on the game. The dance was over at eleven o'clock and we walked home together. She lived in an apartment house a few blocks from me, and I saw her to her door. We stopped and talked about the dance, and suddenly I realized I had had a very good time.

It was about a quarter past eleven. "I've got to go in now," she said. "It's getting late."

"Yes," I said, "it's getting late."

"Good night, Frankie." She smiled up at me.

"Good night," I said. On an impulse I kissed her. She put her arms around my neck; I could smell the clean fresh perfume on her hair. I started to kiss her as I had kissed Julie, but suddenly something stopped me. Her mouth was soft and sweet and gentle—innocent-like. She didn't press herself to me; her lips were not as fiercely violent as Julie's. I relaxed. I put my arms around her back. I had instinctively tried to feel her breasts but had stopped before I got to them. The sweetness of her lips and the softness of her cheek were close to me. She drew her lips from mine and laid her head against my shoulder. I held her closely but loosely. The contact of our bodies was not a sexual one; it was a clean feeling, a young feeling, an "it's-great-to-be-alive" feeling.

"I don't know what you're thinking, Frankie," she said, "but I don't do this with every boy I meet."

"I know," I said. Her perfume was in my nostrils.

She stepped back. "Good night, Frankie." She went into her apartment and closed the door.

I took a few steps down the hall. Then I realized I hadn't found out her name. I went back and looked at the doorbell. "Lindell" it said.

Suddenly I knew her name. It was Janet Lindell. I walked down the hall whistling.

Chapter Four

DURING Christmas week Jerry and Marty came up to my house to see me. Aunt Bertha had taken my cousins to the movies. We sat around in the parlor.

Jerry, as usual, was doing most of the talking. He was trying to convince me that running for class president was a good thing—not that I needed much convincing. "Look," he said, "it can do a lot for you. You'll be on the student-teachers committee and you're given extra credit in civics class."

"Sure!" Marty said. "And besides you'll be a big guy with the crowd. And they'll listen to you. You're a natural leader."

I liked that. "O. K.," I said. "What do I have to do?"

"Not much," Jerry spoke quickly. "We have your campaign all set. We'll take care of the details. All you have to do is make a small speech at the introductory rally the Friday after we get back to school."

"Oh, no!" I said. "I'm not going to get up and make a speech in front of all those people! Not me! I'm out!"

"Look," Marty said, "it's easy. Why we even have your speech written. I have a copy here." He took a sheet of paper from his pocket and gave it to me.

I read it. Halfway through I stopped. "What kind of crap are you guys giving me?" I asked them. "This is screwy. Give this to the other guy if you want me elected. It don't make sense."

"Neither does politics," said Jerry, "and I ought to know! I heard my old man say so a dozen times. It ain't what you do or say that counts. It's how the people like you that gets you in. The best man in the world can't get elected dogcatcher if he hasn't got what you call personality. Marty and I'll coach you in it. You're the last speaker on the program. We'll fix it. The other guys will knock the crowd dead trying to make sense. Then all you have to do is get up, say your piece and you're in."

"Yeah, he's right," said Marty.

"All right," I said, "but if this dosen't come off, you guys are going to have to answer a lot of questions."

"Don't worry," they said almost together, "it'll come off all right!"

Ten nights in a row I practiced that speech. Jerry and Marty coached me until I was sick of it. They told me where to walk, how to hold my hands, what to wear. Two days before the rally they told me to forget about it until I would make the talk.

I couldn't forget it. I thought about it all day during my classes. I lay awake at night thinking about it, and when I fell asleep I dreamed about it. At last the day came. Following their suggestion, I wore a bow tie and a sweater under my jacket.

I felt very self-conscious as I took my place on the platform with the other candidates. I thought the entire assembly was staring at me. Janet sat next to me. Every few moments she would smile at me and I would try to smile back. But I think I must have looked ghastly.

The principal made his speech. It was something about the pupils becoming good citizens and practicing democracy, but I couldn't pay too much attention to him I was so nervous. Then the first speaker got up.

He promised to give the first-term students the best representation the class ever had, and took about ten minutes doing it. When he finished, the cheer leaders got up and ordered a cheer for him. Then they sat down and the second candidate got up. He promised the same things as the first in about the same length of time. I could see the pupils were becoming fidgety and bored. When he had finished, the cheer leaders led a yell for him, and then it was my turn.

My heart was hammering, my throat felt all tight. I didn't think I could speak. I half turned to Janet, she held up both hands to show me her fingers were crossed for luck. I turned and sauntered slowly to the center of the platform. I looked out over the kids' faces and they all seemed strangely blurred to me. I forced myself to speak.

"Mr. Principal, teachers, and fellow students." My voice seemed to echo from the back of the auditorium. "Too loud," I thought.

The pupils all looked half startled, as if I had awakened them from sleep.

"I'm scared," I said a little more quietly, more naturally.

They all laughed—even the teachers. I could feel the tension seeping out of me. I continued.

"Believe it or not," I said, "I don't know why I'm up here anyway."

Then everybody laughed. I could feel all the tension go.

"The other day," I said, "a couple of students (friends of mine) came up to me and asked: 'How would you like to be class president?' and I, like a fool, said: 'Fine.' Now I wonder if they were really friends of mine?"

The audience laughed and some started to applaud. "By Jesus!" I thought, "Jerry is right   They're eating it up." I went on speaking.

"I have just listened to my opponents' speeches, and I'm beginning to wonder if I will vote for myself."

A shout of laughter went up and the students leaned forward in their seats waiting for my next remark. I walked slowly toward the corner of the platform before I spoke again.

"After all, if being on the basketball team or the swimming team is any recommendation for a class president (I opened my jacket to let them see the small orange-and-black "W" on my sweater), then you've got a darn good ping-pong player on your tennis team!"

That didn't go over so well but they still laughed. I walked back to the center of the platform.

"I don't know what to promise you if I'm elected class president. My opponents promised you everything I could think of."

They laughed and applauded that. I held up my hands to quiet them.

"Not that I think they're wrong—they're absolutely right. I agree with them in every respect. I would like to promise you less homework, more study periods, and shorter school hours but I can't. I think the board of education would object to it."

Laughter and applause greeted that. I stole a quick look at Marty and Jerry sitting in the first row and saw them smiling. Jerry held up his hand, fingers circled, showing that everything was all right. I continued.

"Now I don't want to take up much more of your time because I know how anxious you all are to get back to your classes. (Laughter) But I want to assure you, both on my opponents' behalf and my own, that whoever you may elect will give you the best that is in them, and the most any person can do is their best."

I walked to my seat and sat down. The students were on their feet, shouting and applauding.

Janet whispered in my ear: "Get up and take a bow."

"I will if you'll come with me," I said. She nodded. I took her hand and together we walked to the center of the platform. We smiled at the crowd. She looked very pretty in her pink dress. I held up my hand and they fell quiet.

"If you don't vote for me," I said, "don't forget to vote for Janet for vice-president. She'll be the prettiest and smartest vice-president George Washington High School ever had."

They laughed and applauded until the gong rang and the rally was over. We walked down the platform and were surrounded by friends.

That afternoon was election, and while the votes were being counted, Janet and I waited with some friends in the office of the school paper. Ruth Cabell came up to me while I was talking to Janet.

"You ought to come out for the dramatic club, Frankie," she said sarcastically. "I'm sure Miss Gibbs would love to have you." She walked away before I could make a reply. She worked on the paper.

"Who is she?" Janet asked.

"She's Marty's sister," I answered.

Just then Marty came running in. He was all excited. "We're in!" he shouted, "You're both elected! It was a landslide! What did I tell you!"

He grabbed my hand and started shaking it. For a moment I didn't smile—I was thinking about what Ruth had said—then I laughed.

Jerry came running in with about a dozen kids including my rivals. My rivals wished me luck, and soon the room was crowded and I forgot all about what Ruth had said.

Chapter Five

IF I hadn't been elected class president, I never would have met Mrs. Scott and Marty wouldn't have become what he is today. But sometimes I tend to run ahead of myself—my thoughts come much quicker than I can write them.

I met Mrs. Scott at the first meeting of the student-teachers council I attended. We were introduced. I noticed a kindly-looking lady of about fifty with steel-gray eyes and a thin, determined mouth. She was doing some psychological work in connection with the children's welfare bureau.

Most problems at the meeting were petty: children consistently being late or absent, cutting classes, talking back to teachers. We did not punish them; we tried to determine who was right or wrong in these differences: the pupil, the teacher, or the pupil's parents. Every case was referred to Mrs. Scott. She would speak to the pupil and try to get from him the reason behind these actions.

In a school the size of this, the number of petty cases was enormous. The girl that had helped Mrs. Scott keep her records graduated that term. And she asked for someone else to help her. I suggested Marty, knowing he was looking for some extra credits.

Marty and she hit it off right away. And Marty liked the work. It was probably then he decided to become a psychiatrist. He had always wanted to be a doctor, and this was right in line with what he wanted.

Janet and I became very friendly, and around school we were considered as going together. I liked her but thought somehow, after having known Julie, things weren't quite the same, or ever would be. But we continued to go around with each other, continued to kiss each other good night after Saturday night dates, and continued the tedious process of growing up.

School went on. Soon it was Easter, and then summer vacation. I passed all my subjects and that summer went to Rockaway with my relatives.

It was the best summer I had ever had. There was a crowd of youngsters at the beach and we had some swell times. I swam a lot and loafed on the beach all day. I grew tan and dark. I don't suppose I was any different than any other boy at the beach. We looked at the girls in their bathing suits, talked about their physical attributes, and speculated whether they did or didn't. I found out one girl did, and thought I had something exclusive till I found out that almost all the other boys thought the same thing. Then I dropped her cold.

I gained about seven pounds as the summer went by, and soon it was time to close the bungalow and go back to town and school. I guess that was the happiest summer of my life. I often wonder why I can't remember every detail of it, but it was so pleasant that every day seemed to flow into the next and before I knew it, it was over.

School again. This term I was a sophomore. I made the regular basketball team and the swimming team, and before the term was over, I was wearing a big orange-and-black "W" on my sweater. I was now one of the top men in the school and always had a crowd around me, and was catered to and flattered as only a high school hero could be.

All of us had grown that summer, Jerry and Marty and I—Janet too. But I didn't know how much until one day after the Thanksgiving Day football game when I took her home. She was going to her grandmother's for Thanksgiving dinner. Her parents had already left. She was to meet them after she had changed her clothes. I waited in her apartment for her to change because I was to walk over to her grandmother's before going on home. I threw my coat across the couch in her living-room and sat down and began to read the paper.

A few minutes later she came into the room, wearing a bathrobe and carrying a slip over her arm. "I have to iron this," she said. "It wasn't dry enough this morning." She went into the kitchen. I sauntered over to the door and watched her. She let the ironing board down from its niche in the wall, plugged in an electric iron, and then came into the parlor with me. "It takes a few minutes to warm up," she said. "I won't be long."

"That's O. K.," I said. "I have lots of time."

She went over to the window. "Look," she cried, "it's snowing!"

I went over and stood beside her. "Whadda ya know!" I said.

She turned toward me. "First snow this year."

"Yeanh," I said, putting my arms around her and kissing her. "First this year."

For a moment her arms were around me. Then she dropped them. "The iron must be warm," she said, walking into the kitchen.

"So am I!" I said.

She laughed and tested the iron. "Not warm enough."

"Who said so?" I demanded, purposely misunderstanding her. "I'm boiling over."

"Not you, silly, the iron!" Then she saw the smile on my face and walked over toward mc.

I kissed her again, holding her close. She had very little on underneath the bathrobe. Together we moved toward the couch and sat down. I drew her head across my lap and kissed her. She kissed back, her lips growing warm. I slipped my hands inside her bathrobe. Her skin was smooth and soft and tingled my fingers. She drew in her breath suddenly as she felt my hands on her. I kissed her again, moving my hand in circular motions on her back. Her arms went around my neck, holding me close to her. I slipped my hands inside her brassiere and felt her naked breasts and then her stomach. I put my head down and kissed her throat and then her shoulder where the bathrobe had slipped open.

"Frankie, stop!" she said, almost moaning as I touched her.

"No, darling!" I murmured, kissing her breast. Her hands held my head close to her.

"Oh, Frankie, Frankie!" she said over and over as I kissed her.

I tried to loosen the belt of the robe. Suddenly she stopped me. Her hands held mine.

"Frankie, we mustn't! It's not right!"

I tried to kiss her but she turned her head.

"We've got to stop, Frankie. It's so cheap," she said breathlessly.

I held her closely for a minute. Then she pushed me away and stood up, straightening her robe. "We're not children any more, Frankie. We mustn't get so worked up."

I took her hand and kissed it, then rubbed it against my cheek. "No, we're not. I guess you're right."

She leaned forward impulsively and kissed me. "Frankie, you're sweet!" Then she went into the kitchen.

I walked over to the door and watched her. "Janet," I said, half smiling, "you're a wicked woman to tease me so."

She looked up from her ironing board, a hurt expression in her eyes. "I wouldn't tease you, Frankie," she said seriously. "I think I'm in love with you."

"I know you wouldn't, darling," I said equally serious.

She finished her ironing, put the board and the iron away, and went into her room and dressed.

When she came out again I kissed her. Then we left the apartment and walked over to her grandmother's house.

We wished each other a happy holiday and parted. I walked down the street thoughtfully. Janet too had grown up that summer.

Chapter Six

IT WAS three days before Christmas when I heard about Sam Cornell. Oddly enough, though I was on the student-teachers advisory committee, I had not been present at any of the hearings that he had been called to. I had missed many of them because of basketball practice and simply because I was too lazy and not interested enough in them to attend.

Marty stopped me in the corridor and asked me to see Mrs. Scott that afternoon. I asked him why.

"It's about Sam Cornell," he answered. "They're talking about sending him to reform school."

"How come?" I queried.

"He got into some jam. You'd have known about it if you'd attend a meeting once in a while," he replied.

"I haven't time for that crap," I said. "Besides, I've decided not to run again this term. I've got enough to do without bothering about that. I'm on the basketball team, or haven't you heard?"

"All right, big shot," he answered, smiling. "You're going down to see her?"

"Yeanh," I said, "I'll go now while I have a free period."

We walked down to the main floor together. He left me at her door. I walked in.

"Hello, Mrs. Scott," I said to her. "You asked for me?"

"Hello, Francis. I did," she answered. "Where have you been keeping yourself lately? I haven't seen you at any of the meetings."

"I've been too busy to come," I told her. "I've a lot of practicing to do. I'm on the basketball team."

"I was aware of that," she said, "but you should attend meetings; that is one of the reasons you were elected class president."

"I know," I said defensively, "but I've decided not to run this term."

"Because you've decided that you don't want the job is not reason enough to shirk it while you still hold it. That's not being fair to the students who voted for you, and in some ways that is what I want to speak to you about."

"I thought you wanted to speak to me about Sam Cornell," I said.

"Yes, I did," she said, "but I wonder if one of the reasons we failed to get anywhere with Sam Cornell is that you weren't there at the meetings. You see, Sam is one of the boys who voted for you. And when he got into trouble and was sent up to see us, you weren't present. If you had been there he might have had more confidence in us, seeing a friendly face, that of someone he knew who would give him a square deal."

"O. K.!" I said. "So what do I do now—say I'm sorry?"

"No, Francis. That isn't the attitude you should take. You're not sorry—not really. You're a little too selfish and self important right now to feel sorry for Sam. But I'm not concerned with you. You'll get along all right. I would like to help Sam though, and maybe you can help."

"How?" I asked.

She walked over to her desk and sat down. "Sit down, Francis."

I sat in a chair near her desk.

"As you know, Francis, I hate like the dickens to have to

send any boy to the reformatory. I refuse to believe that any child is intentionally bad. The entire theory behind my work is to prove to certain people that incorrigible children are only incorrigible because we make them that way—that their failure is not theirs alone, but ours as well." She smiled at me. "Do you understand what I'm saying?"

"I think so," I said doubtfully.

"Good!" she said, a ghost of a smile twinkling behind her glasses. "We can work better if we understand one another." She picked up a file from her desk and opened it. "All through his first and second terms here Sam was a good student. He had an eighty-five average in his studies and always an 'A' in conduct and deportment. He had a good attendance record: absent only one day in that time and late but twice.

"This term he has already been absent thirty days, has cut innumerable classes, and has been generally annoying in his demeanor. He has failed most of his subjects thus far and no doubt will fail them this term. But this in itself is not a serious enough reason to have the boy sent away. He has also been caught stealing petty things, and in his neighborhood has been accused with several other boys of breaking into stores. Naturally, this has been investigated and we found out that many of his absences had been unwarranted. He had been on the hook, as you would so aptly put it.

"We have spoken with his parents and they seem at a loss to explain it. His mother just tells us that Sam was a good boy and that his friends are spoiling him. And I'm inclined to believe her. I think Sam is still a good boy. But somewhere along the line during the past summer, Sam has changed his ideas of what is good. Sometime during the summer vacation Sam went wrong and didn't get back on the right track. I spoke to him and can't get at the crux of the matter. You see, if I could find out just what it was that made Sam change his mind, I could explain it to him in such a manner as he could see what is right. But Sam doesn't trust me and without his confidence I can't help him.

"He has been under parole from the juvenile court since October, and he has already broken it. Automatically he would go to reform school, but I'm trying to prove that he can straighten out and wouldn't give them any more trouble if I can only get to the source of it and explain it to him. I have already said that I can't. I thought perhaps that Martin could, but he doesn't know Martin any too well either, and Martin didn't get anywhere with him. Then Martin suggested you. He told me that you and Sam had been very friendly the first term you were in school."

"Yes," I said, "I came into the term late and he helped me a great deal."

"You see," she said, "if you could help him, you would only be repaying a favor."

"But how can I help him?" I asked. "I don't know anything about this sort of work."

"You don't have to know anything about it," she said, leaning forward in her chair and speaking earnestly. "Just be friendly to him. Cultivate him. If he likes you, he'll talk to you himself and tell you what he's doing. Then you tell me and I'll show you what to do next. If he has confidence enough in you, then you can help. That is one of the reasons behind this committee. If the offending pupil faces only strangers and teachers, he immediately puts himself on the defensive, which automatically thwarts us and we can't help him. But when he sees his fellow students, he relaxes sufficiently and confides in us, and you would be surprised how many students we have already helped. If a doctor can win his patient's confidence, then he's won half the battle, and if Sam believes in you, then you be the doctor."

"I'll try, Mrs. Scott," I said.

"I think you can do it too, Francis. Would you like to read his file?"

"No, thanks," I answered, "I'd rather hear his story from him."

She smiled. This time she almost beamed. "I'm glad you said that, Francis. That's the way you should feel about him if he's your friend. You seem to have an instinct for what is right. How old are you?"

"Fifteen," I told her.

"Funny," she said, "but at times I feel that you're much older. You have a certain sureness of yourself that most young people your age haven't. It would surprise you if you knew just how much other pupils look up to you. Why, Marty talks about you as if you were something holy."

"I guess that's because we've known each other for a long time," I said.

"It's more than that," she said. "Marty told me how you met."

A picture of Marty as I first met him jumped through my mind—the slightly pale, unafraid kid waiting for me to hit him. "He told you?" I asked.

"Yes, he told me also how you taught him to box and how you used to go swimming off the docks and how you worked after school and in the summer. I know quite a bit about you."

Just then the gong rang announcing the end of a period. The next period was a math class for me. I stood up.

"I've a class," I said.

She stood up and walked to the door with me. "I have a feeling that you'll work things out with Sam."

"I hope so. He's a good kid." I opened the door.

"And, Francis," she stopped me as I was about to step out into the corridor, "think it over about your decision of not running for class president again. It's really a lot more important than other things."

"It's a matter of opinion," I said, stepping into the hallway already crowded with pupils running to their next class. "Goodby."

She smiled. "That's true, but we'll talk about it again some other time. Thanks for coming down."

"*No hay de qué*," I answered, practicing some of my Spanish on her.

She closed the door and I walked down the hall.

Chapter Seven

I RAN into Marty again after the math class.

"Did ya see her?" he asked.

"Yeanh," I said.

"What are you going to do?"

"I don't know," I said. "I don't know where in hell to start."

"You gotta see him first," he said, smiling.

"You're a big help. I know that much myself," I said, "but after that I don't know whether I like the idea of stooling around."

"Look, Frankie," he said in that earnest way of his, "you're not stooling for nobody. You're trying to help him out of a jam like any friend would."

"Maybe, but supposin' he don't want any help and tells me to mind my own business."

"It's up to you to get past that, and if you can't, well, you've tried anyway. But I think you can do it," he said with certainty.

"Thanks, pal, for the vote of confidence. We'll see."

"Sure," he said, "we'll see. I'm going to meet Jerry for a coke. Want to come along?"

"No, thanks," I said, "I have a class this period."

"O. K. Be seein' ya." He walked off.

I started down the hall, and in front of the biology class I bumped into Ruth just leaving the room.

"Oh," she said, "it's you! I might have known it."

I got sore. I was getting sick and tired of her cracks about me all the time, and right now I didn't feel like taking any crap from anybody. "If I'd've known it was you, I would've taken the long way around here. You're the last person in the world I want to run into."

"What's the matter, little boy? Can't you take it?"

"I can take it all right, but I'm getting a little bit tired of it. What have you got against me anyway?"

"Nothing at all, little man," she said half smiling. I recognized that smile. It was so like Marty's. "I just think you're a fake. You're rotten and hard, and I don't like people like that."

I was really mad now. "You're not so hot yourself," I said nastily. "You're nothing but a mean, selfish, little bitch shooting off your mouth about people you don't even know."

She moved her hand up to slap me in the face. She was quick but I was quicker. I caught her wrist and held it, and we looked at each other. Her eyes were blazing. We stood like that for a moment; then I let her arm go. I could see the white marks on her wrist where I had gripped it.

"I wouldn't do that if I were you," I said, smiling now, for this was something I could understand. "It ain't ladylike."

The blaze died down in her eyes, her face relaxed, and she tried to smile. That girl had guts. "You're right, Frankie," she said. "I'm sorry. I guess I never did give you a chance. Ever since . . ."

"Ever since I hit Marty in the parlor at your house?" I interrupted.

"No," she said, "it wasn't that. It was Julie."

"Julie?" I said, surprised. "You knew?"

"I knew that Julie had a case on you and I guess I resented it. We were like sisters until you came along and changed things. She became very secretive and . . . I guess I was a little bit jealous of you. And after she went away she used to ask about you in her letters and send her regards to you, but I never told you."

The gong rang announcing the start of class but I didn't go in. I wanted to know how much she knew of Julie and me. I took her arm and steered her down the hall away from the door. She walked with me willingly.

"Why?" I asked her.

"I told you why," she said. "I was being kiddish. But now that's over. I know. Julie's married."

I felt an unexplained sense of relief at that. "When did you find out about Julie and me?" I asked her.

"Oh, one Sunday when you two had come back from the beach and were standing in front of her door. I heard voices in the hall. I opened the front door of the apartment and looked out and you were kissing her. And that did it, as I didn't like you much anyway on account of Marty."

"Oh!" I said. "Is that all?"

"Isn't that enough?" she said.

I knew then and there that I didn't have to worry about her any more. I felt way older than her. I felt kind of gay and lightheaded. We were off in a corner of the hallway, and there weren't any students around because the classes were in session.

"A kiss isn't anything," I said. "I'll show you!" I took her quickly by the shoulders and kissed her on the lips, then let her go. "See what I mean?"

She started to raise her hand again.

I put up my arm in mock self-defense. "Not that again!" I said smiling.

She shook her head. "No, not again!"

"Friends?" I asked, holding out my hand.

"Friends!" she said, taking my hand.

Solemnly we shook hands.

"Gotta go," I said. "Something about a class, remember?"

I had gone almost half the distance to the classroom when a sound made me turn around and go back to her. She was crying.

"What's the matter, Ruth?" I asked. "I'm sorry. I didn't mean to be fresh."

"Nothing!" she sobbed. "Why don't you go away and leave a girl alone when she wants to be, you—you big dumbbell!" And she turned and ran down the stairway at the end of the hall.

"Women are nuts!" I was thinking as I entered the class and apologized to the teacher for being late.

Mr. Weisbard was a regular guy. He smiled when I told him that class business had detained me.

"Well!" he said in a stage whisper loud enough for them to hear down in the back row of the class. "Confidentially, Francis, I'd wipe some of that important class business off my lips before I sat down, if I were you."

Chapter Eight

SOMEONE grabbed me by the arm as I left the class. I turned around quickly. I was still a little sore about Mr. Weisbard's gag. It was Marty.

"Oh, it's you!" I said.

"Who'd you think it was?"

"Nobody!"

"Look!" he said, "Sam is down in the office now waiting to see Mrs. Scott. If you could kind of drop in casual-like and get to talkin' with him sort of accidentally, it would be much easier for you."

"Whose bright idea is that?" I asked sarcastically.

"Mrs. Scott's," he answered. "She's keeping him waiting outside to give you a chance."

"All right," I said, "but I'm going to need an alibi for my Spanish class."

"Mrs. Scott already thought about that," Marty said. "She gave me a note to take up to your class for you."

"She thinks of everything, doesn't she?" I said, still with sarcasm.

"Almost!" Marty flung over his shoulder as he walked off.

I went downstairs and into the office. Sam was sitting on a bench outside Mrs. Scott's door. I looked at him as if I were surprised to see him there.

"Hey, Sam!" I called across the room. "What are you doing down here?"

"Hello, Frankie," he said, smiling slowly. "I'm waiting to see Mrs. Scott."

I put my books on the table and walked over to him. "I just came down to get some papers," I said irrelevantly, and sat down beside him. "What do you want to see that old bat for, anyway?"

"I don't want to," he said. "I have to. I'm in a jam."

"Is it bad?" I asked.

"Bad enough! It looks like they're going to send me away," he said with a certain tenseness around his mouth and a forced lightness in his voice.

I looked at him. "Say, that is bad!" I said. "Anything I can do?"

"I guess not," he said, looking away from me. He was pretty close to crying.

"Why in hell didn't you see me before!" I asked. "I'm supposed to be class president and have some kind of pull but nobody ever tells me these things. Look, we're friends and you did me some good turns. Supposin' you come over to the other side of the room and tell me what it's all about. Maybe I can help anyway. Can't hurt to try. What do you say?"

He looked at me. Hope seemed to flicker in his eyes. We got up and crossed the room and sat down by the window.

"It all began last summer," he said. "I wanted a job for the summer. We could use the money home. I answered a couple of ads for messenger boys, but they didn't want me because I was colored. I could've got some jobs as porter and things like that, but I wasn't big enough. I could take out the old shine box, but you didn't get much there. In the summer all the kids are out shinin'."

"You're telling me!" I said. "I used to do it myself when I was down at the orphanage."

"You did?" he asked, then smiled. "Then you know how tough that is. Well anyway, one day one of the fellas come over to me and says: 'Sam, why don't you go junkin'?' " Unconsciously his voice imitated the other fellow's. "I said to him: 'There ain't enough in it.' And he says: 'There is the way we do it!' 'What do you mean?' I says. 'Look,' he says, 'you're a regular guy. I know you been lookin' for a job. I also know you cain't get none. An' I also know why. D'ya want me tuh tell ya why?' 'Why?' I asks. 'Cause you a nigger, thass why!' he says. 'Whyn't tell me something I don't know!' I says. 'That ain't all!' he says. 'It's a cold deck we're gettin' up here in Harlem. We get fed a lot of bunk about opportunity an' other crap, but thass all. I studied to be a bookkeeper up in school. I graduated with honors too—highest marks in the class. But when I goes out for a job thass another story. White boys, no matter how dumb they are, gets 'em. All we kin get is the crap, sweepin' up the place. Well, to hell with 'em! Git whut yuh want an' screw 'em!' 'It's easy to talk big,' I says. 'I ain't talkin' big,' he says, 'I'm talkin' straight stuff—top draw! Look, we got a guy who buys secondhand stuff, an' he ain't too particular about where it comes from. An' he pays good money too. Man, don't you ever get tired of bein' screwed? Or are you like the rest of the dopes up here, lappin' up the crap they feed yuh like it was cream?' 'Look,' I says, 'I ain't no dope, but all yuh gotta do is get caught. Up you goes.' 'Balls!' he says, 'thass figured out too. Yuh see only you kids do it. If'n yuh get caught, you is just some kids havin' fun, not realizin' any harm would come of it. So yuh gets the piss balled out of yuh and gets sent home. But yuh don't get caught. It's all fixed.' 'How?' I says. 'Thass my business. Out of my cut I pays off the cops. Whenever a job is pulled, the cop is down at the other end of the beat. But how I fixes him is my business. All yuh gotta do is what you're told. Int'risted?' 'Maybe,' I says, 'I gotta think about it.' 'O. K.,' he says, 'but remembuh. Keep yuh lip buttoned or—!' He made a slashin' motion with his hands across his nuts an' left me. I thought about it and decided to give it a fling. It sounded safe from where I was. But it wasn't. We all got caught. He and the fence are in the clink now, and it looks like I'm goin' to keep them company."

"Boy," I said, "that is a mess! But what has that to do with school here?"

"Well," he said, "after a while I got to thinking about what he said. And I kind of got the idea maybe he's right. There ain't no sense in going to school for an education they ain't going to let you use. So whenever I'd get an odd job I'd cut school. I been on the hook quite a bit and I guess that is going to do the trick. It looks as if they're going to hang me higher'n a kite."

I thought hard. For a while we just sat there not talking. He got up and looked out the window. "What the devil can I tell this guy?" I thought. "He knows more about what he's up against than I." I got up and stood next to him. "Look," I said, "I'm going in to talk with her. I got an idea (I was lying—I didn't have a thought)—maybe it'll work. I'll tell you when I come out."

I left him before he could frame a question, and went in to Mrs. Scott.

She smiled at me. "Well, Francis?"

I told her what he had told me.

When I had finished she asked me if I had any suggestions.

"Not a one!" I told her.

"Well, I have," she said, "If you were to ask him to be part of your class activities, it would help him feel he belongs. If you were to appoint him to one of the different committees you have an elective to, it might do the trick. And if you keep in close touch with him, you might overcome the beginnings of his prejudice."

"How can I do that?" I asked. "My appointments have to be approved by the G.O. council."

"I'll see that it passes," she said.

"O.K., I'll tell him," I said, starting out.

"Wait a minute, Francis," she said. "Don't tell him this was my idea. Tell him it's yours. You see, from now on, you practically will be his guardian. He'll be your responsibility. I hope he won't let you down."

"I don't think he will," I said, walking out. At the door I stopped. "Do you still want to see him?" I asked.

"Yes," she said, "I want to impress him with the fact that if it weren't for you he might not have this chance. You see I'm going to get you deeper into this than you thought."

"I know it," I said, hand on the door, "but I was asking for it."

Chapter Nine

SAM was given a job as assistant cashier in one of the lunch periods, and worked on the accounts of the general organization. He did his work well and was paid for the time he put in as well as given extra credit in his bookkeeping classes. His attendance and his marks improved. I saw him fairly often, sometimes going out of my way to look him up and talk to him. I thought he was doing all right.

The time for election drew close. I did not want to run again. I was too busy with my other activities. At school, I had athletics and other social activities to occupy my time. Outside of school, I was catered to by my family and my friends. I felt the center of all important happenings. My world revolved about me.

One afternoon we all went up to Janet's house to talk things over—Janet, Jerry, Marty and I. We all lounged around. I snagged my favorite chair, her father's easy chair, and put my feet up on the hassock in front of it. I liked the chair, not only because it was comfortable, but because in it I had the dominating part of the room. It was so situated that everyone in the room faced it. Jerry and Janet occupied the couch opposite me, and Marty sat on a small lounge near my right. I spoke first.

"Look," I said, "you all know I don't want to run again. I have too many other things to do."

"But," Jerry countered, "you can win. They know you and you're popular. It's as simple as that."

"Nuts!" I said. "There's too much to do in the job and I don't want it."

"I notice you haven't been spending too much time at it," Marty said. "Janet's been doing all the dirty work."

"If Janet has any complaints," I said quickly, "she'll make them herself." I turned to her. "What do you say?"

She smiled and shook her head. "No complaints."

"That's that," I said to Marty. "If you guys think the job is so good, why don't one of you go after it?"

"You know I can't," Marty answered. "I've a lot to do with Mrs. Scott's work, and it'll be very important to me when I get into college."

"O. K.," I snapped, "then quit your beefing! What about you two?" I looked at Janet and Jerry.

"Janet!" Marty cried, "Why a girl's never been class president before."

"That doesn't mean she can't be," I said. "How's about it, Janet?"

"Not for me!" she said. "I won't stand a chance. But Jerry?" She looked at him.

He sat quiet for a minute, then he smiled. He had a nice smile. "If that is the way you want it, I'm stuck with it on one condition."

Marty bit for the question but I saw it coming. "What's that?" Marty asked.

"Janet runs with me." Jerry looked at her, smiling.

"Of course Janet will run with you," I said, glad to settle the question before she had time to speak.

For a moment I thought Janet looked a little disappointed at my ready acceptance. But I could have been mistaken. It flashed away.

And that's the way it stacked up—through to their senior year.

The next day Mrs. Scott stopped me in the hall. "I hear you're not running again," she said.

I knew Marty had told her. "News travels fast!" I replied, smiling.

"But I thought you had changed your mind after we spoke."

"I didn't."

"What about the things I said you could do? Sam?" she asked.

"Sam'll be O. K.," I said, "and Jerry can do those things. He likes it."

"You know, Francis," she said, "I've a feeling I might have been wrong about you."

"You might have been," I answered casually. "We all can make mistakes."

"I hope I haven't," she said, going into her office. "I liked you."

After Jerry and Janet had been elected I began to see less of the old class crowd than I had before. My abilities in athletics led to my association with more upper classmen, and I became more or less accepted in their crowd. I felt more at home with them than I did with the group in my class because I felt so much older than the children in my class.

I cut down my visits and going out with Janet to about once a week. I went out with older girls. They were a little more wise and I used to get further.

One day as I left school Jerry fell in step with me.

"Hi!" I said.

"Hi!" he answered. "What's doin'? We haven't seen much of you."

"I've been around," I said easily.

"I know," he said. "So I've heard. Janet has too. And I don't think she's too happy about it."

"I'm no baby," I said. "I can take care of myself—and Janet too."

"But Janet . . . ?" He looked uncomfortable.

"Janet and I are not tied together," I said sarcastically.

He grabbed my arm and I turned to face him. He had a serious look on his face. "You know, Frank, I've been waiting for you to say that."

"So I said it! What are you going to do about it, big brother!"

"Nothing. But you better forget that big-brother angle." He let go of my arm and walked down the street whistling.

I looked after him, wondering what was on his mind. "Oh well!" I thought. But just the same I went to see Janet that night.

I got to her house about seven o'clock and rang the bell. She opened the door. When she saw me she smiled. "Come in, Frankie."

"Hello," I said, walking in.

We went into the parlor. Jerry and Marty were there. I was surprised to see them but I didn't show it. I acted as if they were always there when I came.

"Hi ya, fellas!" I said.

"Well, what do you know," Marty said to Jerry, "the gods descend from Olympus!" And then to me with an elaborate bow: "Greetings on thy return, O long lost brother!"

"Wise guy!" I answered. "Don't pay any attention to him, Jerry. The tongue runs in his family."

"What brings you here?" Marty asked.

"I came to see Janet," I replied, smiling easily. "How about you?" I had them. Neither would admit coming to see Janet even if they did.

Marty murmured the old excuse about class business.

"Well," I said, "don't let me interrupt. I'll stick around till you're through." I sat down in her father's chair and picked up a magazine. "Where are the folks?" I asked her.

"They walked over to Grandma's," Janet replied. "She's not been feeling too well."

"That's too bad," I said sympathetically. "Nothing serious?"

"No, just a cold."

The boys gave up. "I guess we might as well run along; we're about through anyway," Jerry said, getting to his feet.

"Don't let me break up anything," I said with a falsely begging-their-pardonish tone in my voice.

"Yes," Janet said picking up my cue, "don't go. I'll put on the radio. Maybe we can get something good."

Marty said something about having promised to be home early, and Jerry said: "Me too," and they left in spite of our protests.

When the door shut on them, we looked at each other and laughed. "C'mere, baby, and give me a kiss," I said, holding out my arms to her.

She came. I kissed her slowly. When we came up for air, I said: "Golly!"

She smiled. "Long time no see."

"I was busy," I said. "But if I'd've known what I was missing, I'd've been around more often."

"Don't lie, Frankie," she said. "Don't ever lie to me, Frankie. You don't have to."

"I know it, baby."

"I love you, Frankie."

I kissed her again but I knew I wouldn't be kissing her long. Something seemed to tell me that she and Jerry. . . . But her kisses were sweet, and we were so young and so serious—even if I told myself I was not.

Chapter Ten

I WAS eating lunch one afternoon several weeks later when Marty slipped into the seat next to me. "Hi, Frankie!" he said. "What do ya know?"

"Nothin'," I said. "You tell me."

"There's not much to tell. You've been making all the news lately."

"Yeah."

"The whole school's talking about your not running for class office again," he said. "They say you think you're too good for them."

I laughed at that. "Let them talk."

"Mrs. Scott doesn't think too much of it either."

"Crap!" I said. I speared the cover from the bottle of milk with a fork.

"What got into you anyway?" he asked.

"Nothin'," I said, drinking the milk. "I'm getting kind of fed up with the baloney she hands out about helping the students. All she's doing is practicing on us. Maybe she's going to write a book and call us experiment 999 or something."

He reached over and picked up my bottle of milk and took a drink out of it. I watched him. "Have some pie too," I told him.

He grinned. "No thanks, I'm not hungry."

"Then what the hell are you doing down here anyway?"

"Well, if you really want to know, I came down to see you. Mrs. Scott thinks maybe you'd like to come back upstairs and work with us. She thinks you're good."

"That's what I thought," I said, standing up. He sat there looking up at me. "You can just run right back upstairs and tell her to get another stoolie. I'm out of business."

"O. K.!" he said, getting up from the bench. "If that's what you want, I'll tell her, but I think you're maybe making a mistake."

"I know," I said, "but don't give it a thought. I make 'em all the time."

I walked out of the lunchroom into the yard and then across the street. There were a row of benches there. I sat down and lit a cigarette. It's kind of on a hill there and you can look out across the river to the Bronx. It was about mid-April and the day was warm and hazyish. I heard the school gong ring announcing change of classes, and I thought: "The hell with it!" I didn't feel like math anyway. I could see some students coming out and others going in. I leaned back against the bench. The cigarette had burned down; I lit another from it and threw the butt away.

A few girls were walking down the path toward me. Janet was with them. I turned my head away, hoping she wouldn't see me; I hadn't seen her since that night three weeks ago. But she did. She said something to them and came over to me. The sun was in her hair and she looked very pretty, but I didn't want to talk to her. I wished she hadn't seen me.

She came up. "Hello, Frankie." She smiled. There was something about her smile that got me. It was like she had said: "Don't be mad at me. If I did something wrong, I didn't mean to."

I smiled back. "Hello, Janet."

"Haven't you got a class?" she asked.

"Yes, but I'm lazy. I guess I got spring fever."

"Oh! It is a nice day, isn't it?"

"Yeanh."

"Mind if I sit down?" she asked.

"No. That's what the benches are here for."

She sat down on the bench, a little way from me. For a while we didn't speak; we just looked out over the river. But it was like holding a conversation. I could imagine her asking me why I hadn't been around to see her and me saying I wanted to, but was too busy and then she would ask if I was going back to help Mrs. Scott because if Marty knew it she would know it working with them and I would say no because I thought Mrs. Scott was a faker and she really didn't give a damn about us and then she would say that I was wrong and Mrs. Scott was O. K. and I would say it's your opinion and you're entitled to it and she would ask me how I was doing in my classes and I would say all right because I had been averaging about eighty and then she would ask me if I was going out for the swimming team again this year and I would say maybe I hadn't made up my mind yet and when I knew that I had made up my mind to go out the coach had asked me and then she would ask me how my aunt and uncle were and I would say they're all right but my uncle has a cold he's been trying to shake all winter but the cough seems to hang on and ask her how her parents and grandmother were and she would tell me that they're O. K. too but her grandmother is getting older and while we were talking I would be thinking of something else how she first kissed me and when she told me she loved me when she was ironing her slip in the kitchen and how the perfume in her hair used to tickle my nose and we would be talking about the kids we knew when we wanted to talk about whether she liked Jerry and I liked her— but we just sat there on the bench looking out across the river to the Bronx.

My second cigarette burned low. I lit another from it and threw the butt over the railing, and we watched it fall over until it was out of sight. At last she spoke.

"You've changed, Frankie—changed a lot in the last year."

"We all do," I said. "We're not getting younger."

"That's not it, Frankie," she said slowly. "Somehow I've got the feeling you're a person I never knew before, you're so different. I know we've all changed—Jerry and Marty and me—but you've seemed to grow cold and hard and selfish. You never were like that before."

I remembered that was what Ruth had said once. I looked at Janet. "That's the way I always was," I said flatly.

We were silent again, and looked out at the river and watched a small boat chugging upstream against the current. I threw my cigarette away. I didn't light another because my mouth tasted lousy. A light wind had come up behind our backs; I could feel it blowing across my head. I looked at Janet. Her hair was blowing in the wind forming small curls around her face. I wanted to touch her hair; it always felt so soft and crinkly.

She looked at me. "You look like a small boy just after an undeserved spanking," she said, gamely trying to smile. She didn't quite make it.

I didn't answer.

"Frankie, why don't you come to see me any more?" There, she said it. I could never know how much courage it took for her to ask that question.

I didn't know what to answer. I mumbled something about being busy. . .

"You were busy before and yet you found time," she said.

I said something about her going around with Jerry.

"I only started to go around with Jerry after you started with that other crowd. What did you want me to do—stay home and mope or wait for you to come back?" Her face was white and tense.

"But Janet," I said, "we were kids and maybe we didn't exactly know what we were saying . . ."

"Maybe you mean you didn't." She was crying now. Tears stood in her eyes, sparkling like little diamonds where the sun caught them. "But I did. I thought you loved me." She covered her face with her hands and leaned forward, weeping soundlessly.

My throat felt funny. I could hardly speak. Nervously I looked around. Thank God there wasn't anyone near us! "But Janet—" I said, leaning forward and touching her shoulder. How could I tell her I was sorry I had hurt her, or that I felt like a fool? I thought of Eve, the girl in the senior class I had been running around with the last few weeks, and her wet, hot kisses and the tricks she had of promising with a look of her eye or a movement of her body—of promising a lot and giving just a little—and teasing, always teasing. How could I tell Janet that I loved her freshness, her simple, direct, honest look, the warmth of her eyes? How could I tell her that I wanted her— and something more?

She shook my hand from her shoulder angrily. "Go away!" she cried. "I feel so cheap—I hate you, I hate you!"

She got up and ran toward the school, wiping at her face with a small, ineffectual handkerchief. I started to get up and go after her. Then I remembered we could be seen from the windows of the school. I sat there and watched her run into the school.

I looked out across the river. The day was getting colder. I shivered. The gong rang announcing change of classes. I was almost glad. I got up and went in. I had a Spanish class coming up. On the second floor I saw Janet coming out of the girls' room. I went over to her. "Janet," I said.

She turned her face away. "Don't speak to me again—ever." She spoke in a low, cold tone of voice.

"All right," I said just as coldly, "if that's the way you want it."

She walked on down the hall. I watched her turn the corridor.

"Damn!" I said to myself. "God damn school, anyway! It's kid stuff." And she turned and walked out of the building.

Chapter Eleven

THE family was just sitting down for dinner when I came in. The kids were all scrubbed up; Irene was already sitting at the table but Essie was helping her mother at the stove.

"Hi ya, folks!" I said as I came in.

"I was wondering where you were, Frankie," said my aunt. "Hurry and wash up. We almost started without you."

I looked at her strangely; this, for her, was almost sharp. Her face seemed to be screwed up in little worry wrinkles. "You know me, Aunt Bertha!" I said trying to get a laugh out of her. "Meals is one thing I'm never late for."

The kids laughed at that. "That's right, Mommy," said Essie, "he's never late for meals."

I went into the parlor. My uncle was sitting there in a chair near the window. He seemed to be staring into space, his hands clenched nervously on the edge of the chair. "Uncle Morris, you surprised me. I didn't think you were home yet."

"Hello, Frankie, I came home early." He tried to smile but it didn't take. It was merely a facial grimace. "I was tired."

I went into the bathroom and started to wash my hands. I called in to him. "You'd better go in to eat; they're starting now."

I could hardly hear his answer: "I'm not hungry."

Something was wrong, I thought. I could feel the tension in the air. I didn't feel quite right. I wondered whether I had done anything wrong. I couldn't tell. I dried my hands and went into the kitchen to eat. We ate the meal quietly. Uncle Morris didn't come in at all. After dinner I helped Essie with the dishes. She washed and I dried and put them away. Then we went inside and listened to the radio awhile. At eight o'clock the kids went to sleep. About nine-thirty I announced I was going to turn in. I kind of felt my aunt and uncle wanted to talk and I was in the way. It had been a quiet, gloomy evening. Usually Uncle Morris laughed and joked and played with the kids. But tonight he was quiet. When they kissed him he let them kiss him on the cheek and didn't kiss them back. I went into my room and shut the door and started to undress. Through the closed door I could hear my aunt and uncle talking in low tones. An occasional group of words would come through. I got into bed and stretched out, my arms behind my head, and looked out the window. It had been a long, tiring day. I dozed lightly, troubled by a strange feeling of depression that had descended on me. Suddenly I became completely awake. My aunt and uncle were talking in the hall outside my door. I looked over at the clock on my dresser; its radium dials said it was about two o'clock. I listened.

My aunt was crying softly. My uncle was speaking. "It's nothing too much to worry about. You heard the doctor. A couple of years in Arizona and I'll be all right," he said. "I'm lucky we caught it in such an early stage. It's completely curable."

She said something about the kids. I could hear my name but I couldn't quite get what she was saying. It was something about my not being sixteen yet.

"Don't worry about that either," my uncle said. "They've got just as good schools out there as they have here. And Frankie will come with us. All we have to do is explain the case to them. I'm sure they'll listen. After all, he's only about four months away, and I guess they'll stretch a point."

She said something else and I heard the door of their room close. I wondered what we were going to Arizona for, and what my not being sixteen had to do with it. I had almost fallen asleep again when the thought hit me. I sat up in bed. Arizona—t.b.—that's what it was! That explained the cough he had all winter. It wasn't a cold. It was t.b.!

I jumped out of bed and slipped into my bathrobe and went out into the hall. I stood in front of their door a moment before I knocked. "It's me," I whispered loudly. "Can I come in?"

"Yes," said my uncle, and I opened the door and went into the room. "What are you doing up so late?" he asked.

"I heard you talking," I blurted out, "and I woke up. Something's wrong. I can feel it. What's the matter?"

My aunt and uncle exchanged glances. My uncle spoke. "Nothing. We were thinking of moving, that's all."

"Yes, I know," I said. "To Arizona. Why?"

They didn't answer.

"Is it because you're sick?" I asked.

He looked at me. "You heard?" It was a question the way he said it.

"Yes. I can guess. I'm no baby."

"Well," he said, "then you know."

"Look," I said going over to the edge of the bed and sitting down, "I have some money in a bank on Broadway if you need it."

He smiled. "No, thanks. We're pretty well fixed. Keep it."

"If it will help," I said, "you're welcome to it. It's more than fifteen hundred dollars."

He was surprised at that. "Fifteen hundred dollars! That's a lot of money. Where'd you get it?"

"I had a job," I said, standing up. "I'll tell you about it sometime. But if you should ever need it, all you have to do is say so."

"No, son, we don't need it. Thanks anyway," he said.

I started out but my aunt called me back. "Come here and kiss me good night."

I knelt over her and kissed her. "You're a sweet kid," she said smiling. "Now go back to bed and don't worry about it. We'll be all right."

I left the room and went back and got into bed. I remembered what they said about my being not sixteen, I had forgotten to ask them about that. I was going to go back and ask them, but then I decided to let it wait until morning. Anyway I thought if it was money I was glad I let them know I had enough to pay my own way. I fell asleep.

Chapter Twelve

I WOKE up late the next morning and had to run out of the house without speaking to anyone. All I had time to say was: "So long, see you after school." I just made the first class. At study period I saw Jerry. We spoke casually for a few minutes; then I left him. At lunchtime I ran into Ruth. I sat down near her.

"How've you been?" I asked.

"O. K. I'm boning pretty hard. I graduate this term, you know."

"Yeah, I know."

"Where have you been keeping yourself lately? You haven't been down with Marty in a long time. You two haven't had an argument or anything, have you?"

"Nope," I said, "we haven't. But we've got different things to do."

"Well, come around sometimes. The folks will be glad to see you." She left.

I looked around the lunchroom. Somehow the school looked different to me. I thought maybe it was because I figured I wouldn't be there long if the family moved to Arizona.

I headed home right after basketball practice. I came in just as the kids were going to play. My aunt was reading the paper in the parlor. She looked up as I sat down. "This is the first chance I've had to sit down and look at the paper today," she said.

"Yes," I said, and then without even thinking about what she had said, asked: "When are we going to move?"

"I don't know," she answered. "There are some things we have to work out first. Your uncle has to sell his territory. We have to arrange for a place to live, schools for you and the children. We'll have to budget ourselves very carefully. Your uncle will have to take it easy for a while."

"I can work," I said.

"I hope it won't be necessary. I want you to finish school and go to college. Have you ever thought about what you wanted to do?"

"No, I don't know."

"I was thinking, if you wanted, you might become a doctor or a lawyer. It would make us happy and would be good for you."

"I don't know. There's time enough later to think about it," I said. "Honestly, how bad is it? What did the doctor say?"

"In some ways we were lucky. Your uncle has tuberculosis. But we caught it in a very early stage, and the doctor said he'll be all right in a little while."

"That's good—as long as he'll be all right. I was worried."

She smiled. "Just between us, I must confess I was too. But I feel better today somehow. I was feeling pretty low last night."

"I know. I heard."

She smiled at me again. "There's very little you miss, is there, Frankie?"

I smiled.

"You're a strange boy. You're kind of old for your age and kind of sweet, but I like it."

I went over to her chair and put my arm around her shoulder. "I kind of like you too."

She patted my cheek. "How about a glass of milk for the growing boy?" she asked.

"Throw in some cookies and you've got a deal."

Just then my uncle came in. She got up and kissed him. "How did everything go, Morris?"

"Pretty good," he said after saying hello to me. "They're going to give me fifteen thousand for the territory, and that is a good price. We'll be able to get along on that for a while. But there's one hitch. I went down to the children's welfare bureau to notify them of my intention to move out of the state, and they asked me why. I told them. They told me that we couldn't take Frankie with us."

I hopped out of the chair when I heard that. "Why?" I asked.

He turned to face me. "It seems there's a rule of the orphanage that says when a communicable disease crops up in a family that has adopted a child, the child's care automatically reverts to them. You may have to go back to the orphanage for a while. But I don't know. I'm going to see my lawyer in the morning, and we'll probably have no trouble at all."

"I don't care. I won't go back to the orphanage." I said.

"You won't have to, Frankie," said my uncle. "We'll see to that."

A week passed by. It was a busy week at home. We had made arrangements for a place to live not far from Tucson. My aunt had started with her early packing. We were to move in about two weeks. It was Saturday afternoon and I had been helping her. It was May. It was swell. We were all excited over the trip. The kids could talk of nothing else.

About two o'clock my uncle came home. He was tired. He sat in a chair in the living room. Aunt Bertha had made him a hot cup of tea, and he was sipping it slowly. I was in the kitchen wrapping some dishes in paper and placing them in the barrels when he called me. I went in.

Aunt Bertha came in with me. "Sit down," my uncle said to me. I sat down on the couch, my aunt next to me. She took my hand and held it lightly.

"I don't know how to tell you this, Frankie," my uncle said slowly, "but I suppose I'll have to, sooner or later, and I think you should know now. You won't be able to come with us."

I started to say something, but Aunt Bertha squeezed my hand and said: "Let your uncle finish." I remained silent.

"As you know," he continued, "I saw my lawyer in hopes that he would be able to straighten it out. But it was no use. There wasn't anything we could do about it. The law was there and, right or wrong, we have to abide by it. I spoke and pleaded with different officials but it didn't do any good. I was told you have to go back to the orphanage until you're eighteen. Then you'll be able to join us."

I had a funny feeling in my throat as if I were going to cry. I hoped I wouldn't. Somehow I had felt all along that I would be able to go with them. I didn't say anything.

My aunt looked at me; she spoke, her voice soft and sympathetic. "In some ways, Frankie, it has its good points. You'll be able to finish school here. You'll be at home with your friends. And Uncle Morris spoke to Brother Bernhard—he's very fond of you—and he promised to look after you and take care of you. In a little while you will graduate school, and then you'll be able to come out with us. You can go to college out there. There are some very fine universities out there. And while you're going to school here, we can pretend that you're away at school, just as if you were away attending some college."

"I don't care," I said dully. "I don't care about pretending anything. I don't care about my friends. I won't miss them, I'll miss you. I want to be with you."

"We want you with us," my aunt said gravely. "You don't know how much. We've become very fond of you and we love you, but we can't do anything about it. We have to do what the law says. We haven't any choice."

I looked at them both. I could feel hot tears welling into my eyes. I started to speak but couldn't. I just looked at them and the tears, filling my eyes, ran down my cheeks. I stood there silently, not sobbing, just crying with the tears running down my cheeks. They watched me, not speaking. Tears came to my aunt's eyes too. I turned and ran to my room and threw myself across the bed.

I heard my aunt and uncle come to the door. I heard her voice through the door. "Morris, I'd better go in and speak to him. Did you see the look on his face? It was as if he was a little boy locked out of his home."

"No," my uncle said. "Let him alone. He'll get over it soon. He's a real man." They walked away.

Vaguely I thought about what he said. I was a real man. Yes, I was. But I was acting like a little boy that had been locked out. I was a man. I tried to control myself. I stopped crying and got out of bed. I went into the bathroom and washed my face. Then I went into the kitchen.

My aunt and uncle were sitting at the table. They looked up when I came in. "Feeling better?" my uncle asked.

I nodded yes. I was afraid to speak—I still didn't trust my voice.

"Sit down and have a cup of tea," my aunt said.

I did. It wasn't until years afterward that I realized my uncle had purposely spoken loudly in the hall outside my door for my benefit. But I didn't know it then. And I felt real bad. I didn't want to go back to the orphanage.

Then I was glad I hadn't told anyone about my going away, for suddenly I didn't want to tell anyone that I was going back to the orphanage. I didn't want anybody to feel sorry for me.

Chapter Thirteen

IT WAS Friday, May 13, 1927. We were all packed. My things were packed. My uncle was going to take me down to the orphanage with my things. They were leaving the next day. I wasn't going to stay at the orphanage until after they had gone; all we were going to do was to take my things down.

"Ready?" my uncle called.

"Yes," I said. I picked up my bag and took it down to the car. We were silent as we rode downtown.

"I didn't think this would happen," my uncle said, as if he were apologizing for what had happened.

I didn't answer. I didn't know what to say. When we got down there I took my bag and we went up to Brother Bernhard's office. He shook my uncle's hand and then mine.

He tried to be pleasant. "You'll get your old room back, Frankie," he said. "Supposing we take the things up there and you can put them away."

We went up to my old room. I put the bag on my old bed and opened it. Some kids came in, looked at us curiously, and then went out. I didn't know them. They were probably newcomers. A boy came in that I knew—Johnny Egan. He came over to the bed. He had grown tall in the time I had been away. He was almost as tall as I.

"Hello, Frankie," he said. "Coming back?"

"Yes," I said.

He didn't answer, just stood there watching a few minutes and then went out.

I opened up the dresser drawers and unpacked the suitcase. I then hung my suits in the closet and put my shoes there. In a few minutes I was finished. I snapped the bag shut and said to my uncle: "I'll take it back home."

"No," he said, "keep it. You'll need it when you come out to join us."

We started back downstairs to Brother Bernhard's office. My uncle had to sign some papers. He signed them and then we got up to go. He shook hands with Brother Bernhard.

"Don't worry about Frankie, Mr. Cain," Brother Bernhard said. "We'll look after him all right."

"I know you will," my uncle said. "Frankie will be here tomorrow afternoon. He's going to see us off at the train first and then he'll come here."

"What time?" asked Brother Bernhard.

"About three o'clock," Uncle Morris said. "We leave about one."

"I'll expect him then. Well, sir, I hope you'll be feeling better soon."

They shook hands again.

"I'll see you tomorrow afternoon, Francis," Brother Bernhard said to me.

"Yes, sir," I said.

We left the room. We walked out, down the stairs, through the gymnasium, and into the street. Some kids were playing basketball in the gym. The old dump hadn't changed a bit.

We drove home just as silently as we had come.

It was the gloomiest evening we had ever spent at home. We went to bed early as we had to be up early.

In the morning the movers came. By ten thirty the apartment was empty, and we all went down for breakfast. The only things they were taking with them were two valises for necessary changes. I went to Grand Central with them. There the train came in a little before twelve. We took the things aboard. It seemed as if only a few minutes had passed, but it was time for me to get off the train.

I kissed the little girls good-by and gave them each a small box of candy I had bought for them.

"I'll miss you, Frankie," Irene, the older one, said, with arms around my neck.

"I'll miss you too," I said rumpling her hair with my hand. I turned to my uncle and held out my hand. We shook. "Good-by, uncle. Good luck. I hope you feel better."

He smiled. "So long, Frankie. Be a good boy. It won't be too long."

My aunt was next. She put her arms around me and kissed me. She was crying. "I wish you were coming with us, Frankie," she said.

"I do too," I said. I felt like crying myself, but didn't because I didn't want them to feel bad. "Thanks for everything."

"Oh! Frankie! Frankie!" she said kissing me again, "don't thank us. We love you and want you with us. I'll miss you terribly."

I didn't know what to say. Just then the porter tapped me on the shoulder. "You'd better be getting off, sir. We's about to start any minute."

I nodded to him. My aunt let me go. I stood up and looked around at them. "Well," I said, "so long." I could feel the tears coming into my eyes, so I turned and got off the train.

I heard their good-bys in my ears as I walked down the platform to where their window was and waved at them. The kids had their faces pressed against the glass. My uncle was trying to tell me something, but I couldn't hear him through the closed window. The train started. My uncle opened the window. I ran along with it.

"Don't worry, Frankie," he shouted, "it won't be so long."

I was running fast by now to keep up with them. "No, it won't," I called back. "It won't. It won't."

I had reached the end of the platform, the train going into the tube. The last picutre I had of them was waving at me and calling: "Good-by, Good-by." I was out of breath. For a minute I stood at the end of the platform, and then I turned and started back. I had never felt so alone in my life.

I got out into the bright sunlight and walked slowly across town. I reached the orphanage. For a little while I stood outside looking in. I shut my eyes and remembered my aunt kissing me good night. I remembered the pleasant little sounds and smells of home. The warming, somehow lovely, evenings we had spent together—me doing my homework, Uncle Morris reading the paper, Aunt Bertha marching the kids in to bed.

I looked again at the orphanage—the bleak, gray, drab building, the old, brown, brick school next to it, the church on the corner, the hospital across the street. I remembered the gong calling us for meals, the carefully planned regularity of all our smallest actions, the preaching, lecturing, confining regulations. I hated the place. I wouldn't go back. I wouldn't.

I looked at my watch. It was two o'clock. I ran over to the bank. I took out my bank book. I went over to the stand and made out a withdrawal slip for two hundred dollars. I went over to the desk and got my money.

I took the subway down to Grand Central. I was going to take the next train to Tucson. As I got near the ticket window I thought that was the first place they would look for me. I was running away. I didn't know where to go I looked up at a sign. It said "Baltimore and Ohio Railroad." There was a picture of a big, moon-faced colored porter grinning next to the words. I went over to the list of trains going out. There was a train going to Baltimore. It left at three ten. I went over to the ticket window.

"Give me a ticket to Baltimore on the three-ten train," I said.

Interlude

JANET

JANET had listened to Martin speak through half-closed eyes. The soft, yellow glow of the candlelight cast quiet shadows on his face, and her mind was playing strange tricks upon her. The room had faded from her mind, and all the things she now held dear were yet to come.

It was Monday at school. She had just come into the building when a messenger was sent up to fetch her to Mrs. Scott's office. She went downstairs wondering why she had been sent for. It might have been something she had forgotten to do. There was no one in the outer office, so she went directly inside.

Mrs. Scott was sitting at her desk. A strange man—a man she didn't know—was seated in front of Mrs. Scott, and Marty and Jerry were standing near them. They looked up as she entered the room. Marty's face was strained and white, and Jerry had a worried look about him.

"Brother Bernhard," Mrs. Scott said rising to her feet, "this is Janet Lindell, the young lady I was telling you about." She turned and spoke directly to Janet. "Brother Bernhard is from St. Therese Orphanage."

Janet smiled politely. "How do you do?"

Brother Bernhard got to his feet. He was a tall man, broad with bushy, grayish black hair and eyebrows. His voice was deep and gruff. He spoke directly, a trifle sharply. "Ha'e ye seen or heard from Francis o'er the weekend?"

"Why, no," she answered, surprised at the question. "Is anything the matter?"

Brother Bernhard sank to his seat dejectedly. Mrs. Scott answered her question. "Francis has apparently run away. As you know, he was to stay at the orphanage beginning Saturday. Saturday morning he accompanied his aunt and uncle to the station to see them off, and didn't come back."

She was bewildered. "Maybe he went with them," she suggested.

Brother Bernhard shook his head. "We sent a telegraph to his uncle, and he isn't with them." His voice had a hurt note in it.

"Didn't he say anything to any of you?" Mrs. Scott appealed to all of them. "Did he ever talk about going away, where he'd like to go?"

They didn't answer. They had no answer. Suddenly Janet sat in a chair and began to weep.

Jerry came over to her. "Don't cry, Janet. He'll probably show up later. You know how he is—independent. Maybe there's something he wants to work out by himself."

"But he may be hurt or sick and no one knows who he is," she sobbed.

Jerry's hand found hers and held it tightly. "Don't worry, Janet. He'll be all right. I know him."

She looked up through her tears at him. "Do you really think so?"

He nodded gravely. She saw something in his face and eyes that caused her to look at him again. She saw his brow was wrinkled with worry. But it wasn't for Francis, it was for her. She saw his eyes were deep with pity. But it wasn't for Francis, it was for her. She saw his face wrinkled with a new look of concern. She caught her breath sharply.

This was the first time she knew how Jerry felt about her. She began to weep again—sorry for Jerry, for Francis, for herself.

The room came back into focus. Martin was still talking, and, oddly enough, while her mind had been far away, she had heard and retained every word he had spoken. Martin took another drink of wine and continued to speak, and her mind went spinning off on another tangent.

She and Jerry had naturally drifted together after that. They never spoke very much about Francis after a while until that night, a few days before she and Jerry were married.

They had had dinner at Jerry's home with his parents. Jerry had just been admitted to the bar and was going to work in a few weeks at the district attorney's office. They were sitting in front of the large open fireplace in the living room, watching the logs crackle and blaze and throw off tiny little sparks. A long time had gone by and they hadn't spoken a word, just sat there, shoulders touching, fingers intertwined.

"What are you thinking about, darling?" Jerry asked quietly.

She turned and looked at him gravely. The light from the fire was dancing on his face. "Nothing, I guess."

He smiled. "You were so quiet I thought you had forgotten I was with you."

"Jerry," she half laughed, "how could you? It's just that—that the day after tomorrow we'll be married, and I guess a girl has a right to look back at her youth and say good-by to it before she settles down into married life."

"You're sure, aren't you?" he asked, a worried look on his face. "You haven't any doubts?"

"Jerry, darling," she leaned toward him and kissed him. "Silly! Of course I haven't any doubts. I love you. I'm just a little moody I guess."

He put his arm around her shoulder and leaned her head on him. "Forgive me, sweet. I'm just being foolish. I love you so much I wouldn't want you to be unhappy. Even if it meant . . ."

"Jerry, stop talking like that. I love you, we're going to be married at St. Patrick's the day after tomorrow at high noon, and we're going to live happily ever after just like it says in fairy tales and movies." She put her finger on his lips.

He bit it gently. "I was just thinking about Frankie. Funny, isn't it? How your mind works, I mean." He turned his head and looked at her. "You don't see a fellow for years and suddenly he pops up in your mind as real as life. Once when I was away at school, a sailor came to the door and asked Robert if I was at home. Robert told him I wasn't. I didn't know who it was; I didn't know any sailors. Then I thought about it, and the more I thought about it the more I was convinced it was Frankie. But I didn't say anything about it to anyone, not even Marty or you, because I was afraid—afraid if he came back I would lose you."

Inside her, her heart was doing strange tricks. She felt a

funny pain around it, and it suddenly began to beat very quickly. She spoke quietly, her voice ringing reproachfully in his
ears. "Jerry, how could you do that! You know how worried his
people were about him? I love you, not Frankie. What I felt for
Frankie was puppy love, kid stuff, not at all the way I feel about
you. You should have told someone." And all the time inside
her she was wondering. It was true the way she felt toward
Frankie was not the way she felt about Jerry. But she loved
Jerry. She was sure about that. Wasn't she going to marry him?

"I know I was wrong, darling," he said, his voice contentedly
belying his words. "I felt like a heel, believe me, but I loved
you—loved you ever since I first saw you, and I didn't want to
lose you."

"You couldn't lose me if you tried." She smiled, and then
added in mock seriousness and twirling an imaginary
mustache: "Not when I've got you in me power, me fine young
bucko!"

He laughed happily. "I love you, Janet."

"I love you, Jerry."

And they were married at high noon at St. Patrick's just as
the invitations had said they would be.

With effort she forced her mind back to the present. Marty
was saying: "He always was the guy I wanted to be, the same as
when I was a kid." He took another sip of wine and placed the
glass back on the table.

Janet spoke quietly. "There was something about Frankie
that was different and attracted people toward him. There was
a tinge of adventure that seemed to cling to him, an air of
deviltry that attracted all the girls when I was young, myself
included." She gave Jerry a fond look and a smile. It was a long
time ago and they could talk about it now.

"But there always was something that escaped you. A look in
his eyes or on his face that would make you think sometimes he
was laughing at you—at himself—or that he was having a great
time playing with you and with life, and you never could be
sure of what he thought—only what he wanted you to know.
There was something in him that made me feel unsteady, not
sure of what I felt, but always trying to find out how I felt.

"Yes," she said smiling at them both, "I think that was what
it was. He kept you forever off balance, never giving you a
chance to thrust back. The things that would hurt your feelings

never seemed to hurt his. He was always the master of himself. He seemed always to be daring you to do something, then laughing at you if you did or didn't. I don't know. I guess you never could really figure him out. He had so many different sides to him, you never knew which side was the real one.

"And it didn't seem to matter. You liked him just the same, and maybe it was the challenge of his personality that got you."

She looked at them both, and suddenly tears came into her eyes. She dabbed at them with a wispy, ineffective handkerchief. "I'm just a fool, I guess—a silly sentimental fool— but I felt so happy to have you both with me. You can't know how lonely I felt with everyone you know away—Jerry in Saipan, you in France, and Ruth. . . ." She dabbed at her eyes again. "Shall we have coffee in the living room?"

Marty smiled. Jerry reached across the table and took her hand. "You're an awfully sweet fool if you are one, darling, and I love you for it."

PART THREE

Chapter One

I AWOKE the next morning in a strange room. Half awake, I looked idly at the ceiling. Slowly my gaze wandered over the room as I gradually realized where I was: Baltimore. I hadn't meant to run away. I wondered about going back. Fully awake now, I got out of bed and began dressing. While I washed my hands in the small basin in the corner of the room, I wondered what they were doing back in New York. Probably when I hadn't shown up, Brother Bernhard wired my folks. As soon as he received their reply, he would report me to the police. They would start checking the railroad stations and sooner or later find out I had bought a ticket to Baltimore. I was too wise to think I would be able to stay out of sight for long. The best thing I could do was first to check out of the hotel I was in, and then lose myself in the city.

I finished dressing, took one last look around the room, and went downstairs. At the desk I gave the clerk the room key and told him I was checking out. He didn't say anything, just tossed the key on a table behind him and went back to reading his newspaper. I bought a newspaper at the cigar stand in the lobby and walked out. A few doors down the block was a small restaurant. I went in and ordered breakfast: juice, eggs, and coffee, twenty-five cents. I spread the newspaper open and turned to the want ads. I scanned the columns for jobs. There were a few listed for boys: office boys, errand boys, store help, and the like. I marked them with a pencil and finished breakfast.

By the time lunch came around I had seen all of them and didn't get a job. I got lost once or twice, but each time I asked a passer-by and received courteous directions from him. It wasn't like New York, where they would tell you how to get somewhere but you would have the sneaky feeling that they were laughing at your ignorance while they were doing it.

I decided I had better think about a place to sleep before I went anywhere else. I opened the paper again and turned to the rooms-for-rent section. They all seemed to be in the same section. I went into a restaurant and with my lunch got some information on how to get there. I finished lunch, grabbed a trolley at the door, and got off at Stafford Street. It was an old run-down section, just off mid-town. Gray and brown stone houses lined the street, in each window were small signs, "Vacancy," or "Room for Rent." I walked along till I found one cleaner than most. I ran up the steps and rang the bell. There was no answer. I waited a few minutes, then rang the bell again. Again no answer. I started down the steps; when I was about halfway down the stoop, I heard the door open behind me. I turned back up the steps. An old woman, her hair tied in funny ribbons, stood there.

"What's the idea waking a person in the middle of the afternoon?" she demanded. Her voice was raucously high pitched with a small waver in it.

"You have a sign in the window, ma'am," I said, pointing to it. " 'Room for rent.' "

"Don't call me ma'am," she said sharply; then following my pointed finger, "Oh, that!" she said more quietly.

"Yes," I said. "Is it still open?"

"No," she said quickly, "it was taken yesterday. I forgot to take the sign out of the window."

"Oh!" I said. "Sorry to bother you." I started down the steps again. About halfway down, she called me.

"Young man," she called, "young man, come back."

Back up the steps I went. "Yes, ma'am."

"Stop calling me ma'am; I don't like it," she said.

"I'm sorry," I said.

She looked at me closely. "You're new here in town, aren't you?" she asked.

I was sore. If she could tell so easily, what chance would I have to stay out of sight? "Yes," I said. "What's it to yuh?"

"Nothing," she said. "Where do you come from—New York?"

"None of your business!" I told her. I was getting madder. "All I did was ask you for a room. I didn't know I'd run into a police station. Forget it!" I turned away.

"Wait a minute," she said. "I didn't mean anything. I'd like help you. Maybe I've got a room. Come inside."

I followed her through the door into a hallway. At the right of the hall was a big door made of two panels. She rolled the door open by shoving them apart, and I followed her into a large room. There were couches and seats all around the room. A large baby grand piano stood in one corner of the room. There were a few empty whisky bottles on the piano. Cigarette and cigar butts were all over the place in ash trays and on the floor near a large old-fashioned fireplace against the far wall. There was a stale smell of smoke and whisky and a something else that smelled like the wind when it blew across from the hospital to the orphanage.

"Boy, it stinks in here!" she said, sniffing the air and then going over to a window and throwing it open. It was at the back of the room. I noticed there were large screens in front of the windows that opened onto the street. Some fresh air began to blow in.

"Sit down, sit down," she said, waving her hand toward one of the couches. She went over to a small cabinet, opened it, took out a bottle of gin, poured herself a drink in one of the tumblers standing there, and tossed it off. She swallowed the liquor without blinking her eyes, then she stood there sniffling the fresh air. "Ah!" she said, "that's better." She made a queer picture standing there in a sort of kimono, her gray hair tied into tight little kinks with ribbons, and color coming into her face from the liquor. I didn't speak. I was tempted to laugh. It all looked screwy to me.

She sat down on a couch and looked at me. For a few minutes we sat there quietly not talking. I was becoming restless under her gaze when she spoke.

"How old are you?" Her voice was more quiet now, controlled.

I hesitated a moment. She noticed it. "Nineteen," I said lying anyway.

"Hmm!" she said. "Why did you leave New York?"

"None of your business!" I said. "I told you before, all I want

to know is have you a room for rent or haven't you?" I started
to get out of the chair.

"Wait a minute. Wait a minute," she said, waving me back
into the seat with her hands. "Don't get touchy!"

"All right," I said. I wondered what the old dame wanted
anyway. This dump looked like a whorehouse to me anyway. It
stank. I wouldn't live here on a bet.

"You in trouble with a girl?" she asked shrewdly, peering at
me.

I shook my head.

"The cops maybe?" Still with that same look on her face.

That could be, I thought. As soon as Brother Bernhard reported me, I would be. I shrugged my shoulders casually. I
didn't speak.

"Oh," she said, smiling now. She was pleased with her guess.
I could see it. "I thought so. What are you going to do here in
Baltimore?"

"Get a job," I said, "and a room if I can ever get the hell out
of here to find one."

She laughed out loud at that. "Going to go straight?" she
chuckled, then stopped and looked at me fiercely. "Don't hand
me that! You know how far you'd get? They'd pick up a punk
like you and ship you back to New York and the can so fast you
wouldn't know what's happening."

I watched her silently. In her excitement she got up and
walked up and down in front of me.

She spoke again: "You're a talkative bastard, aren't you?"

"When I have something to say," I answered. "You're doing
enough for both of us."

She stopped in front of me and bent down and felt my arm
muscles. I thought maybe she was going to try to do something,
so I tightened my arm muscles. "Strong too," she said. She
straightened up, walked over to the cabinet, poured herself
another drink, and swallowed it without a blink of her eyes. "I
like you," she said. "I like that hard, mean look you've got in
your eyes. I got a job for you."

"Doing what?" I asked. Pimping was not my line.

"You know the kind of a place I run here?" she asked,
gesturing with her hands at the room.

"Yes," I said.

"Well," she said, "I need a man here—someone to kind of
keep the customers on good behavior, to keep them from get-

ting too rambunctious. You won't have too much to do. No real bouncing—only once in a while—then it's a drunk and they're easy to handle. All you got to do is stand around and look tough and let them see you. That's enough. And someone to come out to the stores with me, so's they think I'm just another rooming-house operator. Prevent talk. Thirty bucks a week. Room and board. What do you say?"

"Sounds all right," I said, "but it's a little out of line with what I've been doing."

"What have you been doing—a cheap stick-up here and there? And what'll it get you? A bullet in the ass. This is better and pays more." She leaned over me. I could smell the gin on her breath.

"No pimping," I said.

"No pimping!" she said. "What kind of a place do you think I run here anyway? Every Tom, Dick, and Harry can't get in here. I got a nice, quiet home trade."

"O. K.," I said standing up. "When do I start?"

"Right now," she said smiling. "But remember one thing. Leave the girls alone. I don't mean you shouldn't fool around once in a while when you feel like. But don't play any favorites. I don't want any arguments among my girls."

"Yeah," I said, "I understand."

She came close to me. "You do your job and mind your own business, and they'll never find you here."

"That's what I was thinking," I said.

"You got a job," she said, and went over to the cabinet and poured herself another drink. After she swallowed it she looked at me again. "What's your name?" she asked.

"Frankie," I said, "Frank Kane. What's yours?"

"Just call me Grandma," she said, and tossed off the drink.

Chapter Two

SHE walked to the doors. "Mary, Mary," she screeched at the top of her voice. She turned around and walked back to me. "Where's your luggage?" she asked.

"What luggage," I said.

"You must have been in a hurry," she laughed. "That's being young for you. Always shooting off somewhere half-cocked. Not thinking about what you'd need. I suppose you're broke too."

I didn't say anything.

"I thought so!" she cackled triumphantly. "I knew it from the way you looked. I bet you haven't even got enough money to pay for a room if you did get one."

I smiled thinking of the $185 I had in my pocket.

"O. K.," she said, "O. K. When we go out shopping this afternoon we'll buy you some clothes: a suit with built-up shoulders—make you look bigger—some colored shirts." She went to the door again and called Mary. "But don't think you're getting them for nothing," she said coming back to me. "I'll take it out of your first week's pay."

She stopped. A big colored girl came into the room. "What do you want?" she asked the old lady.

"My grandson just got here from New York," the old lady said. "Show him the empty room on the third floor."

The girl looked at me skeptically. The old woman, apparently reading her mind, shouted at her: "What's the matter? You heard me—my grandson! I could have a grandson, couldn't I? I'm the same as the other women in the neighborhood. They got children."

The colored girl sniffed. "I been with you six years, Miz Mander. I ain't heard you mention nobody."

"That's the niggers for you," the old woman said, turning to me. "Treat 'em good and pretty soon they think they own you."

She turned back to the colored girl. She was almost screaming now: "Goddam your black hide! I told you he was my grandson. Look at him. He looks like me. Look at his eyes. They're like mine, I said."

The colored girl looked at me. I could see her hesitate. "If'n you say so, Miz Mander," she said.

The old woman snorted triumphantly. "Well, he isn't. I never saw him before today. But he's going to work here, and as far as anyone else goes, he's my grandson." She turned to me and said: "You can't fool Mary. She's been with me too long. We can't fool you, can we, Mary?"

"No, Miz Mander," Mary said, smiling now.

"Show him his room," Mrs. Mander said. "Then for Christ's sake bring me some breakfast! And then clean out this goddam room! It stinks!" She went to the doorway and then turned to me. "Did you eat, Frankie?" she asked.

"Yes, Grandma," I said.

"All right," she said. "Go to your room then. I'll call you in about an hour. We have to go shopping." She stalked off down the hall, disappearing in the door behind the staircase.

I followed Mary up the staircase. The house was quiet, the hallways dimly lit and somehow dirty. Two flights up she stopped in front of a small room. She opened the door and I followed her in. It was a small room facing the street. Heavy black curtains hung beside the window. A small single bed was over against the wall, a wash stand in the other corner.

"The toilet's down the hall," Mary said, pointing to it. "That room over there is Miz Mander's, mine is upstairs. The girls are all down on the second floh."

"Thanks," I said.

She looked at me a minute. "You really from New York?" she asked.

"Yes," I said.

"But you no relative of hers?"

"No," I said.

She went out. I closed the door behind her. I took off my jacket and threw it over a chair. I stretched out on the bed. I felt tired and restless. I didn't know yet how hard it was to look for a job. I looked at the ceiling and then the wall. I tried to shut my eyes but they were burning. I got out of bed and went to the window and drew the black heavy curtains together. The dimness of the room seemed to suit me better. I stretched out on the bed again.

Let the old dame think what she wants! She was right about one thing. The cops wouldn't find me here. As soon as things were quiet I could beat it and join the folks. I wondered about the family. How were they doing? I could see my aunt all excited over the wire that Brother Bernhard would send her— my uncle telling her not to worry. Brother Bernhard must be mad as hell. Mrs. Mander thought I was tough. In a jam with the cops ... funny ... Baltimore ... Grandma ... whorehouse ... don't play favorites. ...

I started to doze off. The door opened. Mrs. Mander came in. She was all dressed up—nice—like any other old lady. I was completely awake. I sat up.

"Come on, Frankie," she said. "We're going shopping."

I got out of bed and put on my jacket. "O. K.," I said, "I'm ready."

We went out. The first store we stopped at was a butcher shop—then a grocery store. She paid cash for her stuff and they delivered it. Then we went into a small tailor shop.

A little Jewish man came up to us. "Yes, ma'am," he said. "What can I do for you?"

"You got some good secondhand suits?" Mrs. Mander asked.

"I got some secondhand suits, she asks me?" he cried, throwing up his hands dramatically. He pointed at some racks of clothing. "I got the best. Like new they are—hardly used."

"I want a suit for my grandson here," she said.

We fished around for a while until she saw something she liked. "Try that one on," she said to me.

"But, lady," the man protested, "of all the suits I got in my store, she picks the best. I was thinking of keeping that one for myself." Meanwhile, he was taking the suit from the rack and smoothing it. It was a gray cheviot with small stripes. I put on the jacket. It was a little loose around the shoulders and hips. The sleeves were all right.

"It fits him like a glove," he said, patting me on the shoulders. "A little maybe I'll take in around the shoulders. But otherwise—perfect."

"How much?" she asked.

"Twelve fifty," he said. "But only for you."

He settled for nine dollars.

"All right then," he said, "I didn't want to sell the suit, but you bought it. I'll fix it now. The shoulders I should take in, just a little."

"No," she said. "Put some padding in them. I like it large."

"O. K., lady," he said. "It's your suit."

We waited for it. In about fifteen minutes it was ready.

"Put it on, Frank," said Mrs. Mander.

"O. K., Grandma," I said. I put it on and stood in front of a mirror. The old dame was right. The shoulders were broad and I looked older. I tried not to look pleased.

The tailor wrapped up the other suit and we went back to the house. It was nearly six o'clock. I wondered what the rest of the bunch in the house were like. Mary opened the door. I went in.

"We eat at six-thirty," Mrs. Mander told me. "Don't be late."

"I won't," I said starting up the steps to my room—"Grandma."

Chapter Three

A LITTLE while later I heard a bell ring. That must be dinner call, I thought. I went downstairs to the kitchen. I could hear the sound of many voices coming from the closed door. Above them all I could hear the shrill, rasping tones of Mrs. Mander. I straightened my tie in the darkness just before the kitchen door, opened it, and stepped in.

The chatter stopped and all faces turned toward me. There were many expressions showing, predominatly, curiosity. I thought they had been talking about me before I came in. I stood there quietly a moment looking around the table. There was a seat vacant at the foot of the table opposite Mrs. Mander. I walked over to it and sat down.

"That's right, Frank," said Mrs. Mander. "Just help yourself to the food."

I didn't answer, just reached out and began putting some

pieces of meat from the bowl in the center of the table on my plate.

Mrs. Mander turned to the girls. "This is Frank Kane," she said. "He's going to work here—keep things in order." She reached under the table and picked up a bottle of gin from the floor, poured herself a tumblerful, and drank half the glass as if it were water. She turned back to me. "The girl sitting next to you, Frank, is Mary; next is Belle." She reeled off their names nodded to each one. They seemed to vary in age from about twenty-five to nearly forty, all sizes and shapes, from big Mary who sat next to me and was somewhere in her thirties to Jenny who sat next to Mrs. Mander and was small and almost demure-looking in appearance. They were dressed in a varied assortment of house coats and kimonos. Some had their faces all made up with vivid splotches of paint, elaborately mascaraed eyelashes. A few wearing no makeup at all looked tired as if they had just awakened. There was one thing they all had in common: their eyes, bright, beady and sharp, and the corners of their mouths, turned down slightly, even while smiling, petulantly selfish.

Mary seemed to be the leader among the girls. She was a big, hefty woman, dressed in a dirty grayish wrapper—massive-breasted, thick-armed, double-chinned, peroxide blonde. She looked me over carefully. I kept on eating as if I weren't aware of her scrutiny. Finally she spoke to Mrs. Mander. "What's the idea bringing a kid like him into this place for a bouncer? We need someone who can handle himself—a man." She looked at me over her plate to see what I would say. I said nothing, kept on eating.

Mrs. Mander cackled and slugged down another shot of gin. She didn't say anything either.

Mary stood up. I could see she felt more sure of herself since we had said nothing in reply. "He's a punk kid," she said. "Get him to hell out before he busts out crying! Look at him! He's going to cry."

I put down my knife and fork and looked up at her. She must have weighed about a hundred and seventy pounds, almost five feet nine. I didn't speak. I could see the girls watching us. I knew they would act, following her lead, if she were left to say what she wanted. I stared at Mary.

She looked down at me and sat down again in her seat. She leaned forward across the corner of the table and pinched my cheek hard between her fingers. "Look at him, just a baby!" When she stopped and withdrew her hand, I could feel the spot on my face hurt where she had pinched it.

She leaned forward again toward me. "Why don't you run along home, little boy?" she asked. I could see the cowlike brutishness showing on her face. Her voice was nasty and insulting.

I raised my hands and put them back on the table.

"Lost your tongue?" she asked.

Without getting up from my seat I hit her across the face with the back of my hand and wrist. I put all the power of my hundred and fifty-four pounds into it. She went tumbling over onto the floor, chair and all. Blood seeped from the corner of her mouth and trickled down from her nose. She lay there spread out on the floor, one hand raised to her face, looking up at me stupidly. The other girls looked up at me and then down at Mary.

I looked down at her. "You talk too much," I said, and went back to eating. I could see her get up, staring at me. She put one hand on her chair to steady herself, her wrapper was open, one breast exposed like an over-ripe melon, big and heavy. One hand she used to wipe the blood from her face on her wrapper. She seemed to hesitate a little as if she didn't know whether to sit down again. I could sense she was afraid of me.

"Sit down and finish eating," I said to her. "Then get the hell upstairs and clean up your face! You've got work to do." I kept my voice flat and expressionless, like I had heard Fennelli do many times. It sounded hard and cruel, even to me.

She pulled her wrapper closed and sat down.

"I told you, I told you!" Mrs. Mander cackled, "I said to leave him alone." She cackled again.

One by one they finished eating and drifted off. They didn't talk much after that happened. Finally, only Mrs. Mander and I were left at the table. The old lady was half drunk. "She must have the capacity of a camel," I thought, "or else she's pouring it into a wooden leg."

"Frankie, my boy," she cackled, "I always thought we needed a man's touch around here to make it homelike."

About seven thirty the girls came down from their rooms and went into the parlor. They were dressed in shiny, black satin dresses, and made up carefully. I could see there was nothing on underneath their dresses. I could tell from the way their breasts would jiggle when they walked, from the way the dress would cling to their hips and their behinds, from the way they walked. In the dimly lit parlor they took seats in small groups, talking, waiting for the night's business to come and ring the doorbell. Big Mary, as she was called, came down too, nodded quietly to me as we passed in the hall as if nothing had happened. She was called Big Mary to differentiate between her and Mary the colored servant. A few minutes later Mary the servant came down. She was dressed in a loud colored print which contrasted violently with her dark skin and the dresses of the other girls. She sat down at the piano and began to play softly and sing in a low plaintive voice. That was her job for the evening.

From somewhere in the bowels of the house came Mrs. Mander. She was cold sober. I don't know how she did it. When we left the supper table she was so drunk she could hardly walk. And now she was cold sober! She was dressed soberly, almost primly, her hair carefully combed, face powdered lightly, glasses perched high on her nose. Whistler's mother in a whorehouse, I thought, remembering the painting I had seen in the art class back in high school.

She said to me: "Remember, collect in advance, five dollars from a customer—twenty-five if he's going to spend the night. Make sure you get the dough before you let him upstairs. Stay out in the hall here. I'll take care of them inside. In case any of them look good for more, I'll tip you off as to how much." She went inside.

I could see her open up the liquor cabinet and take out some bottles. She lined them up on the piano and placed some empty glasses next to them. She came out in the hall again. "Don't let any drunks in," she warned me. "They only make trouble." The doorbell rang. "Answer it," she said, going back into the parlor. I could see the girls primping up a little, straightening up in their seats, a certain competitive look coming into their faces. The race was on.

I peeped out the hole in the door. A small man stood outside. He looked like a bank clerk or a small shopkeeper. "Mrs. Mander?" he asked. I opened the door and let him in. He was an old hand. He went right into the parlor. I could hear him saying hello to some of them. A few minutes later he came back into the hall with Big Mary. She wore a triumphant kind of look on her face—she got the first customer that evening. He took out some money and gave it to me. It was three dollars. I looked through the door at Mrs. Mander and held up three fingers. She nodded her head.

"O. K.!" I growled—a steady customer.

The doorbell rang again—another customer. I let him in. He went right to the parlor. More customers came in. I could hear the clink of glasses and laughter and soft music coming from the parlor. Some girls went up with their customers. Mary came down with the little man. She helped him on with his coat.

"See you next week," she said to him.

"You bet!" he said. I let him out.

Mary went back into the parlor.

The night wore on without any untoward event happening. It was punctuated with funny sounds: glasses clinking, blue piano, *St. Louis Blues* piano, the flush of toilets, the creak of the door, Mrs. Mander's raspy voice, footsteps on the stairs, coming, going, hello, good-by, clothes rustling, beds creaking, night sounds, dirty sounds. The night wore on.

About three o'clock Mrs. Mander came out. "Any small timers up there?" she asked.

"Nope," I said.

"Close up then," she said. I locked the door. We went back into the kitchen. There was a small safe there, built into the wall next to the icebox. "You should have $315," she told me, taking out a piece of paper on which she had writing. I looked at it. The girls' names were written down, a mark for each customer they had and what he had been charged. I counted out my money. She was right—exactly. I put the thought of larceny away from my mind—temporarily.

She counted it after me and put it in the safe. Then she turned and, opening a closet, took out a bottle of gin. "Have a drink?" she said, holding the bottle out toward me.

"No thanks, Grandma," I said.

She poured herself a drink. She swallowed it. "That's right," she said, "don't touch the stuff. It's poison."

I watched her.

"The first tonight," she cackled, "I never drink while we're working."

I watched her take another.

"Go up to sleep now, Frank," she said, peering at me over the edge of her glasses. "You'll do all right."

I turned and went out of the room and up to my bedroom. I undressed in the dark and threw my clothes over the chair and fell into bed.

I lay there on the bed, staring up through the blackness at the ceiling. I tossed and turned. My eyes ached from tiredness and still I could not fall asleep. I lit a cigarette in the dark and inhaled deeply.

Something was wrong inside me—very wrong. This was the first time in my life I couldn't fall asleep when I wanted to. Suddenly I was afraid: afraid of things I couldn't understand, afraid to be alone, to be without my folks, without Brother Bernhard, afraid to look ahead because my life before me seemed like a pit of slime. I began to cry softly into my pillow.

I felt dirty, somehow incredibly dirty, deep into my skin, through to my bones—so dirty and soiled I would never be able to wash it out.

Why did I ever run away?

Chapter Four

I COULDN'T sleep at all that night. I watched the dawn come into the room. As it grew light I went over to the window and lit a cigarette. The street was empty except for a milk wagon and an occasional early riser on his way down to work. The street lamps began to flicker out. I went to the washstand, filled it with cold water, splashed it over my head and face. Then I dressed. I put on fresh clothes: new underwear and clean shirt. I threw the underwear I had slept in on the bed. I went down the silent hall softly; there were no sounds from the rooms. I let myself out the front door quietly and walked down the steps and then to the corner. Across the street was a small park. I went into it and sat down on a bench. A water fountain near me was spraying water high into the morning air, the drops glimmering in the morning sun, reflecting its light. A flock of sparrows descended upon it in a group, their chirping clatter mocking the early day.

Across the fountain on the other side of the park a sailor was sleeping on a bench, one arm thrown over his eyes to protect them from the light. His white cap lay on the ground near his bench. A policeman came into the park from the entrance near the sailor and woke him up. He shook him gently by the shoulder. He said something to the sailor I couldn't hear. The sailor replied, then picked his cap from the ground and got up and left the park. The cop continued his stroll around the park. I thought about leaving, but thought what the hell, if I'm caught, I'm caught—period! Maybe I was half hoping I would be picked up and sent back. I didn't know I couldn't go back—not after I had run away. I couldn't admit I was wrong—not now. But if I were sent back . . .

"Top o' the mornin', me lad," the cop said to me.

I lit a cigarette. "Good morning," I replied, wondering if he could detect the tremor in my voice.

"A foine morning it 'tis," he said, filling his lungs with air and looking around the park. "Ye're up a bit early, aren't ye?"

"I couldn't sleep," I answered honestly.

" 'Tis very warm for May," he answered, smiling. He had reddish hair and blue eyes—a real mick. "D'ye live around here?" he asked.

"Yes," I said smiling back at him, "I've come to live with my grandmother. She's down the street." I gestured with my hand in the general direction of the house. "I'm from New York."

"A foine place!" he said. "Me brother's there. He's on the force. Sergeant Flaherty is his name. D'ye know him?"

I shook my head. "It's a big place."

"Yes," he said, "it is. I must be going on me rounds now." He took a last look at me. "Good-by."

"So long," I said, watching him saunter off, swinging his club. Cops? I thought. I leaned my head back against the rest at the top of the bench and let the sun play on it. It was good. It felt clean. I could feel it soaking into my skin, warm and penetrating. I drowsed off.

I awoke with a start. A dog, running through the park barking, had startled me. I looked at my watch. It was a little after eight. I felt hungry. I got up and went out the other entrance of the park. I could see some stores a few blocks down. I walked toward them.

I went into a restaurant and had breakfast. About ten o'clock I returned to the house. Mary let me in.

"You up already?" she asked.

"Yes," I said.

"Did y'all have breakfast?" she asked.

"At a restaurant down the block after next," I answered. I went into the parlor. She had a rag tied around her head and had just finished cleaning up the place. The windows were open and a breeze blew through the room. I sat on the couch and began to read the paper I had bought. Through the open doors I could see anyone who came down the stairs. About an hour passed. I could smell bacon frying in the kitchen; so could the others—they began to come down.

Big Mary was the first. She looked in, saw me, and continued on to the kitchen. A few minutes later she came back to the door. "Can I come in?" she asked almost servilely.

"Yes," I answered still reading the paper.

"You're not sore about yesterday?" she asked whiningly, sitting down opposite me, her legs spreading so I could look up her thighs.

"No," I answered. "It was just a misunderstanding." I turned the page.

"That's what it was," she said quickly, seizing upon the word, "a misunderstanding."

"Yes," I said.

"I don't want you to be sore. You know what I mean?" she said, spreading her knees apart still further.

I knew what she meant.

"If there's anything you want—" she asked hesitantly, letting me get a good look.

"No," I said. "Forget about it. We won't have any more trouble."

She stood up. "Well, don't forget—anytime." She went to the kitchen for breakfast.

A few minutes later Mrs. Mander came down. She headed right for the liquor closet and poured herself a drink. Then she turned to me.

"Good morning, up early. Couldn't you sleep?"

"I always get up early," I said.

"Eat?" she asked.

"Yes."

She went in for breakfast.

Jenny was down last. She was the only one dressed in clothes. The others had all worn dressing gowns or wraps, but she had a dress on. It was a gray print. A small gold cross gleamed against her throat.

She came right into the parlor. "Good morning," she said.

"Hello," I answered.

"Have breakfast?" she asked.

"Yes," I answered.

She walked toward me coolly, her hips swaying just a little. "I feel good this morning. I think I'll go to Mass. Want to come?"

"No," I answered shortly. How could anyone go to church from a place like this?

"Why not?" she said. "It'll do you good."

I flared up. "Leave me alone! I don't care whether you go to Mass or to hell, but get out of here!"

She laughed happily, turning and walking to the door. "I will go to hell," she said, still smiling. "So will you. So will all of us. You'll see." She walked out.

"What were you talking about?" Mrs. Mander had come back into the room. I heard the front door slam.

"About going to hell, Grandma." I answered.

"Oh!" she said, helping herself to another drink. "Jenny's always talking about that. She's one of these Catholics who believe in paying for their sins, both now and hereafter. You're not Catholic, are you?" she asked.

"No," I answered.

She lifted a glass to her lips and stopped as if struck by a sudden thought. "Say," she said, "I thought I heard someone moaning last night. She didn't get you to beat her, did she?"

"Hell, no!" I answered.

Mrs. Mander looked at me closely. I guess I looked surprised. "That's right, you couldn't have; she had an all-night customer." She tossed off her drink. "Well, if she ever asks you to," she said slowly, her voice full of hate, "I hope you make it good—the perverted bitch!" She spat the words out. I kept my face impassive as I looked at Mrs Mander, but it was of no use. I was getting sicker of this place every minute.

Chapter Five

IT WAS Thursday night before I came to any decision about what I was going to do. The few days just passed had been comparatively quiet. I had been accepted by the others in the house. I had my place, they had theirs. We respected each other's privacy more or less. I had been restless, somehow unsatisfied with myself, as if I had slipped too naturally into this sort of work. In the back of my mind was the question that this was just another form of pimping. I honestly didn't know whether I liked it. I guess I was a little mixed up as to what I wanted.

Thursday afternoon I sat in the parlor reading the paper, smoking a cigarette. It was raining outside, a glum, miserable rain. Mrs. Mander had gone to the movies with one of the girls. I had gone yesterday. I saw *Seventh Heaven*. I remembered the song the pianist played through the more tender passages of the picture. I left the theater rather depressed and crossed the street for a Coke. I passed a Navy recruiting station and stood at the window looking in. The tall, sunburned officer there was pointing out some of the posters to a tentative recruit. I could see his gestures even if I couldn't hear what he was saying. I followed his arm as it pointed from one poster to another, and imagined myself in those far-off places depicted therein. For a moment I felt like going in and inquiring, but I slowly walked away from the window.

I put the paper down. I had the blues that day for sure. Mary came in and sat down at the piano and began to play. That didn't help either. There was an undercurrent of melancholy in her playing that didn't do me any good. I began to think about home and the folks. I wondered what had happened since I left.

The blue piano got on my nerves.

"For Christ sake," I said, "shut that goddam thing up."

She didn't answer, just closed the piano and left the room.

"What's the matter, Frank?" asked Jenny, who had just passed through the hall. She was dressed in her working clothes: black satin dress with nothing underneath, small gold cross lying on her throat. It was a deceptive cross, lying there with a false promise of innocence. Her skin was very white. She came into the room.

"Nothing!" I snapped.

She sat on the arm of my chair, bending over my shoulder and looking at the paper I was reading.

I closed the paper and put it down. "Why don't you go away?" I asked her.

She looked at me quietly a moment. I felt funny—sick-like, nauseous. It was a distasteful feeling, a cold sinking sensation in the pit of my stomach. It was as if I were two people, one sick at the stomach over the wanting of the other. From the stomach up I was one person, from the stomach down, another.

"Why don't you?" she asked. There was a half smile on her face as if she were reading my mind.

I didn't answer. There wasn't any answer.

She took my hand and rubbed it across her stomach—low. I felt her beneath the dress—warm. "Why don't you go away?" she repeated. "You're a good kid. Do you want to sink as low as we are? Do you want to be damned too?" And all the time she kept guiding my hand over her body.

I pulled my hand away and hit her with my open palm across the face. She fell off the arm of the chair and onto the floor. She looked up at me with a sort of triumphant look on her face as if I had done what she wanted. I made no move to get out of the chair.

"You're strong," she said softly.

I didn't answer. I got out of the chair and stepped across her. She half got up and grabbed one of my legs and kept me from finishing the step. I knocked her hand loose. She tried to grab my hand but I slapped her across the face. I stood there looking down at her. Her eyes were half closed. She moved slightly. I started to walk again but she caught my leg with one hand. With her other hand she lifted her skirt.

She moaned, writhing her hips a little.

I looked at her, stretched out on the floor against the rose-colored rug.

"Now," she said, "now, Frank, now!"

I kicked against her hips and she let go my leg. I walked to

the door and went out on the stoop and stood in the doorway
watching the rain fall. I lit a cigarette. A minute later she was
standing next to me in the narrow doorway.

"You can't go away," she snarled. "You're afraid!"

Suddenly I felt better. It was out in the open now, the thing
that had been in the back of my mind. I smiled.

Her eyes opened wide, she half lifted her hands as if to
protect herself from being hit. For a second she stood there
looking at me. "You're mad," she whispered—"crazy mad!"
She turned and fled through the doorway back into the house.

I laughed out loud into the rain. I took another puff at the
cigarette and threw it far into the gutter.

The rest of the day seemed to fly by. I kept thinking to
myself, repeating over and over: "I was afraid." That's what it
was. And with each saying of it I felt better. Somehow the
saying or the thinking of it would help me feel better. I began
to understand why I had taken the job. I wasn't as smart as I
thought I was; the old lady foxed me. First she had scared the
devil out of me with her crap about the cops. Then she gave
me the job, knowing that if I bit at what she offered, she had
me by the nuts, and I bit. I laughed to myself. Well I wasn't
going to be afraid anymore.

I stood at the door that night in a different frame of mind. I
began to see the cheapness and shoddiness of the place: the
furtive, secretly filthy manner of the customers; the shabby air
of aphrodisiac exuded by the girls; the dirty-minded creak of
the stairs as the customers went up and down; the lazy triumphant look of the girls as they discharged their customers.

About midnight a sailor came in. He seemed to have been
there before. He went upstairs with Jenny and about a half
hour later came down. He laughed as he went out. "What a
broad!" he said.

I laughed with him. "Stuff, brother!"

"You said it, kid!" He smiled. Then he looked closer at me.
"You're kinda young to be creep for this joint."

"I won't be for long," I said. "I'm gettin' out."

"That's good," he said, and went out and started down the
steps.

On an impulse I started after him. "Hey!" I hollered, running down the steps after him.

He turned in the street and faced me. "Whadda ya want?" he asked belligerently.

"Is it true what they say about the Navy?" I asked.

"What's true?"

"Seeing the world—and getting educated—and—" I was excited.

He interrupted me "It shore is. You goin' to j'ine up?"

"If they'll have me," I said.

He laughed shortly. "They'll have you all right. You'll find out."

"What do you mean?"

Again he laughed. "Go ahead, kid, j'ine up. You'll never know till you do."

I missed the sarcasm in his voice. "I will," I said, "tomorrow."

"Do that!" he said. "You'll see the world all right—from a porthole." He started off.

I grabbed his arm. "You're kidding?" I asked.

He looked at me, then looked back up the steps at the house. Suddenly he smiled. "That's right, kid. I was only foolin'. Look at me, I been all over the world—Europe, China, South Seas. It's a great life." He looked up again at the house. "And it's a hell of a lot better'n the one you got here." He turned and walked away.

I watched him go down the street, then slowly climbed the steps to the house. My mind was made up.

As usual Mrs. Mander closed up at three. When we counted out the money she asked me suddenly: "What were you gassin' with that sailor about?"

For a second I thought she had overheard, then I realized she couldn't—not from the parlor with the piano playing.

"Nothing," I said. "He dropped his wallet and I returned it to him."

She looked at me closely a moment, then she reached for her bottle of gin and poured herself a drink. "That's what I like about you, Frank. You're honest." She swallowed her drink. "There's nothing like petty thievery to give a good house a bad name."

Chapter Six

AT TEN o'clock the next morning I was waiting in front of the Navy recruiting station in downtown Baltimore. It hadn't opened as yet, so I had a cup of coffee next door while I waited. Through the window of the coffee shop I saw a Marine sergeant open the door. I finished the coffee quickly and went out into the street.

I walked casually through the door into the office. The sergeant had just sat down at a desk. "I want to join up," I said to him.

"Marines or Navy?" he asked laconically.

"Navy," I replied.

He pointed to a chair over against the wall. "Sit down there," he said, "Lieutenant Ford will be in shortly."

While sitting there I looked around at the various posters. Then I picked up a booklet depicting various scenes of Navy life, at sea, ashore, different places. The officer came in.

The sergeant saluted him. "A recruit to see you, sir," he said.

The lieutenant was a young man. He looked at me and asked me to step over to his desk. I took a seat near the desk. He opened up the desk drawer and took out several forms. Then he filled his pen at the inkwell on his desk and looked up at me.

He began to ask questions in a brisk tone of voice. I answered them as fast as he could ask them.

"Name?"

"Frank Kane."

"Any middle name?"

"Mander," I said, I thought maybe you had to have a middle name to get in the Navy, and I spoke the first name that came into my mind.

"Address?"

I gave him my present address.

"When were you born?"

"May 10, 1909."

"That makes you eighteen now," he said, "You'll need your parents' consent to join."

"My parents are dead," I said.

"Then your guardian?"

"My grandmother," I said. "I live with her."

"That's fine," he said. "We will mail her the consent papers."

I hadn't thought of that, but I had no doubt that I could intercept the papers and sign them before she could see them. I was always the first one up in the house. He continued his questions. At last he was finished. He stood up. I stood up too.

"When your grandmother signs these papers," he said, "bring them down here. Also bring enough clothing to last you three days. You will receive your medical examination, and if you pass that, you will be sworn in and sent to a boot camp immediately."

"Thank you," I said.

He smiled and held out his hand. "Good luck," he said.

I shook his hand and walked back to the house, my head in the clouds.

Monday morning the letter came. I saw it on the hall table where Mary had put it with other letters. It had "U. S. Navy, official business" on it, up in the left-hand corner of the envelope. I picked it up and took it up to my room and opened it. I saw where the recruiting officer had marked an "x" for her to sign. I signed it with a different type hand than I usually wrote. I put it in the pocket of my blue suit, the old one.

My last night there was an ordinary one—the usual routine. When we had finished and closed up I went in the back as usual to settle up with Mrs. Mander. When we had finished I sat back and looked at her.

As usual she had helped herself to a drink. When she saw me sitting there instead of my usual going up to bed, she looked at me strangely.

"What's on your mind, Frank?" she asked.

"I'm movin' on," I told her, "tomorrow."

"What are you going to do?" she asked.

I didn't answer.

"All right, so it's none of my business!" she said sharply, taking another drink. "What about the clothes I bought you?"

"Keep 'em," I said succinctly. "I got enough."

"I don't give a damn what you got! I paid good money for them."

"So what!" I said.

For a second she was quiet. Then she spoke again. "I'll give you a ten-buck raise."

"No dice!" I said. "I don't like the work."

"But look," she said, "stick around and you'll make some real dough. Maybe after awhile I'll cut you in on the take. I like you. You'll get along. We'll make out O. K."

"I'm leavin'," I said standing up.

She looked up at me. "I haven't any relatives and I got a nice bit of money socked away. I'm getting old for this kind of work and I got to have someone I can trust. You're honest with me. Stick around—you'll be rich."

I felt sorry for the old dame; I guess she had a pretty tough life. "I'm sorry," I said, "but I can't stay."

She flared up. She stood near the edge of the table. "Go to hell!" Her voice was shaking.

I turned and started out the door without answering.

She called me back. "Frank."

"Yes," I said, stepping back into the room.

"Need any money?" Her voice was softer now.

I shook my head.

She peeled some bills from her roll and held them out to me. "Here," she said, "take it. I've got more than I need."

I took the money from her and put it in my pocket. "Thanks," I said.

"Come here a minute," she said.

I walked over to her. She took my hand. "You're a fine kid, Frank. There's something wild and hard inside you that needs gentling, but there's also something fine and bright inside you. Whatever you do, don't change. Don't lose that something that keeps you from being hard and rotten." She laughed. "I must be getting old," she said, "to be talking like that." She took another drink from the table.

I was silent. The old dame kind of liked me.

"Well?" she asked.

"Good-by," I said. On an impulse I bent and kissed her cheek. It was old and dry to the touch, like a piece of old paper.

She put her hand to her cheek half wonderingly. She thought aloud: "It has been a long time since—" Her words trailed off.

I closed the door behind me and went up to bed.

The next morning I was sworn into the United States Navy. When I finished my medical examination the doctor goosed me and laughed. "Get used to it, kid. You're in the Navy now."

There were three other men in the office with me being sworn in.

"You will raise your right hands and repeat after me," Lieutenant Ford said.

I raised my right hand. It was so quiet that for a second I could hear my heart pounding.

"I pledge allegiance . . ." Lt. Ford said quietly.

I repeated after him: "I pledge allegiance . . ."

Interlude

JERRY

JERRY settled himself deeply in his favorite chair, took a cigarette from a small cabinet on the side table, and surveyed Marty and Janet who were sitting opposite him. He looked around the room. He liked the simple, rich elegance of its decor, the odd paintings on the walls, the enlarged gay lifelike kodachrome of Janet on the radio.

It had been taken on their honeymoon. They had gone to the Grand Canyon. Janet had been laughing and pointing at some wonder of nature, and he had taken the picture. It was a semi-profile shot and the immense, beautiful canyon served as a backdrop. It was by far the best picture he had ever taken. He was proud of it.

He dragged deeply at his cigarette and listened to what they were saying. The others were still talking about Francis. He felt a little annoyed at the turn the conversation had taken. Then he smiled inwardly. He felt he was acting the fool. One wasn't annoyed by ghosts. Ghosts belong to the past. And Frankie was part of the past.

Marty leaned forward in his chair. His face was earnest and serious. "It's funny, Jerry, but you never told me how you happened to meet Frankie. You've been rather quiet all evening."

Jerry saw they were expecting an answer. He turned the question over in his mind carefully. Then he began to speak with that charmingly simple candor that he had learned to use so well.

"I met him simply enough—about the same as you did: in a fight. We couldn't lick one another, so we shook and called it quits.

"It happened a long time ago. I was attending the Lawrence Academy in Connecticut when one weekend Dad came up there to talk to me. I sat on the edge of my bed in my room and watched him pace up and down before me as he spoke. My dad was a wonderful guy. Even when I was very young he treated me as an equal, asked my opinion on varying things.

"This was one of those things. 'You see, son,' he said. 'In another two years they're going to put me up for Mayor. And the boys seemed to think—'

" 'I should go to school in New York,' I finished for him. I could understand that. I had been brought up in politics. I had watched my father ever since I was a child, and I had learned a great deal from him.

" 'That's it, son,' he said. 'It would mean a lot to me if you'd like to have a try at it. If the people saw you mixing with the other kids, you know how they would feel about it.' He sat down at the edge of the bed and put his arm around my shoulders. 'I know how you feel about this place, son, and I know what it would mean to you if you left it just when you were in so good here and had all your friends around you. But you're growing up. You're almost a man now and you have a right to make up your mind as to what you want.'

"I wanted to be like my father. He was the greatest man in the world to me. He was a leader of men and that's what I wanted to be—a leader of men, a man people would look up to and respeect and admire.

"I knew what I wanted and I knew what had to be done. I didn't want to leave Lawrence but there were other important things in life. So I went to St. Therese.

"I went to St. Therese but I never liked the place. It was filthy and dirty, and most of the kids were stupid and poor and lacked manners and understanding. I never held it against them, but I never got to feel that I was part of the place, the way I had at Lawrence."

He laughed a little. "I suppose I was a bit of a snob. But I tried to get over it. I honestly tried, and I think I did because most of the other kids seemed to accept me. They accepted me and liked me, but I never became the head of the gang because there was another guy. He was Francis Kane.

"They knew him. He was rough and hard and he made the rules and they did what he told them. At first we steered clear of one another, sizing each other up. Then we had a fight. Though neither of us could win physically, I knew inside that he had won. I knew inside that he would have won even if I had bested him.

"You see, at that school I was from the wrong side of the tracks—funny in a way but perfectly true. He was of them, from them, with them, and part of them. That was something I never could be, coming from where I came. He was the first kid I ever envied.

"Well, as the old saying goes, 'If you can't lick 'em, jine 'em.' That's what I did. And as I grew to know him I began to like him. In spite of the way he spoke, the clothes he wore, or the dirt on his hands and face. He and I were a lot alike. But one thing made the difference, he was the leader. It was that in him that I tried to find and see—that tiny spark that made the difference. I never did find it but I knew it was there all the time. Even if I couldn't put my fingers on it.

"Even my father saw it. One day I had him to dinner at the house, and that night Dad asked me who he was. I told him. 'The boy is dangerous,' Dad told me. 'He's smart and tough and he's a scrapper. Don't let the way he talks fool you.'

"I smiled at Dad and told him I knew it. But Frankie was never dangerous for me. He was my friend. He liked me."

A maid came into the room then and placed the electric coffee maker on the table. Next to it she placed three tiny demitasse cups and saucers and little spoons. Jerry fell silent as he watched her.

"I'll serve the coffee, Mary," Janet said, taking the napkins from her.

"Yes, ma'am," the maid said, and retired from the room.

Balancing the small cup and saucer on his knee, Jerry continued. "Remember that time he was running for class president in high school? He was going to make that speech we wrote for him. Remember how bad he was when we practiced it, how afraid you were that he'd muff it? Well, I thought he'd muff it too, maybe even hoped a little that he would so there could be something I could say I was better at.

"Remember what he did when he came to the center of the platform—how he stood there a moment and then started to speak in a voice that was a little bit high? I remember sitting there thinking: 'Here it comes. He's going to blow.' But he didn't. He spoke as naturally as he spoke to anyone—simply, quietly, friendly. It was then I realized fully what Dad had meant when he said Frankie was a scrapper. We all knew he was scared to death at going up there to speak, and there he was wrapping the meeting up in his hands. He was a showman too, the way he turned and brought Janet out with him. It was right—instinctively right. He did the things by instinct that I had to plan. He was the politician I had studied to be since I was a little kid. He was my father and myself rolled up into one, with my father's magnetism and instinct for people and my plans.

"At that moment I think I grew up—watching the two of them on the platform taking bows hand in hand. 'You won't meet many like him', I told myself. 'Watch him and learn from him.' I watched and I learned. And I learned to like him.

"There was nothing complicated about Frankie to me. To me he was the essence of direct simplicity and tact combined with a trigger-quick intelligence. He knew what he wanted and went for it. He told you what he thought, did what he wanted to, no matter what happened."

He raised the demitasse to his lips. The coffee was cold. With an almost imperceptible pursing of his lips, he placed it back on the table.

"So you see," he said, "Frankie wasn't the mystery to me that he was to you. I grew to know him too well. I knew what he would do almost before he did it."

"But," Marty interjected, "you didn't know he was going to run away."

Jerry conceded the point by nodding his head. "That's true. But you must remember I wasn't with him the day he went to the station with his people. If I had seen him but once that day I would have known." But through his mind was running another theme.

"Could I have known? Did I really know him as I say? Or was he as much of a challenge or threat to me as I imagined him to be? The things that happened after could have been predicted by no man. No man could read the future. But he always had had the things I wanted most. He was top man at school, first with Janet. And even though I got the things I wanted after he left them, how do I know I would ever have had them if he hadn't gone away?"

The thing that Janet wanted to do now—was it right or would it be Frank to come back to haunt him? He had no basic objections to Janet's idea and he wondered where it came from. But after all, there had been Frank and though he now belonged to the past, there still was a way open for him to return.

PART FOUR

Chapter One

I STOOD on the steps of the administration building and looked across the naval station. It was December 30th, 1931, and the breeze was chilly as it blew across the San Diego Bay. I turned up the collar of my pea jacket and lit a cigarette. My discharge papers were stuffed into my pocket; the duffel bag with my few belongings lay at my feet.

I was glad to be out. It wasn't that I thought the Navy was bad, but as far as I was concerned it was a better place to bide my time before I rejoined my folks than the orphanage. Maybe I was just swapping one sort of a jail for another, but it was over now and I was glad of it.

Life in the Navy was generally a dull one. The restrictions, the routine, the very detailed planning of every minute of your day led to a certain deterioration of your ability to do and plan things for yourself. It probably did me some good. I read a great deal and was taught many things. I took mathematics for the gunnery classes, bookkeeping for storekeepers duties in addition to English, history and a certain amount of geography.

Now, as far as I was concerned, it was over. I took a last puff at my cigarette, threw it away, and slung my duffel bag over my shoulder and proceeded to the main gate.

At the gate I handed my discharge papers to the chief petty officer on duty there. He took them, flipped them open, glanced at them, and gave them back to me.

"O. K., sailor," he said, grinning, "so long."

"So long, hell!" I said. "This is good-by. I'm out."

"That's what they all say," he said, still grinning. "You'll be back. They all come back."

"Not this baby!" I retorted, "I'm going home." I walked out the gate to the bus stop. A bus came up and I got in and sat down.

I turned for a last look at the station as the bus pulled out, and then settled back in my seat.

The folks would be glad to hear from me. I remembered the last time I had written them. It was from New York. I had a twenty-four liberty from my ship and had wandered around town all morning not knowing what to do with myself. Suddenly I found myself in front of Jerry's house. Without thinking, I ran up the steps and rang the bell.

A butler opened the door.

"Is Jerry in?" I asked.

"No," he answered, "Master Jerry is away at college. Any message?"

I hesitated a moment. "No," I said, "No message," and turned back down the steps as the door closed behind me.

It was then I really got homesick. Here I was in a town I had lived in all my life and not a familiar face around to talk to. I was miserable. I walked around until I came to a hotel and then went in and sat down in the writing room and began to write a letter.

Dear Uncle Morris, Aunt Bertha, Irene and Essie,

I just wanted to drop you a line to let you know I am well and hope you are the same. I especially hope that Uncle Morris is getting better. I am sorry if I have caused you any worry because I ran away, but I couldn't stay in that place anymore, not after living with you. I have been in good health all the time and have been working. I hope some day soon, when I am old enough not to have to go back to the orphanage, to be able to again live with you. Until then I do not want you to worry as I have enough of everything, including money.

All my love to you and I hope you are all well.

                                              Frankie

Looking down at the letter, I got a bright idea. I took the letter and went up to the bank and got a check for the whole balance in my account. I put it in the letter and mailed it to them. Then I turned and went back to my ship feeling better. There was nothing more I wanted from New York.

But all that had happened almost two years before. Now I was out, and I was going to Arizona and join them. I left the bus in downtown San Diego, went directly to the hotel, and registered. Then, even before I went up to my room, I went over to the telegraph desk.

The girl came over with a blank telegraph form and a pencil. I leaned over the counter and began to write, smiling to myself. Things certainly were going to be O. K. from now on. I was going home and I had two hundred bucks in my pocket.

Mr. Morris Cain, 221 Lincoln Drive, Tucson, Arizona.

Received my discharge from the Navy today. Would like to join you immediately. Expect to leave here at end of week. Will let you know what day to expect me. Am eager to see all of you.

Love,
Frank

I went upstairs with the boy who showed me my room. Quickly I emptied my duffel bag into the dresser and went downstairs. I went over to the desk clerk and asked him a good place to buy some clothes. He sent me to a chain-store clothier over on Grand Avenue. I picked up three good suits at nineteen dollars each. He promised to have them for me in a few days. I told him to rush them through, and he said he would have them for me Saturday, the day after New Year's. Then I went next door to a haberdasher and bought about six shirts at a dollar and a quarter apiece. Some underwear, socks and ties rounded out my wardrobe. I bought a small valise for six bucks and went back to the hotel. Now, I thought to myself, I was ready to go as soon as the clothes would get here.

The few days dragged by. I spent New Year's Eve and almost the whole day in my room. The hotel had several parties going on the whole of the night, and I could hear them through the closed doors of the room. Oddly enough, I didn't feel out of things. I had too many things to think about. I could imagine how happy they all were when they received my telegram, how eagerly they awaited my coming. I bet I wouldn't know the kids any more. They must be young ladies by now.

The next day I went down and picked up my suits. I took off

my uniform and donned the brown tweed. I didn't know myself in the mirror. It had been so long since I had worn civies, I felt pretty good with them on. I decided to go out and buy my ticket. I got the ticket for Tucson on a train leaving the next morning. Then I went back to the hotel to check out. While I stood there near the desk, feeling very self-conscious in my new clothes, I saw the clerk put something in my mail box. I stepped up and asked him for it.

It was a telegram from Tucson. I didn't open it there; I was too excited. They had answered me, I thought. I was so nervous that I hurried up to my room to read it. As soon as I was inside the door I opened it.

A copy of my wire had been enclosed; attached to it was a note. It read: "Your telegram of December 30th, 1931, attached has not been delivered for the following reason." Then there was a list of reasons. Next to one, a pencil check had been inserted. "Moved from this address, forwarding address not known."

For a moment I didn't understand it, I sank into a chair, my hopes gone up in smoke. For a minute or two I just sat there too upset to feel anything. I didn't know what to do next. I never thought they would have left without notifying me. But I realized they couldn't. They never knew where I was. Again that feeling of being alone came over me—a feeling of being lost, abandoned without hope. The street noises came in through the closed window. I heard a woman's laugh in the hall. The room seemed to close in on me. I lit cigarette after cigarette. The air became filled with smoke. I don't know how long I sat there in the armchair, but when I looked up it was dark outside. Slowly I got up and looked out the window. The lights were on all over the city. I walked around the room aimlessly. I couldn't seem to fix my mind on anything.

I went downstairs into the dining room. I ordered something to eat—and didn't eat it. I left the dining room after paying my check, and went out into the lounge. I sat there for a while just looking at the people, not seeing them. I wasn't thinking, just in a sort of stupid vacuum. I saw the telegraph desk. I got up and walked over to it. The girl sitting there looked up.

I took the telegram out of my pocket. "Do you know anything about this?" I asked her.

She looked at it. "No, Mr. Kane. As soon as I received it I sent it over to the desk."

"Do you think they could be wrong?"

"I don't think so," she said. "They check these things very carefully."

"Thanks," I said, walking away leaving the girl looking after me thoughtfully.

Next to the Western Union desk was a flight of steps leading up to the telephone lounge. It was less crowded there than in the lobby, so I went up there. I didn't want to be entirely alone, yet I didn't want to be down there in the midst of all those people. I couldn't explain it. I sat down on the chair next to one of the phone booths. I had been sitting there about a half an hour when the girl from the telegraph desk came up. I watched her go into the booth next to me. The door closed. I didn't hear a coin drop into the machine, or hear any conversation. A few minutes later she came out. She stopped in the doorway and acted surprised to see me sitting there. She smiled at me. I nodded back politely; I didn't feel much like smiling.

She took a cigarette from her purse. "How about a light, Mr. Kane?" she said, smiling.

Pretty obvious! I didn't care. I took a match from my pocket, lit it, and held it toward her. She sat down next to me. I moved over to make room for her on the seat. "Thanks," she said.

"It's O. K.," I told her.

"New clothes?" she asked me.

"What?" I asked. For a moment I didn't know what she meant. Then I nodded. "Just got them today."

"How do you like being out of the Navy?" she asked.

"It's all right, I guess," I answered.

"Kind of at loose ends, I suppose." She looked interested.

"That's right," I said. "I'll have to get used to it."

"Too bad, about the telegram, I mean," she said sympathetically.

"I should have expected it," I said. I was beginning to feel better. She was the first person in this damn place to seem interested in me. I looked at her. She was a nice-looking girl: black hair, blue eyes, a trim neat figure. I smiled at her. "I don't want to burden you with my woes," I said. "It's nice enough of you to be interested as it is."

"Oh, I don't mind really," she said. "I've got a close relative in the Navy, and I often wonder how he would feel if he were out."

"I guess it's not too bad," I said, "if you could only make up your mind as to what you want to do."

"What are you going to do?" she asked.

I lit a cigarette over that one. What was I going to do? I didn't know—I hadn't thought about it. "I don't know honestly," I said. "Get a job, I guess."

"Anything special?"

"No, just anything that comes along," I replied.

"Jobs are pretty hard to get right now," she told me.

"I don't know," I said confidently. "I've never had much trouble getting one."

For a while we sat there not talking. Then she got to her feet. "I guess I've got to go," she said. "It's getting kind of late and I might as well get home for supper."

I looked up at her. "Why don't you call home and tell them you're going out for the evening? I mean why not go out with me? I don't mean to be fresh, but maybe we could go out and you could show me the town. I don't know the place too well."

She smiled down at me. "That's nice of you to ask me, Mr. Kane. But I really have to go home."

The hell she did! She had to, like I had to. I played along with her. "Please come," I asked her. "I'd appreciate it very much. You don't know how lonely you can get to feel in a strange town."

She pretended to deliberate a moment. "All right," she said, "I'll go with you, Mr. Kane. But first I have to call home, Mr. Kane."

I took the hint. "Frank, to you."

"All right then, Frank." She smiled. "My name's Helen."

Helen went into the phone booth. I sat there waiting. Again she didn't make any phone call. I laughed to myself.

We went down to some nightclub where they had a pretty good show. We ate and had a few drinks. I never drank very much but this time I didn't care. I was getting pretty high. We danced and drank and danced and drank, and pretty soon it was nearly two o'clock in the morning. We left the cabaret and I hailed a taxi.

"I'll take you home," I said.

"I can't go home like this," she said, giggling. "My father would be sore as hell."

"Where are you going to stay?" I asked her.

"At the hotel," she said. "I often do when I work late."

We got into the cab. "The Berkeley," I told the driver. The cab started off. I was a little bit dizzy but the fresh air from the windows of the car cleared my head. I sank back on the seat and looked at her. She was sitting in a corner of the cab. She giggled.

"What's the matter?" I asked her.

She giggled again. "I feel so silly."

"Do you?" I asked, putting my arm around her and moving her over close to me.

She pressed against me, not resisting my straying hands. I kissed her.

"Still feel silly?" I asked, and kissed her again. This time she kissed back. Her lips were burning flames.

"Not any more," she said, pulling away. "You sure can kiss."

"That isn't all I can do," I told her giddily. "I've got talent." I kissed her again. Then I kissed her throat. She held me tightly. Suddenly she pushed me away.

"The hotel!" she whispered huskily. The cab was stopping in front of the hotel. I let her go. She straightened her clothes. We got out and I paid the cabby.

"Let's go in," I said taking her by the arm.

She held back. "I can't go in there with you. I'd get fired; we're not supposed to mingle with the guests. I'd better say good night out here."

I looked at her. Good night out here! Was she crazy? I didn't go out like this and spend my good dough to say good night on the sidewalk. I looked again. She seemed O. K. Maybe I was wrong. Maybe she was just going along to be nice to me. I shrugged my shoulders. "You sure you can get a room?" I asked her.

She nodded.

"O. K. then," I said, "good night." I turned and walked into the lobby. I was a little sore. The lousy little teaser. But I started to laugh by the time I reached my room. At least she took my mind off my troubles.

I went into my room and took off my jacket and tie. I took out my wallet and counted my money. I had about a hundred and ten dollars left. I decided to pay up at the hotel tomorrow and go out and look for a cheap room. Then Monday I would go out and look for a job. I took off my shirt and went to the basin and washed up, then went back and sat on the edge of the bed smoking a cigarette. There was a knock at the door—a soft knock. I barely heard it. Quickly I stepped over to the table where I had left my money and put it in the dresser. Then I stepped over to the door and opened it.

Helen stood there. I looked at her. I didn't show how surprised I felt. "Well," she said, "aren't you going to ask me in?"

"Oh, sure," I mumbled, stepping back. "Come in."

She came into the room. I shut the door. "I didn't thank you for the good time we had."

"I should've thanked you," I said politely. Hell, she didn't come up here just to thank me! I reached up and clicked out the light on the wall. Only the bed lamp was lit now.

We stood there facing each other in the semidarkness. I took a sudden step toward her. Instinctively she stepped back. I caught her hand and held her. "What's the matter, baby?" I asked, pulling her close and kissing her.

"I'm afraid," she said. "I never did this before."

I slipped my hand inside her dress. Her breast was soft and warm. She drew in her breath sharply. I drew her down on the bed and kissed her again. She lay back across it, her arms pulling my head down. I drew up my head and looked down at her. "There's always got to be a first time, baby," I said, "and I won't hurt you." I ran my fingers up her thigh under her dress—the soft, warm flesh of a young woman's thigh, filled with electricity and fire.

"I'm afraid, Frank," she whispered, holding my hand on her thigh. "But . . ."

I interrupted her words by kissing her breast. When I stopped she continued in a whisper: "But you need me. You need someone. You looked so lonely downstairs—so alone."

I reached up and flicked out the lamp. "I need you, baby!"

Chapter Two

I WOKE up suddenly in the night. Something had stirred in the room. I put out my hand. Helen was gone. I sat up and jumped out of bed. I went over to the dresser and opened the drawer in which I had put my money. It was empty. I swore silently to myself as I dressed. All I had was the ten bucks that was in my pants pocket. I took a quick look at my watch as I hurried down the hall. It was nearly five o'clock. I took the elevator down.

I went over to the desk. "The telegraph operator around?" I asked.

"No," the night clerk answered. "Which one do you mean?"

"The day operator," I said, "the one named Helen."

"Oh, her," he said. "She was only a relief operator. Here for a day. The regular operator's out sick. Is something wrong?"

Is something wrong? Plenty! I was cleaned. I still owed the hotel about twenty bucks and he asked me if something was wrong! "No," I said. "I just thought of a wire I had to send. It'll keep though."

I turned and went back to my room. At least it didn't take me long to get cleaned. I had heard of sailors coming back and signing up a few days after their discharge because they were broke and had been taken for their dough—dough they had spent a whole hitch in getting—and I never could understand it. But it happened to me. I lit a cigarette while I thought over what I had to do next.

About ten o'clock I went downstairs to the telegraph desk. An operator was sitting there. "Do you know where Helen is?"

She shrugged her shoulders. "How should I know?" she asked. "The office sent her over for a trial when I was out. D'ya want I should find out for ya?"

"Could you, please?" I asked. "It's very important."

She got her central office on the wire. Back came the message. "No. She was hired for the day and paid off at the end of her trick. She didn't leave any address."

That was that. I went from there to the desk and asked to see the manager. I was shown into his office. He was a medium-sized, quiet-spoken, gray-haired man.

"What can I do for you, Mr. Kane?" he asked politely.

I told him the whole story. He listened, his hands folded on his chest. When I had finished he asked me what I wanted him to do.

"I don't know what you can do," I answered him honestly.

"I don't know what I can do either," he said, standing up. "We provide a safe for the guests to leave their money and valuables. We have a sign prominently posted: 'Not responsible for money or valuables unless checked with the desk.' If we would listen to every hard luck story handed us, where would we be? I heard plenty of stories like that before. People come in here after spending and losing their money gambling and in other ways and expect us to do something for them. This is a business, the same as any other. We have to run the business right or we lose our jobs. Have you enough to pay your bill?" he asked shrewdly.

"No," I answered, "I told you that bitch cleaned me."

"Tsk, tsk," he said shaking his head. "Very unfortunate!"

"I know that," I said. "But how about giving me a few days. I'll get a job and pay you every cent."

He laughed at that. "Do you have any idea, Mr. Kane, how scarce jobs are? And your room is pretty expensive too—about three fifty a day, I think. No, I'm afraid the owners would never permit anything like that."

"Then how about letting me work it off?" I asked.

"I'm sorry," he said, "I couldn't do that. We're overstaffed as it is, and I expect to have to let some people go this coming week."

"Well," I said, "that puts me right back to where I started from. What do I do next?"

"I don't know," he said. "But in view of circumstances, you'll have to let us have the room immediately. We'll require that you leave your clothing—er, that is, what you're not wearing— with us as security for payment of the rent."

I got sore at that. I stood up. "You lousy bastard!" I said to him. "That's a hell of a way to treat somebody who comes in trying to level with you! If I wanted to fool you, I could have gone on saying nothing and let you find out for yourself. But, no! I have to be the sucker to take the rap for the rest of the cheap tinhorns who are too smart for you!"

He tried to interrupt me but I shouted him down.

"I'm going to take my stuff and get the hell out of here, and you try to stop me! If you do I'll spill my guts out all over this town about how you let your telegraph operators take your customers. See how you like that!" I started out of the room.

He stopped me at the door. "All right, Mr. Kane," he said, "don't get excited. Supposing I let you take your stuff and go. We'll forget the whole matter."

"You bet your life I'm goin'!" I said, still angry "You can

forget it, not me!" I slammed the door behind me. I went up to my room and began to pack my things. When I had everything packed, I went out into the hall and took the elevator downstairs.

I walked out of the hotel. I stopped at the newsstand on the corner. I bought a paper. "Do you know a good reasonable rooming house?" I asked the vendor.

"Sure," he said. He wrote an address on a piece of paper for me. It was a few blocks away, so I walked there. I took a room there for three fifty a week, two weeks on the line in advance. That left me with three dollars and about eighty cents in change. I packed my stuff into the dresser. This place was a dump compared with the hotel, but at least I was good here for the next two weeks.

The next day I went job hunting. I was lucky. I got a job paying fourteen dollars a week delivering groceries and meat for a big market down on Center Street. I came home tired. I stretched out on the bed. It was pretty tough running around all day with grocery orders, and I had been taking it kind of easy the last few months. I got out of bed and sat down trying to figure out how far the money would go. I took a piece of paper and pencil and jotted down figures on it:

Rent	$3
Food	7
Total	$10
Sal.	14
Extra	$ 4

I figured about a dollar a day for food was enough. Breakfast was just coffee and a roll. Lunch was a sandwich and coffee or a plate of soup and coffee. For supper I would take a plate in a cafeteria. I lay down on the bed again. I wasn't worried. I'd get by.

But there was one thing I didn't figure on.

Chapter Three

I USED to come in to work at seven o'clock in the morning. My first job was to get out the early orders. The clerks had them ready the night before, and I would take them out, put them into the pushcart, and deliver them. I didn't care much for the work, but by being careful and saving that extra four bucks a week, I hoped to save up enough to take me back East. I figured that was where I'd find the folks.

But two days later it blew up. I was carrying an order out to the cart when I began to get sick and dizzy. I guess it was the crummy food I'd been eating. The sidewalk seemed to incline up toward the building line. It seemed to be harder and harder for me to keep my balance. I dropped the order on the ground and fell against the side of the building. Stupidly I watched the broken eggs and milk form a mush on the walk. I was sweating. Only by exerting my will power could I keep from falling to the ground. Desperately I fought myself. I must not fall. I mustn't. But the building kept going up and up as the sidewalk kept rising.

The boss came out and looked at the sidewalk, then at me leaning against the building. I was white. Beads of sweat had run down into my eyes and I couldn't see clearly. He made no move to help me. I tried to say something to him but the words that came out were unintelligible.

"Come in and get your time when you've sobered up," he said, turning on his heel and walking back to the building.

I looked after him helplessly. I tried to speak again but couldn't. I just leaned against the building, hoping I wouldn't pass out. The rage and shame and the humiliation were all burning inside of me. The son of a bitch thought I was drunk! I could have wept. But I didn't have time. I had to fight that sidewalk. It was like a tightrope; at any minute I felt I would fall. Slowly I sank to my haunches and rested my head on my arms. I shut my eyes so I didn't have to see that terrible incline I was so afraid of. I tried not to think of it, not to think of anything.

At last it passed. I began to feel a little better. I raised my head and opened my eyes. They were wet with the tears I had suppressed. I had a dull headache. The sidewalk was back to normal. I stood up slowly. I still felt shaky. Holding my hands on the side of the building, I walked around to the door. As I went in, a clerk rushed past me to clean up the mess. I went back to the little glass cage the boss called his office.

He was standing there. "Mr. Rogers," I began.

"Here's your time, Kane," he said. He held out five dollars toward me.

I took it slowly. I couldn't move too quickly. I counted it. "But, Mr. Rogers," I said, "there's only five dollars here. I've worked three days. It should be seven."

"I've taken out what you broke," he said, turning his back on me.

Stupidly I put the money in my pocket. I started to walk away, then turned back. "Mr. Rogers," I said, "I wasn't drunk. I was sick."

He didn't answer. I could see he didn't believe me.

"You gotta believe me, Mr. Rogers!" I said, my voice trembling. "It's the truth, I was dizzy and . . ."

"If you're sick you shouldn't work anyhow," he said, turning to me. "Now beat it! I haven't any time to waste."

I knew he didn't believe me. I walked past the clerks as I took off the apron and put on my jacket. They watched me out of the corner of their eyes. I hadn't worked there long enough to know any of them. I felt that they thought as Mr. Rogers did.

I went directly home. I didn't feel well enough to look for another job that day. Besides, I had a funny feeling of shame that seemed to cling to me. I thought everybody on the streets looked at me strangely. I went up to my room and lay down. I stayed inside for the rest of the day. I wasn't hungry and didn't feel like eating anything.

The next morning I went out again. But that day passed and I didn't get a job—and the next day, and the day after that. I was pretty low on dough. I had cut down to one cheap meal a day. By the middle of the next week I was broke. I could see no job in sight, and Sunday I would have to pony up three and a half for the room.

I was on the street when the idea hit me. I would go back to New York. I had friends there. I knew my way around that town. They would help me find the folks. I turned back to my room. I got all my clothes together—the new suits I had bought a few weeks ago and all my shirts but one—and put them into the valise. On the way downstairs I told the landlady I was giving up the room at the end of the week.

I looked around for a hock shop. I found one down on lower Main Street. I walked into the shop and dumped the stuff on the counter. An old man, wearing glasses, came forward to wait on me. "What can I get for this, uncle?" I asked him as I opened the valise.

He took out the new suits and looked at them carefully. Then he put them down "It can't be done," he said. "I'm not handling hot goods."

"Uncle," I said, "this stuff ain't hot. I just bought it last week. But I lost my dough and I want to blow out of this burg."

"You got maybe a bill of sale?" he asked, looking at me shrewdly.

I fished in my wallet. I found the one for the suits. I showed it to him. He looked at it. "Five dollars apiece I'll give you for the suits—fifty cents for the shirts."

"Holy Christ! I just paid twenty bucks for those suits a few weeks ago, and you offer me five bucks."

"Business is bad," he said with an expressive gesture of his hands, "and suits is a drug on the market."

I began packing the stuff back into the valise.

"Vait a minute," he said. "You want to sell the stuff or hock it?"

"I want to sell it," I said, still packing. "The valise too. I told you I'm leaving town."

"In that case," he said, "I'm offering you seven fifty for the suits, since I don't have to hold them, and two fifty for the valise."

We settled for thirty bucks and a pair of blue denim work pants and shirt. I changed in the back room. I gave him the suit I had on as well as the others. I walked out of the store and went to the nearest restaurant and had me a good meal. After I had eaten I bought me a pack of cigarettes and lit up. I walked back to the rooming house, feeling a little bit better. I went upstairs and went to sleep.

Early the next morning I was down at the freight yards. I was heading home—back to New York.

Chapter Four

IT WASN'T too tough a trip. There were many others like me riding the rods for one reason or another, some heading nowhere in particular—people without anchors, just drifting along. Others were going some place definite—home or to a new place where a job might be found.

They too were like other people, some nice and helpful, some nasty and mean, but on the whole I got along. I minded my own business, never stayed on one train too long, jumped off at an occasional town along the route to hole up for a day and night in a cheap room and eat a few decent meals, and then I'd be on my way again.

I didn't have much dough left when I tumbled off the sleeper in Hoboken, just across the river from New York, but it didn't worry me. I knew I could get along once I was there.

It was four blocks from the freight yards to the ferry, and the rain that had been falling when I first got off the train turned to a heavy snow by the time I boarded the ferry.

It was late in the evening and the crowds were coming back from work. There were mostly trucks going back to New York. I swung up behind one of them and climbed inside. Once the truck was on board the ferry I hopped out.

I could feel the lurch of the ferry and the slush of the water against the pier as the ferry went out. I walked into the closed-in passenger part. I sat down and looked forward through a glass window, trying to see New York in front of us, but I couldn't. All I could see was white snow falling—falling in a thick blanket between the water and the sky.

When the boat suddenly came near the dock and the tall

buildings and the lights of New York began to shine in front of me, I felt as if I'd come home—really home. This was one town and one set of people that I could understand.

I heard the clank of chains as the gate rolled open, and I walked forward. The trucks began to roll off and I joined the crowd pushing their way on to the dock. I was cold but too excited to mind it. The blue denim work trousers and heavy work shirt I had on weren't enough protection against this kind of weather, but at the time I didn't mind.

The ferry docked at Forty-second Street. I walked crosstown to Times Square and stood on the corner, just like any other hick for the first time in New York, and gawked up at the big sign on the Times Building as the lights went on.

"Seven p.m. February 10, 1932."

Suddenly I was hungry. I ducked into a cafeteria and ate a pretty good meal. It wasn't until I paid my check that I realized I had only about forty cents left. But I didn't worry about it. I slept that night in a cheap hotel down on the Bowery for two bits. That left me with only fifteen cents for tomorrow. I remember smiling as I fell asleep. This was my town and I didn't need dough to get along here.

It was still snowing when I woke up. I turned out of the flophouse and went up toward Sixth Avenue to the agencies. At each corner as I walked I saw a man, generally with his over-coat collar turned up around his neck and a cap pulled down over his face, and a little wood fire burning in a medium-sized tin can, over which he almost always held his hands, and a crate of apples in front of him, with a sign on it: "Buy An Apple From A Veteran."

That night I slept in a hallway, and when I woke up in the morning the snow had stopped falling. It was piled high in front of some stores where the sidewalks had been cleaned, and everywhere men and women were pushing and shoveling snow from the street into the gutter.

I stopped in front of a newsstand on the corner and read the headlines. They said: "Expect 30,000 Work On Snow." That gave me an idea. I stopped in a restaurant near there and got rolls and coffee for a nickel, for breakfast.

I went to the Department of Sanitation office on Eighth Street for a job on the snow. But the line of vags there was a block long, and while I watched them, it kept growing larger and larger. I took a cigarette out of my pocket and lit it and walked toward the Third Avenue El. The exit gate was closed, so I invested my last nickel in a ride uptown.

I left the train at 125th Street. At a D.S. office on West 126th Street I got a job and was sent right out with a crew of men to work. The man in charge of about fifteen men was a well-fed-looking Italian street cleaner. We all looked at him rather enviously, thinking how well off and contented he must be to have a good, steady-paying, city job.

"All right," he said, "Yousa fellas afolla me."

I had a big scoop-shaped snow shovel, which I threw over my shoulder and followed the rest of the men. At 135th Street and Amsterdam Avenue we stopped.

Big trucks were lumbering up and down the sides of the street, pushing snow into great piles. There were other men working out in the middle of the gutter, shoveling snow into a manhole. At the far end of the block more men were throwing snow up into a big dump truck.

The Italian in charge of our group led us into the middle of the road where the other men were shoveling snow down the manhole. He spoke a few words of Italian to the man in charge of the others, and then the other group picked up their shovels and walked down the hill.

My job was to push snow up to the manhole, where other men were waiting to shovel it down. When the foreman thought we had satisfactorily started our work, he left us and went to a big fire burning at the side of the road down the block, where a number of D.S. men were standing. They would stand there, warming their asses against the fire, and call orders to their groups.

One of the two men that were working right next to me was a thin-lipped, pasty-faced Irishman, and the other was a short powerfully built Negro. Most of the men wore lumber jackets or sweaters or coats, and gloves to keep their hands warm. I didn't feel the cold so much, but my hands got pretty stiff, and soon my shoes and feet were soaking wet. When my fingers were so cold that they hurt, I put down my shovel and went over to the fire where the D.S. men were standing. They fell silent as I approached them, and my foreman, who was smoking a Guinea stinker, watched me closely.

"Wassa da matta, boy," he asked, "you a lazy kid?"

"Jesus!" I said, showing him my hands, "my fingers are froze."

I put my hands over the fire. The foreman reached into his pocket and took out an old pair of work gloves which he gave me.

"Thanks," I said, and put them on.

There were several holes in them but they were warm. I left the fire and picked up my shovel and went back to work.

About an hour later the Mick said to me: "A few minutes more and we knock off for lunch." Looking enviously at the D.S. men standing around the fire, he said: "Just watch them babies scatter when the head fink comes around."

And sure enough, a few minutes later, a small coupé pulled up and a man got out who seemed to be some kind of a boss. As soon as he showed his nose outside his car, all the foremen went over to their groups and got busy shouting orders and directions.

A whistle blew and our foreman said: "All right, boys, putta the tools by the truck and 'a go to lunch."

He turned and walked away.

Some of the men began taking packages of sandwiches out of their coat pockets and scattering to different hallways on the street to eat their lunch, while others headed for near-by restaurants and lunch counters.

It was about two o'clock. I walked quite a way down the block before I found a doorway empty so that I could get in it and out of the cold.

I walked all the way back in the hallway and sat down on the steps. I took a cigarette out of my pocket and lit it, and the moment I relaxed I began to shiver. It wasn't that I felt cold or particularly hungry, but without something to do, my body just seemed to feel the cold more intensely.

A few minutes later the hall door opened and the man who worked next to me came into the hallway followed by a colored boy about my size. They didn't see me at first since the hallway was dim.

The older man said: "What did Mom send for lunch, Sam?"

"Y'all got some hot soup an' baloney sanwiches an' coffee," the kid replied.

"Man, I'm sho' hungry!" said the older man. "Let's go sit on the steps while I eat."

They walked back toward me and stopped short when they saw me sitting there on the steps.

"Whut chu doin' here?" the older man asked.

"Smokin'," I replied.

"Ain't chu eatin'?" he asked.

"I'm not hungry," I said.

They sat down on the steps beside me. The older man tore open a paper bag and took out two milk bottles—one half filled with soup, the other half filled with coffee—and several sandwiches. The smell of the hot soup made my mouth fill with water.

"Ya workin' hard?" asked the kid.

"Nope, Sam," said the older man. Then turning to me, he said: "This yere's my kid brother. He brought m'lunch."

"That's good," I said.

He began to drink the soup out of a bottle. Holding the bottle against his lips, he leaned his head back and the soup just seemed to go down his throat in great gulps. I moved several steps up the stairway to give him room, and looked down at him. His brother was watching me, and I tried to look in another direction so that I wouldn't see him eating. The cigarette burned down to my fingers and I threw it over the bannister without putting it out.

As if some unspoken word had passed from the boy to the older man, the older man turned around and looked at me. "Man, I'm not as hungry as I thought I was," he said. Then turning to the boy, he said: "Mom gave me too much soup. I can't eat all this." And he turned back to me. "Why don't you drink it? It's a shame to let it go to waste."

I looked at him for a minute, not saying anything. Then I took the bottle out of his hand. "Thanks," I mumbled, and began drinking the soup. I don't know what kind of soup it was, but it was good. A few minutes later while I was still drinking the soup, he reached behind him without looking around and held out a sandwich in his hand toward me. When I took the sandwich from his hand, it seemed that we had made a bargain. He knew, instinctively perhaps, of the circumstances and condition I was in, and with the extreme gentleness of the really simple and without trying to make me uncomfortable, he offered me help. I didn't utter any further thanks. It was unnecessary. He didn't expect any.

When we finished the coffee I reached in my pocket and took out three cigarettes. Putting one in my mouth, I offered each of them one.

The boy shook his head. The older fellow explained to me:

"He's goin' to high school—he's on the track team"; and took one himself.

I lit his cigarette and then mine, and we sat back smoking.

"You in New York long?" the old fellow asked.

"No," I answered; "just got in yesterday."

"Damned cold out today!" he said.

I grunted: "Uh-huh."

"My name is Tom Harris," he said.

I told him mine. We sat there without saying anything for a few minutes, and then we heard a whistle blowing in the street.

"That's us," Tom said. "Let's go!" As I started to get up, he said to Sam: "Give him your coat. You'll be in the house all day and you won't need it. I'll bring it back tonight."

Without saying anything, Sam took his coat off and handed it to me. I put it on. I don't think I could have thanked him if I tried. I just walked out into the street ahead of him and up to the gang already assembling in the middle of the block.

The afternoon passed by a little more quickly than the morning had. I began to feel somehow that the day would turn out right. In the evening just before we knocked off, the colored fellow asked me: "Where you staying?"

I said: "I haven't got a place yet."

"Why don't you come over to my place for a couple of nights—at least until you get paid?"

"You might not have any room," I said weakly.

"Sho', we have!" he said. "We got a big place."

And suddenly the day was over. We followed the foreman back to the office and handed in our tools. The colored fellow tapped me on the shoulder and I walked with him up to 126th Street and into a tenement between Convent and St. Nicholas Avenue, where I saw their "big place." We entered a dimly lit hallway. Somehow, on walking into the hall you'd know, maybe by the shadows or by the odor of pork or even by the dim lights that hung high on the ceiling, that it was a nigger house. We went up about three landings, and I followed Tom into one of the apartments.

The door opened up into a kitchen, in which there were a table, some chairs, a dirty wooden closet, and a coal stove, on top of which a big pot was cooking. There was a gray-haired colored woman of about fifty standing in one corner of the room.

Tom went over to her and said: "Mom, this is Francis Kane. He hasn't any place to stay and he's gonna stay here with us tonight."

I didn't know it at that time, but that night lasted almost a month. She came close to me and looked at my face and I watched her. I don't think that we were going to pass judgment on each other, but I knew that unless she said it was all right, I couldn't stay.

For a few minutes she looked at me, and then she said: "Sit down here, Frankie. We're goin' to eat now."

I thanked her and we had supper and then sat at the table. The heat from the stove began to make me drowsy, and my head and eyes felt so heavy I had to keep shaking my head in order to stay awake.

It was about seven o'clock when she said, "Tom, you and your friend better go to sleep because at ten thirty you have to be over at the other station."

I looked up at Tom. He explained: "I kin get night work in the snow at 129th and Third. They don't know I'm working in the daytime over here. You want to come along?"

"Yes," I answered, "thanks."

"I can get you on," he said smiling.

I didn't see the younger boy anywhere around, and on asking his brother where he was, found out that the kid was working in a near-by store in the afternoon.

We went to sleep in a big double bed in a room where there was another bed, which he told me was his sister's.

I took off my clothes and shoes and stretched out. The next thing I knew, someone was shaking my shoulders and saying: "Get up, boy, get up! Time to go to work."

I opened my eyes and sat up. I could hardly see in the room because there was no light in it—light came from the next room into this just through a cut in the wall. Half asleep, I began to dress. As my eyes grew accustomed to the darkness, I saw the other bed was occupied. I saw the head of a girl just outside the blanket, and the whites of her eyes as she watched me move around the room. I felt no self-consciousness, and when I left the room I said good night to her. She didn't say anything. I followed Tom down the street, both of us carrying the lunch that had been packed for us. We worked until five thirty in the morning. The work was about the same as I had done earlier in the day, and at five thirty when we quit, we went back to Tom's place and went right to sleep. At eight thirty we got up again and worked the day through.

Chapter Five

ALTOGETHER we worked two and a half days before we were laid off. And when we got paid I actually received pay for five days' labor because I had worked two shifts. I had $17.50, and I think when I walked back from the paymaster I felt as if New York was my oyster. It wasn't so hard to make money or find work. For the first time in weeks I became aware of other people—not regarding them as a class set aside or apart from myself but thinking of myself as one of them. I too had worked —for a while.

I stopped off at a hock shop and bought myself a suit, two shirts, an overcoat, and a pair of shoes, all secondhand, for eleven dollars. I left my old clothes there.

When I got to Tom's place, I went to Mrs. Harris and offered her half of what I had left, because she had let me stay there, but she wouldn't take it. She said I'd need it.

It was about two o'clock in the afternoon when Tom and I went right to sleep. We didn't wake up until about nine that night. When we got up we ate and while we were eating their sister came in, and for the first time I saw what she was like. She was about fourteen with hard, straight, black hair that was combed down in back of her ears. She had a long face and a dark-brown skin, and wore a purple-colored lipstick. Her shoulders were wide, her arms and legs thin and slightly muscular. She sat down at the table and spoke to Tom. "You all laid off?"

"Uh huh," said Tom, "we sho' is!"

"What you going to do now?" she asked him. But she didn't mean him; she meant me.

Tom didn't answer her.

"I don't know," I said. "I don't know what I'm going to do. Guess I'll go out and get a job."

She tossed her head. "The hell you will! There ain't no jobs to be had nowhere."

"I don't know about that," I said, "I got this one easy enough."

"You was lucky," she said, "but you ain't going to be that lucky now."

"Where's Mom?" Tom asked her, tactfully changing the subject.

"She and Sam went down to the meeting," Elly told him. "She sent me back for you to go there soon as you woke."

"All right," said Tom. "Guess we better go." He took his coat and they went out the door together.

We all knew that I could not go with them, and so I wasn't asked. About an hour passed. I read the paper and smoked and began to get drowsy when the door opened and Elly came in.

She came over to the table and sat down. "You still up?"

"Yes."

"They're goin' to be at the meetin' for another couple hours. I got tired so I come home early."

I didn't say anything. I sat by the window and looked into the courtyard. They used to leave the window open just a little bit because one of their neighbors had a radio and they would sit there and listen to the music. But that night the radio wasn't playing.

"Well, good night," Elly said.

"Good night," I answered.

She went into the other room and I could hear her moving about.

She called through the open door: "Ain't you tired? Why don't you go to sleep?"

"No," I said, "I'm not tired. I think I'll wait till Tom gets back before I turn in."

"They won't be back till late. You know how those meetin's are," she said.

"That's all right," I said. "I'm not tired."

For about fifteen minutes we didn't say anything. Then with her coat thrown around her nightgown, she came through the kitchen to go into the hall to the toilet. A few minutes later she came back and went into the bedroom. When she walked through the room she looked at me but I looked away. For another few minutes there wasn't any sound. Then she called: "Frankie, would you bring me a glass of water, please?"

"All right," I answered. I went over to the sink and took a tumbler and filled it with water and took it into the bedroom and gave it to her. She took it from my hand and drank, sitting up in bed holding the blanket around her. When she reached back to give me the glass the blanket fell and the top of her nightdress was down. I could see her shoulders and her breasts against the grayish white sheet. She looked at me.

I started to turn and she put her hand on my arm. She said: "What's the matter with you, boy? Are you afraid?"

"No," I said. Then, "Maybe I am."

"Nobody will know," she said.

"That's not it," I said. I started to walk out of the room thinking about Tom and her mother and how it would be a pretty low trick to pull on them after what they did for me.

She jumped out of bed and caught me by the shoulder, throwing herself against me. She was stark naked. I tried to shake her off but she wouldn't let go. Somehow I think the fight did something to me. The struggle to get away was not a struggle to escape her, but an attempt to fight off going to her. Finally I batted her across the face.

She stepped back. She snarled, her body rigidly tense: "If you don't I'll scream and I'll holler. The whole house will come down and I'll tell them that you tried to."

I stood there for a minute and then turned and started to walk towards the door. She opened her mouth and started to scream something. I turned back to her and, putting my hand across her mouth, told her to shut up or I'd kill her. She bit my hand. I picked her up and threw her down on the bed, and once again I started to go out.

She said: "I'll scream."

I walked back to her. "All right," I said. "All right."

It was about twelve thirty when they came back from the meeting. Elly was asleep in the next room, and I was sitting at the kitchen table trying to read the *Amsterdam News* in the dim light.

Sam and Tom came over to me, and Sam said: "It's goin' to be cold tonight. It's blowin' up."

For a moment I didn't answer them, and then I said: "I guess it is. It's going to be a cold night."

Sam called to his mother: "Do you want something hot to drink?"

"No," she said. "Maybe Tom and Frankie would like some coffee. There's some made that you could have."

We didn't take any but went right to sleep.

Early the next morning I went out looking for a job, and I don't think there was any to be had. I spent thirty-five cents and didn't have any luck. Even the nine- and ten-dollar-a-week jobs were not to be had. I went to the agencies on Sixth Avenue, and there, like many others, could find nothing. About seven o'clock I got back to Tom's house and told them what I did.

"You'll get something," Mrs. Harris said. "Don't worry, boy, the Lord will provide."

I smiled at her. I said: "Thanks, Ma, but the Lord can't provide barely enough for you folks, and I guess one extra might be a little too much for you."

"Don't talk like that, boy," she said. "We got enough to go around."

Chapter Six

WE ATE grits three days. Grits is a good food but a damned tiring one. At the end of a week I still had no job. I had about three dollars left.

Saturday night Tom asked: "Would you like to go to a party?"

"I sure would," I told him, "but maybe—"

He interrupted me. "You come."

"For a quarter you go to this 'ere rent party and there's music, eats, and drinks." He took my arm. "And man," he added, "they is some gals."

I smiled. "Yeah," I said, "but—"

"But nothing," he interrupted again. "That's an ofay junction. They'll probably think you some playboy coming up to Harlem."

About an hour later we put on our coats and went out. Sam was sitting at the table reading.

"That's a smart boy, my brother," said Tom. "He's at the head of his class now. He goes to Haaren High School downtown."

I said: "Yeah, he always seems to be studying."

Did you ever drink gin and beer? A tumblerful of beer with two shots of gin thrown in—that was what they were drinking at the party. I think I was drunk after the first drink and could barely tell what went on. There were about thirty people in the apartment on St. Nicholas Avenue. A man was strumming a guitar, and several white men and girls were there. The white men and women seemed to avoid each other and talked only to the colored. When I spoke to one of the white girls, she turned her back on me and went to speak to a good-looking nigger.

About three o'clock it finally broke up. Tom was so loaded he could hardly move. I put his arms around my shoulder and helped him down the steps and home. The cold air cleared my head a bit and by the time we got home I was sober.

Tom was singing and gurgling happily as we staggered up the steps and went into the house. As we started up the stairway he passed out. I tried to lift him but I couldn't. The light in the hall was out. I struck a match, and just over the bannister near the steps I heard a movement. I looked.

Elly was there and a white man of about 40. They both looked up at me. The white man's face looked strained and frightened. His coat and jacket were open and Elly was standing there looking at me. The man started to walk out of the hall.

Elly grabbed him by the shoulder. "Give me the other quarter!" she said.

He reached in his pocket and gave her a coin and hurried out of the door.

Then she calmly walked up the steps toward me and looked down at Tom.

"Did he pass out?" she said.

"Yeah. Give me a hand and get him up," I told her. "I can't lift him."

She took one shoulder and I took the other, and together we hauled him up into the apartment and dumped him into bed. It was about three thirty. Sam was sleeping, and from the other room we could hear her mother snoring. I went back into the kitchen.

Elly came back behind me. I looked at her. "You won't tell?" she asked me.

"No," I said, "I won't tell."

"We got to get some money some way," she said desperately. "Sam only gets $1.50 a week at the store and tips, and the food voucher is only $13.50 every two weeks, and it ain't enough. We got to get some more money."

I looked at her. "How do you explain it to them?"

"I tell them I work three nights a week at a ribbon factory on 132nd Street. But I got laid off a few weeks ago."

"How long is this going on?" I asked.

"Why don't you mind your business?" she snapped.

"All right," I said, "I will." I looked out of the window and felt a little sick.

She came over to me and stood by my side. "Have you any money," she asked.

"No," I said, lying for a reason I didn't understand.

She held out a quarter to me. "Maybe you'll need it tomorrow. It's Sunday—when you go to church."

I said: "No, thanks." I looked at her. "No!"

There were tears in her eyes. We looked at each other for a few minutes. And the tears began to roll down her cheeks. Her eyes got puffy, like niggers' eyes do when they weep, and red and bloodshot. I touched her on the shoulder.

"Don't worry," I said, "it will be all right."

She went into the other room and went to sleep. When I went in to sleep, I saw the bed that she had occupied in our room was empty. I looked into the next room and saw her sleeping next to her mother. I went back into our room and went to sleep in her bed.

It was Sunday and I awoke early. For a while I lay in bed listening to the snores of Sam and Tom. Finally I got out of bed and went into the kitchen. It was six o'clock. I splashed some water over my face and started to rub some soap into my skin. It was still dark outside, so I turned on the dim kitchen light. I began to shave. While I was shaving Sam came into the room and sat down on a chair watching me.

"What are you doing up so early?" I asked him.

"I got to go down to the store to deliver the breakfast orders," he answered.

We were silent a minute. "How old are you, Frankie?" he asked.

"Twenty."

"You're not much older than me," he said. "I'm almost eighteen. I thought you were older."

"Yeah," I said turning to look at him. He was really a good-looking kid—fine black skin, tight kinky hair, thin features, large expressive eyes.

"Frankie, what do you think of us? I mean, really—Tom and Mom and Elly. Don't you feel different?" His large, brown eyes were earnest.

"You people are really swell. You couldn't be better if you were ..."

He interrupted me: "If we were white, you mean?"

"No," I told him. "Even if you were my kin, I couldn't ask for any more kindness or sympathy."

He stood up. "I gotta be goin'. I'll see you later. I'll be home at ten when we close. We'll go to church."

"See you then," I said. I finished shaving, got dressed, and went out. It was cold outside. I lit a cigarette and walked over to 125th Street. I passed the store where Sam worked and it was full of people. On impulse I stepped in. I saw Sam: he was busy packing orders into cardboard cartons. The store was full of women, mostly Irish, who had just come from the church on the corner, their brogue mixed with the hebe accent of the three clerks in the store. Sam nodded to me. I nodded back.

When it was my turn I bought a dozen of cheap eggs and a pound of bacon and a dozen rolls and a package of cheap cigarettes. I paid the bill—it was seventy-two cents—and put the package under my arm and went home.

Mrs. Harris and Elly were in the kitchen, but Tom was still asleep. I put the package on the table.

"I bought breakfast."

"You shouldn't," Mrs. Harris said.

We didn't eat until Sam came back. Tom was up. He had a big head.

"Man, we sho' had fun!"

"Swell party!" I said. We ate.

"Goin' to church?" Mrs. Harris asked me.

"Unh-hunh."

We all went out together. The church was in a little store down the block. It was heated by a big stove in its center. I felt queer going to church in a store. To me a church always meant a big building with impressive ceremonies. Mrs. Harris looked at me. I think she read my mind. "God is everywhere, son," she smiled gently, "even with the poor folks." I felt a little ashamed of myself.

The people looked at me but, seeing who I was with, paid no further attention to me. The Harrises knew everybody there and after the services I was introduced around. I met the preacher. He had a very warm smile. I felt a little better when Mrs. Harris told him I was their friend.

We went home and sat around the house. Sam took out his schoolbooks and began to study.

Tuesday, Tom and I got some work delivering coal from a truck. We made three dollars each. But we didn't get any more work that week.

Thursday night was meeting night and I was left alone.

Elly came home early but we sat around not talking. There were too many things to think about but not enough things to talk about. When the folks came home we turned in.

The days flew by. Soon it was March and the weather became a bit milder. I saw that things became a bit more stringent at home, and began to think of leaving.

One afternoon when Elly and I were alone in the house, I said: "I guess I'll have to be going soon."

She looked up at me, kind of surprised.

"I can't stay here forever, you know," I said.

She came over and took my hand. I put my arms around her. The thought of that night and the nearness of her did things to me. She was instantly aware of it and led me into the other room. Somehow in her giving of herself, the fierce jumping of her thin body, I could sense her not wanting me to go. It was not love, not even passion; it was a warmth and kindliness and understanding.

We arose from the bed breathless, her hands clinging to my hips. I still held her breast, her hard nipple in my palm. I suddenly threw her back on the bed, falling on her.

"I've got to go, understand, I've got to go! I can't stay here taking everything, giving nothing." I was rough.

She moaned as I hurt her. She could hardly speak, her breath coming in long shuddering gasps. "You've ... got ... to ... go. ..."

That night at supper I told them I was leaving. They asked me not to. "I'll have to get a job somewhere," I said, "and there's none here. I'll leave tomorrow."

The next morning I shook hands with Tom and Sam and kissed Mrs. Harris and Elly good-by. I thanked them.

Mrs. Harris said: "Be a good boy, Frankie. Don't forget us if you need help."

"I won't," I said, and went to the door. I looked back at them and smiled. "So long."

I shut the door behind me quickly and walked down the stairs and into the street. It was a bright sunny, almost warm, day, and somehow I felt sure that things would brighten up for them.

I looked around, not knowing which way to walk. My few extra shirts were in a paper bag under my arm. I decided to walk east. I began to walk toward Eighth Avenue.

Mrs. Harris's gentle voice rang in my ear: "Don't forget us if you need help." I smiled to myself. They needed so much themselves. Yet they had so much to give me. I stopped on the street a moment; there was a lump in my throat. "You're getting soft," I told myself accusingly. Then I laughed and walked on.

Chapter Seven

I WALKED down Eighth Avenue. I stopped in every store on the way down asking if they needed help. Some people were nice about turning me down. Some weren't. It all depended on how they felt. At Seventy-second Street and Columbus Avenue, I got some work in a cafeteria, washing dishes for the afternoon. I was paid off after four hours with a dollar bill and supper. I put the dollar in my pocket. When I had finished eating, I went over to the manager and asked him if he needed anyone for tomorrow afternoon.

He looked at me quietly for a moment before he spoke. He

was a short, fat little man with friendly eyes and smile. "I'm sorry," he said, "it was only for the afternoon. I didn't really need you but I wanted to . . ."

I smiled back at him. "I know," I interrupted. "Thanks a lot anyway." I went out.

It was getting dark. I had better find myself a place to flop or I'd be out in the street all night. I went down to a Mills Hotel and got a small private room for fifty cents. In the lobby they had a few papers. I sat around reading them for a while, and then turned in. I was wondering what I should do about looking up my aunt and uncle. I didn't want them to find me broke and shabby the way I was. I was half afraid that I would bump into someone that knew me and I would have to explain my circumstances.

I was up early and on Sixth Avenue at seven-thirty in the morning. The agencies were crowded as usual and nothing seemed to turn up. I was sent on several jobs but when I got there, they were either taken or the boss had someone else in mind. I ate in a cheap restaurant on Sixth Avenue near Forty-sixth Street and had large franks and beans and coffee for thirty-five cents. I went back to the hotel and took a bed in the semiprivate room. This room I shared with about ten other men. They were mostly a different type from the men down at the Bowery flops. These were men who as yet had not hit the extreme bottom. A few of them were playing cards. I watched them awhile and went to sleep.

The next day I tried the wholesale market section. I was lucky. I went into the warehouse of a small retail grocery chain store and was hired almost immediately. The delivery boy had just quit in a store on Columbus Avenue and Sixty-ninth Street.

The supervisor looked up at me from the desk. "What do you want?" he challenged rather than asked.

"A job," I replied simply.

"I haven't any," he said shortly. Just then the telephone on his desk rang. He picked it up and barked into it. "Rayzeus talking." A voice hummed excitedly through the earphone. I stood there waiting.

A few seconds ticked by. The supervisor didn't speak, just listened to the voice crackling electrically through the phone. I don't know how I knew that this meant a job. Whether he glanced at me, or told me to beat it, or the way he listened—I don't know. But suddenly my hands were sweating, my heart began to hammer excitedly. I just knew there was a job and I wanted it.

The supervisor hung up the receiver. A truckman came up to the desk and showed him a bill of lading. They spoke a few minutes and then the truckman walked away. The supervisor looked up at me. "What are you hanging around for?" he snapped.

"A job," I said again.

"I told you I haven't any," he replied.

"You just had a call about one," I ventured.

He looked at me questioningly a minute. "Got any experience?" he asked.

"Some," I replied. "I worked in a big food market in San Diego." I didn't tell him I only lasted two days.

This time his glance was appraising. "How old are you?" he shot at me.

"Twenty."

"You wouldn't want it," he said, turning back to his desk. "It's a delivery boy's job—pays eight dollars a week."

"I'll take it," I said.

He looked up at me again. "It pays only eight dollars a week," he repeated.

I put my hands in my pockets so he wouldn't see them trembling. "I'll take it," I told him. Christ, how I hoped he wouldn't turn me down! I never wanted anything more in my life.

"You wouldn't be satisfied on eight bucks a week," he said to me. "You're not a kid. You need more than that to get along on."

I still kept my hands in my pocket. "Look, mister," I said, the tension cracking my voice a little: "I got to have a job. I need it bad. I'm flat. I worked on the snow about six weeks ago, and that's the last work I've had. Eight bucks a week is a lot of dough to me."

He tilted back in his chair and turned a little away from me. "Do you live with your folks?" he asked.

"No," I said, "I haven't any. I live at the Mills Hotel right now."

"Why do you want to work for eight bucks a week?" he asked. "Surely a big, strong young man like you ought to be able to get something better paying."

"I tried to, mister," I said desperately. "Honest, I tried, but there isn't anything. A man's got to have something."

He was silent for a while. I was going crazy. This cat-and-mouse business was driving me nuts. Suddenly he turned his chair toward me. "O. K.," he snapped, "you got it."

I felt weak. I sank into a chair near the desk and took a cigarette from my pocket. I put it in my mouth and tried to light it, but I couldn't strike the match; my hands were trembling too much. He struck a match and held it toward me. Gratefully I accepted his light. I dragged deeply at the cigarette. "Thanks, mister," I said. "Thanks a lot."

For a minute I felt dizzy. I thought I was going to be sick. My stomach heaved and the bitter taste of gall came into my mouth. Desperately I swallowed. Not now, please God, not now! I put my head in my hands. He got out of his chair and came around toward me. He put his hand on my shoulder. "It must have been pretty bad, son," he said. His voice didn't have that aggressive snap to it now.

I nodded, my head still in my hands. I felt better, the flash of nausea had gone. I looked up at him.

"You all right now?" he asked.

"Yes, sir," I said, "I'm O. K. It was just the . . . well, you know what I mean." He nodded. I continued: "When do I start and where?"

He went back to his desk and sat down. He wrote out a slip of paper and handed it to me. I took it and read the address.

"You can start now if you want," he said.

"I'd like to, sir," I told him, "if it's all right with you."

He took another sheet of paper from his desk. "What's your name?"

"Frank Kane, sir," I replied.

He wrote a few words on the paper and gave it to me. "That will do it." He smiled. "Give that to the manager of the store, and if he has any questions tell him to call Rayzeus at the office."

"Thank you, Mr. Rayzeus," I said. "Thank you very much."

"Good luck, Frank," he said, getting up from his chair and holding out his hand.

I shook hands with him and went out into the street. It was a wonderful day. I felt different already. A job made all the difference in the world how you felt. I swore to myself that I'd make good. I couldn't let a right guy like Mr. Rayzeus down. I looked at the note in my hand. It was the most beautiful note I had ever seen.

Harry—

This will introduce Frank Kane. Put him to work. He will get $10 a week.

J. Rayzeus.

I just couldn't fail the man now. An extra two bucks a week! I'd cut off my right arm to the elbow for him! I walked to the subway at Franklin Street whistling.

Chapter Eight

I LEFT the subway at the Sixty-sixth Street station and walked over to the store. It was about noon, and the sun cast queer, irregular-shaped shadows from the el onto the street. I walked up to the store and stopped in front of it. It was a small store with one window. Over the front of the store hung a gray-and-black sign: "The Wonder Tea and Coffee Stores." The window had a small display of groceries, and people walked by, not even looking at it. The store was set in a renovated house a little way from the corner. Next to it on the corner was a drugstore, and on the other side of the grocery store was a malt-and-hop store. Down the block a little farther an ice-cream parlor and a vegetable market and a butcher were all lined up to make this a marketing section. Upstairs over the store was a club. On its windows there was imprinted "Workers' Alliance."

I went into the store. There was a customer picking some canned goods from a small display in the store; a man, white apron tied around his middle, was waiting on her. I waited until she was through and had walked out before I went over to him. "Mr. Rayzeus sent me down from the office," I told him.

"Fine!" he said. He seemed to be expecting something.

I gave him the note. He read it and put it in his pocket. "O.K.," he said smiling, "I'm Harry Kronstein." He held out his hand.

I shook it. "Glad to know you, sir."

He reached under the counter and grabbed an apron and gave it to me. "Here, put this on. The first thing you can do is sweep out the place. My boy didn't show up this morning."

I took the apron from him. There was a broom in the rear corner of the store. I went back to it, took it, and started to sweep. I swept from the front of the store, starting at the door, sweeping down in front of the counter to the corner of the back room, and then swept down behind the counter to the corner. I used the end of a cardboard box to gather up the dirt, and dumped it in an empty box just inside the back room. Then I came out. "What next?"

Harry looked at me approvingly. "Where did you learn how to sweep out a store like that?" he asked. "Most guys don't know where to start."

"I worked in many stores," I told him.

There were many cases of canned goods lying on the floor in front of the counter. The truck had just left them there. He pointed to them. "Unpack those on the shelves where you can and take the rest in the back," he told me.

I looked around at the shelves. They were pretty well filled up, but certain items seemed low. I looked at them to see what they were, then looked for a case of the stuff. When I found it, I put the case on the floor near the shelf. In a little while I had quite a few of the cases spread around the floor. The rest I couldn't find a place for, so I took them in the back room and stacked them up. Then I came out and started to unpack some of the cases. I had to ask him where a ladder was so I could reach the top shelves. When I had emptied about three cases onto the shelves, he stopped me.

"Come on," he said. "We close for lunch."

We went down to the ice-cream parlor for lunch. We sat in one of the booths there and talked. I had a good chance to look at him while we sat there. He was about five six, about three inches shorter than I. He had watery blue eyes almost hidden by thick, heavy-framed glasses. He was bald with a fringe of reddish-brown hair around the sides of his head, and a red mustache covered his rather full lips. He had a long, round chin that came almost to his Adam's apple. He spoke slowly, moved casually, and smiled carefully. His smile was warm, but it never had the air of spontaneity I ordinarily associated with laughter.

He spoke quite awhile. I told him of some of my recent experiences and I learned from him that the store had no clerk.

I was to be both clerk and delivery boy. I had a sandwich and a cup of coffee for lunch, and then we went back to work.

About four o'clock I had finished unpacking the canned goods. By that time he had accumulated a few orders, which I delivered. I got about forty cents in tips, and when I got back to the store, he told me to start emptying out the window. The window was on a display made of empty egg crates. It was a small window and I emptied it quickly. Then I removed the window signs and washed the windows, inside and outside. I remembered washing the windows at Keough's. I wondered what the old bunch were doing now. When I went inside he took me over to the icebox and showed me the different cheeses and butter and told me how to cut them. He then unpacked some eggs into the display case, showing me how to do it.

I thanked him for showing me how. He smiled slowly. "The quicker you learn the better. You'll be more useful around here, and I'll need all the help I can get."

"If there's anything more I can do, Harry," I said, "just tell me. I want to be all right here. I need the job."

"You'll be all right," he said. He took out his watch and looked at it. It was seven o'clock—time to close up and go home. We took off our aprons and went out.

I walked over to the hotel and took a private room again. Then I went out for supper. After supper I felt better, so I took a little walk around the neighborhood and then turned in for the night. I asked the desk to wake me at seven in the morning because I didn't have an alarm clock and I didn't want to be late for work.

The next day I was waiting outside the door of the store for him to open up. He came walking up the street slowly and said good morning. We went in and I swept up. He sent me over to the ice-cream parlor for coffee. I got a container of coffee and we had coffee and buns. About an hour after we had opened at eight o'clock, Mr. Rayzeus came in. I was washing the front of the counters. I looked up and said good morning to him. He nodded and walked on back to the register where Harry was standing.

They talked for a while and I heard my name mentioned a few times. Later Mr. Rayzeus went out and got in a car and drove off. I had finished the counters and Harry told me to

bring out certain cases of canned goods. We were going to dress
the window.

We finished dressing the window before lunchtime, and we
went to the ice-cream parlor for lunch. After lunch we went
back to the store and I delivered a few orders. I got about
twenty cents in tips. Our trade was a mixture of the very
poor—those on home relief—and the middle class—those
making about twenty or thirty dollars a week. We carried a
cheap line of groceries and always had specials to sell. To
bolster up our weekly business, Harry had a few restaurants we
called wholesale customers. They bought a case of eggs, a bag
of sugar, cases of cheap canned vegetables. He sent me out to
see them and pick up their orders. At seven o'clock I made
ready to leave. He stayed open a few minutes later. I waited
until he closed, then I had supper and went back to the hotel.

The next day was Saturday. It was a long day, according to
what Harry had told me. We were to be open until twelve
o'clock at night. Saturday, Harry had decided, would be the
first day I would wait on customers, and I looked forward to it.
It was also payday.

The day dawned bright and clear. I was at the store early
again and waited for Harry to come ambling up. We opened
and had our coffee. Then I stacked away the bottles of milk and
cream in the icebox and waited for customers. About nine
o'clock a few drifted in. Harry nodded and I went forward to
wait on one of them.

She was a tall, dark, Italian woman, who spoke with a harsh-
sounding voice that seems to be a characteristic of the poorer-
class Italians. The first few things she asked for were fairly
simple. Then she asked for some cheese; I turned to the icebox
and took it out. She wanted half a pound; I cut a little more. On
the scale it weighed almost three quarters. At forty cents a
pound, I thought, this piece was thirty cents. I started to tell her
the price, but Harry came up behind me and whispered: "Thir-
ty-six."

I took the cheese from the scale and told her the price that
Harry had given me. She said it was all right and I wrapped
it up. She bought a dozen of the cheapest eggs and a pound of
the cheapest coffee. I took out a large bag and started to write
the prices down on the bag. I totaled them when I had finished
listing them. It came to $2.38. Harry had been standing near
by as I marked down the prices, checking me as I ticked the

items off. I had an idea he might like to check my addition, so I passed the bag to him. He ran his eye quickly down the column of figures and handed it back to me without comment. I knew it was correct. I packed the bag and the lady gave me a five-dollar bill. I placed it on the register and called out: "Two thirty-eight out of five."

Harry registered the sale and gave me the change. I counted it out to the lady and said: "Thank you. Call again." I had made my first sale. I turned to the next customer but Harry had cleared them up. He came over to me.

"You'll be all right," he said with a smile. "There's still a few things to learn, though. When you cut cheese and it's a little over the weight called for, don't be afraid to charge a little more than it registers. The customers don't know it anyway and most of them can't figure, and it helps to make up for what we eat in the morning and other things, such as egg breakage, that the office doesn't give us any credit on."

"I understand," I said. I sure did! This only confirmed my ideas. Everything had an angle. All you had to do was look for it.

Chapter Nine

IT WAS Sunday and I slept late. When I woke up I looked over at the dresser where I had placed the new sixty-cent alarm clock I had bought last night. It showed a few minutes after eleven. I looked over at the floor where I had placed the bag with some groceries in it. It was there. I turned over in bed, reached out and took a pack of cigarettes from my pocket, placed one in my mouth, and lit it. I lay back comfortably on the pillow and looked at the smoke swirling up to the ceiling. I felt relaxed and at ease, and put one arm under my head while I thought about the day before.

The past few weeks seemed far away. I had never been cold and worked on the snow and been hungry. I felt good.

I remembered the night before about ten o'clock when Mr. Rayzeus had come around he had another man with him. Harry told me it was the boss, the Mr. Big who owned all these stores that we and others like us worked in. He was a quiet, smiling, little, gray-haired man who nodded pleasantly to me as he came in the door. I was waiting on a customer and I had smiled back at him, not knowing then who he was. He went over to the register and looked in. Then he turned to Harry, and they shook hands and talked for a few minutes. He walked around the store and then left. Mr. Rayzeus spoke a few words to Harry after Mr. Big left, and then he too went out. He said: "Good night, Frank," to me as he walked out, and I felt pretty good that he remembered me.

And later after we had closed up and I had swept out the store, Harry called me over to the register to get my pay. He handed me seven dollars and asked me if that was all right.

For a moment I was confused; then I said: "You gave me too much. I only worked three days. That's half a week. Five dollars."

Harry smiled, "The extra two is for me. I always let the boys take home a package of groceries Saturday night. But you don't need any, so I thought this would come in handy. You play square with me and I'll treat you right."

I looked at the money in my hand and then at Harry. "Thanks," I said, "I'll do my best to earn it."

"You will," Harry said, and laughed.

"If it's all right with you," I said, "I would like to get a grocery order for some people. They've been nice to me. I'll pay for it."

"Pick it out," Harry said, turning back to the register to balance his cash.

I took a dozen of the best eggs, a pound of real butter, a package of lean bacon, some old-fashioned American cheese, sugar, flour, some cans of good vegetables, and a few packages of cereal. I figured out how much this amounted to, and I added to it two loaves of white bread and a large twenty-five-cent cake. I went over to Harry and gave him the bag. I had written down the name of each article and the price next to it. It came to three dollars and ten cents. I put three dollars and ten cents on the register and started to pack it up.

Harry came over to me, still holding the money in his hand. "Who are the groceries for?" he asked.

"Friends of mine," I answered. "When I got to New York in February, I was broke and they took me in. They're pretty poor and I couldn't stay too long, but without them I would have been licked."

He was silent a few minutes while I tied up the bag and put a wooden handle on it so I could carry it better. Then he held out the money to me. "Here," he said, "keep it."

I didn't take the money. "I want to pay for it," I said. "I got enough money. I made over two bucks in tips today."

"Take it," he urged. "We'll make it up in the store this time."

I took the money and put it in my pocket. "Thanks again," I said, "I appreciate this."

"Forget it!" He smiled. "Come on over to the restaurant and have some coffee with me before we go home."

I had been sitting there in the ice-cream parlor an hour with him before we left for home. It was near two o'clock and I rode down on the trolley to the hotel. The night clerk recognized me as I came in, and handed me my key. He saw the package and smilingly said: "No cooking in the rooms, Mr. Kane."

I laughed. "Don't worry!" I called over my shoulder as I strode toward the stairway, "I won't."

The cigarette was almost out. I put it out in a small plate on the dresser, shaved, and then went down the hall to the shower. It was late and there wasn't a line. I went right in, turned on the warm water, and soaped myself. The warm water felt good as it ran the soap down my back. I stepped out and dried myself on the rough towel, rubbing till I could feel my skin turn red and tingle. Then I went back to my room and dressed. I took the subway and went uptown. At 125th Street I got off and walked over to the Harrises. It was near one o'clock. I walked up the stairs in the dimly lit hallway, smelling that old fried-porky smell, and knocked on the door.

Tom opened it. His face broke into a smile as he saw me. "Man!" he said, grinning, "we was jus' tawkin' about you. Come on in."

I stepped inside as he called into the other room, "Maw, guess who's here?" He turned back to me and grabbed my hand and shook it enthusiastically. "How ah yuh, boy?"

I managed to grin and rescue my hand before he crushed it. "Fine!" I said, "just fine!"

Sam and Elly came running into the room, followed more

slowly by their mother. I shook hands with Sam and Elly and kissed Mrs. Harris. From the way they greeted me, a person would think I hadn't seen them in years, instead of just five days. When the excitement died down a little, I put the package on the table.

"I got a job," I announced proudly, "a real job, in a grocery store, like Sam. I thought I'd bring something up to you." I opened the bag and took out the food. "The best eggs," I said, "real butter and cheese and cake and...." I stopped. Mrs. Harris had sat down in her chair and was weeping.

I went over to her and put my arm around her shoulders. I could feel the thin bones of them near her neck. "Why, Maw," I said softly, "what's the matter?"

She looked up at me and smiled through her tears, "Nothing, Frankie," she spoke softly. "Nothing—I'm just glad I guess. I was a-prayin' for you evvy day—A-prayin' fer you to git somethin' that would let you smile again an' kinda turn the cohnehs of youah mouth up a little."

I was silent—I didn't know what to say. I looked at Sam and Tom and Elly. Tom nodded his head. "Thass right, Frankie. She tole us evvy day to pray fer you. An' we did—all of us." He looked at his brother and sister. "Didn't we?"

They shook their heads in silent assent. I looked around at them and down at Maw Harris. "I don't know what to say."

Maw Harris smiled at me. "Don' say nothin'. You don' have to say nothin'. It's just that the Lawd has heard us an' all we can say is: 'Thank you, Lawd. Thank you foah all youah kindnesses.' "

Later when we had eaten and I had told them all my story—how I got the job and how much I was making and what I was doing—and we were sitting back and I was smoking, Mrs. Harris spoke again: "This has been a good week foh us folks too."

"What do you mean?" I asked.

She looked proudly at Elly. "Elly's done got herself a good job too—thass what! She is wukkin' over at anothuh ribbon fact'ry an' makin' mos' fifteen dollars a week."

"That's swell!" I said, automatically looking at Elly, happy for them. Elly was sitting there, her face stony. She stared right back at me almost defiantly. I knew instantly what Elly was doing, and yet couldn't say anything. I had to play along with the old woman.

"She has to wuhk pretty late some nights though," the old woman continued. "But Elly's a good girl. She doan' mind that." She looked at the old clock on the closet shelf. "My, my!" she said, getting to her feet. "The day does fly. It's mos' fouah o'clock an' I mus' go down to the Sunday aftehnoon meetin'. Come on, Tom, and you too, Sam. You has to go with me. Elly went this mohnin, an' she can stay an' keep Frankie com'ny till we gits back. Hurry now!"

They left, the two young men and their mother, one on each side of her, holding her gently as they went down the steps. The Queen of England couldn't have been held with more care, more respect, and more devotion than the touch of their hands on her arms or the soft, tender look on their faces. I closed the door behind them and turned to Elly.

She was sitting on the edge of the window sill, looking out into the dirty brown courtyard. I sat down in a chair near her and watched her. We didn't speak. I lit a cigarette. "So you got a job, Elly," I said quietly.

She didn't look at me. Her voice was low and bitter. "You know I haven't."

"I don't know anything," I said. "Supposing you tell me."

She didn't answer for a while. Then she spoke, her voice tense and strained, but controlled. "I wuhk oveh at an apahtment with some women." Her dialect was more pronounced than usual. "We splits with the ownuh."

"There must be something else you can do," I said.

"Is theyah?"

I had no answer for that question.

After a minute she continued, her voice deliberately mimicking mine. "Thcyah mus' be somethin' else you can do. Sho' they is. I can go intuh the five-an'-ten or the depahtment stoh on One Hundred and Twenty-fifty Street an' say: 'I is white an' you can hiyeh me to sell youeh muchandise to the poh nigguhs who cain't git jobs because they is black an' oney white people is hiyed heanh in this stoh.'

"An' Tom wouldn' have to sit in the house all day an' look at his hands—his big, strong, capable han's while they opens an' closes oveh a piece of wuhk he ain't got until he gets filled with feelin's he don't know he's got inside him. An' yuh throat huhts just sittin' theeyah an' watchin' his min' slip down an' down an' down until they fixes an' comes up with an ansuh. An then he goes out an' drinks—cheap rotten gin, made by some white

man who is kind enuff to sell to poh nigguhs foh a nickel a drink
so they kin inflame they min's until the fiyeh buhns them up inside an' they doan' remembeunh anymoh they is black. But foh
a few minutes they is white an' the worl' is they oystuh and they
laughs an' is happy until they falls down. An' when they wakes
up the next mohnin, they head bustin an' they throat raw an
they stummic buhnin, they brings they han's to they heads an'
holds it tight an they sees they han's is black an' dirty and has no
wuhk to keep them busy. They cries to themselves, not with
teahs, not with they eyes but with they hearts an' ask themselves: 'Wheanh is the beautiful white, busy han's I had yesterday?'

"An' Sam wuhkin in a stoh evvy mohnin befoh school. He
knows evvythin' in the stoh—all the prices, all the stock. An' all
he does is delivuh groceries. He cain't wait on customehs. He
ain't allowed to cut buttunh or cheese. His black might come
off'n his hands and git in some nice white cream cheese that has
to go down on nice white bread that has to go down some nice
white throat. Sho, there mus' be somethin' else I kin do."

She turned toward me. Her face was grim and hard, her eyes
as wise as time. "I kin lay me down on a nice white bed, naked,
and squirm so that the customeh will think I'm hot foh him an'
cain't wait foh him to come oveh to me. An' he kin lay down on
me so's I kin change his luck. An' he nevuh worries whether the
black'll come off an' when he gits up an' begins to pull on his
trousehs, his knees kind a shakin' a little, he'll look oveh at me
an' say: 'You suah you all right, girl? If'n you ain't, tell me. I
won't be mad. I just want to know so's I kin git to a doctuh
befoh anything happens.' An' I'll look oveh at him an' say: 'I'm
all right, mistuh. Doan't you worry yoh head none. I may be
black outside, but inside I'm as clean an' white as any white
woman you have evah known.' But that ain't the way it comes
out. It comes out low and husky and full of tears. 'I'm all right
mistuh.' "

She stood up straight and looked at me. "I'm all right, mistuh," she repeated.

The way she said it went down deep inside of me. I put the
cigarette out and stood up, holding my arms out to her, "You're
all right with me, lady," I said.

She came into them and laid her head against my chest and
cried and cried and cried. I let her cry herself out. After a while
she stopped. For a few minutes we stood there silently.

"I'm sorry," I said.

She stepped out of my arms and took a cigarette from the pack I had put on the table and lit it and sat down. "I don't know why I tell you these things," she said so softly I almost couldn't hear her. "It's not your fault that's the way they are. But I got to tell somebody and I can't tell them."

"I know how it is when you got something on your mind and have no one to tell it to," I said. "I felt the same way many times."

She went over to the sink and washed her face, then combed her hair. Her hair was kinky, but she had used some cream to soften it out so that it framed her face loosely. Her black skin was thin and fine and shone with a pale blue translucence that seemed to give it a white undertone. Her body was thin, her breasts pointed, a little stomach, a high boogey behind, and thin legs in high-heeled shoes that made them look even thinner. She sat down and picked up the lit cigarette and puffed at it. "I feel better now," she said in a normal tone of voice.

I felt rotten. We sat there silently awhile, waiting for the family to come back. We heard Tom's booming voice downstairs in the hall. She put out the cigarette and went over to the sink and rinsed out her mouth.

"Maw doesn't like fer me to smoke," she explained.

I left there about seven o'clock before they ate supper. I didn't want to take anything from them. My portion would only have come from their scanty share. I promised to come up to see them next week and went to eat in a cafeteria on 125th Street. Then I went into the Loew's Victoria and saw a picture called *Skippy*. It was based on the comic strip in the *American*. But it wasn't real. Nobody lived like that.

Chapter Ten

AT THE end of the next week life had settled down into a routine of a sort for me. Friday evening after coming from work, I spoke to the desk clerk about a permanent room. For three dollars a week I got a room with an adjoining bath. It was a larger room than the one I had before. It had two windows facing the street and a large closet. There were two easy chairs and a regular chair and a small table next to the bed. A dresser on one side and a chest of drawers opposite it completed the picture.

Saturday was a tough day. I was busy running around all day and had made out pretty well on tips during the week. The customers seemed to like me and I was very careful to be polite and do everything I was asked. I found out I had a fair gift of selling. I could talk easily to the customers—joke with those who wanted to, but respectful to those who demanded it. I worked pretty hard but I liked it.

Sunday at the Harrises was a quiet affair. Tom was reading a paper when I walked in. I put my package on the table.

"Where are the folks?" I asked him.

"They gone out for a walk," he replied.

"Anything new?"

He shook his head. "Naw, I worked on the coal truck one day. But they ain't anything."

"That's tough!"

"Sho' is!"

I gave him a buck. He took it quietly. "Buy yourself some cigarettes, pal," I told him. "Or maybe go to a show or somethin'. What you need is a little change. Sitting here and worrying about it ain't goin' to do you any good."

"Who's worryin'?" he demanded, his shiny black face crinkling into a scowl. "Not me, I ain't worryin'."

We waited until the folks came back from their walk, then we sat around and chewed the fat awhile. I left about six o'clock and went downtown to eat and bought a paper and went up to my room. I undressed slowly and stretched out on the bed and read the paper. After I had finished the paper, I put out the light and lay there in the darkness, smoking a cigarette and thinking. I wondered if I could do anything about finding a job for Tom. I fell asleep with the glimmering of an idea in the back of my head.

The weeks went by, one dissolving into the next with a smooth, melting routine that let them slip through my being. I made about enough money to get by easily if I was careful and the only extra money I spent was for the Harrises' Sunday package. I went up there every Sunday and always left with a vague feeling of defeat.

March slipped into April, April into May, and May into June. I bought myself a few articles of clothing that I needed, but for the most part I used a pair of work pants and a shirt all through the week. I bought a new suit for Sundays but had no place to wear it except to the Harrises.

One morning when helping to unload the truck from the warehouse, the driver told me they were putting on another truck.

"Who's going to run it?" I asked.

"Tony," he said. Tony was his helper.

"That means you're going to need another helper," I said.

"Yep," he said. "We'll need two—one for me and one for him."

I went to the store thoughtfully. This was a job for Tom. I decided to speak to Mr. Rayzeus when he came the next morning.

When Mr. Rayzeus came in, I asked him if I could see him a minute before he left. I told him about Tom and he asked me if he was reliable.

"He sure is!" I said, "and he wants to work too. He needs a job."

He shook his head. "I've had bad luck with niggers," he told me. "The first few weeks they're O. K., but the minute they have a few bucks in their pocket they go off on a drunk and don't come back till they're broke."

"I don't know about the others," I told him, "but I know this guy. He'll do a good job. He's not a bum."

Mr. Rayzeus looked at me strangely. "You know the guy pretty well?"

I nodded. "I worked with him before. I know he's all right."

Mr. Rayzeus shrugged his shoulder, "O. K., send him up to me next week. I'll talk to him."

"Thanks, Mr. Rayzeus," I said, and went back to work. I felt pretty good. Now maybe things will be a little better for them. I could hardly wait until Sunday so I could go up and tell them.

Sunday came bright and clear and warm. I put on my new suit and went uptown. All the way up I kept thinking how happy they'd be to hear the news—Mrs. Harris especially. I walked over to the house from the station and went upstairs.

The old dump never changed. It smelled the same. Its rickety wooden steps still creaked underfoot. The electric bulb was too small for the large hallway and didn't throw enough light. The paint peeled dryly off the walls.

I opened the door and walked into the apartment. Elly was sitting there reading the *Sunday News,* the colored page of comics spread out on the table before her. The window, open wide behind her, allowed many of the sounds of the courtyard into the flat. Somewhere a kid was crying and a man and his wife were shouting at each other and a radio was playing, a jazz band—blending hideously together to make a kind of song of poverty.

Elly looked up at me. "Hello, Frankie."

"Hi!" I said. "Where's everybody?"

She spoke slowly, tiredly. "Maw is down to church with Sam. Tom went out early this mornin' and won't be back till later this afternoon."

I put the package on the table and opened it. "You'd better put this stuff away," I told her. "Some of it might spoil."

She got up and started to put the butter in the icebox. She didn't speak. It was hot in there. I took off my jacket and hung it carefully over the back of a chair and watched her. She was wearing a new dress. It was a shiny black satin, fitted fully around her breasts and yet shaped to them. It fitted closely to her skin all the way down. I could see she didn't have much on underneath from the way it clung to her thighs as she walked around. When she had finished she went back to her chair and sat down without speaking.

Time dragged by. The perspiration was running down my neck, wilting my collar. I could feel little trickles of it running down my back under my undershirt. I opened my collar.

She put her head on her arm on the table and just stayed there silently. I could see the lighter tan of her breasts down the front of her dress as she bent forward.

"What's the matter, Elly?" I asked. "Don't you feel well?"

"Un-unh," she said, "I'm sick."

I got out my chair and walked over to her. "What's bothering you?"

She didn't answer but got out of her chair. "Got a cigarette on yuh?" she asked.

I took out a package from my pocket and gave them to her. She put one in her mouth and I lit it. She leaned forward to take the light from me, and I looked down inside her dress. On impulse I pulled her close to me. I could feel her body against me. She made no move to stop me, just let me hold her and she remained stiff and wooden in my hands. I felt her breast inside her dress, trying to arouse some response in her. She stood there impassively holding the lighted cigarette in her hand. I let her go and went back to my chair feeling oddly defeated. I sat down and lit a cigarette. I didn't look at her.

She walked over to the window and sat down on the sill looking out. After a few minutes she got up and walked over to me. I didn't look up.

"It's not that I don't care, Frankie," she said softly. "I'd rather be with you than anyone else. But I'm sick."

"If you're sick," I burst out savagely, "why don't you go to a doctor?"

"I did," she said dully. There was an undercurrent of fear in her voice.

I looked up at her. Her face was set, impassive. "What did he say?" I asked.

She walked a little away from me. A few minutes passed before she answered. "I got a dose."

I was shocked. "Clap?" I asked.

Another minute passed before she could bring herself to answer. "Syphilis," she said, and suddenly sat down in her chair and stared dully at me.

I started to speak, but a thousand things flashed through my mind that I couldn't say. I opened my mouth like a fish but no sounds came out. She looked at me a little defiantly. We stared at each other. I didn't know much about it but I knew it was pretty bad. "What are you going to do?" I finally managed to ask.

"I dunno," she said. "The doctor says I have to report for treatments down at the hospital."

"You're not going back to the. . . ." I stopped.

She stood up. "Why not!" she snarled. "Why shouldn't I go back? That's where I got it."

"But you'll give it to someone."

"Why should I care?" She paced across the room. "They didn't care about giving it to me. It's their tough luck. I ain't goin' to see us go hungry just on account of that."

"You won't have to think about that," I said, "My boss wants to see Tom about a job on one of the trucks."

She looked at me in open disbelief. "Youah jus' talkin'."

"No," I said, "I mean it. He wants to see Tom. He told me."

She was convinced.

"So you see," I continued, "you can go to the doctor and get cured. You won't have to worry about them."

She looked as if she were going to cry, but she didn't. Instead she came over toward me and took my hand. "It's so good, Frankie," she said, half smiling, half crying, "I just can't believe it."

Maw Harris came in. She stood in the doorway a minute looking at us. Elly ran over to her. "Maw, Frankie tol' me his boss wants to see Tom about a job!"

The old lady's face broke into a smile. "She right, Frankie?" she asked me.

I nodded. "Yes, Maw, she's right. He wants to see Tom right away."

Mrs. Harris turned to me in simple wonder. "The Lawd was a-lookin' out for all of us when Tom brought you home."

I looked at them. Elly was smiling happily; her mother too had a quiet, happy air about her. Sam came in. They told him the news. We all felt good. After a few minutes had passed, I asked Sam if he would go down for a pack of cigarettes and a large bottle of soda pop. It was hot and we could stand a cool drink. Tom hadn't shown up yet. Elly went down with him.

Mrs. Harris sat in her old rocker. The chair squeaked on the bare wooden floor as she rocked it gently to and fro. She waited until the footsteps in the hall died down, and then she spoke. "You been a real friend to us, Frankie. We appreciate deeply whut you done foh us."

I was a little embarrassed. "I didn't do anything," I said. "You did more for me than I ever could do for you."

A few minutes passed before she spoke again. "Ah never asked you befoh, Frankie—maybe it ain't none o' my business —but haven't you any friends besides us? I mean some white folk that you know?"

I thought of Jerry and Marty and the folks before I spoke. "No," I said, "and if I did it probably wouldn't do any good. It's been so long ago."

"Didn't you cvunh try to look them up an' fin' out?"

I shook my head. "It wouldn't do any good. It was a long time ago. They probably have forgotten about me by now."

"Real frien's never forgets," the old woman said, "no matter

how long it is you don' see them. Besides you should have some
white frien's." She hesitated a second. "You should know some
people you kin go out an' have some fun with—some young
boys an' girls youh own age."

"There's nothing the matter with you folks," I said. "You've
been as nice to me as anyone I know of."

"But," she said, "you can't go out with us. You can't go
dancin' with us. We is colored. That ain't the way things is
done."

"I don't care how things are done," I said, "and I don't like
dancing anyway."

She smiled at that. "There's another thing I thought I'd tell
you about. It's Elly. I think she kinda likes you, an' they is
nothin' but grief in it foh us if'n she gets the idea wuhkin' ovah
in her haid. I don't want to huht yoh feelin's none but things
ain't that way eithuh."

I thought that over. While I was turning that thought over in
my mind, the old lady continued to speak. "She kinda waits all
week foh you to come up, an' on Sundays she dresses herself up
in her bes' clothes cause yoah comin'."

I knew more about Elly than the old lady knew, and yet she
never said anything to me about what she felt or thought. I
knew I didn't love her, and I didn't think for a minute that
she might be in love with me. There was a feeling between us,
but I thought it was a mixture of a sort of camaraderie and
sex—an indefinable solution that had blended so well it defied
all attempts at analysis. Finally I spoke. "I see what you're
tryin' to tell me, Maw. I'll do what you think best. I don't want
to make any of you unhappy."

She smiled again at me. "I knew you'd say that, Frankie.
Youah a good boy. We'll think about it an' decide later what to
do."

Sam came in with the soda. We opened the bottle and each
drank a glass. Then Sam asked me if I wanted to go up to the
park near City College and watch a ball game with him.

I didn't know what to do. I wanted to wait around for Tom
so I could tell him about the job, but Mrs. Harris urged us to
go. She said she was tired and wanted to lie down and take a
nap, and that she wouldn't tell Tom till I came back. I put on
my jacket and went out with Sam. On the way down the stairs
he told me that Elly had gone over to see a friend of her's but
she'd be back later. We went up to the park.

Chapter Eleven

IT WAS hot up there in the park. The sun beat down on us unmercifully. There was a good game going on up there though, and we had a good time watching it. We bought some hot dogs and lemonade from one of the pushcart vendors and ate them while we watched.

When we got back to the house it was nearly six o'clock and Tom hadn't come back home yet. Elly was there and tried to urge me to stay for supper, but I begged off and went over to 125th Street and ate. Then I went to see a picture and came out a few minutes after ten. I decided to go over to the Harrises and see if Tom had come back. I turned up St. Nicholas Avenue and walked over to their house.

As I turned their corner a fire engine whizzed past me, its bell clanging and men pulling on their coats over their shoulders. I looked after them. There was a fire down the block. Smoke was pouring from a building. I stood on the corner staring at it foolishly a few minutes before I realized it was Tom's house. Then I broke into a run down the block.

There was a crowd of people gathered already and being pushed back by the cops. The firemen were running up a long ladder to the sixth floor, and powerful streams of water were gushing into the blazing building. I pushed through the crowds of people to the front and looked around for one of the Harrises. It was dark and I couldn't see very well. There was a great deal of excitement. A hand grabbed me by the shoulder.

I spun around. It was Tom. "Frankie!" he shouted, "where are they?"

"I don't know," I shouted back at him. "I just came from the show. Weren't you home?"

"I just got back."

Just then Sam and Elly came running up. They had been running and were out of breath. "Where's Maw?" they shouted at Tom.

"I jus' got home," he shouted. "Ain't she with you?"

"No," Sam answered. "She was feelin' kind of tired an' she went to bed early."

We moved over to one of the policeman. He was a big colored man.

"Did they git my mother out?" Tom asked him.

"What she look like?" the cop shouted back.

"An old woman—Mrs. Harris—about sixty-two—gray hair." Sam told him.

He shook his head. "I didn't see nobody of that description come out," he said. "You'd better go ask the fire chief over there."

We ran over to the fire chief and repeated the question. He shook his head. "No one like that came out," he said. "But don't worry if she's in there we'll get her out."

Tom turned to the house. "Maw's still in there," he shouted. "I'm a goin' to git her." He started toward the house. A couple of cops grabbed him.

"You can't go in there," one of them said. "The firemen'll get her out."

"My maw's in there," he shouted, struggling to get himself loose, "in the third floor back. I gotta git her!"

"You can't go, goddammit!" hollered one of the cops.

Tom shook one hand free. He aimed a punch at the other cop holding him. The cop sidestepped it and hit Tom in the jaw with his fist. Tom went out on his feet. The cops lowered him gently to the ground. "We can't let him in," the cop said apologetically to some of the crowd that had gathered around. "He'll get himself killed in there. The building's going up like a matchbox."

Someone in the crowd yelled. I looked up at the building. Elly had broken from the lines and was running toward the open door of the house. I looked over my shoulder. Sam was kneeling on the ground near his brother, his face streaked with tears. I turned and sprinted after Elly.

"Come back! Come back!" I yelled after her.

She disappeared through the door. I ran up the steps to the door after her. Just as I reached the door, a stream of water hit me in the back. One of the firemen had turned the hose on me. I tumbled through the doorway into the building. It was dark in the hallway filled with smoke. The water was spraying around over my head; I crawled under it to the staircase and ran up the steps.

"Elly!" I hollered. "Elly! Come back!"

There was no answer. I ran up to the third floor. Elly had just gone into the kitchen. I jumped through the doorway and grabbed her. I tried to pull her back. The flames were blazing all through the back of the flat. The smoke was so thick we could hardly see each other. She was coughing. "You gotta come back," I said hoarsely, pulling her with me.

Her coughing had stopped. She struggled to keep me from pulling her with me. "Maw's in there!" she screamed. "Maw, Maw, d'ya hear me? I'm comin' tuh git yuh." She raised her hands and scratched at my face. I tried to hit her but missed. Then she kicked me and broke loose and ran into the bedroom.

The flames sprang up behind her. Their hot, livid fingers burned at my face. I started to follow her. I could hear her screaming somewhere there in the dark: "Maw! Where are you, Maw?"

Then I heard a crash and a long scream that stopped in the middle. For a minute the fire in front of me died down, and I saw the wall between the rooms had fallen with part of the ceiling blocking off the entrance. Then the flames sprang up again, and I turned to the hall, the scream still ringing in my ears. The hallway was blazing. I headed for the stairs and tripped on the top step and rolled down to the first floor. Bits of flaming wood were falling around me. I turned and ran down the last landing. The entrance was blazing in front of me but there wasn't any other way to get out. A stream of water came splashing into the hallway. I got down on my hands and knees and crawled out into the street under it. In the street I got to my feet and ran toward the fire lines.

One of the firemen grabbed me. "You all right?" he asked harshly.

"Yes," I said, coughing.

He held on to me as I walked back to the lines. The crowd was being pushed back. "Back up!" the cops were shouting. "She's going to cave in. Back up!"

I was near Tom and Sam. Tom was still stretched out on the ground but he was beginning to come to; he was shaking his head from side to side. He started to sit up. Just then the building came down with a roar.

We looked at it. A cloud of dust hung in the air over it, occasional tongues of flame licking up into the black night sky. Tom got to his feet. He didn't know that Elly had run into the building too. He stepped toward the building and roared, his head thrown back shouting to the night sky: "They'll pay for this, Maw. D'ya hear me? They'll pay for this, every goddam one of them! The lousy bastards in the banks, the goddam people who won't let us live in better places! I'll make them pay for this, Maw. It's a promise. D'ya hear, Maw? It's a promise."

A cop ran up to him and tried to pull him back. Tom turned on the policeman. He grabbed him by the neck and began to choke him. The cop's face was pasty white in the light of the fire. "You're the first!" Tom screamed, a wild look in his eyes. "You're the first but you won't be last! Evvy goddam one of you'll pay!"

The colored policeman we had first spoken to ran up to them. He tried to pull Tom off the other cop but couldn't. Finally he stepped back and picked up his club and brought it down on the side of Tom's head. Tom went down like a felled ox. The other cop stood up gasping for breath.

Two white-dressed men came up, rolled Tom on to a stretcher, and took him over to an ambulance. They put him in the back. Sam and I ran over to the driver. "He's my brother," Sam said. "Kin I go with you?"

The driver nodded. "Hop in the back."

We got into the back of the ambulance. The intern sitting there looked at me curiously as we got in. "You look pretty well messed up," he said.

I looked down at my new suit. It was dirty and torn and soaking wet. I would never be able to wear it again, but it didn't register. I looked back at him dully.

"You the guy that ran in after the girl?" the intern asked.

I nodded.

"You'd better let me have a look at you." He reached behind him and picked up a stethoscope. "Take off your jacket."

Automatically I took it off. I was watching Sam as he sat down near his brother. His face was frozen. The full realization of what had happened as yet had not permeated his mind. He didn't cry, just sat there looking down at Tom. I think he didn't even know we were in the ambulance with him.

I was soaking wet through to the skin. My face felt dry and burned, the hair on the back of my hands was singed and my hands felt hot. The doctor gave me something to drink after he had taken my pulse. I drank it.

"You're damn lucky!" the intern said. "You haven't got a serious burn on you." The ambulance started off.

Two hours later in the hospital I was sitting outside with Sam, waiting for the doctor to come out and tell us about Tom. Tom had had quite a wallop over the head, and for a while they didn't think he would pull through. As it was, it would have been better if he didn't.

When we were ushered into the room, Tom was sitting up in bed crying. Long tears began to roll down his cheeks. Sam, who until that moment had scarcely spoken, ran over to him crying: "Tom, Tom," and put his arms around his older brother.

Tom looked at him, no recognition in his dim eyes. He just kept on crying, mumbling undistinguishable, incoherent sounds to himself. He pushed Sam away. "Go away," he mumbled. "I want my mammy. Wheanh is she?"

I turned to the doctor, a question on my lips.

The doctor answered before I could speak. He shook his head. "I'm afraid he'll never be the same. He's had too many shocks. It did something to him. What he needs now more than anything else is rest and quiet."

Sam had been standing just behind me when the doctor spoke. He had his back to us looking at Tom, but he heard every word the doctor said. That did it. He turned to me, tears in his eyes, his mouth twitching with controlled sobs. It took me back a long way, that look on his face—to another Sam who had turned to me in his time of need.

"Let 'er go, kid," I said gently. "There's times even men cry."

He sat down in a chair and put his head in his hands, and his body shook with sobs. I couldn't say anything to him, so I went over to him and stood there awkwardly with my hand on his shoulder. After a while he stopped and we went out into the hall. We sat down out there, not quite knowing what to do next.

About half an hour passed before he spoke. "Frank," he said, his voice suddenly older, more mature, "kin you get me that job that you were goin' to get Tom?"

I looked at him before I answered. "What about school?"

"I'll get working papers. I'm old enough and I'll have to do something," he answered. "Can you get it for me?"

"I guess so," I said.

"It's strange," he said, almost as if he were talking to himself, "just a few hours ago I had a home—and a family, and a place to go. And now I don't know where to go or where to stay."

"How about coming down with me until we can straighten things out?" I suggested.

He looked at me gratefully. Just then a tall colored man came into the corridor excitedly. He came over to Sam. I recognized him as the preacher I had once met in the little church in the store.

Sam stood up as he came over to him. "Hello, Reverend," he said quietly.

"Sam," the Reverend said, and put his arm around the boy. "I heard about it and came over right away. You're going to come over to my house and stay there. You're not alone. You've always got the Lawd."

"You know my friend," Sam said, motioning toward me.

The preacher looked at me and nodded. "Yes," he said, "we've met." He held out his hand and we shook. "You did a very brave thing," he told me.

I didn't answer.

Together we walked down the hall. At the doorway we parted. The preacher took Sam into a taxi. He asked me if I wanted to be dropped anywhere. I thanked him and assured him I could get home all right. I watched the cab speed off into the night. I started for the hotel.

Elly and Maw Harris were buried two days later on a rainy Tuesday morning. The services were held in the little church, and then we rode out to the cemetery. As the earth began to fall on the coffins, the preacher closed his book and spoke. Sam and I stood near each other and I watched him. He was standing alone at the edge of the graves, the rain falling on his bared head. Tom was still in the hospital, and would be for a long time.

Thump—a wet clump of earth fell on the coffins.

The preacher stood there too, his head bared, looking up at the dark-gray sky while the rain beating on his face mingled with the tears in his voice. He looked like a big black ebony statue against the sky.

"O Lord!" he cried. "Look down on us, thy people, who turn to thee for strength and understanding and hope. . . ."

That was the word I could hear ringing in my ears the next few days. It had a never-to-be-forgotten world of meaning— the way his rich baritone resonance had sent it winging on its way to the sky—the way Sam looked at him as he spoke.

Hope—that was the word. Where would we be without it?

Interlude

RUTH

"IT IS strange," Marty was thinking, "no matter what Jerry said, he still didn't know Frank. Stranger still, none of us seem to think about him in the same manner. He was a different person to each of us. Each of us saw him differently in the light of his own experience and knowledge. I wonder who is right? Perhaps none of us. I don't know. Maybe Ruth did. She was the first to see—"

His thoughts were interrupted by Jerry asking him if he wanted a drink. He leaned back in his chair and watched Jerry mix the highballs. As he turned his head he noticed Janet looking at him. She smiled at him. He smiled back gently. Old friends—you knew them, knew everything about them, and yet had much to learn about them.

He took the drink from Jerry and drank it slowly, savoring the mellow smokiness of good Scotch, the carbonated water tickling his nose a little.

Janet turned toward him. "I wonder what Ruth thought about him?" she asked, putting her highball on the table and lighting a cigarette.

"It is odd," Marty said, still holding the glass in his hand, "I was just thinking about that myself.

"I think that Ruth was the first among us to see the real person beneath Frank Kane. The first time she met him, the very first day I brought him home with me, she knew him—and didn't like him. She was a little afraid of him, in an unusual sort of way.

"She caught me alone for a minute. 'He's not like a boy at all,'" she told me in a puzzled sort of way, 'He's more like a man. The way he looks at you, you feel old and aware of what you are.'

"Poor Ruth! In a way, he affected her more at that time than any of us. She was several years older than we were and much more adult than we knew. It was a long time afterward that she told me about him.

"You may recall that we had a girl working for us that summer. Julie, I think her name was—anyhow, it's not too important. This girl was about twenty and good looking in a sexy kind of way. Anyhow, Frankie saw her and probably was 'smitten with her charms' as the poets say.

"That evening Frankie had given me a boxing lesson and a shiner, and Ruth was pretty sore about it. She gave him hell when he went home and regretted it the moment she closed the door behind him. 'For after all,' she thought, 'the poor kid is an orphan and probably never had any friends.' She came into my room to find out how I was getting along and stayed for a while talking.

"Later she left and went to the kitchen to get a glass of water. She let the water run for a few seconds to cool it, then drank a glass, and when she put the tumbler down she thought she heard some sounds coming from Julie's room. She went to Julie's door, thinking that Julie was up and they would chat for a while. When she put her hand on the doorknob, she heard another voice in the room. The voices came toward the door.

"She was upset and a little nervous, so she ran from the door into the little hall near the kitchen and stood there, her back to the kitchen. At first she hadn't intended to eavesdrop, but there was a mirror on the wall opposite her, which gave her a clear view of what was going on in the kitchen. She saw the door of Julie's room open and Julie look out for a moment, then Julie stepped into the kitchen followed by Frank.

"Julie let Frank out by the servants' entrance, and at the door he kissed her. Ruth, watching, knew it wasn't any kid stuff. This was the real thing. And though she tried to look away, she couldn't. She was fascinated by the reflection in the mirror. To her mind it was the epitomization of the sordidness of sex, but it was also a trap into which she fell unknowing.

"She had felt the intensity of Frank's emotions by proxy, and she was lost and didn't know it. She didn't have enough experience at the time to evaluate her emotions properly or attempt to analyze them. She only knew simply that the thing she had felt about him had been felt by others and that nothing would make her whole again until she knew what there was in him that she wanted.

"She tried to laugh herself out of it saying he was just a kid. But her mind kept telling her that Julie knew that too and felt the same way she did about him.

"Ruth went back to her room, crying. She didn't know why. If I had known it then I would have called it 'emotional shock.' She didn't sleep that night, and the next morning when she got out of bed tired and upset, she had unconsciously decided on a plan to belittle him in her mind.

"After that she continually ripped into him—made wisecracks at his expense, laughed at his *faux pas,* gibed at his achievements. I wonder if Frankie knew why she did that. Until one day in school in the hall, he kissed her. And all the things she had set up in her mind about him scattered to the winds.

"She knew then that he was the only man she would ever settle for, knew then that it wasn't child's play, but serious, honest, adult emotion, desirous of finding adult expression.

"It was years after that she came to me and told me what had happened. She had just started working with the hospital unit of the welfare department. You remember, don't you, Jerry? Your father had helped her get the job. I was interning at Manhattan General, was on the late trick and got home about three in the morning.

"The first thing I noticed was a light on in the living-room. Wondering why it was on, I went in there and found Ruth, asleep in the big chair. I shook her gently to wake her up; I didn't want to frighten her.

"She opened her eyes. The first words out of her mouth were: 'I just saw Frank.'

"I could only gape stupidly. 'Frank,' I said, 'Frank who?'

"I don't think she even heard me, the words came tumbling out of her so fast. 'You wouldn't know him, Marty; you wouldn't know him at all. He's so changed. His hair is almost white, and he looks tired and lonely and beaten, and he was hungry. That's what they brought him into the hospital for; he had passed out on the street. The doctor said he hadn't eaten for days.'

" 'Wait a minute, girl,' I said, 'Take it slow. Who are you talking about?'

"She looked up at me as if she were surprised that I didn't know what she was talking about. Then she said slowly: 'Francis Kane.'

"Suddenly I was as excited as she was, 'Frankie,' I yelled forgetting the time of night. 'Where did you see him?'

" 'That's what I'm trying to tell you,' she replied. 'I saw him at the hospital tonight.'

"I was still excited. 'What did he say? Did he remember you?'

"At that she burst into tears, 'No,' she sobbed. 'He denied he ever knew us. He denied he was the Frank Kane I knew he was—even after I told him I loved him.'

"This was a little too much for me. I sank onto the couch. 'You what?' I asked. I still thought I was hearing things.

"Her tears had stopped and she looked at me steadily. 'I told him I loved him and that he had once kissed me in the corridors up at high school and all he did was wisecrack and say he wasn't the guy I thought he was. Then I told him that I would bring you down in the morning and you would know him, that maybe he had amnesia and couldn't remember, but I knew inside me that he did remember, that he was lying, that he had put that old high wall around himself and hung a sign on it that said "No trespassing" and he would let no one in at him, let no one crack that wall. Then I was really sure it was Frankie because I remembered when we were kids and I would say something that cut into him, a veil would drop down like a curtain over his eyes and face and an invisible wall would come up suddenly from the ground between you and you would know there wasn't any use in going on, because nothing you could say or do could get past that invisible wall and all you succeeded in doing was hurt yourself.'

"I watched her silently for a while. Many little things about her began to fall in place—why she never went steady, why she never married. She was almost twenty-five then and I had known her all my life, seen her almost every day of it, and now I first began to know her. That's funny in a way. Yet there is so little we know about ourselves, it's not surprising that we first begin to know each other after we had lived so closely together for twenty-five years.

"Finally I spoke, 'We'll go down there in the morning and see if we can talk some sense into him.'

"She shook her head slightly. 'It wouldn't be of any use. He won't be there in the morning. I could see it in his face.'

" 'Then we'll go now,' I said, standing up.

"She put her hand on my arm and looked up at me. 'No, Marty, we'll not go now,' she said softly, 'If we do, he'll never forgive us. The only thing he ever really had was his pride, and we couldn't take that from him. If we did, we might just as well not call him back, for he wouldn't be the Frankie we knew. We have to let him work this out himself, just as he always had.'

" 'But, what about you?' I asked.

" 'I can wait,' she said simply. 'He has to have this chance.' She drew me down to the chair beside her and rested my head on her shoulder where I could hear her fine, soft breathing. 'You see,' she said reflectively, 'he never had a chance to really be young; he had too much to fight, too hard a world to face. He was never an adolescent in the literal sense of the word. He sprang from childhood directly into manhood. That's why he seemed old to us kids. That's why some of us liked him and others didn't. There weren't any halfway measures in the way you felt about him. It was one way or the other. But beneath it all he was just a little boy hungry for someone to like him, to love him.'

"I turned my head and looked up at her. 'But if he goes away this time, he may never come back.'

"Her eyes looked across the room over my head. 'That's a chance I'll have to take, but,' she smiled slightly, she seemed to know much more than she was saying, 'I believe he'll come back. And when he does, I'm going to marry him and I'm going to take the lonely lines from his face and the bitter corners from his mouth. I'll knock down that wall around him and build one of my own—with bricks made of love, not suspicion.'

" 'But it may be years,' I said.

"She looked down at me, her eyes were warm and clear with an inner confidence. 'We can wait,' she answered. 'We're young and we can wait. Meanwhile there are others I can help. There are many children like Frank in this world—too many kids that have to by-pass their youth in order to provide themselves with necessities. Every child deserves a break. I'd like to take part in seeing that they get one.'

" 'So we won't go to the hospital tonight?' I asked.

" 'No, Marty,' she said, 'we won't go tonight. Let him get all the rest he can. He needs it badly.'

"We went down there in the morning and as Ruth had expected, he was gone.

"Time went by. I finished school and hung out my shingle. You two were married, and Jerry went to work in the district attorney's office. Ruth became head of her section of the child welfare department. We were growing up, all of us. But we knew and could see each other grow. I knew where you were, and you knew what I was doing during that time.

"But none of us knew about Francis—not even after he came back into our lives. Not even after he had married Ruth, did we know. Maybe he told her, maybe he didn't, but she never told us. Francis was passing through what I like to call, 'the lost years.' 'The lost years,'—I wonder what they were like for him, the years in which we grew up. Does anyone know? I wonder if they do."

Marty finished his drink and got up and walked over to the window and looked out. There were clouds in his mind, and he felt curiously depressed. The evening had lost its magic for him.

"Marty," he heard Jerry's voice calling him.

He turned around. There was a new look on Jerry's face, a certain strain had gone from it. His face looked brighter now and he seemed more sure of himself.

"Maybe I can fill them in for you," Jerry said.

PART FIVE

Chapter One

SAM quit school and went to work on the truck. He got about twelve dollars a week and lived with some relatives of his in upper Harlem. By midsummer I had become well integrated into the work at the store. Though Harry didn't say anything to me, I could tell by his manner and the way the customers spoke that I was doing all right. Work took up most of my time, and on Sundays, my one day off, I used to lounge around generally and go to a show.

I didn't make friends with the facility I used to, so my outside interests were rather curtailed. I didn't care very much; I was content just to go along in a routine sort of way. The few moments of discontent I had, I relegated to the back of my mind with other indefinable longings. I made several attempts to locate my uncle through his former place of business, but the whole family just seemed to drop out of sight. Business was slow during the summer, and Harry told me that he would get me a raise in the fall. My salary was ten dollars a week, to which I added the extra two dollars Harry used to give me and about three dollars in tips that I used to average, which made a comfortable total of fifteen a week and was enough for me to get along on. I could use more money, but then, who couldn't? Jobs were pretty hard to get and I thought I was doing pretty well. It wasn't as much money as I had made years ago when I worked for Keough, but somehow I wasn't too interested in trying to get back into that work. I had the idea that I would eventually work my way up into a better paying job. The Horatio Alger idea was still a good one as far as I knew.

In July, Otto, the owner of the ice-cream parlor on our block, asked me if I wanted to work for him on Sunday afternoon, when he was pretty busy. He told me he'd give me two dollars for the afternoon, which was from one o'clock to eight o'clock in the evening. Since I didn't have anything else to do, I took him up on it. In a few weeks I had become a fair soda clerk—about good enough to get along—and I enjoyed talking to the young people that hung around there. Quite a few of them came down from the club that was upstairs over the grocery store.

I always wondered about that club. The sign on the windows said "Workers' Alliance," but the name to my mind never seemed to fit the place because all its members were on home relief and didn't work. I know every Saturday night when we were working late in the store, we'd hear a lot of noise coming from upstairs.

One Saturday night about midnight after we had closed up, I decided to go up and see what their rackets were like. I had been asked to come up several times by some of the members but had never felt like going up there before. I guess I was a little restless and maybe lonesome for some human laughter.

Their meeting place was a large, unpapered apartment that had had the walls knocked out to make one big meeting room. They had a four-piece band in one corner of the room and a table stacked with cold cuts and bread on the other side of the room. They had a barrel of beer, a punch bowl, and some big gallon bottles of red guinea wine next to the table. The band was playing some unfamiliar and unharmonious music, and some younger people were dancing while the older people formed little groups and stood around talking with sandwiches in their hands.

I stepped over the threshold and into the room looking for some familiar face. I spotted one that I knew. A fellow named Joey who bought in the store—I didn't know his last name— came over.

"I didn't expect you here," he said in a surprised sort of voice.

I shook his outstretched hand and laughed. "I thought I'd come up and see what kind of a racket you guys were running."

He took me by the arm. "Come on," he said, "I'll show you

around." He introduced me to several young men and girls and I nodded to several people I knew from the store. Then he led me over to the table, stuck a sandwich in my hand, said: "Enjoy yourself," and rushed over to the door to greet someone who was just coming in. I gathered he was kind of an officer of the club or something because he seemed to know everybody there.

After a while I saw a girl I knew talking to a fellow. I knew her from the store because we had a standing joke between us. She always used to come into the store and ask for a bottle of ketchup and she used to say it fast. It sounded funny the way she said it. I walked over to her, took a bite out of my sandwich so that my mouth was full, and mumbled: "Did you get your katship today?"

She turned around and saw me. She too seemed a little surprised. "What the hell are you doing here?" she asked.

I swallowed my mouthful. "I'm a member of the party," I retorted.

"Like hell you are!" she said with conviction.

"All right, then I came up for the free eats."

"Ain't that the truth?" she said with some scorn. "Didn't we all?"

The fellow walked away and began to talk to some other jane. "Want to dance?" I asked her.

"O. K., I'll risk it," she said.

I put the sandwich on a chair and we began to dance. "It's a nice racket they're running," I said.

"It's free," she answered.

People kept coming in while we were dancing even though it was late. I kept stepping all over her feet. It had been a long time since I had danced.

"You might be able to cut cheese," she finally said in disgust after I had stepped on her feet for the sixth time, "but I'll be damned if you know how to dance!"

I held her tight, close to me. "That's just an excuse," I said.

She pushed me away. "Oh!"

The music stopped. "Now come the speeches," she told me.

"Do you want to duck out?" I asked her. I had some other ideas.

She didn't want to. We walked back to the chair where I had parked my sandwich. I picked it up and we sat down. "Stick around," she said, "you might learn something."

I looked out across the floor. Joe was climbing up on a big

table he had dragged out in the middle of the floor. He held up his hand. "All right, everybody," he shouted, "I want all your attention. As you know, we have a guest speaker down here tonight who you all know and have heard before. I don't have to introduce him. His work in this section and part of the city is known by all of you. His efforts on your behalf and that of the party are widely known. So, I give you Gerro Browning."

He jumped down, and to my surprise a tall young, redheaded Negro climbed up on the table. I looked around at the people. They were a pretty mixed bunch. Micks, Italians, Spicks, Polacks, everything. He was the only Negro I saw there but what a reception he got. Everybody began hollering and stamping their feet while he looked around quietly, smiling a little.

Then he held up his hands and they all fell quiet. "Friends," he said—his voice was unusually free of accent—"I see a lot of new faces here tonight—faces that I haven't seen before, but they're warm faces and they're human faces and they're people like us, who want the same thing out of life that we do and I want to thank them for coming here tonight." Everybody applauded. He waited for the applause to stop and then he continued.

"I'm not going to talk tonight about the party or its principles. I'm not going to repeat the things you all know so well. I'm going to tell you instead the story of a man who lives down the block.

"He has never been up here. He has never come to any of our meetings. Though I have asked him and others have asked him, he has not come. He, like many of you, had for a while been on home relief and lately got a job out on Long Island for the power-and-light company. Maybe one of the reasons he never came up was because he was afraid if his bosses heard he belonged to our club, they would fire him or lay him off and then he would have to go back on relief until another job came his way. Anyway, he has said at different times that he had been warned to stay away from us and have nothing to do with us—that we were a radical bunch of bastards and he would lose what little he had gained and had.

"Last week while working digging a ditch to lay a new cable, his pick bit into the ground and hit a live wire. The shock of the electric current ran through him and flung him about ten feet, injuring him and burning him severely. Tonight he is still in a hospital and we don't know whether he will live or die.

"When I heard of the accident I went to his wife and asked her if there was anything we could do to help. She didn't think there was anything we could do, and told me when and where her husband was injured. That night I reported back to the office. They sent a doctor, who specialized in that type of work out to the hospital, and an investigator to the scene of the accident.

"The doctor is trying now to save the man's life.

"The investigator's report, which I have here in my hand, clearly shows that this man was not injured in an ordinary work accident, but an accident that was caused by the neglect and carelessness of the company that employed him. I quote from the report: 'The law requires that power and live current lines are to be laid a certain distance below the level of the street. These lines were not laid at the prescribed level as directed and specifically stated in the law. They were three feet higher than they should have been.' Mind you, friends, three feet higher than they should be! These three feet may make the difference between life and death for this man. These three feet spell the difference between hunger and food for this man's family.

"I have already spoken to our lawyers and they are going to bring suit against his employers and see that justice will be done in this case."

The people began to applaud that, but he held up his hands for them to stop. His hands high over his head, he appeared almost like a prophet.

"Friends," he said, "this man's wife is here tonight. The money she will receive from the compensation board will barely give her enough to buy her children food. It will not pay her rent. It will not pay her gas and electric bills. I know that you can ill afford to give even a few pennies to help her from your own meager pockets, but I want you to do just that.

"The party will assume the legal expenses in connection with this action. But you are big enough, and I know you are, to do with a little less and help this man's wife and family. You've got to remember what has happened to him can happen to you. And what happens to anyone of us hurts all of us.

"We've all got to work together. We've all got to fight together."

His voice grew more quiet, more determined, more positive. "We are entitled to live and to work and to eat. We will not gain those rights unless we are willing to go out and get them.

Remember, the stronger the party is and the more members it has, the more recognition and respect we will get for our fundamental rights. I want you to make every effort to bring in new members. I want you to sell or give away our paper and literature. But more than anything else, I want all of you to put your entire support behind this club so that the club can put all its support behind you."

He got down from the table, and a crowd of people gathered around him, all talking.

I looked at the girl next to me. I never thought very much of her. As a matter of fact I never thought very much about the members of this club. I had heard Harry say many times that most of them wouldn't work even if they got a chance. Now I didn't know.

I looked at her again. Her eyes were shining. Her face was pale, and her rouge and lipstick stood out like splashes of paint. She turned to me. "Come on," she said. "You're working. Get it up." She held out her hand.

I took out a quarter.

"You can give more than that," she said. "I want a dollar."

I laughed and gave her a dollar. "I thought you said this was for free, and here I am paying for it the same as I would anywhere."

"You dirty bastard!" she said to me coldly. "Would you like that to happen to you?" She took the dollar and walked over and gave it to the man who had just finished speaking. Apparently he asked her where she got it because she pointed to me.

He detached himself from the crowd around him and came over to me. "Thanks for what you gave," he said, holding out his hand. "It was more than anyone else gave."

"I'm working," I said, shaking hands with him.

"So would the other people here if they only had a chance," he replied quietly.

"I didn't mean it that way," I said. "I can afford it."

"You're new here. I haven't seen you before."

"I'm Frank Kane," I said. "I work downstairs."

"Glad to know you," he said, smiling, "I hope I'll see more of you."

"You will," I said politely.

He smiled again and walked away.

The girl came over to me. "I see you were talking to Gerro," she said in the same tone of voice as if I had spoken to God.

"Yeah," I said. "If the speech is over let's go. Maybe we can catch a late show on Forty-second Street. And by the way, I don't know your name."

"It's Terry," she said. "I know yours from the store—Frank."

"So you know," I said. "Get going or do you want to hang around here all night?"

"O.K., O.K.!" she said. "Wait a minute. I'll put some powder on." She walked away.

I watched her walk over to the ladies' room. Suddenly I wanted to go out with her. I hadn't been out with a dame for a long time. "It's not bad," I thought, looking after her, "and who knows? I might be lucky tonight."

Chapter Two

I MADE a date with Terry for the next afternoon. We were going swimming out to the island. She was a cute little thing but strictly no dice. She was a natural-born teaser. She'd say bold things and make bold motions, but it was all a front, part of the act. She'd neck with you till you saw stars, and the minute you'd reach for a little more, she'd slap you down.

"I don't know," she'd say with a cute little half smile, as if she were laughing at your torment, "but all you fellows are alike. You seem to think if you take a girl out for a good time you're entitled to everything. Why can't you just have a good time without it?"

I'd explain, feeling foolish: "But baby, you can't do those things. Why, you can drive a man nuts that way! Come on, baby, be a sport! Nothing'll happen."

I was right about that. Nothing did happen. But through her I became one of the crowd upstairs. I began to feel that I wasn't the only person in the world that had to break his ass in order to get by with a few pennies. Other people had the same problem—all of them, no matter who or what they were. They all had to make those lousy few pennies or go hungry. I saw the funny look on some of their faces. Time and circumstance had imprinted defeat upon their faces. Charity had left its mark in the loss of pride they felt. They all showed it in different ways.

Some would come into the store with their food voucher, laughing, gay, putting on a big act. "We eat again!" they'd chortle gleefully, and walk around with high abandon buying food, food, and more food, until their voucher was used up. Some would slap the voucher openly down on the counter and say in a half-belligerent tone of voice: "Do you take these?" And others would come in quietly, wait around until you were through with the other customers and the store was empty. Then they would lean over the counter with their voucher in their hand and ask hesitantly, half ashamed: "Do you take these?" And still some others would come in and take their order, and when it would be all wrapped up, they would take out the voucher and say, in a tone of voice that seemed to dare you not to: "Do you take these?"

One thing though they all had in common. They would never refer to the food voucher by its full name, "Emergency Relief Voucher." They would always say "these" or "it." "How much is left on it?" And if they had bought what they thought would last them for the period until the next voucher came, some would buy a piece of cake or some candy for the kiddies. Some would ask for cigarettes or cash for the remainder of the voucher. We weren't allowed to give cash or cigarettes. But we did. Occasionally some one would come in and offer a $13.50 voucher for five or six dollars in cash. We bought them. So did all the other storekeepers in the neighborhood. There were lots of things being on relief did to people. But most of all it took away their pride.

Upstairs in the club, however, it was different. The club was fighting for the people to get cash instead of vouchers. It claimed that many stores were charging the reliefers higher prices than the cash customers. I heard some storekeepers justify that by saying they had to wait ninety days for their money. Anyway, there were always complaints on it upstairs. There were other things going on too. The club had heard that the government was going to institute a vast works program to help out the people on relief. Every day new rumors were given voice. But meanwhile the people just stood around and tightened up their belts.

I dated Terry Wednesday nights. I didn't want to go out on Sundays with her because it took too much money and there was nothing in it for me. Not that I didn't like her. She was O.K. But I'd leave her all steamed up, and I'd lie in bed and toss all night, not sleeping, thinking all kinds of thoughts. I couldn't bring myself to go to the whores to escape those feelings, not after what I'd seen of them. So I'd lay there and toss and swear at the bitch and say I wouldn't go out with her anymore and think of knocking her off anyway. "I'll bat her ears off if she tries to stop me," I'd promise myself, but somehow I never did. I did one thing though. I stopped seeing her weekends and went out with her Wednesday nights. We'd go to a show and then I'd take her home and I'd spend a few minutes in the hall at her house and grab a few kisses and a little feel and then I'd leave. I was tired after a day's work and at least I'd go to sleep and sleep through the night—sometimes.

It was Thursday afternoon and I was delivering an order up to a house. I was pretty steamed up that day. The night before I had gotten my hand inside Terry's dress and felt her warm, soft breast. She let me keep my hand there awhile, and when I tried to slip my other hand up inside her knees, she pushed me off. I kept thinking about how she felt. No matter how hard I'd try, that thought would persist in coming back.

I rang the bell. A young woman answered. She had faded blondish hair, a narrow face, and wore an old dress. She was a new customer. She had used up her relief ticket and had bought some stuff, asking for it to be sent up later in the day. She expected to get some money.

"Groceries," I said, standing in the hallway. "One twenty-five, collect." I remembered Harry telling me not to leave it if I didn't get the dough.

"Bring it in, please, and put it in the kitchen," she said in a low, quiet voice.

I went into the apartment, put the package down, and turned toward her.

She was looking at the box hungrily. "My husband's coming home in a few minutes," she said. "He's getting some money. Can you leave it here and I'll bring the money down later?"

"I'm sorry, ma'am," I told her. "I'd like to, but I can't. It's marked C.O.D., and the boss would can me if I didn't do what he said." I began to pick it up.

"Wait a minute," she said nervously. "Can you wait a few minutes? He ought to be right along." A child about six walked into the room. It was her daughter. She picked the kid up. "You can sit down if you like."

I sat down in a chair near the package and lit a cigarette. I offered her one. She refused. I waited until the cigarette was burned down before I got up. "It's getting pretty late, lady," I said. "I'll have to be getting back to the store or the boss will wonder what's happening to me."

"Wait a few minutes more, please," she said. "He ought to be right along." She walked over to the window and looked out on the street. "He'll be right along," she repeated nervously.

The hell he would! Even if he did show up, he'd be broke too. I'd have to take the package back anyway. But I waited another five minutes. Then I got up.

"I'm sorry, lady," I said, "but I have to get back. If your husband comes in, send him down to the store. We'll give him the stuff." I picked up the box and put it on my shoulder.

"Please," she said, "don't take it away. Leave it. When he comes in I'll send him right down to pay you—honest!"

"Look, lady," I said, "I believe you. I'd like to leave the package here but I can't. If I did the boss'd fire me." I was getting a little bit sore at her whining. Maybe I was a little sore at myself for not leaving it. But nobody was going to put anything over on me. I heard enough stories about guys getting gypped on their orders.

"But we didn't have anything to eat all day," she said, "only the baby. My husband went downtown to get a job. We'll pay you."

"Lady," I said, "why tell this to me? Tell it to my boss. If he wants to trust you I'll leave the package here."

"I did," she said, putting the child on the floor and sitting down.

I knew his answer from the way she said it. "Well then, what can I do?" I asked, turning toward the door. Then I had an idea. I turned toward her. "Unless?" I spoke only that word but the silence afterward was full of meaning.

At first she looked up at me with a glimmer of hope in her eyes, but it faded quickly as she looked at my face. Her face grew red and she looked down at her hands nervously gripping each other.

I looked at them too. They were red and ugly from work. They were the hands of a young woman aged before their time from housework—all the housework.

"No," she whispered. She spoke so low she almost might have been talking to herself. "No! No! No!"

"O.K., lady," I said cruelly, "if that's the way you want it. But don't kid yourself. We both know how much of a chance there is for him to get a job today." I walked over to the door and put my hand on the knob.

"Wait a minute," she called. "Let me think." She put her head in her hands while the little girl stared solemnly at the both of us.

I relaxed. I could practically see the wheels go round inside her head. But I knew what the answer would be. What it had to be.

At last she looked up at me. Something more had gone out of her face—I didn't know just what, but she looked different. She spoke to the child: "Laura, run downstairs and wait for Daddy. Call me through the window if he comes."

The child solemnly walked through the door I held open for her. She looked back and waved at us and started downstairs. I waited until she was downstairs before I closed the door. Then I put the package down and faced her.

She looked at me a moment and then led the way into the bedroom. It was a small room with a small window. There was a neatly made three-quarter-size bed and crib in one corner. A small statue of the Virgin and the Child hung opposite the foot of the bed. A picture of her husband and herself was on the dresser. She stood there a moment and then said: "Not in here," and walked through to the parlor.

I followed her. She sat down on a couch, took off her shoes and stretched out.

I sat down on the edge of the couch. I could feel a pulse hammering in my throat and a tightness across my groin. I put my hand on her body near her thighs just under her stomach. Her skin was as cold as ice, and she started as I touched her. Then I made a mistake. Involuntarily I looked at her face.

It wasn't a woman I had there, it was an empty shell. I looked at her for a full minute. In that minute she didn't even move a muscle; she lay the way I shoved her, staring at me.

I jumped to my feet and straightened my trousers. At first

she looked at me as if she didn't believe what she saw, and then she stood up. "Thanks for the sleigh ride!" I said. "You can keep the groceries." I started for the kitchen.

She took a step forward. "Mister," she said, and suddenly slumped toward me.

I caught her before she hit the floor. She was suddenly warm. I could feel the cold of her skin give way to the rush of heat that seemed to flow through her body like fire. Her head was against my shoulder and she was crying—this time without tears. I held her tightly but impersonally, all the strength seemed to have left her legs.

"Mister," she sobbed, "mister, you couldn't know what we've gone through—how many times Mike has gone hungry to give the food to the kid, how many things he's done without, cigarettes."

She was cracked. Here I had a dame in my arms and she was crying about what her husband sacrificed. I suppose she didn't think she had done anything for the kid either. I was suddenly ashamed.

"Take it easy!" I said, interrupting her babbling. "Take it easy! Everything will be all right."

She looked up at me. Her eyes were wide pools of gratitude. I gave it back to her, look for look. "You're O.K.," she half whispered.

"I know, I know." I laughed shortly. Sucker Kane, number one patsy!

We walked silently through to the kitchen. At the door she stopped me.

"Thanks again, mister," she said.

"Forget it, lady! Courtesy is our motto."

I walked down the stairs and out into the street. About half-way down the block I saw the little girl. A man ran up to her and picked her up and tossed her in the air.

"Daddy, Daddy!"

He did a little dance with her, "Laurey," he sang out, "Daddy's got a job!"

I walked past them. "Congratulations, Mike!" I said. "You got more than that." And kept on going.

He looked after me for a second and scratched his head. I guess he was wondering if he knew me. Then he turned and ran for his house with his baby in his arms.

I was getting madder and madder as I walked back toward the store. That teasing bitch Terry would pay for this! The next time I had her out, she wouldn't get away with it.

And she didn't.

Chapter Three

THE next morning the lady I had left the groceries with came down to the store. She came over to me. The kid was tagging along with her. She looked different than she had looked the day before. It was the way she held her head or maybe the way she moved—more sure of herself. The defeated look had vanished from her eyes.

"My husband got a job," she said without any preliminaries. "I was wondering if you could let me have a few things till payday, tomorrow."

"I know," I said. "I saw him on the street. Wait a minute, I'll ask the boss." I went over to Harry and explained the situation to him: that her husband had just started work and they would like a few things to carry them over until the next day when he'd get paid. I was ashamed of what I had done yesterday. I didn't know just how bad off I was until this morning. And now I was anxious to make it up to them. He told me it was O. K. if I thought they were all right.

I went back to her and gave her what she wanted. While I was wrapping the package I tried to apologize for my action yesterday. I spoke in a low tone of voice so no one else could hear me but her. "I'm glad your husband got something," I said.

She didn't answer.

"I'm sorry about yesterday," I continued. "I don't know why I acted that way, but I heard so many stories about different things. I don't know who to believe any more. I don't know who to trust."

"Why can't you trust everybody until you find out differently about them?" she said simply, her face reddening.

I felt worse than before, but there was no answer to what she said. I couldn't explain to her some people would cheat you and some wouldn't—that the bad ones made it tough for the good. I wrapped up the package and gave it to her. She took it and left.

Later in the afternoon Terry came in. She smiled at me. "Gimme a bottle of katship."

"Christ!" I said to her, "don't you ever eat anything else?" I knew she wasn't sore at me. I could tell from the way she acted. I should have knocked her off a long time ago I thought, and then I wouldn't have been in the swindle I got myself into. I took the ketchup from the shelf behind me and put it in on the counter. "Anything else?" I asked.

She shook her head.

I put the bottle in a bag. "Ten cents, please."

She gave me the dime. "Coming to the meeting tomorrow?" she asked.

"I'll be there," I said. "Wait for me."

She left.

Harry came over. "How come you're going to those meetings?" he asked. "They're a bunch of reliefers. Most of them don't want to work anyway."

"I don't know," I told him. "They seem like pretty decent folks. The breaks are against them, that's all. Besides I have some fun up there."

He looked at me. "Don't tell me you're going communist!"

I laughed at that. "I don't even know what communism is. I wouldn't know one if I saw one. The people upstairs look the same to me as other people. They seem to want the same things other people do. They want jobs and food and a good time. I want the same things and I'm not a communist."

"They believe in free love," he said. "They don't believe in getting married if you want it."

"I don't know about that," I replied. "Most of them up there are married."

"Well," he said, "if they were decent, they wouldn't let their kids run around the way they do—like that Terry, for instance. I bet they bang her off plenty up there."

That got me sore. I started to answer him hotly but controlled myself. Instead I grinned slowly. "She's the kind that everybody would bang—if they could."

A customer came in then and Harry turned away to wait on her and I got busy unpacking and we forgot all about what we were saying.

The months went by. Sam quit his job and went to live with some relatives of his in Hartford. I became a full-fledged grocery clerk and was raised to fifteen dollars a week. I became a pretty good soda clerk too on the Sundays I worked for Otto. I saved a few bucks and bought some new clothes, gained a little weight, felt a little better, more friendly toward people. I knew everybody in the neighborhood. Between the store and the club I kept pretty busy. Not that I was active in the club, but being there seemed to bring me closer to people in general.

One evening about a week after Thanksgiving Gerro Browning called me as I left the store. I waited for him to catch up to me and then we walked downtown.

"Where do you live, Frank?" he asked.

"At the Mills," I said. I was wondering why he was interested.

"Where you going now?"

"I'm going to eat and then home," I told him.

"Mind if I eat with you?" he asked.

"No, not at all," I answered, surprised that he should ask to eat with me. "I'd like it, as a matter of fact—have someone to talk to for a change."

He looked at me curiously. "Haven't you any folks?"

I shook my head.

"How old are you?"

"Twenty-two," I told him. I looked at him questioningly. "Look, I don't mind your asking me these questions, but maybe you can tell me why the sudden interest?"

He laughed shortly. "I don't know exactly why myself. You interest me, I guess."

"Why should I? I'm no different than any of the others."

"You don't think so?"

"No, I don't," I said. We turned into a cafeteria.

We went down the counter and picked up our trays and food. Then we sat down at a table and began to eat.

For a few minutes we ate in silence. Then, between mouthfuls of food, he said: "Your hair, for instance."

Instinctively I raised my hand to my temple. "What about my hair? It's combed, isn't it?"

He began to laugh. "No, that's not it. It's different. You asked me, didn't you?"

"It's no different than any other hair."

"It is," he said, smiling. "It's got gray in it—not much, but enough to see. And you're kind of young to have gray hair."

"Maybe I worry a lot."

He shook his head. "No, you're not the kind. But you've been through a lot."

"How can you tell?"

He swallowed a mouthful of food before he answered. "By little things mostly. The way you act. You seem to sit back and watch people with a glint of amusement, or superiority, or something in your eyes. The way you talk—positively, tersely, always surely, never indefinitely. A certain way you move around, on the edge of your feet, so to speak, ready to jump one way or the other—like an animal, always wary, always on guard." He took another mouthful of food. "Like when you sat down here in the restaurant—your back against the wall. The instinctive way you look at everybody that comes in or walks past while we're talking and eating. Who are you looking for, and what are you on guard against?"

I smiled. "I didn't realize I did that," I said. "I'm not on guard against anything. It's just a habit, I guess."

"There are reasons for habits," he said. We were through with our meat. I got up and went for the coffee and brought it back to the table.

He was sitting back in his chair and smoking, absently twirling a small pin attached to his watch chain around his finger.

I put the coffee down on the table. "What's that?" I asked him, indicating the watch chain.

He took the watch from his pocket and gave it to me. I looked at it. "That's a Phi Beta Kappa key."

I turned it over in my hand. It had some strange lettering on it. "It's the funniest-shaped key I ever saw," I said. "What does it open?"

He laughed. "It's supposed to open the world of opportunity. But it doesn't. Sometimes I think it's a fake." He saw I didn't understand him. "You get it in college. It's a very snooty club that admits you only if you've maintained the highest standing."

"You went to college?"

He nodded.

I handed the watch and chain back to him. I thought of Marty and Jerry: they should be pretty nearly through college by now. "I have some friends that are going to college."

He looked interested. "Where?" he asked.

I smiled at him wryly. "I don't know," I confessed. "I haven't seen them for a long time."

"Then how do you know they're going to college?"

"I know them," I said.

"It's funny how people lose track of each other," he said reflectively.

That seemed to break the ice between us, and everything came easy afterward. We sat and talked for over an hour. I told him about myself. I hadn't ever told anyone before, and he seemed to be really interested. We parted pretty good friends.

Chapter Four

THE winter of 1932-3 was a bad one. People were out of work, on relief. It was becoming more evident, even to me who was safe in a small way, that steps would have to be taken to insure the livelihood of the people around me. Every day the papers screamed "New Crisis." People were hungry. People were cold. Bonus for the veterans. Jobs for the people. Stop kidding yourself, neighbor, "prosperity" isn't just around the corner.

But in some strange way it didn't seem to affect me. I was safe. I wasn't hungry. I wasn't cold. I had a job.

When I went upstairs to the club the complaints of the people attending never seemed quite real. The speeches I heard never seemed to have an effect. The demands that were made were never listened to. And gradually the people seemed to despair, to lose their hope of ever getting a job again. It reflected itself in many ways. Men who would religiously go out to look for work every morning stopped going. They adopted a what's-the-use attitude. Theirs was a standard complaint.

"Don't you know there's a depression on? Buddy can you spare a dime?"

Several stores on the avenue went out of business. Nobody seemed to care. The stores stood vacant on the street with big to-let signs in their windows. The byword was cheap: "Cut rate," "half price," "fire sale," "anniversary sale." Any excuse for a sale. But there weren't any sales.

The people were bewildered, confused. They didn't know who to blame. Small stickers were pasted on the subways, store windows, doors: "Buy American." The *Morning American* and the *Evening Journal* were plugging a nationwide campaign: "Bring back prosperity by buying American." At Columbus Circle men were speaking against the government, against the President, against the Jews, the Negroes, the Catholics, against anything. They lashed out savagely at everybody—at unions, at strikes, at strikebreakers, scabs, bosses, Jew bosses, Jew bankers. Aimlessly, savagely, stupidly, they struck at the people around them.

Buy Gentile. Buy American. People walked the streets amidst news of riots in Harlem—food riots in Hell's Kitchen. Tempers were being frayed, the latent savagery in people was being stirred. The whole mess was being stirred, as if by some master hand that stopped every few minutes, to add a little bit of seasoning, hatred, suspicion, calumny, insinuation.

Put the nigger in his place. White men need the jobs. You don't want your sister raped by a nigger, do you?

Look around you. Who owns all the businesses? The Jews. Who have the banks? The Jews. Who have the best jobs? The Jews. Who has the most doctors and lawyers? The Jews. Who are the communists? The Jews. Who are the strikers? The Jews. Is this our country or theirs?

The niggers are like cancer. Let them into one house in your neighborhood and they came swarming in like flies. They ruin real estate values. They'll ruin your neighborhood. They'll ruin you. You'll be afraid to walk the streets at night if you let the niggers in. You'll worry about your little girl coming home from school. The niggers are like cancer. Once you get it, you're through. They'll kill you if you let them.

It was a bad winter in more ways than one. I remember the night in February—the night of Lincoln's birthday—the night I heard Gerro cry.

I stood way in back of the room. The club was half empty

and the members were standing around talking quietly. There were no more bands or dancing. The money was needed for more important things. People had stopped coming to the meetings. They had lost hope or had listened to others' whispering lies, and had been seduced away by coarse, loud-mouthed corner orators.

I had been talking to Terry. As usual, she was complaining. "I'm late again, goddamit! Are you sure you were careful?"

I laughed at her. "Sure, I'm careful. Stop knocking yourself out. In case you get caught, I can always trip you up on the stairs and you can lose it that way."

She was mad. "I don't know why in hell I bother with you! You don't give a damn about me! All you want is your nooky."

"Is there anything else I'm supposed to want?" I asked her brightly.

"O.K., wise guy!" she snarled through curled lips, her eyes flaming. "Some day you'll find out I won't be around to give it to you. Then try and get it!"

"There's other dames," I said noncommittally.

She exploded. "Goddamit! Joke about it! I'll get married."

"Who wants to marry you?"

"There's a guy," she said, suddenly sure of herself. "Got a good job too! Driver on the Fifth Avenue bus. He's a real gentleman. He wouldn't push over a girl when she didn't want to."

"It only proves the old saying," I said, " 'There's a sucker born every minute.' Why don't you marry him?"

"I don't know why I don't," she snapped back. Suddenly she changed her tone of voice. It became soft and friendly. "Did you ever think of getting married, Frankie?"

I raised my hands in mock horror. "Do you think I'm nuts? Why make one dame unhappy when you can make all of them?" I laughed. "Is this a proposal? This is so sudden."

She was mad again. "Go ahead and laugh. If I show up this month, I will marry him and you can whistle for it." She walked off.

I looked after her thoughtfully. You never could tell when she was serious. But hell, I didn't want to get married to anyone!

Gerro had climbed up on the table to speak. He held up his hands for silence. "Friends," he said, but that was as far as he got.

Just as he spoke, a rock smashed against the window and into the room. More rocks followed. For a minute we stood still, not being able to realize what was happening. Gerro stood there on the table, his mouth open.

I was nearest the window. I moved toward it and looked out. There were twenty or thirty men outside in the street; they were looking up toward us. I didn't recognize any of them. I felt a hand grab mine. It was Terry.

"What do they want?" she asked. She sounded frightened.

I didn't have to answer that. Someone in the crowd downstairs did. "We want that pimpin' nigger. He cain't go aroun' screwin' white women in this neighborhood. We'll teach him how to act around white people."

I looked back at Gerro. He was standing in the center of the room. Somehow he seemed to stand alone there. With white frightened faces, the others shrank against the wall. A woman drew in her breath with half a scream. "Why don't someone call the police?"

"I'd better go down and talk to them," Gerro said quietly. He started for the door.

"Don't let him go, Frankie," Terry whispered. "They'll kill him!"

I reacted to her statement automatically. "Gerro, wait a minute. If you go out there, it may not do any good. Let's get the women out first."

He stopped near the door and came back toward the window.

"Stay where you are!" I told him.

He stopped in his tracks and stood there looking at me.

I turned back to the window. "If we let you have him," I shouted down into the street, "will you let the others out?"

I could see a few men talk. "O.K.!" someone shouted.

"All right then," I hollered. "The women will come out first, then the men. When they're all gone, you can come up and get him."

"No!" someone shouted. "You come out last with him."

"O.K.!" I hollered back.

"Frankie, you can't do that. You can't turn him over to them like that," Terry whispered.

"Shut up!" I whispered. "They won't get him. When you get out, call the cops. Then go home and stay there until I get in touch with you." I spoke loud now. "You people will get out of here, so don't worry. Go out single file. Keep your hats off so they can see you're white. Go home and stay there until morning. And don't open your mouth to talk to anyone. Just get out and beat it!"

One of the men protested. "We can't leave Gerro here."

"I won't," I said. "Now get out, you don't want any of the women to get hurt, do you?"

They began to move toward the door.

A voice from the street shouted up: "Bring the nigger to the window so we can see he ain't getting away."

That put a monkey in my plans. I had planned to tell Gerro to hotfoot it up to the roof and over to the other buildings. Now they wanted to see him and that would slow us up. Gerro started over.

I stopped him. I saw Joey. I called Joey over and told him to go up to the roof and open the trap so we could get right out, and then to come down and go out with the rest. He nodded and left.

"Now," I told the others, "go out single file and slowly. We need all the time we can get."

They began to move out of the room slowly. There was no confusion. Quietly, stolidly, they went downstairs and out. I looked out the window and saw the first of the group emerge from the building. They hurried along the fringe of the crowd and went to the corner and disappeared from sight.

Someone in the crowd hollered: "Where's the nigger?"

I motioned to Gerro with my hand. He came to the window. His face was set and hard, his lips drawn together firmly. If he was afraid, he didn't show it. I saw Terry walk down to the corner. She stopped there and looked back at us and lifted her hand in a half wave and went out of sight. A rock came hurtling to the window. I instinctively ducked it, and it hit Gerro on the side of the face just under the cheekbone. He didn't move under the impact.

I looked at him without speaking. His cheek had been cut by the rock and it was bleeding. He didn't turn his head. He didn't show any signs that it had hit him. The blood ran down his cheek and neck, and stained the clean white collar of his shirt a dull, soggy red. I gave him my handkerchief, which he pressed to the side of his face with as little emotion as a barber applying a hot towel. He stood there at the window looking out at the crowd.

"You know any of them?" I whispered.

"Yes," he said simply, his voice trembling a little, "I know most of them."

Some of the bastards were probably members here at one time or another, I thought. I didn't say anything. I hoped Joey would get back quickly before the last of the crowd filed out.

"Frank!" Joey's voice came from the doorway.

I didn't turn my head from the window. "O.K.?" I asked.

"O.K.!" he whispered back.

"Beat it!" I said, still looking out. "Don't forget to go out last."

I heard him move toward the stairway. "Get ready to run for it," I told Gerro. "Follow me when you see Joey come out."

He didn't answer.

A few more rocks came flying in. I dodged them but Gerro just stood there motionlessly. I saw Joey come out of the building.

"We're coming out!" I hollered. I stepped back into the room. From the corner of my eye I could see some of the crowd surge toward the entrance. Gerro still stood at the window. I grabbed him by the hand and yanked him toward me. "C'mon, goddamit!"

I started to run toward the doorway, half dragging Gerro with me. We got to the hall. I could hear footsteps on the lower staircase. I turned the other way and ran up the steps to the top floor. There was a ladder leading to the roof. I saw the square boxlike cover of the exit had been removed, and I could see the stars in the sky above. "Good boy, Joey!" I thought.

I pushed Gerro up the ladder ahead of me and saw him disappear through the vent; then I started up. There was hollering on the flight below us in the clubroom. I could hear furniture being smashed. There was more noise on the stairway coming up to us. I was almost at the opening when I felt a hand clutching at my feet. I looked down. A man was partly up the ladder grabbing at me. I kicked viciously at him. My foot landed in his face. He fell off the ladder to the floor, and I went up and out of the vent.

I looked around. The roofs were covered with the remains of the last snowfall. I saw the cover lying near the vent, and next to it an old rotting mattress that some tenant had probably left there after sleeping on the roof some summer night. "Gimme a hand with this," I snapped at Gerro.

His face was still bleeding, but he bent and helped me replace the cover. Then I threw the mattress over it, hoping it would delay them a little more. I straightened up and looked around. Some of the roofs had regular entrances to them. I started over the buildings toward them. The first one was about two houses away. I ran up to it and tried to open it, but it was locked.

I looked back over my shoulder to the building we had come from. The cover was still on the vent, but I could see it move as they tried to open it. The mattress was moving up and down and sliding off a little. We ran to the next building.

We were luckier there: the door was open. We ran inside the building. I turned and locked the door behind me. There was a little hook that fastened into the door and held it closed from the inside. We ran downstairs and out of the building. We came out on Sixty-eighth Street and ran up toward the park.

I looked down the street. There weren't any signs of pursuit. We picked up a cruising cab on Central Park West and piled in. "Keep rolling!" I told the driver. "I'll tell you where to go in a minute."

Gerro sank back into the seat and covered his face with his hands. The handkerchief he held in his hands was covered with blood by now. I turned to him and pulled his hands away from his face and looked at the cut.

"That's a bad one," I said. "We'd better get you to a doctor." I leaned forward and told the driver to take us to the Roosevelt Hospital.

At the hospital we got out and I paid the driver. We went into the emergency ward. I got one of the interns to look at it. It needed several stitches. While the doctor attended to Gerro, I answered the questionnaire the nurse had to fill out. The doctor finished and put a bandage over the cut. He told Gerro he had better go home and lie down for a while. He gave him some pills to take, and we left the hospital.

A clock in a store window across the street showed it was eleven o'clock. I looked over at Gerro. "You'd better go home now. You look a bit wobbly to me."

He tried to smile. "Yes, I'd better. I guess I can make it home all right by myself. Thanks for everything, Frank. You were swell!"

"Forget it!" I said. "Do you think you can make it all right?"

"Sure!" he told me. "Sure I can." He seemed to sway a little.

I put out my hand to steady him. "I think I'll go along. We might as well finish the night together. We started that way."

He didn't protest.

"Where do you live?" I asked.

He appeared to be trying to think. "Maybe I shouldn't go home. My folks will be too upset if they see me. I'd better go down to a friend's house."

"Anywhere you say," I told him. "Only let's get going. You need a little rest."

We climbed into a cab. He gave the hackman an address in Greenwich Village. The cab started off. He leaned back against the cushions. For a while as the hack went downtown we didn't speak; he just sat there looking out the window. I looked at him from the corner of my eye every few minutes.

At last he leaned his head forward and put it in his hands. He began to cry. I know it wasn't the pain. It was the hurt, the humiliation he felt that was expressed in his hard, choked-back sort of sobs. "The fools," he said, "the poor misguided fools! When will they learn?"

Chapter Five

THE taxi stopped in front of a small renovated apartment house. There was a sign over the doorway, "Studio Apartments." I got out and paid the driver. I turned to Gerro and we went into the building. We stopped at a door about two flights up. He rang the bell. The cut was beginning to pain him now. I could see the way he stood there that he was very uncomfortable.

I rang again. We waited about a minute but there wasn't any answer. "Maybe your friend's not in," I said.

He shook his head. "I have a key," he told me, and taking it from his pocket, he opened the door.

I followed him into the apartment. He put on a light. In one corner of the room there were a typewriter and some torn

sheets of paper lying near it. On the other side of the room
there was an easel with a half-completed portrait of a man on
it. There were a table and several chairs scattered about the
room. Off in one corner near the window was a small kitchenette, containing a small stove and refrigerator and pantry.
There was a door on the opposite side of the room. Gerro went
over to the door and looked into the room. I could see a set of
twin beds and a small vanity table over his shoulder. He closed
the door and came back into the room.

"It looks like they aren't at home," he said. He stood there
uncertainly a moment as if he didn't know what to say next.
"Well," he continued, "I guess I'll be all right now. You might
as well go home. It's pretty late and you must be exhausted."

"I'll go," I told him, "after I see you in bed, and after you
take a hot drink and those tablets the doctor gave you."

"I can make it all right," he protested.

I got the feeling he wanted me out of here. "Nix!" I said. "Go
inside and get into bed. I'll put some water on to heat. You got
any tea here?"

He nodded. "There's some tea bags in the pantry."

I went over to the small range, filled a pot with water, and
put it on the stove. I turned and saw him standing there
watching me. "Go on in and undress and get into bed," I said.

He turned and went into the other room and closed the door
behind him.

I waited a few minutes until the water began to boil. Then I
looked through the pantry until I found some cups and the tea
bags. I put a bag into one of the cups and poured the hot water
on it and started for the bedroom. I stopped outside the door.
"The tea is ready," I called through the closed door.

"Come in," I heard him answer.

I went into the room. He was in a bed at the far end of the
room near the window. He had put on a pair of blue pajamas.
His dark face shone against the pillow, the white bandage
adding an incongruous look to the scene. "How are you feeling?" I asked.

"A little better," he said, "but I'm getting a terrible
headache."

"Drink this and you'll feel better," I told him. "You got those
tablets the doctor gave you?"

He held out his hand; they were in his palm.

"Take them," I commanded, "then drink this."

He swallowed the pills and held out his hand for the cup of tea. I gave it to him, but when he took it I could see his hand was trembling so much he could hardly hold it. I took the cup back and fed it to him by the spoonful. At last he finished and laid his head back on the pillow.

I sat there watching him for a while. He looked back at me. "Anything else I can do for you?" I asked.

"No, thanks," he said, "you've done enough."

We were silent for a little while. I could see him drowsing off. Suddenly he opened his eyes and asked: "Frank, were you afraid back there in the club?"

I smiled at him. "I was scared green."

"You weren't," he said. "I was watching you. You never turned a hair. You almost seemed to enjoy it."

"You weren't so bad yourself," I said. I imitated his voice, "I'd better go down and talk to them."

"I was," he said seriously, "afraid, I mean. I was really afraid. Deep inside of me I knew I was afraid and I was ashamed of it. I was ashamed because I thought I had mastered that fear a long time ago. It's a peculiar Negroid fear in character—fear of a mob of white people. It goes back a long time, I guess."

"Well, you didn't show it," I said. "You'd better forget it and try to sleep. In the morning everything will seem different."

"Will tomorrow be different?" he asked speculatively. "Will it ever be any different than today? People don't change overnight. When something goes wrong it's natural for them to look for a scapegoat. They forget anything a person has ever done for them in their foolish stupid search for vengeance."

I got to my feet. A note of determination crept into my voice. "Put it out of your mind and go to sleep. A little rest is what you need right now." I walked toward the door and opened it. "I'll be out here if you want me. Just call."

He nodded. "You're a funny guy, Frank." He smiled a little. "I told you that before, didn't I?"

"You can tell me again tomorrow," I said, "when you've had a good night's rest. Good night."

"Good night," he said.

I closed the door softly behind me. I rinsed out the cup and put it back in the pantry. Then I sat down and lit a cigarette. About halfway through with it, I thought I heard him call me. I got up and peeked into the room. He was asleep. I went back inside and sat down.

There was a small portrait of Gerro on the table near the easel. I went over and picked it up. It was a good portrait. I didn't notice it before, but Gerro was a good-looking guy. He had a firm, sensitive cast to his face, high cheek bones, large, intelligent eyes, and a long, clean line to his jaw. I put the painting back on the table and returned to my seat. I remember looking at the clock and noting that it was after one o'clock, and then I must have fallen asleep in the chair.

I awoke when I heard a key turning in the lock. A quick glance at the clock told me it was three thirty. I waited for the door to open. I heard the tumblers click, and then a girl stepped into the room. She stopped short in the doorway when she saw me.

She was a beauty—small, dark-red hair, deep-brown eyes, a small, beautifully curved mouth. Her coat was open and I could see she had a terrific figure—sexy. The right things in the right places—nice legs, a soft, creamy-white skin. I blinked my eyes. This was why Gerro had tried to shake me. I stood up.

"Who are you?" she asked. Her voice matched her figure. It was a soft, deep voice.

"Frank Kane," I said. "I'm a friend of Gerro's."

"Where is he?" she asked.

I gestured to the bedroom. "He's in there asleep. He had a bit of an accident and I came along with him."

She closed the door and came into the room, taking off her coat. She looked at me a moment, and then went to the bedroom and opened the door and looked in. I could see he was still asleep. She went into the room and stood over the bed looking down at him. Then she quietly came back into the room I was in, and closed the door softly behind her.

I saw she was a little pale. "Don't be upset," I said. "He'll be all right."

"What happened?" she asked.

I took out a cigarette and offered her one. She took it and we lighted up. Then I told her. When I had finished she sank into a chair.

"It must have been terrible," she said.

"It could have been worse," I said.

"I mean for him," she said. "You don't know how much of himself he put into that club. How proud he was of it! How proud he was of the way he was accepted there! He always said that it was only the beginning—a forerunner of a better tomorrow. When everyone, no matter what their color or creed would be, would get along with each other. He must have taken a terrible beating."

I looked at her. "It wasn't a bad cut."

"The physical side of it, he will forget soon enough," she said. "It's the other side that really was hurt—his pride and spirit—and it won't heal as well as the cut on his face."

I picked up my coat. "I'd better be going now," I said. "I only waited for someone to come so I could tell them not to disturb him."

"No," she said quickly, "don't go. It's late. I don't know how far away you live but why don't you stay here tonight. You can sleep inside with Gerro. I'll sleep out here on the couch. You look terribly tired."

"No," I said slowly. "Thanks just the same but I think I'd better go." I walked toward the door.

She came to the door with me. "Why don't you stay?" she asked. "I don't mind sleeping out here—honestly. I'll have to do it anyway."

I just looked at her questioningly.

She blushed, the hot, red color running up her neck and across her face. She looked down at the floor. "Wait a minute. You don't understand. I'm his wife."

I almost smiled. "Look, lady, I don't want to seem rude or small-minded. It's your business, not mine. It doesn't make any difference to me who or what you are. Gerro is a great guy. He may even be a great man. I'm just one of the people who are lucky enough to know him, that's all."

She sat down on a chair. She seemed to be furious with herself. "I'm sorry I said that," she told me. "I lied. I'm not his wife." She picked her head up and looked at me proudly. "I wish I were, though. I wish I had the nerve to make him marry me."

I looked right back at her, staring into her eyes until she began to color up again, but she didn't look away. I threw my coat across the room. "This is a hell of a way to treat a guest!" I said. "Haven't you anything to eat in this place? I'm starved, Miss—?"

"Marianne Renoir," she said.

"How about something to eat, Marianne?" I asked, smiling.

"Eggs?" She smiled back. "You'll have to take that. It's all there is." She turned toward the kitchenette. "Fried or scrambled?"

Ten minutes later we were sitting at the table eating—that is, I was eating, she was talking.

"Gerro wouldn't have liked what I said to you. He doesn't like me to lie about us. The truth is always much simpler, he says."

I nodded agreement.

She lit a cigarette. "I met Gerro when we were juniors in college. And you know how those things are. One minute you're talking about a common problem of classwork, and the next minute you find out that there are more important things to talk about.

"But I was the brave one. We'll defy the world, I said. What the hell are standards? What do we care what people say or think? We'll show them. But Gerro never said anything. He'd just smile in that sweet, quiet, sincere way he has and not say a word.

"I guess he knew, even then, that I was just talking to keep from facing the facts. My folks wouldn't allow it. I come from Haiti, and though there was a touch of Negro in us, somewhere back in my great-grandmother's time, they were even more proud of their color than those who were pure white.

"And Gerro's family was the same way from exactly the opposite point of view.

"Gerro always wanted to be a writer—a journalist. He studied journalism in school. But the inequity of his opportunity as compared with his training soon became apparent to him. Then he turned to this. He thought if he worked hard enough at it and if others worked hard enough at it, people would grow to accept him in the way they would accept anyone else of equal talent. That's why I think he must feel so hurt over what happened tonight.

"He's kept so busy that he hasn't had time even to see me more than once a week. And when he does come he goes over to the typewriter over there and starts to write things, so wonderful and beautiful and compassionate that I don't see how anyone who reads them can keep from weeping. He pours out his heart and soul into that typewriter, and then when he's finished, he looks up at me and smiles and gives it to me to read. And while I read it, he walks up and down nervously, smoking one cigarette after the other, and tries to read my mind as to how I feel about it.

"And when I'd look up at him and tell him how wonderful it is, he takes the pages back from me and he holds them in his fist and shakes them at me. 'Is it the truth, Marianne?' he would ask, 'Is it the truth?'

"It is the truth all right. The truth—naked, raw, honest, uncompromising. The truth—the misery of a man's soul, his sensitivity to his fellow man's feelings. But the truth—a torch— a bright, shining torch on a foggy night in a world beclouded with prejudice and stupidity."

She got up and picked up the little portrait of Gerro that I had looked at before. "I painted him one day while he was working. He never knew it until he had finished his work, then he looked up and saw me. I smiled at him and showed him the painting. And do you know what he said?

"He said, 'Lord, darling, you make me beautiful!' As if I could make him beautiful—he who is beautiful and kind and honest in his own right."

She put the portrait down and stared at it a few minutes. I had finished the eggs and I watched her. She was oblivious to my gaze. "Christ!" she said. "Christ! I wish we were married!"

I started to speak but a voice interrupted me. It was Gerro, and he was standing in the bedroom doorway smiling at us. "I see you two have met," he said. "But as usual she only tells you her side of the story. She didn't tell you she won the Ross Scholarship in Art, did she? She didn't tell you her family is one of the wealthiest in Haiti? She didn't tell you if I married her we wouldn't have a penny to live on?"

She got up and ran over to him. "Gerro, I was so afraid for you."

He smiled at her gently. "Afraid, Marianne? Not you. Maybe I was. But not you."

I got up from the table. "Look," I said, "I'm tired. Court's adjourned for the night. I'll listen to your side of the story, Gerro, in the morning. Let's go to sleep."

I slept on the couch in the studio. I had almost fallen asleep when I heard someone come out into the studio from the bedroom. I looked through the darkened room. It was Marianne. "Marianne," I whispered, "is he asleep?"

She came toward me and stopped near the couch looking down at me. "You still awake?"

"Yes."

"He told me what you did. I wanted to thank you. I didn't realize," she laughed suddenly to herself.

"What are you laughing at?" I whispered.

"You know what I thought when I first came into the apartment and saw you sitting there in the chair? I thought you were a burglar who had fallen asleep in the chair and just woke up when I came in. There was something on your face that seemed to be laughing at me. It seemed to say: 'All right, I'm caught. What are you going to do about it?' I was afraid to come in but I couldn't go away. I just stood there not knowing what to do. Some day I'm going to paint you—even though I know now you are such a nice boy."

I didn't answer.

She bent down and kissed my cheek. There was a perfume about her, a femaleness I was instantly aware of. "That was for being so kind to Gerro."

I put my hands under her arms and pulled her toward me. "That was for Gerro," I whispered. "This is for me."

I kissed her on the lips. At first she was too surprised to stop me. Then she kissed back. Her arms went under my head and held my face close to hers. When we separated I whispered: "For whose benefit was that speech while I was eating—mine or yours?"

For a second she held her face close to mine. We looked into each other's eyes. Then she straightened up. "You dog!" she whispered evenly. "You dirty dog! I can never paint you now. You are a burglar. I was right the first time." She moved toward the doorway and stopped there. "I'll never see you again," she said definitely.

I turned over on my stomach and looked at her. "Marianne," I whispered, "would you say that if I weren't Gerro's friend?"

She went into the bedroom without answering. I turned over on my back and looked up at the ceiling, half smiling to myself. She was right. I would never see her again, not as long as Gerro was my friend. It was too dangerous for both of us. I liked her—more than I had ever liked anyone before. There was something about her—about us—that seemed to draw us together. I sensed it when I first saw her. I knew she did too. I liked her voice, her mobile, expressive face, her hands with long, capable, sensitive fingers. I liked the way her lips felt against mine, the corners of them moving a little. But I would never see her again, not as long as Gerro was my friend.

I left early in the morning before either of them had awakened. It was Monday and I had to be at work. I slipped out of the apartment like a thief—a burglar.

Chapter Six

A FEW minutes after we had opened, Terry came in. She was as mad as hell. "I thought you were going to get in touch with me last night," she said furiously.

"I couldn't," I said, trying to cool her off. Harry was looking at us curiously. "Gerro was hurt pretty bad and I stayed the night with him. What happened after I left?"

She cooled off quickly. "I don't know. I called the cops like you said I should, and then went home. I guess the place must be wrecked. How is Gerro?"

"He'll be O. K.," I said. "We got away over the roof."

"What are they going to do about the club?" she asked.

"I don't know," I answered. We went out into the street and looked up at the club. All the windows had been smashed. We went upstairs. The little furniture that had been there was thoroughly smashed. Obscenities were chalked on the walls. We went outside again. Terry had a funny look on her face.

"I guess it's all over now," she said slowly.

"Maybe," I said. "You never can tell. If it means enough to the members, it will open again."

"If it does mean enough!" she answered.

I was curious. "What did it mean to you?" I asked. "What did you get out of it?"

She hesitated a moment before she answered. "It was a place to meet people, to make friends, and talk about things. It was a place to get together."

"Wasn't it a place where you could help share what you had? Didn't it mean more than just a place to have fun?"

"I guess so," she said doubtfully.

I was right. Most of the people that came there didn't know what in hell the score was—it was just a place to go. Any good work that came out of it was only through the planning of its officers, men like Gerro. The ordinary member didn't really know how important it was for them. I said good-by to Terry and went back to work.

Wednesday afternoon, Harry answered a phone call. "It's for you," he said, holding the receiver toward me.

I took it. "Hello."

I recognized Gerro's voice. "Hello, Frank. This is Gerro."

"How are you feeling?" I asked.

"O. K. now," he said. "I just wanted to call and find out if you can have supper with me tonight."

"I'd like to, thanks," I said. "Where'll we eat?"

"Down here at Marianne's," he said.

I didn't expect that. I didn't know what to say. I didn't want to go down there; I didn't want to see her. That is, I wanted to see her, but I knew I had better not. I had thought too much about her the last few days—more than I thought I would. It was funny the way she had crept into my mind. "What time?" I asked.

"About seven-thirty."

"Wait a minute," I said. "I just remembered. The truck comes tonight, and I have to wait around for it. I won't be able to come. I'm sorry."

"Oh!" He sounded disappointed. "Marianne wanted you to come down. We'll both be disappointed that you can't make it."

It was funny the way my heart jumped when he mentioned her name. "Tell her I'm sorry I can't make it, but you understand."

"Yes," he said, "I understand. Maybe some other time."

"Yeah, some other time." We said good-by, and I hung up.

I felt good after that call. I knew she had thought about me too or else I wouldn't have gotten that invitation.

Gerro called me again next week, and I had dinner with him at a restaurant on Fourteenth Street. We had a nice talk. I was beginning to like the guy a hell of a lot. He was the first guy I had met who I seemed to cotton to in a long time. He was smart and friendly.

"What are you going to do now?" I asked him while we were having our dessert.

"I'm being transferred to a club uptown," he answered, "up in Harlem."

"I don't know why in hell you bother with that bunch! Most of the people don't know or care what you are really trying to do. All they're looking for is a place to have a good time." I thought I was telling him something he didn't know.

"I know that," he said readily. I looked surprised. He continued: "I know that most of them don't understand what we are trying to do. But that isn't any reason why we shouldn't try to help them. Sooner or later everyone will realize that what we're trying to do is the right thing. It may take a little time but they will learn."

"So you're going uptown," I said ruminatively. I was thinking about the Harrises. There was a hell of a lot he could do up there. He was the right kind of a guy too.

"Yes," he said. "The organization feels I'd be able to do a better job up there among my own kind."

"You did a hell of a good job down here!" I said.

"I thought so too," he said, shaking his head, "but now I don't know. I had hoped that by working with the people, we would forget the old animosities and differences. That's the only way for us to get along: by working together in a common effort. That way we'd get to know each other and understand that each of us are looking for the same thing. Then we wouldn't have any differences."

"I guess you're right," I said. I didn't know how right he was, but I did know you couldn't make people change overnight.

I met him once a week after that, and it was the most interesting evening of the week for me. I looked forward to it. We had become fairly good friends.

I began to see less of Terry. The club had moved to new quarters about five blocks away, and I didn't attend any of the meetings there. Somehow since I had met Marianne I had changed. I was beginning to feel there were more things I wanted from a woman than the mere physical possession of her body. Terry was a nice kid but she didn't have what I wanted. There was no pretense of love between us. Our relationship was purely physical. In some vague manner I began to feel that I wasn't being given all that I wanted. I didn't have that feeling of lift, excitement, curiosity or awareness that I felt when I thought of Marianne. I began to wonder whether I had fallen in love, but I laughed it off. The idea of falling in love was a foolish thing to me. It was something you read about in books and saw in the movies, but it had no place in real life. I felt sure I hadn't fallen in love.

One evening in March when we were standing in the hallway of Terry's house, I had kissed her and she had pushed me away. This time I didn't press myself on her. She stood there in the dimness looking at me. At last she spoke.

"You've changed, Frank," she said.

I laughed.

"No," she said seriously. "You've changed. I mean it. There's something on your mind."

"Nothing that I know about," I told her flippantly.

"You may not know it, but there is." She looked at me, trying to see what expression there was on my face. "And I've been thinking too. This thing we've been doing will have to stop."

I didn't answer.

"I was right," she said, more sure of herself now than before. "A few months ago you would have argued with me. Now you don't say anything. And I'm glad. I was going to stop even if you didn't. I'm going to get married."

She misunderstood my sigh of relief. I had expected something else.

"To that fellow I was telling you about. He's a bus driver, and he has a pretty good job and makes about forty a week. He loves me, and if I marry him, I can move out of this dump and have all the things I want. We can live on Long Island in a nice steam-heated flat, not this cold place. I won't have to worry about bills and food. We won't have to try to stretch pennies."

I tried to look unhappy but I had a hard job doing it.

She put a hand on my arm. "Don't feel too bad about it, Frank. It's something we couldn't help." She sounded like a dame in a picture we had seen last week. "We had a lot of fun together and some laughs. Let's part friends."

I looked at her strangely. She really didn't believe that crap she was handing out. Her face was perfectly serious; she meant every word of it. I cleared my throat of a wild desire to laugh. "If that's the way you want it, Terry," I said. My voice sounded strangled to me because of the attempt to control it.

She thought I felt bad. "This is good-by, Frank," she whispered.

I played the game. "No," I said, "you can't mean it."

"Yes," she said, "I mean it. This is good-by." She was so carried away by what she said there were actually tears in her eyes.

I bent over and kissed her on the cheek. "I guess you're right, baby," I said. "I'm not good enough for you. I hope you'll be very happy. Good luck."

She burst into sobs and ran upstairs crying. I watched her go and then walked out into the street grinning.

A month later as I walked into the restaurant to meet Gerro, I saw Marianne sitting at the table with him. I stopped a moment in the doorway and then walked over to the table as he caught my eye. I sat down.

"Marianne is having dinner with us." Gerro smiled.

"So I see," I said. "How are you, Marianne?"

"I'm all right," she replied, smiling at me in a way that set my pulses to racing. "How have you been?"

"Pretty good." I nodded, looking down at the menu so she couldn't see what was going on in my mind.

"If you will excuse me," Gerro said, standing up, "I'll be back in a minute. Order some tomato juice to start for me." He walked toward the men's room.

I spent an awkward moment looking at the menu.

"What's the matter, Frank?" Marianne asked with a smile. "Surprised that I came?"

I nodded. "A little."

"Well," she said, "don't let it bother you. I was just curious to see what you looked like in the daylight."

I looked out the window of the restaurant. It was dark. It had been dark over an hour.

She followed my gaze and laughed. "You don't believe me then?"

"No," I said succinctly.

She laughed again. "Frank, I think you're afraid of me—that you think I'm a wicked woman."

"I told you before," I said, "who you are and what you are doesn't interest me. I'm Gerro's friend."

"*Touché!*" she said, then leaned forward earnestly. "Frank, it's possible for a woman to be in love with two men at once.

Gerro is wonderful—he's sweet and kind and everything a
woman should want in a man. I wish we were married, and I
mean it. But you're different. You're wicked, selfish, dishonest.
I can see it in your face. You seem to want everything that
someone else possesses. But you attract me. I want to take you
apart and find out what makes you tick. But you're elusive. I
knew you wouldn't come down to see me, so I talked Gerro
into taking me along. I had to see you again. I had to know how
you felt about me. And now I know. I can see that in your face
too, under that mask you keep in place."

"Well then," I spoke quietly, "maybe you can also see that
you're Gerro's girl, and that he has a hard enough job to do
without my messing up his personal life. For years the thought
of you has kept Gerro alive. I'm not going to take that away
from him."

She looked down at her plate and bit her lip. I could see the
color pour into her face. She blushed very easily. She started to
answer, but Gerro came back to the table and we dropped the
conversation.

When I left them after supper I walked slowly uptown. "If it
weren't for Gerro," I thought, "I'd—" Resolutely I put the
thought from my mind and went back to the hotel.

Chapter Seven

APRIL came, and with it the first soft touch of spring. Spring in
New York! It kind of did something to you. It wasn't anything
like spring was supposed to be. It was the first onslaught of the
dull, hot days to come. It was the first sign of hot, uncomfortable summer. I went through the days automatically—one
day after another, the same thing every day. I didn't know
whether I was happy, but I knew that I was content in some
strange, unsatisfied fashion. There were other things I longed
for, but I never could define those feelings even to myself.

One evening Gerro asked if I could come down to Union

Square on May Day. He was scheduled to make a speech there and he wanted me to hear it. I didn't know whether I could go because May Day fell on a Monday. I told him I'd ask Harry if I could have a few hours off that afternoon. If I could get the time off, I would come.

I hadn't seen Marianne since that last meeting in March. I vaguely wondered if she would be there. I don't know whether that was the factor that finally influenced me to go to the May Day affair. But I know it must have played some part in my decision because I didn't care for speeches.

Anyway, Monday, May 1st, I got time off to go. There was a big crowd down at the square, and they had erected a temporary platform for the speakers. Men were going around handing out slips of paper on which was printed the program for the day. I looked over the list and I saw Gerro was the fourth speaker. His subject, as announced by the program, was: "Equality—A Birthright."

I pushed my way down to the front of the crowd. A man was talking. I didn't know who he was, I didn't care. I was trying to locate Gerro. At last I saw him. He was sitting up there on the platform with some other men, all plainly awaiting their turn to speak. I waved to him.

His eyes, which had been wandering restlessly over the crowd, came to rest upon me. He grinned and nodded his head to show that he saw me. I waved again. I began to look over the crowd to see if I could locate Marianne. She wasn't there.

A hand tugged at my sleeve. I turned around. It was Terry. "Hello," I said, smiling. "I didn't expect to see you here."

She smiled back when she heard me speak to her. "I came down to hear Gerro," she said. "I'm with my folks."

"That's good," I said awkwardly, not knowing what else to say. "How have you been?" It was a stupid question because I saw her almost every day in the store. But there was a feeling of strangeness between us, and we didn't talk very much.

"I'm O. K.," she said. "Nice crowd, isn't it?"

"Yes," I replied, looking around again for Marianne, "big crowd."

We were silent a few minutes: we didn't know what to talk about. Finally she said: "I'll have to get back to my folks."

"Yes," I agreed brightly, "I guess so."

"So long," I said. I turned back to looking over the crowd but didn't see Marianne. I looked at the speakers' stand, and saw Gerro get up and move toward the steps. I walked over there.

I shook hands with him. "Hi, ya, boy!"

He grinned at me. "I was glad you came down. I was nervous as hell until I saw you. This is the first time I've made a speech to so big a crowd, but when I saw you I felt better. I knew everything would be all right. I always like to talk to someone in the crowd I know. It takes your mind off the other people."

"Then I'm glad I came," I grinned. I looked around and asked him casually: "Did Marianne come down?"

"No," he shook his head, "she can't stand big crowds like this."

I concealed my disappointment. We spoke a few minutes, and then he went back on the stand. I stood around waiting for his turn to come. There would be two more speakers before he appeared.

There were all kinds of people there—poor of every race, every color, every creed, dressed in their Sunday best. Poverty wasn't exclusive. You didn't have to be born here to be broke. Around the edges of the crowd were mounted policemen to keep order. They were astride beautiful reddish-brown horses, and gripped clubs firmly in their free hand. They looked ready for trouble.

I looked back at the speakers' stand. The first man had finished and another was speaking now. I felt warm, so I went back to the edge of the crowd and bought a bottle of Coke. Then I pushed my way through the crowd again to the front. Gerro was now sitting in the front row on the end nearest the steps. I edged closer to the platform. I had finished the Coke. Now I looked around for a place to put the bottle down, but couldn't find any so I stood there holding it in my hand.

The first I saw of the fight was a surge of the crowd toward the steps of the speakers' stand. Then I heard some people hollering: "Fight! Fight!" Gerro got up from his chair and looked over the railing. I moved over to where I could see better what was going on, and I saw a few men fighting. I looked up at Gerro and saw he had started down the platform steps into the crowd. From the other side I saw a cop come riding into the crowd, the people melting away before his horse.

Things happened quickly after that. Gerro leaped in between two of the fighters and was trying to hold them apart. The cop came riding up, swinging his club at the fighters. He was shouting at them, but I couldn't hear what he was saying because of the noise the crowd was making. I saw Gerro jump up and try to grab the cop's club arm. I knew he was trying to stop the cop from hitting anyone, just trying to hold the club arm. The cop wheeled his horse viciously and broke his arm loose from Gerro's grip. Then he brought his club down twice, once on each side of Gerro's head. I saw Gerro slip crazily along the side of the horse, trying to keep himself up by holding on to it. He was near its rump when the cop turned the horse toward the crowd. The horse in turning kicked Gerro in the chest. Gerro fell in back of the horse, and the crowd pressed toward the cop. The horse backed up. I could see its rear hoofs step on Gerro, who was writhing there on the ground.

I tried to push through the crowd to get to him, but there were too many people in front of me. "Why don't they get him out of the way? He'll be killed!" I heard myself screaming.

The cop didn't seem to know Gerro was under the horse's feet. He was swinging his club around at anyone trying to get near him. I picked up my hands in helpless rage and suddenly realized I still held the bottle in my hand. The next thing I knew I had thrown the bottle. It spun crazily over and over in the air and hit the cop on the side of the face. He swayed dizzily in the saddle a moment. Suddenly blood poured from his nose and mouth, and he slipped out of his seat and fell to the ground. I could hear the whistles of the other cops tooting shrilly as they came riding toward the scene.

I looked around wildly a moment before I realized I had better get out of there quickly. My gaze fell on Terry. She was looking at me through fear-widened eyes, her hand to her mouth. I turned and plunged back into the crowd. If the cops ever picked me up and found out I was the guy who had thrown the bottle, I'd get the beating of my life.

I got to the subway entrance breathing hard, and turned to look back. The crowd was still milling around. I couldn't do any more for Gerro by hanging around, so I decided to go back to the store until I heard from him.

It was a few minutes before three o'clock when I walked into the store. I had taken a few minutes to go into a bar and get a drink before I went back. Then I had some black coffee, and I could feel my nerves ease off. I went in calmly, put on my apron, and went to work. I felt glad that Harry was too busy to ask any questions about the speech.

The next two hours dragged by. I was waiting for the phone to ring. I don't know why I expected to hear from Gerro, but I thought he would call if he was able to. About six o'clock it rang. Harry answered it and called me over.

"Hello," I said.

"Frankie," I heard her voice crackle excitedly, "this is Terry. You'd better beat it. The cops are after you."

"Wait a minute," I cut in, "how do they know? You were the only one down there that saw me."

"There were others, Frankie," her voice came back nervously. "There were some people from the club, and they saw you. The cops were questioning everybody, and any minute now they might find out who you are. That cop's in the hospital and he might die. If he does . . ." Her voice trailed off.

I didn't want to think about that either. "Do you—do you know how Gerro is?" I stammered.

"Didn't you know?" she asked. She began to cry. "He's dead. The horse crushed him."

I stood there a minute. The store seemed to whirl around. I got hold of myself. "Are you still there?" I heard her ask wildly.

I forced myself to answer: "Yes, I'm here."

"You better hurry," she said. "There isn't much time."

"Yeah," I said. "Thanks." I hung up the phone and stood there.

I don't know how long I stood there before I could rouse myself to go over to Harry and say: "I'm quitting."

He was slicing some cheese on the machine, and was so surprised he almost cut off his finger. "Why?" he asked. "What's wrong?"

"I'm in a jam," I said simply. "There was a fight down there at the meeting. And I gotta beat it."

"Oh!" he said. "That bad, hunh? I told you to stay away from those bastards, that they'd get you in trouble."

"That don't do any good now," I said. "And besides, it wasn't their fault."

He finished slicing the cheese and wrapped it up and gave it to the customer who was standing in the front of the store and couldn't hear me. Then he came back to me.

"I'm sorry, Harry," I said. "I didn't mean to quit like that and leave you stuck, but I can't help it. You've been very decent to me, and I want you to know I appreciate it. Will you tell Mr. Rayzeus that for me too?"

He nodded, and I went in the back room and took off my apron. I hung it on a nail on the wall and came back into the store. I went over to him and held out my hand. "Thanks for everything, Harry."

He shook hands with me. "I'm sorry to have you leave, kid. You were a good boy, and I liked you."

"I'm sorry too," I said, turning toward the door.

"Wait a minute," he said. "You forgot something."

I turned toward him. He held out his hand. "Your pay," he said simply.

"But," I said, "this is only Monday."

"Take it," he said. "You earned an extra week's pay many times over."

I took the money and shoved it in my pocket. "Thanks," I said, "I can use it." I could. I had only a little over a hundred bucks saved up in the box in my room at the hotel. You couldn't save any dough on the money I made.

"It's O. K., kid," he said, coming over to the door with me. "I hope everything turns out all right."

I held up crossed fingers to him. He grinned and held up his hand to me. He crossed his fingers too. I stepped out into the street. I looked up and down the avenue; it was quiet as usual. I hopped into the subway and went down to the hotel. There I packed everything I had into the small secondhand valise I bought some time ago and checked out. I was about to go over to the railroad station when a thought struck me.

Marianne! Who would tell her? I hoped not a stranger, someone who didn't know of their feeling toward each other. I hoped she wouldn't read it in the newspaper, printed there coldly for the information of anyone who was mildly interested. With each step I took, I began to realize that I would have to tell her. But I didn't know I would until I stood in her doorway, valise in hand, ringing her bell.

I hoped she was home. She was. I could hear her quick footsteps coming to the door. She opened it and saw me. She looked puzzled for a moment when she saw my suitcase. I stepped in without waiting for her to ask me.

She closed the door and looked at me. "Going away, Frank?"

"Yes," I said, "but first I have something to tell you." My face was serious.

She couldn't know what I was talking about, so she misunderstood what I was going to say. She came up close to me, and her face had a soft look on it. With surprise I saw that her eyes were gray, not brown as I thought, but a dark, smoky gray. "What do you have to tell me?" she asked softly. "What is it that you couldn't go away without telling me?"

I put the valise down and gripped her by the shoulders. Savagely, I thought she would understand quick enough.

"Frank, you're hurting me," she said.

I loosened my grip. The savageness I felt disappeared. "You'd better sit down," I said more gently.

"No, I won't," she said, her eyes beginning to widen in fear. "What is it?"

"Gerro is dead," I said bluntly.

For a moment she looked at me uncomprehendingly, then her face went pale and her eyes rolled up. I caught her as she slumped toward me. I picked her up and carried her into the bedroom and placed her on the bed. I went into the other room and got a glass of water and came back with it. She was beginning to stir. I held the water to her lips. A few drops trickled down her throat. I loosened her blouse and sat there waiting for her to come to.

Her eyes fluttered open. "I didn't want you to find out from someone else," I said gently. "I thought it would be better if I told you, but I'm afraid I messed it up."

She shook her head weakly. "How—how did it happen?"

"There was a fight down there at the square. A cop hit him and he fell under the cop's horse. I threw a Coke bottle at the cop and the cop's in the hospital and I have to beat it."

"But Gerro—," she said faintly, "was there—any pain?"

"No," I said as gently as I could, "it all happened too quickly. He couldn't have felt anything." I didn't know whether he had or not, but it didn't make any difference to him now and it was better for her if she thought that was the way.

She sat up in bed. "I'm glad it happened that way," she whispered, "quick—if it had to happen. He couldn't stand any pain." She covered her face with her hands and began to cry.

I let her cry for a few minutes. Then I got up. The longer I stood here, the more dangerous it became for me. I couldn't stay around much longer. She stopped crying and looked up at me.

"You were his friend," she said. "He was so proud that you had fought for him. He told me so many times. And you fought for him even at the last."

I didn't know what to say to that. You just couldn't say nonchalantly: "It was nothing. I was glad to do it." A thing like that just happened, and no matter what you did, you couldn't stop it.

"I'm sorry," I said. "You don't know how sorry. He was a swell guy."

"There will never be another like him," she said.

We were silent a minute, then I went into the other room. "If you think you are all right," I said, "I'll be going."

"I'm all right, I can manage," she said dully.

"Good-by," I said from the bedroom door.

"Good-by," she answered.

I turned and started for the apartment door. I heard footsteps run behind me. I turned. Marianne ran into my arms.

I held her close to me, her cheek to mine, her tears against my face. I ran my fingers through her hair. "Marianne."

Her lips were close to my ear. "Be careful, please. And come back. I'll need you now that . . ."

I didn't let her finish what she was about to say. "I'll come back," I whispered huskily. "When the summer's gone and this thing is forgotten, I'll come back."

"Promise?" she said like a little child.

"Promise!" I answered looking into her eyes. They were wet with tears—and were violet, not gray as I thought. "Stay here and wait. I'll be back." I let her go without kissing her.

"Be careful, darling," she said as I closed the door behind me.

It was dark in the street, and I thought it would be too dangerous to go to the railroad station. If the cops had found out who threw that bottle, they would be looking for me there. My best bet would be a hitch across the ferry to New Jersey.

She had called me darling! For a moment I felt a twinge of conscience as I thought of Gerro. Then I realized he was gone and that these things didn't matter to him now. And besides, I had done my best. I had never gone near her while he was around. Darling!

I got a ride across the ferry easily. A truckman going to

Newark gave me a lift. At the Newark station I bought a ticket to Atlantic City. It was a summer resort and the best spot to get a job, if there were any.

I looked wryly around the station while I was waiting for my train to come in. I was on the same old merry-go-round again. I wondered if I would ever catch the brass ring. Then I chuckled to myself.

"Darling," she had said. For the first time in my life I was really in love.

Chapter Eight

I GOT a job two hours after I reached Atlantic City. Jobs were still plentiful: it was the beginning of the season. I got a job at a soda fountain on the boardwalk. I was to work nights, coming in at three in the afternoon, leaving at one in the morning. The salary was twenty bucks a week and meals, seven days a week and would last only until September. That was all right with me; I had some place to go when the summer was over.

After I got the job I took a room at a cheap hotel for eight dollars a week. The hotel was only a few blocks from work. After a few days of breaking in at the fountain I was all right; the work I had done at Otto's had paid off. I was a fair soda clerk. After a while I became a good one because I learned to move with a certain economy of motion that made for quicker service and faster sales and was less tiring for me.

I generally would spend my days on the beach until it was almost time to go to work. Then I would go back to the hotel and dress and go to work. I ate lunch at the fountain, worked until closing time, and then went to the hotel to sleep.

The summer went by slowly. I worked hard but felt good. The days at the beach had turned me a dark brown, and I put on a little weight. I didn't bother very much with friends, either men or women. I didn't feel any need for them. For the while I was very content just to be alone. There were plenty of girls I

could have gone out with—girls that I met on the beach or at
the fountain—but I didn't bother.

I would get the New York papers, morning and afternoon,
but beyond the original mention of the fracas and the fact that
the cop was in the hospital, there was never another word
about it that I could find. I wasn't taking any chances however.
I didn't write or call Marianne for fear the cops would be
watching her for some clue as to Gerro's background. I just
bided my time and waited for the season to pass.

I did a lot of thinking that summer too. I thought about
myself, my aunt and uncle, Marianne. I wondered what there
was between Marianne and me that made us the way we were.
What was there inside each of us that would allow so quick a
change-over in our feelings, almost as soon as Gerro had left
the scene? The only explanation I could find was one for myself—that I was a realist; that what had happened was done,
and nothing I could do would change the fact; that I was an
opportunist; that I saw what I wanted and when the chance
came, I took it, regardless of my previous sentiment about the
matter; that I wanted Marianne—that she had an attraction no
other woman had ever had for me, something that vaguely
eluded me, something I wanted to pin down and secure for
myself; that I was in love with her—which seemed like a vague,
silly and futile explanation to me, one which I accepted only in
part and rejected in the light of reason.

But I wouldn't know how Marianne felt until I would see her
again.

July passed, and August was drawing to a close. I had about
three more weeks to work, and then I would go back to New
York. Everything seemed safe: there hadn't been the furor
made over the fight in the square that I thought would be. I was
ready to go back to New York as soon as the job folded.

It was the last Wednesday in August. I was lying on the sand,
one arm thrown over my face to shield my eyes. I was half
asleep, drowsing in the sun, when suddenly I became wide
awake. What if Marianne wasn't waiting? I got up and went to
a telephone and put a call through to her.

It was about eleven o'clock in the morning. I wondered if she
would be at home. I began to feel silly and, was about to hang
up when a voice answered: "Hello." It was clear, warm, musi-
cal.

I almost stuttered in my eagerness to speak. "M— Marianne?"

"Frank!" she cried out in surprise. "Oh, darling! Where are you? I was beginning to think you would never return."

I was happy over the feeling I could hear in her voice. "I'm in Atlantic City. I've been working here. I had to call and find out how you were."

"I'm all right," she answered. "Are you all right?"

"Just fine," I replied.

"When are you coming back?" she asked.

"In about three weeks," I told her, "when my job here is finished."

"Can't you make it sooner?" she asked. "I want to see you. There are so many things . . ." She left the sentence unfinished.

"I'd like to," I said, "but I can't. I promised to stay here until the close of the season." I changed the subject. "Is everything all right there?"

She knew what I referred to. "Everything's normal around here," she replied. "Darling, can't I go down there to see you? We could spend a few days together. I don't want to wait here any more."

"I don't know," I said hesitantly. "I work from three in the afternoon until one in the morning, and we wouldn't have much time together."

"We'll be able to squeeze out a few minutes, and I need the rest. I've been working very hard the last few months. There were a lot of things I had to straighten out in my own mind."

"You too?" I smiled into the telephone. "I've done a lot of thinking about us the last few weeks."

"You see?" she said. "I've got to see you. I've got to know if you feel as I do. I'm going to go down there. Where are you staying?"

I told her.

"I'll drive down there tonight," she said. "I'll leave in a few hours as soon as I pack a few things."

"I'll be at work until one," I said. "Maybe you'd better come to the fountain. It's on the boardwalk in the Victoria Hotel."

"I'll be there tonight," she told me.

"O. K.," I said, "I'll see you then. So long."

"Darling, I love you," she said.

For a moment I was still, the words ringing around in my ears. "Marianne," I said, "Marianne."

"Yes," she said softly. "Do you love me, Frank?"

"You know I do," I said.

"I knew it," she whispered. "From the moment I first saw you in my room, from the first kiss, I knew it. It wasn't fair. It was wicked. But I knew it, and you knew it, and there was nothing we could do about it." She seemed to sigh through the phone. "I'll see you tonight, darling. Good-by."

"Good-by," I said. I hung up and went back to the beach.

At twelve o'clock midnight, by the time I had started to clean up the fountain, she still hadn't arrived. I had given her up, thinking she would be down in the morning. Charlie the boss was working the far end of the fountain, and I was cleaning the end nearest the door. I was washing the syrup pumps, and we were talking. There weren't any customers in the place.

Charlie had kidded me several times in the past about not going out with any of the dames here, and I never bothered to explain to him. Business after this week would begin to drop off. Labor Day weekend was the high point of the year. He had a place in Miami Beach where he planned to go when he had closed up here. His partner ran that in the summer while he ran this one.

I finished with the pumps, stacked all the glasses neatly on the shelf, and glanced up at the clock. It was twelve thirty.

"Want to get off early, Frank?" He grinned. "Got something lined up?"

I shook my head.

One o'clock came and we closed up. I waited a few minutes outside the store for her to show up, but she wasn't there. I walked over to the edge of the boardwalk, sat down on one of the benches, and lit a cigarette. I guessed she couldn't make it. The boardwalk was nearly empty; only a few people were out walking. I looked out at the ocean. A ship was way out there, its lights blazing gaily across the water. It looked like a Mallory boat going to Florida. Maybe she was only talking, I thought. Maybe she won't come down at all.

A pair of hands covered my eyes. A soft voice whispered in my ear: "Guess who?"

I knew who it was; I could feel it. It was a sort of knowing, an awareness of person. I played the game. "Jane?" I said.

"No," Marianne answered.

"Helen? Mary? Edna?" I began to laugh.

"I'll give you one more guess," Marianne said. "If you're not right I'm going home. Maybe I shouldn't have come down in the first place. You seem pretty well occupied."

I reached up and took her hands down from my eyes, kissed her open palms, and then rubbed them along my cheek. I turned and drew her around the bench and down beside me. "Marianne," I said, "I thought you'd never come!"

She smiled, her white teeth beautifully even, her soft, reddish hair shining in the moonlight. "I couldn't stay away once I knew where you were, darling, even if I had wanted to."

I kissed her. It was soft, tender, warm and passionate, all at once. It was as if the moon and all the stars had come down and started to whirl me around from one to the other. It was like floating on air, like walking on clouds. I was a little boy again and a man full-grown and complete all thrown into one. I was gay and there was a little catch in my throat and I couldn't speak.

I looked into her eyes, and they were soft and swimming in tears. I held her close to me and felt the pounding of her heart against me. I kissed her again. It was like magic, with the world fading away from eyes, its sound fading from ears. That soaring ecstatic feeling!

"See what I meant when I spoke over the phone?" she whispered. "It's us, our feelings—they're one and the same. You can't escape it by running away. Gerro told me a lot about you. I know you ran away from a home. I thought you might do that again and run away from me. But now I know. You can't run away any more."

"Marianne, I love you. You're all the things the world has ever offered. You're everything in everything to me. Marianne, I love you."

She put her head on my shoulder. "I wanted you to say it. I love you. I love you. I love you."

We arose from the bench and began to walk down the board-walk. We went down on the sand and spoke about a million things and then we walked and talked. And as we walked and talked, we had our arms about each other's waist, or our hands would touch and glances meet.

And later when the moon was far in the sky to the west, and we stood near the window of my room and looked out at the sea and smoked a cigarette, I suddenly realized that time had caught up with me. I had made love this night, and the difference was in giving, not taking.

And in the early dawn when I suddenly awoke, aware of her
sleeping at my side, I was overcome with wonder that I could
possess all this beauty and passion. She must have felt my gaze
for she half awoke and putting her arm around me, whispered:
"Don't ever leave me, Frank. Never!"

"I'll never leave you, Marianne," I answered, sure of myself
for all of time.

Chapter Nine

WE WENT swimming the next morning. She had a beautiful
new bathing suit, and she looked good enough to eat. She was
the kind of girl that looked as well in little or no clothes as she
did when fully dressed. She had a slim, rounded figure and long,
well-shaped legs. She was graceful of movement and had a
quick, alert look about her. She looked wonderfully and vividly
alive, and I was proud to be with her. I could see the looks that
men gave her, and boy! I felt good as I thought of their envy.

And she knew how she looked. She knew she was dynamite
in a white bathing suit. She fished artfully and shamelessly for
compliments, and would smile at me happily when I told her
how beautiful I thought she was.

After swimming we lolled around the beach and lay on the
sand and laughed and were happy. The feeling of completeness
that I felt when I was with her was something I had never
known before, and I gave myself up to it completely.

About noon I bought some hot dogs and brought them out
on the sand to eat. While we were eating I asked her about New
York. It was the same old town she said. About herself—she
had just completed two commissions and was so exhausted. I
had just called at the right time because she didn't know what
she was going to do next. She was so glad to be here, so glad to
be with me, so glad just to be alive.

I took her hand and we lay back quietly. After a while I
asked her if she had gone to Gerro's funeral.

She answered slowly: "No."

"Why?" I asked.

She spoke quietly, candidly. "Because I'm a coward. Because I couldn't bear to see what was being done to him. Because I didn't want to think of him gone and me still alive and enjoying life. Because of you, and the way I felt about the two of you. I loved you both and didn't know who I wanted most. Because I loved you for one set of reasons and him for another. Because you two were so far apart and yet so close together. I couldn't bear to go."

"He was a great guy," I said. "It's too bad he had to go. There aren't enough people like him."

She looked at me strangely. "Do you really mean that, Frank? Honestly, deep inside of you, aren't you a little bit glad over what happened?—secretly I mean, for if it never happened, there wouldn't have been . . . us."

I never thought of it in just that way. Maybe she was right. If she was, that was why I had gone to see her before I left town and not for what I thought was the reason. I felt a little confused. I looked at her. She was stretched out on the sand, lying on her back, her hair glowing like fire around her head, her firm, rounded breasts swelling against her suit, her little stomach flat and melting into the softness of her hips and thighs. I looked at her and wanted her, and then I began to understand my feelings.

I spoke rather slowly; I wanted to think out clearly what I said and say it articulately and definitively. "No. That's not what I feel. I am what I am. I want what I want. But I want it for myself and not at the expense of other people, no matter how much I want something. I feel that you and I were going to be what we are now. The fact that circumstance made it possible doesn't alter the fact that I still am sorry about Gerro. You and I would have found a way, even if Gerro were still here."

She looked at me wickedly. "Not from the way you were acting. Not from the way you avoided me. It never would have happened, and look what you would have missed!" She gave a small wave of her hand. "All this. And you and I. Perfection and rhythm and harmony and happiness. Some people were just made for one another, physically and mentally and (she laughed a little) morally. You and I, we're cut from the same die. We're predatory, we're selfish, we're spoiled. I don't mean in the sense that you got everything you ever wanted merely for the asking in the same manner I did. But in your own cute way you are spoiled, in the way you have had only yourself to consider and so always aimed directly for what you wanted. You know we're wicked, don't you? You know what we're doing is considered wrong by most people. And yet you don't care. You go right ahead and do it anyway. You're an animal: you walk like one, you act like one, you think like one—in terms of black and white. There are no intermediate shadings for you. And that's what I love about you. You're an odd contradictory mixture, and I love every crazy little facet of your personality. Plus which you're not too hard to look at with that gorgeous tan. I just bet the girls couldn't leave you alone."

I laughed at that last remark. Not many of them had bothered with me. "I had to fight them off every minute," I said. "They just wouldn't leave me alone."

"You're mean," she said, rolling over against me.

I put my arm around her and kissed her.

"Nice work if you can get it," I heard a voice exclaim. I looked up and saw my boss Charlie. He had just come in from the water and was dripping wet and looking down at us. I grinned up at him.

"Hi! Charlie," I said.

"Hi! Frank," he retorted, sitting himself down beside us.

I had to introduce them. I was a little sore because he had run into us, but there was nothing I could do about it. This was a public beach.

"Marianne, this is Charlie," I said.

They said hello. Marianne was smart. The minute I explained he was my boss she went to work on him.

"I don't know why Frank has to finish off the season if things slow down after the holiday," she said to him. "He ought to take a few weeks off to rest before he goes back to New York."

Charlie looked at me cagily. "It's up to Frank," he said. "He can do what he wants after Monday."

That was the fastest swindle I ever got into, I thought, looking at Marianne with a new respect. She certainly knows what she wants, and she doesn't want me to work while she's down here.

"We'll talk about it later," I said, putting off the answer and getting to my feet. "Come on, darling, I've got to go and get dressed. It's almost time to be at work and the boss'll be sore if I'm late."

I pulled Marianne to her feet, and Charlie got up. He was grinning; he could see the game between us. "See you later," he said, walking off.

When I came out of the shower she was already dressed and combing her hair in front of the dresser mirror. I had the towel wrapped around my middle, and walked across the room toward her. "What's the idea pulling that stuff on Charlie?" I demanded, half smiling.

She turned to me and grinned mischievously. "I told you I was selfish, didn't I? Well, I don't want you away working all day when the weather is so beautiful, and you could really rest yourself and be with me."

"You're a witch!" I laughed. "But you forget, if I don't work I don't eat. We all haven't got rich folks to support us."

"You don't have to worry about that." She smiled. "I've got more money than I know what to do with. Why don't you quit? We could move out of this dump and over to the Towers and really have a wonderful time."

I looked at her quizzically. "Just like that!"

"Just like that!" she answered, coming close to me. "Darling, there are so many things I want to do for you. I want to see you in the right clothes; yours are something terrible. You have a fine figure, and in the right sort of things, you'd be a knockout. And I'd like to teach you the proper way to eat; you wolf everything down as if someone were going to snatch it away from you. I want to make you over and not change you a bit. I'm a perfectionist and I'm crazy about you."

"So you want to change me and support me!" I said. "That's bad. Just what are your intentions, madam?"

She grinned at me and pulled the towel off my waist. "Guess!" she said, coming into my arms.

Later in the store when the evening rush had died down, Charlie asked me who the dame was.

"My girl," I said. "She came down from the city to spend a few days with me."

He whistled. "She's O. K. She must have a bad case on you. With a doll like that no wonder you never chased the chippies around here. I was beginning to wonder if you were sick or something."

I didn't answer.

"You going to knock off like she wants?" he asked.

"I don't know," I said hesitantly. "I haven't made up my mind yet." But that was so much crap; I knew she had me jumping through the hoop right this minute, and that if she said quit, I'd quit.

And that's just what I did—Monday night.

Chapter Ten

WE SPENT three weeks in Atlantic City. We moved to the Towers Hotel and took a suite of three rooms on the thirteenth floor, with a terrace overlooking the ocean. We had our meals sent up to us by room service; Marianne had an aversion to hotel restaurants, or so she said. It cost her plenty; I don't know how much because she paid each bill promptly in cash from a seemingly inexhaustible supply of money she carried around with her.

I bought her a little sterling-silver novelty bracelet at one of the souvenir shops that lined the boardwalk. It cost eleven dollars, and I had it inscribed: "To Marianne, with love, Frank." I gave it to her one morning about three o'clock. We were on the terrace, getting the cool breeze from the ocean. She was wearing a light, flimsy negligee, and I had on a pair of shorts and was smoking a cigarette. I had just remembered my gift and had been looking for an opportunity to give it to her. So I had gone inside and brought it out.

I felt rather funny as I gave it to her. I hadn't given very many gifts before, and I didn't know just what to say as I handed it to her. "This is for you, Marianne," I said awkwardly, holding it out toward her.

She seemed surprised and took it with a little gleeful sound. "Frank, it's lovely," she said, reading the inscription aloud, "To Marianne, with love, Frank." She looked up at me and smiled. "It's sweet—and an original saying too."

I thought I could detect a faint note of sarcasm in her voice and I felt a little hurt. I spoke quietly. "It is original. I've never said and meant anything like that before."

She reacted quickly to the sound in my voice. "Oh, darling, I didn't mean it that way. I didn't mean to hurt you. I'm sorry. I do love it and I'll wear it always. Please put it on." She held out her arm.

I took the bracelet and fastened it on her wrist. She had a ring on her small finger; it had a diamond offset with two small rubies. It sparkled in the moonlight, and I felt funny as I fastened it awkwardly on her wrist. It looked so cheap in comparison with the daintily simple expensiveness of the ring. I cursed myself for buying it. It only accentuated the difference between us. When I got back to town, I promised myself, I would make some real dough and get her something that wouldn't suffer by comparison with what she already had.

We went back to New York September 20th. I moved into her apartment, and after settling down for a few days, decided to go out and look for a job. Jobs were still hard to get, and I didn't have very much luck the first few days.

She, meanwhile, was very busy. She had several jobs to do, and was in a constant state of energy and work and effervescence. When she was working she was an entirely different person. She would give me some money and chase me out of the house, telling me to go to a movie or some place and not to come back until later. At first it was all new to me. The queen could do no wrong. I loved to watch her paint; she had such a curious air of concentration about her. Her head and eyes and body would appear tense and pointed toward her work. If I spoke to her she would answer in monosyllables or not at all, and very often woud go about the studio as if I weren't there. When she actually was painting, she would dab furiously at the painting and mutter curses under her breath if some effect was particularly difficult to get, and blotches of paint would appear on her face and forehead from her hands as she lifted them to brush away her hair from her eyes.

But if a day went well and she was satisfied with her painting, she would appear at night sweet and loving with a sort of childish gaiety. She would joke, and we would drink champagne and I would make her some nice things to eat. I did most of the cooking, for she said she was a horrible cook and never could eat anything she herself prepared. And occasionally some of her friends would come in to visit—artists like herself, writers, men and women of a varying intellectual capacity that seemed to live in a world of their own. When I was introduced to them, they would look at me politely and inquire what I did. When they found out I was not one of them, so to speak, they would politely turn from me and ignore me and exclude me from their small talk, unless they wanted another drink, and then they would call me as if I were a servant.

But I was hopelessly, madly, crazily, in love. The queen could do no wrong. The queen took me out shopping with her and spent about three hundred dollars on me for new clothes. I had suits and coats and shirts made to order. I wore underwear of an unaccustomed luxury and had silk pajamas. At first, I tried to get a job, and when there was a chance of getting one and I had come home all excited and told Marianne about it; she frowned and asked: "How much does it pay?"

"Nineteen a week," I told her confidently.

"Only nineteen dollars!" she cried out, flinging her hands into the air dramatically. "What on earth would you do with that kind of money? It wouldn't even be enough to keep you in cigarettes."

"It's a job," I said stubbornly. "It's better than nothing."

"It's worse than nothing," she retorted emphatically. "It's an insult to your intelligence, to your brains, to your ability to do things. You're worth much more than that. Besides, darling, why work for that kind of money when you don't have to? I can give you twice that each week if you want it."

I began to lose my temper. "But I can't go on like this all the time. It just isn't right that's all. And besides I feel funny asking you for money all the time," I ended up rather weakly.

"You don't have to feel funny about it, darling." She came over and kissed me. "If you had the money and I didn't, I wouldn't feel funny about taking it from you."

"But that's different," I protested.

"No, it isn't," she said. "We're in love, and everything we have is to share between us "

There was no arguing with her about it when she made up her mind to be sweet. And that was the way it went for a while. It was easy living, and I liked easy living. I had had too much of the other kind, and besides I felt that sooner or later I would get a break and get a decent job. So I let it ride.

About a month later as I came over to the small table where I kept my cigarettes for a smoke—it was the table where

Gerro's picture had stood—I looked down and saw that Gerro's portrait had gone. It was replaced with one of me. I looked at it. It was all right, I guess. I didn't know very much about those things. Somehow in looking at it, I felt it didn't seem as if it were me. I was too relaxed, too casual, too at ease. I had a vague feeling it was wrong.

"Like it, darling?" I heard Marianne's voice behind me.

I turned to her. "It's very nice," I said politely.

"It's for you—a present; for being what you are: wonderful, and making me happy." She came over and kissed me.

"Thanks," I said.

"Don't thank me," she answered. "I wanted to do it. The hard job was getting it done so you wouldn't know I was doing it. I had to paint you at the oddest moments."

"I guess so," I said.

"You don't sound happy?" she asked, concern in her voice. "What's wrong?"

"Where's Gerro's picture?" I asked.

"Oh that!" she said, turning and sitting down in a chair. "The agent saw it and said he could get a good price for it, so I gave it to him to sell."

"Get it back," I told her. "I want it."

She looked at me, her eyes widening. "What on earth for?"

"I just want it," I said. "Get it back." I didn't know myself why I wanted it.

She was beginning to get angry. "Give me one good reason and I'll do it," she said heatedly. "But why the devil you should want it is more than I can see!"

I turned to my portrait and picked it up, "This is a very nice portrait. But that's all it is—a very nice flattering portrait. It tells you nothing. It's my exterior, my outside. Maybe there isn't anything to me inside to put on canvas, but there was in Gerro. You caught it in him. And if you couldn't face what you caught in that painting, and tried to replace it with this soporific thing of me, you're mistaken. You just don't bury things like that. And if you don't want it, I do."

She stood up suddenly, violently. Her chest was heaving. I could tell from the way she acted that, as little as I knew about painting, I had hit the nail on the head. "I won't get it back." Her voice was loud, and she shouted: "Who do you think you're telling what to do? You're in no position to be giving orders."

I took the small frame off my painting. Slowly I began to tear it into small strips. "Stop shouting like a fishwife," I said to her quietly, though I was boiling inside.

She came at me when she saw I had torn the painting; her hands were small fists, striking and scratching at my face, she was screaming, shouting, crying all at once. "You ignorant fool! Because I cater to you and play up to you, you think you own me. Why I've a mind to throw you back in the gutter where I found you!"

Suddenly something exploded inside me. I hit her across the side of the face with my hand. She fell back across the couch, and looked up at me.

I towered over her, my voice was as cold as ice. "You get that portrait of Gerro back, or I'll beat you within an inch of your life!"

Suddenly the expression on her face changed; it became soft and her eyes grew smoky in color. "You'd do it too!" she said, her voice familiarly husky. "I believe you really mean it."

"I mean it," I said easily. "I want that portrait."

She put her arms around me and drew me down beside her. "My lover, my strong, wicked, simple darling, of course you shall have it back. I'll give you anything you want."

She kissed me, and her lips were burning flames that turned the world all upside down for me. But the next morning Gerro's picture was back on the table.

Chapter Eleven

IT WAS while I was sitting in the big easy chair in the corner of the room, smoking the pipe Marianne had given me, that I made up my mind. I took the pipe from my mouth and looked at it distastefully. Some of the bitter soup from its bowl had come back into my mouth. I don't know why I smoked the damned thing anyway. I didn't like it. I would never like it.

But Marianne had said: "Darling, why don't you smoke a pipe?"

And I had answered: "I don't know. I never tried one."

"There's something about a pipe that's so manly," she smiled. "It has a definitely masculine touch to it. It's one thing no woman would smoke. Would you like one?"

"No," I said, "I don't think so. I'll stick to Camels."

But the next day she went out and bought me not one but a set of four matched pipes and a humidor and rack. She also bought some specially blended aromatic tobacco to go with it, and made quite a ceremony over giving it to me. She couldn't wait until I had filled it with tobacco and put it in my mouth.

"Let me light it for you," she said, standing over my chair, her head tilted charmingly to one side, a packet of matches in her hand.

She held the match to the pipe while I sucked and drew the tobacco to a flame, and then she backed off and looked at me. The pipe was bitter. I knew I had to break it in before it would taste good, and shuddered at the enthusiasm that had given me four pipes to break in. I drew a deep breath of smoke and blew it out.

Suddenly she sat down on the floor and looked up at me. "You look marvelous," she said, staring up at me with an adoring look on her face like a little child. "You were meant for a pipe "

After all that there was nothing I could do but smoke it. I didn't want her to know I didn't care for it, that it made me sick. So I continued to use it, but as time went by I cared for it less and less; many were the times I put it down and would light a cigarette to take the taste of the pipe out of my mouth.

As I looked at the pipe in my hand, it became a symbol to me—a symbol of all the things I had become. Here was I, young, strong, healthy and filled with the desire to do something and not doing it. It wasn't that I cared particularly for work—I liked that no more than the next man—but suddenly I felt my uselessness. I was content to let things drift along just as they were; content to live, to be close to Marianne, to make love to her and let her make love to me; content to give in and let things drift because I was too lazy to do anything about it.

Unconsciously my gaze drifted to the portrait of Gerro on the table. The lamp was tilted so that the light fell upon it and left the rest of the table in the gloom. His strong, vital look exerted a queer pull upon me. I half shut my eyes, and once again I could hear his voice saying: "I have a job to do. And all the things I want will never be possible for me unless I do this thing first. The world is willing to give you, not what you tear from it, but what you put into it."

I remembered him saying: "What are you looking for, Frank? What are you on guard against? What do you want? What are you doing to get it?"

I remembered him saying: "You are big enough to do with a little less, to help—Thank you, it was more than anyone else gave—Strange you should have gray in your hair—Only by working together can we earn the things we all desire—To live in the world as men, among men and with men—"

I came out of my reverie when Marianne spoke. "What are you thinking about, Frank?"

I half smiled, still looking at Gerro's portrait. "Him."

She followed my glance to the painting. "I thought so," she said. "You had an expression on your face as if he were talking to you."

"Maybe he was," I said. "Maybe he was giving me some good advice."

I put the pipe down and lit a cigarette. As it burned down I came to a decision. I would never smoke the pipe again. And once I thought that, another thought came to my mind. "Marianne."

She got out of her chair, came over to me, sat down on the floor at my feet, placed her arms around my legs, and pressed herself against me. "Yes, darling," she said.

"I'm going to get a job."

She looked at me closely. "Is that what you were thinking about?"

"Yes," I answered.

"But, darling," she protested, "why waste yourself on little, piddling things when you don't have to. Aren't you happy? Don't you have everything you want?"

"Yes," I replied, "but—I feel useless, so out of things, out of touch with what goes on around me. I never felt like this before."

"What do you care what goes on around you? It's not pleasant anyway," she argued. "It's so much nicer here: just the two of us in our own little world, no one to bother us, to inflict us with their troubles, their petty little problems. Don't you love me?"

I looked down at her. Her head was resting, her chin on my knees looking up at me. "Of course I love you," I said, "but that has nothing to do with it. I love you, I adore you, I'm very happy with you; but that isn't all there is to it." I cast around in my mind for something that would make her understand what I was trying to say. "Look," I said. "Supposing you didn't have your painting to occupy your mind, then how would you feel?"

"That's different," she said. "That's art. It's a feeling, an absorption. It's something beyond you, something you can't help. It's not just work."

"But it's work nevertheless," I said, "and you would feel quite empty if you didn't have it. What I want to do may not be art, as you call it, but it brings to me the same sort of satisfaction your work does to you."

She got to her feet and looked down at me. Her voice had taken on a little edge that I had learned to recognize. She didn't like to be differed with. "I'm beginning to believe he was really talking to you."

I was curious about that remark. "What do you mean by that?" I asked. "Did he ever say that to you?"

She didn't answer right away. She was thinking. "Yes," she finally answered, "many times. I begged him to do as I asked, begged him not to throw away our chance for happiness, but that was just what he did. And it was so silly, so terribly futile— after all, we had all we could ask for. And yet he wasn't satisfied. And look what he got as repayment for his ideals. And now you want to do the same thing—destroy our happiness." She sat down in her chair and began to weep.

I went over to her and put my arms about her. "Don't cry, sugar. I'm not trying to destroy us. I just want to make myself whole again. Now I'm only a shell with no inside. I feel so wasted when I walk down the street and see men going and coming from work. I feel so empty when I spend my afternoons in the movies, watching pictures on the screen go through the motions of living. I just want something to do, something to keep myself busy."

She stopped crying. "Then why not do something here at home?" she suggested. "Why not do as Gerro did? Try to write.

You are expressive, you can say what you want; why not try to write?"

I couldn't keep from laughing at that. It was so absurd. Me—write! "No," I said with a laugh, "I don't think I will. It's sweet of you to think that I can, but I know better. No dice! I'm going out and get me a job."

But jobs were no easier to get at that time than they had been before. It was getting colder now, and I would come back from looking for work, chilled and angry with myself for my failures.

And she would stop her painting, or whatever work she happened to be doing at the moment, and come to me. "Any luck?" she would ask.

And I would shake my head. "None."

"Why don't you stop torturing yourself and put an end to all this wasted effort on your part?" she would tell me. "Sit back, take it easy. We have enough of everything."

I would look at her and not answer. But, bit by bit, hope faded from me, and in a month I stopped looking for work and began to stay home again.

Marianne was happy about that, but I was bitter. It galled me to think that I couldn't land even a lousy two-bit job. I would sit in the big chair and stare at Gerro's picture, and it would stare back at me. I would sit there for hours on end looking at it and going over my failures in my mind.

One day while I was sitting there in the chair looking at the portrait and Marianne was working over her newest painting, a voice within me began to whisper: "You're through. You will never be anything. You will live on handouts the rest of your life."

The voice was so real and so strong that involuntarily I answered it aloud: "I will not." My voice was loud and rough, and shattered the stillness of the room.

Marianne threw her brush and palette on the table furiously. I had broken her mood of concentration on the painting. "Didn't I tell you a thousand times to be quiet when I'm working!" she screamed at me.

I looked up at her almost in surprise. I had forgotten she was in the room. "I'm sorry," I said.

"Sorry!" she mimicked me nastily. "He's sorry, he says! You

fool, do you know what you've done! You've ruined my painting—that's what you've done. I'll never get it now."

Suddenly I was angry too. It was like a spark thrown to dry
tinder. I blazed up before I knew it. My voice went flat and
hard with the rage that was in me. "No," I said, "I'm not
sorry—not really. I won't take the blame for you if you find
that you're trying something outside your reach. You can't
blame your inadequacy on me."

"Inadequate, am I!" she shouted. "Who are you to tell me
I'm inadequate!" She turned, picked up a palette knife from the
table near her, and advanced on me threateningly.

I laughed coldly. "You're not going to try that!" I asked
contemptuously.

She stopped short and looked at the knife in her hands and
then at me. She threw the knife to the floor. Rage and shame
seemed to flow over her face, one chasing the other like clouds
across the face of the moon. "You no-good-son-of-a-bitch!"
she yelled. "You dirty, rotten bastard!"

I could feel the blood leave my face in a rush. I felt cold and
white and taut with anger. For a moment I could have mur-
dered her, but we stood there and stared at one another while
the seconds ticked by. I could feel a pulse beating madly in my
forehead. My hands were clenched.

Suddenly I opened them and could feel them at my side, wet
with sweat and trembling. I turned, snatched my hat and coat
from the hall tree, and stamped out the door. I could hear her
voice calling after me: "Frank, Frank, come back!"

It followed me as I went down the hall into the street, ringing
in my ears with the oddly fearful sound of her saying after me:
"Where are you going?" and the slam of the door, and the
words, "Please come back!" as if torn from the bottom of her
soul and filled with a fear of losing me.

I knew I would be back, but for the while I felt a savage glee
in making her suffer and feel pain and humiliation as I did.

It was late when I came back, and I was drunk for the first
time in my life; but not so drunk that I didn't know what I was
doing—that is, not altogether know what I was doing. I paused
a moment outside the door before I went in and listened. I
heard no sound, and put the key in the door and went in.

I staggered over to the table and picked up Gerro's portrait.
"Gerro, my frien'," I whispered, "my frien', I mish you," and
began to weep drunken tears. I slumped toward my chair and

fell into it, still holding the picture. I held the picture up and
looked at it, still weeping. "My frien', tell me what to do. I feel
sho losht."

The bedroom door opened and Marianne stood before me in
her negligee. I could see the black nightgown she wore beneath
it. "Marianne," I cried, holding the picture to her, "he won'
talk to me."

She looked at me speculatively for a moment. Then she took
the picture from my hands and put it back on the table. She
helped me to my feet and led me into the bedroom and undressed me. I lolled helplessly on the bed while she took off my
shoes.

"Oh, darling," she whispered, as she unbuttoned my shirt and
then helped me into my pajamas, "why did you do it? It's all
my fault—my bitchy temper."

I looked up at her. She was never so beautiful as then, her
face furrowed with small lines of worry and remorse. "Marianne," I said solemnly, "you're a bitch, but I love you," and
rolled over on my stomach and fell sound asleep.

Chapter Twelve

IT WAS a Thanksgiving party given by one of her friends that
really began to break us up. Time moved on slowly, and while
I wasn't completely satisfied, I was fairly content with letting
things go as they were. Marianne had become possessive about
me. I didn't object to it. Matter of fact, I liked it. I loved her,
loved the way she spoke, walked, acted. I loved the way she
held her hands, her feet. I loved the way she pressed against me
when we danced that made it seem so intimate, so personal, so
daring.

But this was another party and the usual crowd and the usual
thing. Marianne and I alone were one thing—close and warm
and understanding—but Marianne and I and a group of people
were another. She would gravitate naturally to her crowd of

fellow artists and talk shop. I would be excluded from such conversations—not intentionally, but naturally—as I could offer nothing in the way of talk on that subject. So I would stand around, drink in hand, and wait, bored and tired and left out, until the party would break up and we could go home.

Going home was a silent affair. We would cut through Washington Square, where the double-decker buses waited for their passengers, our breath cutting frostily into the chill night air, and wouldn't talk until we got home. Then Marianne would say: "Nice party, wasn't it?"

I would grunt: "Unh-hunh."

And she wouldn't answer. She probably knew that I didn't care for them but would never admit it.

This party was no different than the others. Marianne got busy talking and I held up the wall. The evening dragged by. About ten o'clock a few new people came in and more groups formed. I was beginning to get fed up with my silent role, and was thinking about walking out and going home. I put down my drink and started over to Marianne to tell her I was leaving. Someone caught me by the arm. I turned to see who it was.

It was a model who occasionally worked for Marianne. "Remember me?" she asked smiling.

"Why yes, of course," I said, pleased to have someone to speak to. "How are you?"

"Stiff," she said flatly. "The party stinks."

I laughed. It made me feel good to know that someone else felt the same way about it as I did. "Why do you come then?" I asked her.

"Have to," she answered succinctly. "My business—I have something to sell." Her hands made a gesture down her body.

"Oh," I said, "I see." I sure did. She had something to sell.

"Dance?" she asked.

I nodded. We moved off together in a corner where the radio was playing. She danced well and made me look better at dancing than I actually was. Several of the people stopped talking and watched us. From the corner of my eye I saw Marianne and her group fall quiet as we danced by them.

"They make an unusual couple," I heard one of them say to Marianne. "Why don't you do them?"

We moved out of hearing and I didn't hear Marianne's reply. "Why do you?" the blonde was asking.

"Do what?" I asked, looking down at her.

"Come to these parties?" she said. "You're like a fish out of water."

I shrugged my shoulders. "There's nothing better to do."

"I see," she said knowingly, looking over my shoulder at Marianne. Her meaning was plain enough—orders from the boss.

Suddenly I had enough of dancing. I was a little angry with myself. "How about a drink?" I asked.

We stood against the wall watching the others. I could see Marianne looking at us—a quick glance and then away—as we stood there.

After a while I couldn't take that any more. "How about some air?" I asked the girl.

She nodded and we took our coats and went out. We walked silently through the park and then around it. Once we stopped and looked up at the people getting into the bus. We didn't talk, we just walked, her hand on mine.

Then we started back. At the door of the party I stopped. "I'm not going in," I said. They were my first words since we started to walk.

She looked at me. "I don't feel like it either," she said, "but I have to. Someone I promised to see about some work tomorrow."

I got the impression that if I asked her, she wouldn't go back at all. I didn't say anything.

She stood there a moment watching me, then she smiled and stepped back. "Moody cuss, aren't you?"

I didn't answer. She turned and went into the building, and I went home.

I sat down in the easy chair at home and read the morning papers. A little after one o clock Marianne came in. "Hello," I said, "how'd ya like the party?"

"Why didn't you stick around and find out?" she said heatedly.

I could see she was angry so I shut up. I didn't feel like fighting tonight.

She went into the bedroom and came out a few mniutes later. "Where's Bess?" she asked.

I guessed she meant the model. I looked up at her and smiled. "At the party, I guess. I left her at the door and came home."

"I didn't see her come back."

"I don't know what she did after I left her," I retorted. I smiled again. "Take it easy, baby. I'm beginning to think you're jealous."

That was the wrong thing to say. She all but hit the ceiling. "Jealous!" she hollered. "Of that two-bit bitch! The hell I am! I just didn't like it, that's all. When you come with me, I expect you to stay with me. How would you like people to talk about you?"

I was beginning to get a little steam up myself. "Let them talk. There's no way you can stop them. Anyhow, what do we care what they say?"

"I don't care!" she yelled, "but how do you think I feel? They know about us, and you run out with that little blonde bitch."

"How do you think I feel?" I countered. "At every party I'm shunted to one side like an overcoat, and picked up on your way home. For Christ's sake don't be such a goddam fool!" I lit a cigarette. "Forget it."

"That cheap whore made a play for you the minute she saw you."

"She seemed like a nice kid to me," I said defensively. "And besides, what's wrong with that? What did you do?"

"I didn't do that," she said, walking over to the door of the bedroom. "But if I'd have found her here, I would have cut her heart out."

I began to laugh. This was getting a little funny. "Is that why you looked in the bedroom when you came in?" I asked. "You don't think I'm dumb enough to bring her here, even if I wanted to?"

She came back to me and stood in front of my chair, looking down at me furiously. Her voice was tense but controlled. "Look," she said, "remember this. You belong to me. Everything you have, everything you are, everything you ever will be, is because of me—because I gave it to you. And because I gave it to you, I can take it away just as quickly. I can throw you back where I got you from like that." She snapped her fingers. "When you go anywhere with me, remember that. You stay with me, whether you're bored, whether you like it or not. You'll go when I tell you, not before."

I was mad, but I sat there coolly and held on to the edges of my temper. She was right. I had nothing of my own. Even the clothes I wore and the money in my pocket belonged to her. "O. K. baby," I said evenly, "if that's the way you want it."

She looked down at me, curiously disappointed, as if she had expected me to flare up and I didn't. "That's the way I want it," she said a little bit unsteadily.

I got out of the chair and went into the bedroom and undressed and got into bed. I fell asleep. I don't know what time it was that I awoke. She had called me "Frank, are you awake?"

"I am now," I said. Suddenly my eyes had opened wide. The dimness in the room wasn't the only thing I could see through now. I could see myself the way I really was—kept, a sweet man! I writhed a little inside.

"Come over here, darling," she whispered.

"Yes, master," I replied, getting out of my bed and sitting on the edge of her bed.

"Not there, darling," she whispered, her eyes luminous in the darkness. "Lie down here, beside me, and kiss me."

I stretched out beside her and took her in my arms. Her body was warm and soft, and I could feel the sparks of fire shoot out when we touched. I was bought and paid for, and I gave her her money's worth that night.

I loved her. I knew I would always love her. No matter what she said or did. But all night long someone just behind me and over my shoulder was watching me and laughing and whispering in my ear.

"Jump when she tells you," the voice giggled obscenely in my ear. "Dance when she pulls the strings. But remember, something is gone. He! he! he! You'll never get it back. Never! Never! Never!"

She was sleeping when the gray of dawn beat its way into the room. I looked at her. Her hair was framed round her head like a living flame on the pillow. Her mouth had a half smile and her face was relaxed and happy.

I looked at her and my heart went out to her in a funny, lumpish sort of way. I loved her, but something vital had gone, had been lost. And way down deep in the hidden recesses of my mind, I knew it would not be long before I too would follow. And I knew that it would come as sure as day after night and yet—.

Chapter Thirteen

HOLIDAY week—that slow-moving, gayly exciting week between Christmas and New Year's. The week that children were out of school and even the men and women who worked had a different air about them—an air of excitement, of repressed gaiety, of looking forward to the new year and wondering what excitingly great things were going to happen to them in the year that was coming.

I spent most of the week sitting in the window of the apartment looking out—watching people as they hurried to and from work, watching children as they played, watching street cleaners shovel snow, watching mailmen deliver letters, watching the milkmen deliver milk, watching cops walk their beat, watching, watching, watching the world move around before me through a pane of glass. This business of watching the world and not being a part of it was beginning to get me in my craw. It was beginning to choke in my throat, make me nauseous and sick to my stomach. The inactivity began to tear at my nerves. The end was coming. I could see it. It had to be soon. And it was—sooner than I had expected.

It was New Year's Eve and horns were blowing. And everyone was half lit—except me. I don't know why. I tried to get lit up like a Christmas tree, but the more I drank, the less effect it had on me. We were in a nightclub in the Village. Marianne and all her friends and I. And suddenly it seemed as if I were outside myself, looking upon the scene as an outsider would, ironically tolerant, sarcastically amused at the foolish, childlike behavior of these so-called adults trying ever so hard to pretend they were glad at the coming of time while inwardly they were afraid. Afraid of tomorrow! I laughed aloud. That's what I was—afraid of tomorrow!

Marianne looked at me quietly, her eyes half amused. "Having fun, darling?" she asked.

I didn't answer. I laughed again. She thought I was a little drunk. I pulled her to me and kissed her. It was sweet and warm, and I felt strong and powerful. What did I have to be afraid of? I was young and strong—ever so strong. She kissed me back. I kissed the side of her neck down to her shoulder.

"Frank," she half whispered huskily. I could tell the passion in her voice. "Not here, Frank, not here!" Her arms were around me.

I let her go and laughed again. She laughed with me. We laughed together. We laughed and laughed and laughed until we were out of breath, and then we looked at each other soberly.

Her eyes were haughty and proud. "He is mine," they were saying. "Mine! He belongs to me. I belong to him. I'm proud of him as he is of me." Her hand found mine and gripped it tightly under the table. Currents seemed to flow between us—feelings without words, emotions without language. We looked at each other and were proud. The evening wore on.

The lights went down dim and then out. The orchestra began to play *Auld Lang Syne*. And suddenly she was in my arms and we were holding each other close, savoring each other's warmth. We kissed.

"I love you, darling," her lips murmured under mine. "Happy New Year!"

"I love you," I heard myself saying. "Happy New Year!" I kissed her cheek. It was wet with the salt of her tears. I could taste it on my tongue, in my mouth. And I realized she had known all along what I was thinking.

She kissed me again, her mouth half open against mine, her arms holding me tightly to her—ever so tightly. "Don't go, darling, please don't go."

"I must," I whispered. "I've got to. I can't help it."

The lights went on again, and there we were, staring at each other. She was pale and her eyes were wide and filled with tears. There was something in my throat and I couldn't speak. Just our hands clung together tightly as we sat down.

We left the party a few minutes later and walked home silently. The night was bright and clean and new, and a million stars were out blinking brightly. The air was new, everything was new—it was 1934. Silently we went into the apartment. I took off my coat and threw it over a chair. I went to the closet and took down my valise and spread it open on the bed.

Silently she began to hand me my things: shirts and shoes

and stockings and ties and pajamas and suits. I pressed one knee down to close it. I heard the clasp lock.

I straightened up and faced her. My voice was trembling a little. "I guess this is . . . good-by."

She flung herself violently into my arms. "No! Frank, no! You mustn't go! I need you!" She was crying—the first time I had really seen her cry.

I held her to me and didn't speak for a moment. "It's better this way, darling, much better. Believe me," I whispered shakily. "In time we'd grow to hate each other. It's better now than when we've both grown bitter."

"But, darling, you're my world, my life." She kissed me. "And what will you do? You have no job—nothing. How will you live? I can't bear to think of you going back to those cheap little jobs. Here with me you are safe. I can look after you, protect you. I can give you the world—anything you want."

I remembered something I had read. "What does it profit a man," I quoted, "if in gaining the world he loses his own soul?"

She looked at me strangely a moment and then kissed me hard on the lips. "Say good-by to me gently, darling," she whispered, her hand reaching for the light and turning it off.

I said good-by gently, sweetly, passionately. And time whirled around past us and through us, carried us all through a lifetime together, and put us back in the little apartment in Greenwich Village at the door. I stood there awkwardly, valise in one hand like a stranger just leaving after a long, unexpected visit.

"Wait a minute," she said, and brought me Gerro's portrait and placed it in my free hand. "Take him with you," she said, "because you have something of him inside you—and something of me. And all of us together mean something more than just people—more than just living. There is a brightness in you, an incandescence you have now, you've never had before—until tonight. I saw it fuse and harden back there in the nightclub, and I knew then, at that very moment, you were lost to me—and that nothing I could do would stop you."

For a split second she stood there, and then she kissed my mouth hard, quickly. And I stepped outside the door, and she shut it gently. I could hear a soft sobbing sound behind me as I went down the hall and out the building.

I looked up at the sky. The stars were still blinking, but over in the east the first tinge of dawn was breaking. It was a new day coming—a bright new day. I walked toward it confidently, my mind full of thoughts about Marianne. I had no plans for today or tomorrow. They could take care of themselves.

Chapter Fourteen

I MUST have walked about five blocks before I realized I still held Gerro's picture in my hand. I put it in my pocket. I was beginning to get a little hungry, and I was tired for I hadn't slept at all that night. I saw the lights of an all-night cafeteria at the next corner and went in. I had some coffee and toast while I kicked around some ideas in my mind.

By the time I had finished I had decided to go over to a hotel and get some sleep; tomorrow I would start looking for work. I felt sure this time I would do all right. The morning was brisk and clear, and I started toward the nearest subway station. The streets were almost empty; it was New Year's Day and not many people had to go to work. There was a man hurrying down the street in front of me. I didn't notice him very much as he was sticking pretty close to the building line as he walked.

Suddenly he disappeared into a doorway. I walked along. A car drove slowly down the street toward me. I noticed it only because of the slow manner in which it proceeded. There was a short, staccato burst of gunfire from it as it passed the doorway the man had ducked into. Then it speeded up and turned the corner. For a second I stood there frozen in my steps. Then I ran toward the doorway. The man came bungling from it toward me. I dropped my bag and caught him. A moment passed while we stared into each other's faces.

He recognized me. "Frankie!" he gasped, blood oozing from the corners of his mouth, "help me!" and sagged against me.

For a full minute I couldn't think; I could only stand there stupidly staring at his quickly whitening face. The clock had turned back ten years, and again Silk Fennelli was spilling blood over my shirt front. Again, as then, I was paralyzed with fright. Ten years—ten years and the clock turned back!

Only this time I didn't run away.

I got him to Bellevue. I left my valise there on the sidewalk where I had dropped it, put him in a cab, and got him to the hospital.

I didn't hang around there. I beat it as soon as I had him set. I didn't want to hang around to be questioned by the cops. Once in the street again, I lit a cigarette. Then I remembered my bag. I took a hack back to where I had picked him up, but the bag was gone. I looked up and down the street but it was gone. I laughed bitterly to myself. I should have known better than to expect to find it.

Suddenly I was tired. I went to a hotel, checked in, and went to sleep. It was nearly evening when I awoke. I sat on the edge of the bed and counted my money. All I had was about ten bucks. It would have to do until I got something, I told myself. I went down and got something to eat. I sat around for a while, read the evening newspapers, and then went upstairs to bed.

I tried to sleep again but I couldn't. I was all slept out. I lay there in the dark tossing and turning and thinking. Finally I got out of bed, put on my trousers, and sat near the window smoking.

Ten years! It was queer. Fennelli hadn't changed much in ten years, but I knew I had. I wondered how he recognized me so readily. Maybe it was something about the way I looked; maybe it was the situation. I don't know. I couldn't understand. I went back a long way. For the first time in a long while, I thought about the folks and wondered what they were doing and where they were, and about the kids I used to know—Jerry and Marty and Janet. What had happened to them? But it was such a long time ago it was hard to remember.

I remembered breakfast with the folks: the smell of the rolls, slightly warm from the bakery after I had just brought them in—the way my aunt would smile at me. I remembered high school and the kids laughing as we crossed the big yard going home. I remembered so many things, and all of a sudden I began to feel old and tired.

I went back to bed and stretched out. My tiredness left me, and I was wide awake again. I tossed and thought about Marianne, and about how she would sense that I couldn't sleep and come into my bed and lie down beside me and we would talk and I would feel her warmth near me and I would become quiet and begin to relax and she would fall asleep and carelessly throw one long white leg over mine and then I would begin to fall asleep.

But Marianne wasn't here and I couldn't sleep. I could see her standing in the doorway saying good-by. I could hear her voice, low and husky and controlled. What was it she had said? I tried to remember. And then I heard it and saw her say it, the shadow of the door half falling on her face.

"There's something of Gerro in you—and something of me and all the other people you have ever known. But mostly there is you. . . ."

But what about me? I had never turned to look inside myself. What about me? Of all the people I knew, I knew myself least of all. Why did I do things? What did I want? Why was I content to drift, never really searching for an answer to myself? I wondered. What did I want? Money? Love? Friends? Respect? I searched through my mind for the answer, but none was forthcoming.

I had read a lot while I lived with Marianne. She had quite a few books, and I had devoured them— Some good, some bad —but the answer wasn't in them. What did people think about me? What was there in me that they liked? Why did they take me into their homes and hearts when I had so little to give in return?

I missed Marianne. During the day I had slept. I had been exhausted. But now, with the night, came a new, a peculiar feeling of loneliness. I longed to go to the phone, pick it up, dial her number, and hear her low, soft voice answer: "Hello, darling."

"Hello, darling!" But I couldn't do that. You can never go back. That was something I learned a long time ago. You can never go back— Never! At last I fell asleep. Marianne, Marianne, even my sleep was filled with you! My night was warm and alive with you. Would you ever let me go?

I woke up. The sun, streaming through the window, had hit my face. At first I threw my arm over my face, reluctant to get up and face the reality of the day. But bit by bit I came alive. I could feel it surging through my legs and up my body to my mind. I could feel the thoughts coming, stronger and stronger. This is tomorrow. This is today—your day. Get up. You've got to face it.

I went down the hall to the shower, and then came back to the room and dressed. I handed in my key at the desk as I left.

This was too expensive a place for me with my pocket. Two dollars a day was too much. I would have to go back to the Mills Hotel. It was more my speed.

I bought a morning *Times* and glanced through the want ads. I didn't know what kind of a job I wanted, but there wasn't anything likely in the papers. I took a trip up to Sixth Avenue to the agencies, but no luck there. I wasn't worried. I felt sure I'd get a break. This was tomorrow and it was mine.

Two months later it was still tomorrow. But I was beginning to wonder if it was mine. I was beginning to wonder if I would ever have the tomorrow I had promised myself. It was early March and still bitter cold. My new heavy, warm coat had long since gone the way of my watch and everything else I could hock. I hadn't eaten a square meal in weeks. I had stood in bread lines, soup lines, work lines—all kinds of lines—but I hadn't worked, not even a day.

Last night I had slept in a hallway. I was chased early in the morning, when I was cold and damp and chilled and miserable, by the super as he came to clean. I could still hear his hearty, full-voiced threats muttered in some guttural, foreign-sounding English. He stood there waving his broom at me. "You bums!" he had shouted. I scurried from the hall like a thief. I had only been stealing a night's rest—a little peace.

I was hungry. I was cold. Automatically I reached for a cigarette, but I didn't have any. I walked along the curb looking for a butt. At last I snagged one. A man came walking down the street. He looked like he'd be good for a little tap. I watched him come toward me and then walk past me while I stood there motionless, frozen to the spot. After he had gone I was bitter with myself. Why didn't I tap him? There's nothing to it. All you have to say is: "Mister?" with a little whining sound in it. You didn't have to say any more; they knew the rest. But I couldn't bring myself to do it—not any more. There was something inside of me that seemed to stop me. I couldn't do it. The man turned the corner. I walked on.

Fool! I kept saying over and over to myself. Fool! Fool! Aren't you ever going to learn? Stop kidding yourself. You're nothing special, no more than anyone else. Beg. Plead. Kiss an ass or two. That's the way to do it. That's the way to get along.

Go back to Marianne—Marianne. She'll take you back. You'll be comfortable again. Warm and full of food and a woman. God, what a woman would feel like just now! I began to laugh. Which would you rather have, I asked myself, a woman or a steak? I laughed again. My mouth watered as I could smell a steak sizzling as real as that lamppost ahead.

I stopped in front of that door again and pulled the bell. I wondered what I could say to her. "Marianne, I'm hungry and tired and cold. Please let me in. Please take me back. I won't ever go away again—not any more. Please, Marianne, please."

What if she would say: "No! Go away!" But she couldn't. She was mine. Didn't she say so? After an age, the door opened.

"No, Miss Renoir doesn't live here any more. She went home to Haiti last month. I'm sorry."

The door closed. I stood there staring at it and then walked out. I crossed the street and began to walk uptown. I felt tall—terribly tall—like that time I had been tight, only taller. I laughed, thinking I was so big now I could look into second-story windows as I walked by, and surprise the people. My head began to float through the air, and pretty soon it was pushing its way through the clouds. But the clouds were damp and dark and I couldn't see and it was only a matter of minutes before I stumbled and began falling. And then it was night—New Year's Eve—and I was strong and a million stars were out, all of them winking and blinking only at me. This was tomorrow— my tomorrow!

Chapter Fifteen

THEY put me in a bed in a long, gray room with about forty other beds in it. The doctor came around in the evening and looked me over. The nurse was with him. He stood at the side of the bed and looked down at me. "How do you feel now?" he asked.

"Better," I answered.

"This not eating is a bad business," he said with a wry attempt at humor.

He wasn't telling me anything. I didn't answer.

He turned to the nurse. "Better send for the registrar. We'll keep him here for a day or two." He turned to me and spoke again. "Take it easy for a while. Is there anything else you want?"

"Smokes?" I asked, afraid it might be too much to ask for.

He fished down into his pocket, dragged up a half-used package of Camels, and tossed them on the bed with some matches. "Keep them. But don't let the nurse catch you. And don't burn the place down," he shrugged his shoulders expressively and looked around the room, "even if it looks like it should be."

He walked off and the nurse followed him. He looked like a nice young kid. I was sorry I didn't think to thank him for the smokes. I waited until they left the ward before I lit a cigarette, and then leaned back puffing it slowly. Cigarettes from a package have a better flavor than those you snag from the street.

The cigarette burned down, and I put it out in a plate on a stand next to the bed. I then leaned back against the pillows and enjoyed their comfort. It was amazing how good you can feel with a full belly and a soft bed and the tender, acrid smoke of a cigarette still in your nostrils. I shut my eyes.

A voice beside the bed spoke softly, "Are you awake?"

I opened them quickly. A girl was sitting near my bed, a pad and pencil in her hand. "Yes," I answered.

"I'm Miss Cabell," she said. "I didn't want to bother you if you were asleep, but we have to fill out these forms."

"It's O. K.," I answered. "Go ahead." There was something familiar about her. She wore a brownish salt-and-pepper suit, very mannishly tailored, white blouse, and large horn rimmed glasses.

"Your name, please?" she asked, and added apologetically: "There wasn't anything in your clothes to tell us."

"Kane," I answered, still slowly trying to place her, "Francis Kane."

She wrote the name down. "Address, please?"

"None."

"No home address?"

"No," I said. "Make it New York City." I was beginning to feel a little irritated. There was something about this girl. I knew her, and it was one of those things that stood right at the edge of your mind and you couldn't get it out.

"Age?" she asked not looking up from the pad.

"Twenty-three."

"I'm sorry," she said. "I meant when were you born? What date?"

"June 21st, 1912."

She said, almost to herself: "Sex, male; color, white; eyes, brown." She looked up at me, "Complexion, dark; hair, gray black." She stopped. "You seem young to have such gray hair."

I answered shortly: "I worry a lot."

"Oh!" she said, "I'm sorry. I didn't mean to be impertinent."

"It's all right," I said. "Forget it."

She continued, "Your height?"

"Five nine."

"Weight?"

"One forty when I weighed myself last," I answered.

She looked at me and smiled. The smile did it. It was a familiar smile—Marty. I knew her now—Marty and Ruth—Ruth Cabell. I hoped she didn't remember me. I didn't want anyone to see me like this.

"That must have been a while ago. We'd better make it one fifteen."

"As you like," I said, trying to keep the excitement out of my voice.

"Where do you work?" she asked.

"I don't," I answered. "I'm unemployed."

"What kind of work do you do?"

"Any kind," I said, "that is, any kind I can get."

"Where were you born?"

"New York."

"High school or any education?"

I almost dived into that. If I'd have said Washington High, she would have had me spotted.

"No," I answered.

"Sure?" she asked.

I noticed she wasn't writing this down. There was a little glint of excitement in her eyes. "I should be," I said.

She got up and walked to the foot of the bed and looked right into my face. I looked back at her. "Francis Kane," she said to herself, reflectively. "Frank Kane. Frankie, Frankie, don't you remember? I'm Ruth, Marty's sister."

Remember? How could I forget? Poker faced, I replied, "I'm sorry, miss, you've got me mixed up with somebody else."

"No, I haven't," she said half angrily, walking up the side of the bed to me. This was more like the old Ruth that I knew, that little show of temper. "You're Francis Kane, aren't you?"

"Yes," I admitted, shaking my head.

"Then I'm right. I must be right." She took off her glasses. "Look, you went to George Washington High School with my brother. You were in the orphanage—St. Therese. You must remember."

"I'm sorry," I said. "You're mistaken. I never went to any of those places. I don't know your brother."

"But your name is Francis Kane. You must be," she insisted.

"Miss," I said, trying to act patiently resigned, "the name's not an unusual one. There must be quite a few of them." I tried another tack: "Besides, what did this guy look like? Not much like me, I'll bet."

She looked at me for a few seconds before she answered. Then a little doubt crept into her voice. "No," she answered, "not much like you, but that was eight years ago."

"See?" I said, a slight note of triumph in my voice.

"No," she said, "I don't. I don't see at all. You must have forgotten. You were sick. You could forget, you know. It's happened before."

"A man doesn't forget his friends," I said, "no matter how long it's been since he's seen them."

She sat down again. "But maybe you had a touch of—" she hesitated at the word.

"Amnesia?" I filled in for her and then laughed. "No, I don't think so."

"I can't be wrong," she insisted. She tried a new tack: "Remember Julie? She used to work for us. You gave my brother boxing lessons. And Jerry Cowan? Janet Lindell? Your aunt and uncle, Bertha and Morris Cain? Don't those names mean anything to you at all?"

I shook my head and closed my eyes. Those names meant the world to me—a world of perfection and love. I opened my eyes again and shook my head from side to side. "No," I said, "I never heard of them before." I let my head sink back against the pillow.

She leaned forward, suddenly solicitous. "You're tired. I've upset you. And you're a little pale. I don't want to upset you. I want to help. Please try to remember. Remember there was Julie and then Janet, and I was a little jealous of them—a little jealous of you, of all the people that liked you and why they liked you. I didn't know why. Maybe because it was that I liked you so much myself—more than I knew, more than I admitted myself. I used to pick on you and insult you. And one day in the hall of the school you kissed me. You said we'd be friends, remember?"

She turned her head away a little and continued to speak, "When you kissed me, I suddenly knew how I had felt about you—how I had always felt about you and I was ashamed of all the things, the nasty things, I had said to you. You must remember. You couldn't forget."

I laughed a little and injected a little sarcasm into my voice. "If I had ever kissed you, I wouldn't forget very easily."

Her cheeks began to grow red. She sat there angry with herself for blushing. I could see it. After a few seconds she controlled herself and turned back to me and spoke in an impersonal tone of voice again. "I'm sorry," she said, "I could be wrong. I didn't mean to offend you. I was only trying to help."

"I know," I answered softly, "and I appreciate it. I'm a little bit sorry I'm not the guy you're looking for."

She stood up, pad and pencil in hand, her voice still cool and impersonal. "You might be wrong too, you know. Tomorrow I'll bring my brother down and ask him to look at you—maybe Jerry Cowan too. They'll know."

"It won't be any use," I said. But I knew differently. They'd know in a minute, no matter how I had changed.

"My brother's interning at a hospital uptown and he won't be able to get here before noon, but we'll see. I hope you are the one. There are many things we have to tell you." She stood there waiting.

I almost went for that. There were many things I wanted to know—my folks. Questions ran through my mind quickly. I fought them down. Ruth hadn't lost any of her cleverness.

"As you like, lady," I said as if I were tired with it all, "but I tell you it won't do any good."

Disappointment flashed across her face. It was gone almost immediately. "Maybe," she said, turning away. "Good night."

I watched her walk down the ward and out without answering. Then I reached for a cigarette with trembling hands and lit it. Noon tomorrow! That meant I would have to get out of here by then. I didn't dare stay and try to bluff my way past them. I made up my mind to put away a big breakfast before I left. They couldn't keep me here; I wasn't a criminal.

I leaned back, trying to think why I had failed to get a job—why I seemed to be messing things up. Maybe it was because I didn't have a plan. Maybe it was because I tried to grab at anything. That must be it. I must have a plan this time. I couldn't afford to miss again. This time it must be it. But what could I plan? What could I do that couldn't miss? There had to be something, something solid and sure and indestructible.

I turned one thing after another over in my mind. One wild thought after another. They chased themselves through my head. And as soon as I had thought of them, I threw them out. I looked around the ward. Down at the end of it near the door was a small placard. It read "Ward 23—Bellevue Hospital." And then I had it. It raced through my mind so quickly I was surprised I hadn't thought of it before. This one couldn't miss. It was sure-fire. I put out the cigarette and went to sleep.

I stood on the street corner and looked at the clock in the window across the street. It was eleven o'clock. Close call! I thought. I had a little trouble convincing the doctor I was all right. But what could he do if I said I was O. K.?

He had looked a little worried when I asked him to let me leave. "You should stay here a few more days," he said. "You really need the rest." He was putting it mildly.

"But, doc," I said, "I feel better. Besides I have some friends that will look after me. I'll be all right."

"Well," he said, "if you say so. We can't force you to stay here, but you'd better take it easy. You're more run down than you think. When you get up there with your friend, stay in for a couple of days and rest."

"Don't worry, doc," I assured him, "I will."

I watched him sign the discharge slip and give it to a nurse. "Don't forget to do what I told you."

"I'll do it, doc," I replied. "Thanks a lot. Thanks very much." I held out my hand.

For a moment he looked at my hand in surprise, then he took it. The nurse returned with my clothes. I got dressed and walked toward the exit and out.

I looked at the clock again—eleven o'clock. Now I had a job to do. I started to walk uptown. I had to find Silk Fennelli—today. He would remember what I did. I probably saved his life by getting him to the hospital in time. Today would tell the story. If I had to go back, I'd go all the way back.

He couldn't turn me down.

Interlude

FRANCIS

JERRY walked over to the sideboard and mixed another drink. He held it up to the light reflectively. Just right: liberal with the Scotch, but just a splash of soda. He turned toward Marty and waved him to a seat. "The lost years," he spoke quietly. "The way you said the phrase summed it up for me. Somewhere in that period of time, from the time he ran away until the time we saw him next, Frankie was growing up too. Maybe not in the same sense that we were. But in another way. Something must have happened to him during that time that turned him back to the only way he knew for certain he could get along.

"I don't know what it was. Probably no one does or ever will know now. But there are traces of his start on the way back into our lives. Faint traces, meager traces—but enough to give us clues as to what was happening to him and what he was doing.

"It started, oddly enough, a little while after I had gone to work as an assistant D.A. It was in April 1936. The police were investigating a gang shooting in one of the midtown hotels. There were rumors around that involved certain well-known gamblers. We were checking all the angles and were getting nowhere, when one of our stoolies came in with a strange story about a man who worked for Fennelli—a man we had never heard of before. But according to the stoolie, he had moved up in a few years—maybe two, maybe three—from a bookie's runner to one of the top spots in the organization. A guy by the name of Frank Kane. I was busy on another case at the time and was in court, and so I missed it completely until several years later when I picked up the file."

The boys were sitting around playing penny-ante poker when the door opened and a man came in. They stopped their game for a moment to look at him. His age was hard to tell. He was thin and his face gaunt almost to the point of emaciation. He wore no overcoat though it was bitterly cold outside. There was a youthful quality about his complexion that gave the lie to his eyes and gray-black hair. His eyes were brown, almost black, and had no depth, no expression. His mouth was small and he spoke through thin, compressed lips. It was a strange voice— old and tired and empty of expression as his eyes. It had a flat, hard undertone. He stood there in the doorway looking at them, meeting their gaze unwinkingly.

"Where's Fennelli?" he asked.

Piggy Laurens, who fancied himself as a wisecracker and jokester generally, got out of his chair and walked over to the stranger. "Screw, punk!" he said. "Fennelli don't give no hand-outs."

The stranger quietly closed the door behind him, stepped into the room, and placed himself in front of Piggy. His hands dangled loosely at his sides, no expression crossed his face, his voice was even, flat, controlled, hard and quiet. His eyes gazed unblinkingly into Piggy's face. "I don't take advice from the cheap help," he said.

Piggy flushed and took a step forward toward the stranger, and then he looked into the man's eyes. Piggy was by no means a coward, but he didn't like what he saw there. However, it was too late to turn back; it was his move. He took another step forward.

The boys looked up from the table with interested eyes. They wondered how long it would be before the stranger would back down and beat it.

Piggy's hands began a threatening move toward his pockets. The stranger's voice froze them into an empty gesture.

"If you do that," he stated in the same tone of voice, "I'll kill you." His hands still dangled easily at his sides, but his lips had drawn back in a half smile that resembled a snarl and lights seemed to flicker in his eyes.

Silk's voice came from the door of the back room. "Sit down, Piggy."

Piggy went back to his chair and sat down uneasily.

The stranger and Fennelli stared at each other across the length of the room. For a moment the room was still. Then the silence was broken by the stranger's footsteps as he crossed the room.

"I came for the job you promised me," he said, stopping in front of Fennelli.

Fennelli looked at him appraisingly, then stepped out of the doorway and motioned for him to go in. The stranger crossed into the room and Fennelli followed him in.

"You took a hell of a long time getting here, Frankie!" the boys heard Fennelli say as he shut the door.

They went on with their card game.

Jerry took another drink of his highball. "The stoolie said that this man was organizing the entire gambling setup in the city; that he was going to put an end to the constant wrangling and warfare between the different gangs that was drawing the public's attention and ire. There had been a period of gang war that the newspapers had played up, and they were raising hell with the department for not stamping it out. Kane had the answer all figured out. He was going to establish a cartel, an organization that would set up territories for the different groups, and enforce them. He had asked the principal leaders in the city to come to a meeting."

If Fennelli had known what was to happen, he might never have given Frank a job. He started him out as a runner, but Frank didn't stay at that long. He was too much of an organizer. In a little while he had others out picking up the bets for him, and he split commissions with them. Then Silk took him into the group and put him in charge of all his runners.

To the others in the business, Frank Kane always remained a stranger. Fennelli was the only guy who knew who he was and where he came from, and Fennelli didn't talk.

Frank sat at Fennelli's right at the table. The city was well represented at the meeting: Madigan and Moscowits from the Bronx, Luigerro from South Brooklyn, "Fats" Crown from Brownsville, "Big Black" Carvell from Harlem, Schutz from Yorkville, Taylor from Richmond, Jensen from Queens, Riordan from Staten Island, Antone from Greenwich Village, Kelly from Washington Heights.

They met in a hotel room and it looked as if it were a

board-of-directors meeting of some large company. A pad and pencil were on the table in front of each man. Cigars and cigarettes and ashtrays were there. It was about two o'clock in the afternoon, and the sun came streaming in the open windows when Fennelli got to his feet to talk.

"You all know why you were asked to come down here. There is talk of the Governor appointing a special prosecutor to clean up the city. If a guy comes in that we can't get to, we're sunk, unless we first clean house ourselves. His voice was low, pleasant and well modulated. His manner of speaking was simple. He was one member of a group of business men talking to the others in hopes that they would see the light and protect their business. The fact that he had it in his mind to be kingpin was incidental. When Frank had first suggested the idea, he had laughed. He was convinced when Frank had explained it further. He decided to give it a fling when public indignation began to mount and two of his boys were knocked off.

"Under this plan here," he continued, "we'll all be able to operate without interference by the police. We can eliminate friction between ourselves by laying our differences before the commissioner." He liked the sound of that word. It made him think of Judge Landis and how well baseball was organized to the exclusion of outside interests. "No more shooting, no more publicity, no more pressure from the people to clean up the city.

"There's lots of dough in it for all of us—more than enough if we're smart. Even if being smart isn't what we thought it meant, we'd better get smart right away. We're a big business— one of the biggest in the country. If anything happens to a business that threatens its interests, they take steps to counter it. That is all I'm suggesting—a way to protect our investment." He sat down.

Madigan was the first on his feet with a question. "It all sounds very pretty to me but who's going to make a guy stay in his territory if he feels like expanding?"

Fennelli answered, "The commissioner."

"How?" Madigan persisted.

"By talking it over with the people involved."

"And if that don't work?"

"Torpedo!" Silk answered.

Madigan made his point with an air of triumph. "Then we're right back where we started."

Fennelli was stumped. He hadn't thought about that.

But Kane had. He got to his feet quickly. "That's just what we're trying to avoid," he said, "and we can avoid that by agreement. If all you men are willing to work together on this, we can work it out.

"My idea," he said, boldly taking away the credit from Fennelli, who had called the meeting, "is this: You men will appoint the commissioner. He will open operations in an office that eventually will become the nerve center of the business. He will set up an exchange to help you control prices, apportion layoffs, fix odds. He will see to it that you get your fair share of the business and your fair share of the combined profits. He will be your representative and will operate solely to protect you."

"And who will this guy be?" asked Madigan.

Fennelli relaxed in his chair. He knew what was coming—Frank would suggest him.

"Me," said Kane flatly.

Fennelli bolted upright. "You!" he almost shouted. "Who the hell are you, anyway!"

Kane faced him quietly.

"The first double cross!" thought Moscowits. "This will go the way of all the other attempts." He was getting a little tired of this business anyway. He wanted to retire and go away somewhere—far away. But if there could be a little peace instead of this dangerous play and counterplay, he might be tempted to stick it out a little longer.

"I'm the right guy for the job," Kane answered evenly. "I'm the only one here who has nothing to protect. I don't owe any of you anything. I don't benefit if any of you guys get more or less. Besides, none of you will agree on any of the others. The only choice you have is me—or the special prosecutor."

Fennelli relaxed. "By Jesus, the kid's right!" he thought. "I wouldn't trust any of them no more than they'd go for me. Besides, I can control him and that's all I need." "O.K.," he said aloud, "I see what you mean."

Kane faced the table. Excitement was simmering deep within him. "This is it!" a voice was saying over and over in his mind, but none of this showed in his manner. "Any other objections?" he asked.

"How much will it cost us?" Antone wanted to know.

"It will vary according to the business you do," Kane answered. "The shares will run from five to twenty-five hundred a week to start. In your case the amount is written on a slip of paper in an envelope in my pocket. I have one for each of you. Your name's written on the outside. You can talk about it or not. It's up to you if you want to keep your business to yourself or not, because it's based on the amount of business you do." He took a group of envelopes from his inside jacket pocket and tossed one to each man around the table.

The men opened the envelopes quickly and looked with varying expressions at the amounts written on the paper enclosed.

"Two G's a week," Moscowits thought. "It's not too bad."

"Fats" Crown got to his feet ponderously. "This is a lot of crap to me! I don't like it. Nobody's going to tell me what I can do and can't do." He looked over at Luigerro as he spoke. The war between them was well known.

Kane spoke to him. "What you think is your business? In front of each of you is a pad and pencil. Write on it yes or no and sign your name, and then we'll see what we're going to do."

The men wrote and passed the slips up to Kane. He looked at all of them carefully and then up at the men. He spoke directly to Crown. "Yours is the only no. Do you want to change your mind?"

Crown shook his head. "It won't work. Nobody is going to ..."

Kane interrupted him. "If you want it that way, it's your choice. But the rest of us aren't going down because of you or any fool like you." He spoke almost gently, "You may withdraw from the meeting."

Crown looked around the table. "I'm getting out but I'm warnin' yuh. Stay out of my territory, that's all!" He stamped angrily to the door and went out.

The other men looked at Kane. It was important to see how he handled this situation. What he did now would indicate what course he would take in the future.

Kane walked over to the side of the room and picked up a telephone. He dialed a number. A voice answered. " 'Fats' walked out of the meeting," he said quietly into the phone, and hung up.

He came back to the table and sat down. "The rest of us are in business," he said. "Now the first step is to pick a headquarters. I've got a place over in Jersey City. . . ."

"Christ!" Fennelli thought bitterly as Kane elaborated on his plan. "The son-of-a-bitch has an organization ready!" And mixed with this thought was a certain amount of reluctant admiration.

"No one would believe the story the stoolie told," Jerry said, watching Marty's face closely, hoping to catch an expression of surprise there. Marty's face remained impassive, a doctor hearing a case history. His opinion would be formed later when he had heard and assimilated all the facts.

"It was ridiculous, the police claimed. They wouldn't believe 'Fats' Crown was rubbed out by an organization of all the big operators in the city. They tried to find a way to pin the rap on Tony Luigerro but couldn't make it stick.

"After the killing of 'Fats' Crown the city grew quiet. The mob wars seemed to stop, and gradually the public's attention turned to other matters. The pressure turned off, and the idea of a special prosecutor fell by the wayside for the time.

"And all the while Frank continued to consolidate and build his empire. He started his organization in a two-room office in a building in Jersey City. The name on the door read: 'Frank Kane, Enterprises.' But it was growing. From that little two-room office, tentacles were reaching out all over the country, to Chicago, to St. Louis, to San Francisco, to New Orleans. North, east, south, and west, they were reaching out in all directions, blanketing the country. Organized gambling became one of the biggest and most powerful businesses in the country.

"By late 1940 the two-room office had expanded into fifty rooms on four floors, had employed over two hundred people, bookkeepers, secretaries, clerks. Their eight operator telephone switchboard had direct wires to every gambling center in the country. It was big business in the American concept. There was nothing small about it.

"It had department heads, minor executives, top executives. It had an expensive and elaborate legal department. At its head was one of the top legal business counsels in the country. It had a public-relations department, with a man from one of the leading public-relations agencies heading it. This was the department whose job it was to maintain public interest in the venture. I know it sounds odd, almost crazy, to believe that a business as illegal as this one was interested in publicity, but it was true. This department saw to it that stories appeared in the newspapers and columns about killings made at the track, at the fights, at all games, by personalities that the public was interested in. They planted stories on how the bookies wept when so and so laid down his bets. They had competent sports writers writing articles on all angles of sports. They didn't miss a trick.

"And at the top of it all was Frank Kane. Under his direction the organization called Frank Kane, Enterprises continued to expand. A department was set up having miniature tote boards for every important track in the country. The pari-mutuel machines at the track were duplicated in this office by electric calculators, operated by trained men, which reflected at every minute the bets received in his office on any one race in the country. It was a routine matter to check his play against the track by telephone, and if the prices weren't right, a man at the track would begin to tumble money into the machines to get the price to where a profit could be made by the organization.

"He set limits upon which the bookies would pay off. Twenty-to-one to win. Fifteen-to-one to place. Ten-to-one to show. Fifty-to-one on parlays. One hundred-to-one on daily doubles. Before that, the prices bookies would pay were on a competitive basis, depending on how much business they needed or wanted. Sometimes one or the other would go over his head and fail to pay off. Frank Kane stopped this. A limit was set for the bookies according to their financial basis; all over that limit had to be turned into the organization, which would then split the profits with the bookies on a commission basis. It was a place where bookies not only could, but had to, lay off their bets if they went in over their heads. This had a stabilizing effect on the business. They began to brag that not one of them had failed to pay off in two years. It was a great deal like the Federal Deposit Insurance Corporation guaranteeing the deposits in banks.

"Perhaps the most amazing thing about the entire setup was that, despite its size, comparatively few people outside those connected with the organization knew about it. And even less people knew about Frank Kane, when suddenly one day the newspapers broke forth with the news. A joint interview with the Governor and the Mayor resulted in the statement:

The City and the State of New York, even the country, is in danger of falling into the power and hands of one man. One man, who has so organized gambling as a business that it is vitally affecting our entire economic welfare, whether we gamble or not.

He has so involved many of our citizens in economic bondage, forcing them into debt to small and large usurers and bookmakers, that the amount of money involved is greater than we can imagine.

His business has led him into fields of corruption never before equaled in our history. He does business in millions not in pennies. He had bribed or attempted to bribe large and small public officials. He has so organized nefarious activity that no longer is murder necessary as a threat to those that would oppose him, though there can be no way to estimate the murders and suicides that have resulted from his activities. He has substituted for this another weapon. The threat of economic enslavement for those who dare to oppose him. This man must be stopped.

Within a few days the governor will announce the appointment of a "Special Prosecutor" whose sole function it will be to stop this man and put him where he belongs. Behind bars.

This man's name is Frank Kane.

The job of the special prosecutor will have but one function.

To get Frank Kane.

"The newspapers were in an uproar. They had long been aware of the fact that a great story was to break, but this caught them almost unprepared. They searched frantically in their files for pictures of Frank Kane and couldn't find any. He was described variously as tall, short, fat, thin, and so on. To the public, he was a ghost, a wraith, a name without a body. He had never been arrested, never fingerprinted, never described. The question on everyone's lips was, 'Who is Frank Kane?' 'Where is Frank Kane?'

"Frank was in Chicago when the story broke in New York. He had gone there alone for two days, and for reasons no one seemed to know. There was never any business involved that we could find out, no woman, none of the usual things that would take a man to another city halfway across the country for only two days.

"I don't know whether he was aware of what had gone on in New York after he had left, but I rather imagine he was. Anyway he boarded the train with his usual nonchalance, took his seat in the Pullman and opened his copy of the *Chicago Tribune* to the first page. And there I came back into his life—or rather he, into mine.

"Right there on the bottom of the page, next to an item that told of the accidental death of a Chicago railroad detective, was a small squib which read—

New York, N.Y.
September 9, 1940 (A.P.)

Jerome H. Cowan, son of the former mayor, A. H. Cowan of New York, has been appointed to the position of Special Prosecutor by the Governor of New York. It will be the job of Mr. Cowan to get Frank Kane who is designated as the currently top man in the gambling racket of the country by New York's Governor.

"Yes, that was my job—to get Frank Kane. A funny way to get your big chance—nail your friend to the wall and let the buzzards pick at his carcass!

"I didn't want the job, really. But my father, who had wangled it, said: 'This is your opportunity. Friendship be damned! You may never get another like it.'

"So I took it. I was a fool, I guess, but then I couldn't know what was to happen. My first order was to bring Frank in for questioning. You know what happened to that. He stood politely across the river in Jersey and thumbed his nose at us.

"At the end of three weeks of intensive investigation, we had gotten nowhere and I was getting frantic. The newspapers were slugging away at me. They thought I had been given a wrapped up case, that all I had to do was get it into court. They were wrong. I had nothing to start with and nothing after three weeks.

"I decided to see him and talk with him. So one afternoon I picked up the private phone on my desk, not the one that went through the switchboard, and dialed the number of Frank Kane, Enterprises. If I couldn't get him over here, maybe I could make him see the hopelessness of his position and get him to quit before it was too late. 'After all,' I thought, 'he was my friend.'

"A voice answered the telephone: 'Frank Kane, Enterprises.'

" 'Mr. Kane, please,' I said.

" 'Thank you,' the voice replied. I heard the clicking of the transfer then another voice came on: 'Mr. Kane's office.'

" 'Mr. Kane, please,' I repeated.

" 'Who is calling?' came the voice over the phone.

" 'Jerome Cowan,' I said.

"I could hear the faint note of surprise in the voice as it said: 'Just a moment please'; then a click, then the voice again: 'Mr. Kane, Mr. Cowan on twenty-fi-uv', then another click and—

" 'Kane talking.' His voice came expressionless through the receiver. It was like talking to a ghost."

Jerry put his half-finished drink on the side table—he had long forgotten that he held it in his hand. He got out of his seat and walked over and stood in front of Janet and Marty, looking down at them.

Janet looked up at her husbnd with slightly widened eyes. He had never mentioned this before. He was agitated and nervous as he seemed to relive the moment in his mind.

He began to talk again, his voice was harsh and nervous. " 'This is Jerry Cowan,' I said.

" 'I know,' came Frank's reply through the phone. His voice exhibited no more emotion than if I spoke to him every day; he didn't seem affected by the strangeness of my call, by the fact that I had been appointed to put him in jail. It betrayed no curiosity as to the reason for my call; it was polite, casual, disinterested.

"I spoke quickly. I was afraid he might hang up and cut me off before I could finish what I wanted to say. From the way I acted, one might think that I was the accused, not the accuser. 'Jerry Cowan,' I repeated, 'Remember?'

" 'I remember.'

" 'I want to talk to you,' I said foolishly.

" 'You are,' he pointed out in the same cool, casual voice.

" 'You've got to get out of this,' I said. 'You know people are gunning for your scalp and that you can't beat them forever. We were friends once. Take it from me—get out while you can.'

" 'Is that all you called up to say?' he asked.

" 'Yes,' I said, 'Frank, for Christ's sake, listen to me!—'

" 'I have listened,' his voice replied, and now a hard note had come into it. An underlying quality of steel crept into his inflection. 'Mr. Cowan, I know you have a job to do. It's your job. You took it. You do it. Don't expect me to do it for you.'

" 'But, Frank,' I protested, 'that's not it. I want to help you.'

"He laughed shortly. 'You can start in helping by minding your own business.'

" 'All right,' I said, 'if that's the way you want it.'

" 'Is there anything else I can do for you, Mr. Cowan?' he asked. There was a hidden quality in his voice that I couldn't understand.

" 'No,' I said, suddenly exhausted, 'nothing. I was just thinking. When we were kids, everything was so simple and we were friends and you and Marty and I were—'

" 'I know,' he answered. Suddenly his voice had changed; it was gentle and friendly. 'I was thinking too.' He rang off and left me staring at the receiver in my hand.

"I put it back on the rocker and sat there in a sort of daze. I must have sat there for almost an hour, while a feeling of despair slowly crept over me. I was licked and I knew it. It was the same old story, and he was always better at it than I. I had the feeling I would never beat him down—never.

"I looked around the office. I hated it, everything it stood for, hated everything I wanted to be ever since I was a kid. What a fool I was, wanting to be something I wasn't! I had to get out of the office, had to go out in the air by myself and think. I grabbed my hat and left. 'I'm going out for the afternoon,' I snapped at my secretary as I passed. 'I won't be back today.' I jumped into my car and drove up into the country, and—and—" His voice seemed to choke up in his throat and he couldn't speak. He stood there looking down at them silently, his throat working convulsively, his Adam's apple jumping up and down.

Janet reached up and took his hand and drew him down to her. He sat between them, his face in his hands. "You know the rest of the story," he muttered between clenched fingers.

Janet looked at Martin over his bowed head. There was a look of understanding, of love and sympathy for him on her face. She spoke to Jerry, but it seemed to Martin that she was talking to him. "We know, darling," she said softly. "And that's why we're going to do what we are."

A strange look came into her eyes; they seemed to be seeing far ahead into the future. Her voice took on a mystical quality. She spoke to Martin. "What would you do if you had your life to live over again? What would you do for Francis?"

For a moment Martin thought he was crazy. He jumped to his feet. "Why, that's preposterous! We all know that Francis is dead."

The flame in Janet's eyes glowed brighter. "What would you do if I told you he wasn't?" she asked softly.

PART SIX

Chapter One

FENNELLI was waiting in my office when I got back from lunch. He jumped to his feet when I entered the room. I crossed the office and sat down behind my desk. I turned the switch down on the inter-office phone so that my secretary would know I was in—I had entered by the private elevator. The one-o'clock report was on my desk. I picked it up and looked at it before I spoke to Fennelli.

Then I looked up at him; he was standing in front of my desk. He seemed to be a little nervous. Perhaps someone who didn't know him as well as I did wouldn't detect it, but I did. There were little signs: the studied stillness of his hands, the slightest pressure of his lips—little things that gave him away.

I smiled. "Sit down, Silk." I lit a cigarette and watched him seat himself. "What's on your mind?"

He jumped to his feet again. "The pressure's really on, Frank."

He was telling me! For the last six weeks I didn't dare cross the river into New York and he was telling me the pressure was on! I didn't speak.

He put his black Homburg on the desk. "I mean it, Frank. They've really turned on the heat. Cowan saw the Governor the other day and got permission to start on us first since they can't get to you."

I knew that too. I was paying a guy right in the Governor's office two C's a week to keep me posted. I knew when Cowan made the appointment and when he kept it. I even had a transcript of their conversation in my desk. There was still nothing for me to say, so I kept my mouth shut and smoked my cigarette.

Silk was watching me. When he saw I didn't speak, he spoke again. "We've got to do something. The boys are worried."

"What boys?" I asked.

"Madigan, Moscowits, Kelly, Carvell, the whole bunch."

"You too?" I asked.

He sat down again and nodded his head. "Me too."

I laughed. I remember when I used to think these guys were tough and that nothing fazed them. Now I knew different. They were tough enough in their own cute way, but if anything went wrong they came running to papa.

"What do you want me to do," I snapped, "hold your hands?"

Silk flushed a little. "Can't you get to Cowan in some way?"

"I told you I tried that and it can't be done." I was lying. I didn't even try. If I had, I didn't think he would bite anyway.

"How about the guy himself?" Silk asked. "Maybe he's got something hidden away somewhere he don't want anybody to know about?"

I laughed again. "That guy's led so decent a life it's disgusting. There's nothing there."

"How about his family?"

"You know his old man yourself," I pointed out. "Do you think you can hang anything on him that would stick? New York's grand old man of politics!" I laughed derisively. If they ever started in on the old man, they would pull themselves down with him and they knew it.

"His wife?" Silk asked.

"No dice there," I said. "I checked that too. They've known each other a hundred years—ever since they were kids. They were engaged since they left high school. There's never been anyone to nail there."

"There's got to be a way to stop him," Silk muttered.

I stood up and walked over in front of Silk and looked down at him. "Sure, it's very simple. All I got to do is walk into his office and say: 'O. K. boys, here I am, what can I do for you?'" I stopped for a second and ground out my cigarette in the ash tray. Then I turned back to Silk. "Just like that!"

Silk held up his hand. "You know we don't mean that, Frank."

"How do I know what you bastards mean?" I snarled. "All I know is that you guys come whining over here every goddam time something goes wrong.

"Can't you dopes see that that's what they want you to do—play you around till one of you cracks wide open? Then they'll have all of us.

"Sit tight. Keep your goddam mouths shut! Leave the thinkin' to me and stop crappin' in your trousers every time the wind blows cold!

"You guys put me here to do a job for yuh and I'm doin' it." I turned and looked him straight in the eye and put a different inflection in my voice. "That is—unless you guys ain't satisfied?"

"Oh, no, Frank. We're satisfied all right," Silk protested a little too quickly.

I knew about the talks the boys in New York were having too. If I gave them a chance they'd throw me to the wolves as quick as the next guy.

"Then go back there and tell them to stop shiverin'. You can tell them that I'm on top of every goddam move they make and that I want them to do what I say.

"I've made arrangements to get every guy out that they pinch, within a few minutes after they book him. You tell them to keep operatin' until I tell them different." I went back to my desk and sat down.

Silk picked up his hat and moved toward the door. "I'll tell them what you said, Frank." His voice was respectful but his eyes were showing green.

I changed the subject. "You're nine G's behind on your share of the pool last week. While you're here, go down and see Joe Price and square it."

"I'll do that, Frank," he said, his hand on the door, his eyes shifting around the office.

I threw another punch. "And Silk," I said quietly, "don't forget that I remember you once wanted this job for yourself —and that I got a good memory."

He took his hand off the door and held it toward me. "Don't forget," he said in a queer tone of voice for him, "if I didn't give you your first break, you never would have got this setup."

"I'm not forgettin'," I answered quietly. "That's why I'm talking to yuh so polite."

He hesitated in the doorway a moment. He looked as if there

were something else he wanted to say but couldn t get the moxie up to say it. He went out and closed the door behind him. The trouble with these guys was that they'd been pushing others around for so long that they forgot they were human enough to stand a little shoving themselves.

I reached for the phone. "Get me Alex Carson." Carson was the top shyster for the firm. I had to tell him to follow through on the idea I had when I was talking to Fennelli—the one about setting up bond and bailing the gee's out as soon as they were pinched. Sometimes a little talk went a long way toward clearing things up. I was always ready to talk things out. The trouble was I couldn't trust any of them enough to talk with, so I had to dope the whole works out myself. I could only tell them a little at a time or else they would know as much as I did and soon begin to get ideas.

When I was through with Carson, I hung up the phone and turned back to my desk. There were a lot of things I had to do. I smiled a little to myself. Easy living was hard work.

A girl came in with the five-o'clock report and stood there waiting while I read it. I looked up at her. "Anything in from Tanforan yet?" I asked.

"No, Mr. Kane."

I picked up the phone and asked for Joe Price. Joe Price was the controller—a very smart guy with the numbers. When I picked him up, he was making a hundred fish a week as head accountant for some lousy little company. He had gone into the bag for a few G's, and I thought I could use him, so I pulled him out. He was worth it. I wasn't paying him a grand a week because I liked his looks.

He answered.

"How'd we make out on the first at Tanforan?" I asked. Tanforan was in California and was three hours behind us.

"We're down about eight thousand," he spoke in that clipped accountant's voice of his, "and the pool is down about thirty."

"How does it look for the day?"

"We'll be lucky to break even," he said.

"O.K.," I said, and hung up the phone. You couldn't make it every day.

My secretary was still standing near the desk. I looked up at her. "There is a woman outside waiting to see you—a Miss Coville."

I looked puzzled. "How did she get past the front desk?" I asked, "I don't recall the name."

"I don't know, Mr. Kane," the girl replied. "I guess she just walked by." She picked up the report from the desk. "She said you'd know her, she was Marty's sister."

"Oh, yes!" I knew her all right! What the hell was she doing here? I hesitated a moment. To cover my thoughts, I asked: "Is Allison in yet, Miss Walsh?"

"No." She started to go. "Shall I tell her you're busy?"

I hesitated again, then answered: "Yes."

She went out. I looked down at the desk. I had been tempted to see her, but nothing would be gained by it. She probably would recognize me as the guy that was in the hospital, even though I had put on a little weight and a two-hundred-dollar suit. It was better this way.

A few minutes later Allison came in. He was my night secretary. I needed two—one for day, one for night—and a woman was hard to get to work nights. I generally was around the office until pretty late and all the tabulations were in. So I had hired Allison.

"What do you want?" I asked.

"There's a lady waiting outside to see you, a Miss Coville," he said. There was a funny look on his almost effeminate face. I never did like him. I could never trust a man who could take shorthand.

"I thought I told Miss Walsh to send her away," I said.

"She's still waiting, sir." He rarely looked directly at me, but now he did. I was surprised to see how strong his jaw line was. "She said you had promised to see her."

I gave up. I'd see her and get it over with. "All right," I snapped, "send her in!"

I stood up as Allison opened the door for her. She stood there in the doorway a moment looking at me. She was dressed in a smoky blue-gray suit that seemed to set well against her blue eyes. Her gaze was level and direct. Her mouth was firm and her jaw almost mannishly square.

She waited until the door closed behind her before she spoke. "It is you." She walked toward me and held out her hand.

I ignored it. "Who did you expect it to be?"

She dropped her hand self-consciously to her side. Doubt flickered in and out of her eyes like shadows on a wall. "I don't know," she said with a suggestion of nervousness in her voice.

Then it grew calm. "Anyway, you were at the hospital that time. I wasn't wrong."

"What does that prove?"

"Why, nothing, I guess," she answered. "It's just that I thought—"

We had remained standing, facing each other across the desk, like fighters in a ring. "What do you want here?" I asked.

Her nervousness had gone completely. "I wanted to see you— to see if you were at the hospital—to see if you were the same person that had come into our house."

"Now that you see who I am, is that all?"

She set her chin. She hadn't changed very much. "You're still the same person now that you were then. Only you're older— and harder."

I didn't answer.

She began to speak again. "I shouldn't have come. Marty and Jerry warned—"

With a bound I leaped across the space between us and put my hand over her mouth. "Shut up, you fool!" I whispered harshly. "Don't you realize that I'm watched every minute, that everyone that comes here is watched? Why in hell you couldn't leave well enough alone, I don't know!

"Don't you know what will happen to them if I'm ever tied up to them?" I didn't use their names but she knew who I meant. I let go her mouth, her lipstick was on my hand. I wiped it off on a handkerchief and looked at her.

She was close to tears. Her eyes were filled and her lower lip trembled. She sank into the chair in front of my desk.

"I didn't know," she said. "I didn't think."

"That's just the trouble! You didn't think!"

"I only wanted to help," she said.

"Who, me?" I asked sarcastically. "A lot of good you can do me! And if you're ever traced to them, it'll be tough. The best thing you can do when you get out of here is to never come back."

She had gained control of herself. She stood up. Her voice was cool again and formal. "I'm sorry. I made a mistake. It was a mistake to even try to help you. You haven't changed a bit. No one can help you. You won't let anyone try. You'll just go along until you're knocked down. I'm sorry I came." She moved toward the door.

I watched her. I wanted to tell her I was glad to see her,

wanted to tell her I missed the old bunch. But I didn't dare. Maybe Jerry had sent her to me, looking for an angle. I couldn't know.

"I'm sorry I was so rough with you," I said gently.

"That's all right," she said, "I deserved it. I should have known better." She was at the door. "Good-by."

I went to her and took her hand and smiled. "Anyway," I said, "thanks for coming."

We stood there a moment, our hands locked, looking into each other's eyes. She leaned toward me, I felt a kiss brush my lips. "Remember what you said long ago," she said. " 'Now we're friends.' "

"Good-by," I said, and watched her close the door.

I called Allison for the Tanforan report, and while I waited on the phone for him to read the figures, I was thinking. It was nuts. It was screwy. This was no time to fall for a dame, no matter who she was.

Or was it?

Chapter Two

I HAD been seated at the desk a long time, lost in thought. Allison had come in, turned on the lights, and left. Time flickered by without notice. I had come a long way in the last few years. All the things I had ever wanted were now mine. I had money. I wore good clothes, ate well, lived well. What more did I need?

A woman? Hell, all I had to do was snap my fingers and I had the best tail in the country! No, it wasn't that.

Friends? Maybe. But I learned a long time ago I couldn't afford them if I was to get what I wanted. For everything I gained, I had to give up something else. Besides, friends don't give you what I got.

I turned my chair around toward the window and looked out. Across the river the lights of New York flickered tantaliz-

ingly in my eyes. It was funny. There was nothing I really
wanted across the river I couldn't have here, and yet I wanted
to go across the river. Maybe it was the pull of invisible chains
restricting my actions that made it seem important. I got out of
my chair, lit a cigarette, and stood near the window looking
over at New York.

Ruth would have to come and see me just at the time she did!
I wondered why? Did Jerry really send her? I had found out
you couldn't afford to take chances in this business. Your first
mistake was generally your last.

But still if Jerry hadn't gotten that job things might have
been different.

The phone rang. I went to the desk and picked it up. It was
Allison. "I've got the Tanforan report for you."

I looked at my wrist watch. It was nearly ten o'clock. I didn't
think it was that late. I was tired and hungry. "O. K.," I said,
"what are they?" I listened to him and then hung up.

New York was still just across the river.

I sat there for a moment wearily; there was one thing I had
to do before I could leave. I took Allison's personnel record
from the top drawer of my desk, where it had been since the
day before, and looked at it. Then I pressed the buzzer for him.

He stood in the doorway. "Yes, sir?"

"Come in and sit down," I told him. "I want to talk to you."

A puzzled look crossed his face. In a second it had gone.
"Yes, sir," he said, crossing to the chair in front of my desk and
sitting down.

I held up his service record for him to see. "I've just been
looking over your record," I said. "It's a very unusual one."

He tensed slightly in his chair. "In what way, sir?" he asked.
Despite his efforts to control it, his voice betrayed some pertur-
bation.

"You can drop the 'sirs' and 'misters' when we're alone,
Allison," I said. "That's a lot of crap anyway. People only use
titles of any sort to disguise their own feelings about the people
they're talking with. Everyone calls me Frank."

He nodded. "My name's Edward. Ed."

I looked at him. He was no dumbbell. No matter how much
he wanted to know the answer to his question, he threw it away
when he saw I didn't reply. Just that afternoon his jaw had
impressed me. Now I saw other lines of strength in his face: the

set of his mouth, his eyes, blue and determined, the furrows on
his brow.

"You don't care much for this sort of job, do you?" I asked.
"With the background you have, it seems odd to me that you
should have stooped to working in a place like this, for a guy
like me." I read from the record. "Columbia School of Business
'31, Columbia School of Law '34."

"A fellow has to eat." He smiled at me, feeling more sure of
his ground. "Hunger is no respecter of degrees, especially college degrees."

I liked that. I found myself liking the man in spite of what I
knew about him. I liked the way he didn't deny my allegation
that he was sinking below his standard. I liked his saying what
he had instead of something like: "Oh, no, Mr. Kane! This is
just what I want!"—or something equally stupid. I smiled back
at him. "Don't tell me that, Ed! Your folks seem to have been
pretty well fixed."

He tried another tack, seeing the first hadn't gone over.
There was a mocking tone in the back of his voice. He tried to
give the impression that I had him. "I wanted to do something
different," he said. "I didn't want to go into the dull routine of
an ordinary law or business office."

"So you came here." I smiled.

He nodded. "Yes."

"And was it?" I asked.

"In a way," he answered. "But it wasn't quite what I expected."

I laughed aloud. "What did you expect—blood on the car-
pets? Be your age, man, this is a business, just like any other."
It was my turn to be mocking. He was beginning to show the
slightest signs of having a temper. I made a mental note of that.
He didn't like to be laughed at. I changed the subject. "How
long have you been working here, Ed?"

"About eight months," he answered. I saw he didn't call me
Frank, but then he had dropped the "sir," and "Mr. Kane."

"How much do you get?"

"One hundred a week," he said.

"What would you say if I made it two hundred?"

He looked a little surprised. "Why—why I'd say thank you."

I laughed again. It was a good answer. "What would you do
for it?"

He was puzzled again. "What do you mean, sir?" There it was back again.

"Supposing I were to tell you that the Department of Justice was trying to find someone in the office close enough to me to give them a line on my activities. Supposing you were that guy—I might be able to fix it. Would you send them the reports I would O. K.?" I looked over at him quietly.

He stood up and looked down across the desk at me. "Then you know?" he asked. He leaned forward against the desk, his hands gripping the edge, his knuckles white from their pressure.

"Know what?" I asked softly.

"That I'm from the Department of Justice," he said. There was a sense of failure in the sound of his voice.

I felt a little sorry for him. Why did I always have to feel sorry for the wrong people? If I hadn't caught on to him, he might have been able to hang me higher than a kite. "Oh, that!" I spoke lightly, as if it were unimportant. "I knew that when I hired you."

"And yet you hired me?" His voice was still tense.

"Of course!" I smiled, seeing the surprise on his face. "I needed a secretary." He tried to say something. I wouldn't let him interrupt. "Sit down," I said in a slightly bored manner. "There's no need for dramatics. I'm not going to have you bumped off—that isn't the way I operate. I told you just a minute ago that this is a business."

He sank back into the chair silently.

I continued. "You've been here eight months. In that time you've learned nothing on which your department can base a case. I run a business. The business has many and diversified interests as you already know. We operate and have interests in various industries, such as coin machines, juke boxes, clubs and restaurants, and small manufacturing. I like to gamble a little. Who doesn't? All my profits from all phases of my activities are properly reported on my income tax. I commit no crimes. There, in a simple form, you have a picture of my company.

"It's just what the name says on the door: 'Frank Kane, Enterprises.' "

He was silent for a moment, then he looked directly up at me. The hidden things—the things that had made me distrust him, that I had sensed rather than seen on his face—were gone.

They were replaced with a reserved kind of candor. He smiled. "I'm rather glad that's over," he said.

I laughed and lit a cigarette. I was too. If he could have known how close he had come! But that was something else. It wasn't until yesterday that I had known about him, and with all this breaking now, I would have wound up behind the eight ball. I was silent.

"I guess I might as well go now." He stood up.

"Suit yourself." I watched him move slowly toward the door before I spoke again. "I could still use a good secretary."

"What do you mean?"

I was deliberately vague. "You might turn in your badge and work for me. Or, then again, you might continue on the old basis; I really don't care what you tell them about me."

He looked incredibly young as he stood there. "I couldn't do that."

"Why not?" I asked. "No one but ourselves need know what we spoke about."

"No," he said, "it wouldn't be fair."

Fair, hell! What did he think spying on me was—fair! I laughed. "It's up to you," I said.

He went out.

I turned around in my seat and looked out across the river.

New York was still winking at me, giving me the old come-on, come-hither look.

Chapter Three

IT WASN'T until I had gone halfway across the bridge to New York that I began to realize just how much of a fool I was.

I had left the office about ten forty-five and had gone to the garage for my car. Then it happened. "Mike," I asked the old garageman, "have you a car I can borrow for the evening?"

The ten-dollar bill I pressed upon him with my question brought a ready assent. "Sure thing, Mr. Kane!" His smile showed toothless gums. He went off into the garage and in a few minutes came back driving a small Plymouth sedan.

I got into the car behind the wheel and looked at the dashboard. There was a full tank according to the gauge. "By the way, Mike," I asked before I drove off, "whose car is this?"

He cackled, "The boss's. It'll be O. K. I'll tell him."

"Thanks, Mike," I said, putting my foot on the gas and driving off. I went to the bridge, rather than the ferry which was closer. I didn't want to park where I might be recognized.

I slowed down as I came to the driveway leading downtown. I turned off Riverside Drive at 135th Street and went to Broadway. I parked there for a few minutes while I went into the drugstore on the corner and looked up Ruth's address. I ran my finger down the page.

"Cabell, Ruth—100 E. 40th St.—Murray Hill 7-1103."

A few minutes later I pulled up in front of the building. It was a large, white apartment house on the corner of Park Avenue. I went into the lobby of the building and looked at my watch. It was a few minutes past twelve. I pressed the button for the elevator.

A sleepy-looking elevator operator opened the door. I stepped in. "Cabell's apartment, please."

"Yes, sir," he said, sliding the doors back and starting the elevator up. "Doctor Cabell's on the fifth floor—apartment five twelve." He opened the door expertly and watched me walk down the hall. When I looked back at him as I stopped in front of the apartment door, he shut the door of the elevator and I saw the indicator move down. I pressed the bell.

I put up my coat collar and pulled my hat down over my eyes. What if she weren't home? I almost walked away.

The door opened. A strange man stood there.

"Miss Cabell?" I asked. I could hear the subdued tone of voices coming from the apartment. From the sound, there were quite a few people there. "I'm from her office," I added by way of explanation, "Mr. Coville."

"Come in." He stood aside as I passed him. "I'll tell her you're here." He looked at me curiously before he went.

I kept my collar up and my hat on. I was standing in a small foyer. At the end of the foyer on the right was an open door where the voices were coming from. I watched him enter that room.

I could hear his voice. "Ruth, some man is here from your office—a Mr. Coville."

For a second there was silence, then I heard her say: "I'll be back in a minute. I'll just go see what he wants." Then she came into the foyer. Her face was pale. She came directly to me.

"Why did you come here?" she whispered. Her voice was anxious.

I smiled. "I'm repaying your visit."

"You must go. You can't stay. Jerry's in there." She still whispered.

"You wouldn't leave my place until you saw me," I said. "I'm entitled to the same right."

She put her hand on my arm. "But you don't understand. Jerry's inside, and if he sees you he'll have to turn you in. You've got to leave."

"I don't think he will." I smiled. I was beginning to enjoy this. You get a feeling of exhilaration from treading where the ice is thin.

"He will," she said, coming closer to me. There was a scent about her that was faintly nostalgic. At first I couldn't place it. Then I remembered—Marianne used it. "He will," she repeated. "You don't know him."

"Don't I?" I asked, recalling my conversation with him of a few weeks ago. "I'll take the chance."

She was disturbingly close now. The perfume went ping, ping in my nose. "Please, please go away."

Then I kissed her. For a moment she was still. I could feel her lips in shocked surprise under mine. Suddenly they were warm and clinging, her arms around my neck holding my lips down to hers. I had kissed many women since Marianne, but I had never felt their kisses inside me, the way I felt Marianne's. But this—this was different. It was so like, and yet so different from Marianne's I couldn't explain it. I didn't try. It was tender, warm, sweet and passionate.

She withdrew her lips from mine. I still had my arms around her. Her eyes were deep blue pools in which I let myself sink. "Now, please go," she whispered. Her hand was half raised, her fingertips caressing my chin.

I smiled, more sure of myself than ever. "Not for this kind of pay-off!" I whispered. "Maybe, if you'll come with me?" I let the question hang in the air.

She didn't answer.

I made a motion to take off my coat.

"All right," she whispered, "I'll go with you. Now wait outside."

"I'll wait here," I said.

She hesitated. "All right, but be careful." She turned and disappeared into the room from which she had come.

I could hear her explanation through the doors. I could see two shadows coming toward the door. I turned my face toward the wall and examined a small painting hanging there and kept my back toward them. From the corner of my eye I could see it was Marty. He didn't look at me. I couldn't hear what he said—he was speaking quietly. I just caught his last phrase, telling her to be careful. She had a coat thrown over her arm, and I could see her eyes flicking glances at me. She laughed and sent him back to the party or whatever it was, and came toward me.

I smiled. "Can I help you with your coat?"

She looked at me. Her face was troubled and serious. "I'll put it on outside. The quicker you're out of here, the better I'll feel."

I laughed and held the door open for her.

The elevator boy eyed us strangely as we went out. We were silent all the way down. We walked silently out to the car. I opened the door for her and closed it after her. Then I went around the other side and got in.

Suddenly she smiled. "This car is rather anticlimactic, isn't it?"

I laughed. "I see what you mean. You must have expected a large flashy job. Well, I'm sorry to disappoint you, but I couldn't use mine. It's hotter than a firecracker right now."

Her smile faded quickly. "You were crazy to come."

"No more than you!" I replied, starting the car. I turned on to Park Avenue. "Where to?" I asked.

"Where can you go?" she asked.

I thought that over. She was right: New York wasn't the healthiest place in the world for me right now. "I know just the place. I'll be all right, there."

She didn't realize where I was taking her until we were on the bridge heading for Jersey. I pulled into the garage and we changed over to my car.

"This job suit you better?" I asked, smiling.

She nodded. "It's more in line with what I expected." It sure was—a large, black, twelve-cylinder Caddy roadster. I drove over to my place.

I lived in the Plaza Hotel. I had a three-room suite that just suited me fine. Hotel service took care of the place, sent meals up when I wanted it, and left me free of any servant problem of any kind. I liked it that way. It kept people from coming too close to me. I let myself in.

"Won't you step inside my parlor?" I smiled at her.

She looked at me quizzically as she passed into the apartment. I stepped inside and shut the door.

I reached for her and put my arms around her and drew her to me and kissed her. I hadn't been wrong. This was different.

Suddenly she pushed me away. Her voice had a breathless quality to it. "Is this why you came to see me?"

I smiled into the dark. I was beginning to wonder about that myself. I reached over to the wall and flicked on the lights. I threw my coat on a chair and went to the telephone and picked it up. "Room service."

While I waited for the connection to be made, I looked over at her. Her coat was pulled tightly around her as if she were afraid to take it off. "No, darling," I said lightly, "I was hungry and I wanted someone to talk over old times with, while I ate."

She grew angry at that. Her old temper flared up. Her lower lip trembled as if she were ready to burst into tears. "You're still the same," she spoke bitterly. "You know all the answers." She started for the door.

A voice on the phone answered: "Room service."

"I'll call you back," I said hastily, and hung up the phone and dashed after her. I caught her at the door and grabbed her shoulders. "If I didn't want to see you so much, I wouldn't have gone into town after you."

She let me draw her back to the center of the room. I saw there were tears in her eyes. "Then why don't you say what you feel?" she asked in a small voice. "Or are you so used to hiding your feelings you don't know how to express them any more?"

I kissed the corners of her eyes. Maybe she had something in what she said. Suddenly she put her arms around me and kissed me. "I love you—you selfish, stupid animal!" she whispered against my mouth. "I've loved you all my life. There never could be anyone else for me."

I held her close. The sudden, sweet pain I felt inside me at her words told me of the truth in what she said. But it wasn't anything new. I had known that ever since I saw her in the hospital. I kissed her again.

The phone rang. She looked at me, startled. I smiled reassuringly and let her go so I could answer it.

"This is room service, Mr. Kane, did you call us?"

I looked at Ruth. "Room service," I said, mostly for her benefit. She smiled at me. "Some cold chicken for two and a bottle of Piper Heidsick '29, please." I placed the receiver back on the hook and walked toward her. "Now, how about taking off your coat?"

She slipped it off and gave it to me. Her eyes were glowing and her skin had a rosy hue from the cold November air. I looked at her. She wore a simply cut, black dress. "What are you looking at?" she asked, smiling.

"You," I answered. "You're beautiful." She was beautiful.

"The man speaks from hunger," she said.

"Both kinds!" I answered. We smiled at each other and suddenly felt very close and near to each other. Instinctively she held her hand toward me; I took it. I threw her coat on a chair next to mine.

We sat down on the couch in the center of the room. Her hand was folded through mine; her head rested on my shoulder. We were quiet for a long while. I shut my eyes. This was the first time in years I felt deeply satisfied and contented. It was as if I were a boy again and had come home to my aunt and uncle and we were sitting in the parlor, no one speaking, yet everyone happy and aware of each other's happiness. It was like that with Ruth and me.

I buried my face in her hair. She turned her face toward me. We looked deeply into each other's eyes. There was a question in hers—do you love me? She didn't have to say it, I could see it. Apparently she was content with the answer she saw in mine because she kissed me.

Then she turned her head once more and placed it on my shoulder. She spoke softly, almost in a whisper. "I'm not mad, darling, just deliciously insane. This is only happening because I've dreamed it so often." She turned suddenly and looked at me, her fingers raised to my cheek, her eyes round with half a fear, "This may be a dream. You may be gone when I wake up."

I caught her hand and turned it palm up and kissed it. "This is no dream," I said.

She sighed contentedly and leaned her head on my shoulder again. The quiet, peaceful, happy, contented feeling stole over me again. The world moved far away. It was true: I had come home again.

Chapter Four

THERE was a soft rap at the door. "Come in," I called, not getting up. A waiter came into the room, pushing a small tea wagon before him. He rolled it over to us.

"Shall I serve, sir?" he asked politely, handing us napkins and uncovering the food on the table.

I looked at Ruth. She shook her head slightly. "No, thanks," I said, giving him a tip and signing the tab. "We'll manage."

He bowed and withdrew from the room. Ruth leaned forward and placed some chicken on my plate while I opened the wine and poured it. Then we sat back and began to eat. I was hungry and ate quickly. I was busy with my food and didn't speak.

Ruth watched me. "You really haven't changed. You still wolf your food down. I remember when we were kids you used to do that."

"I'm hungry," I said, picking up a chicken leg and gnawing at it. "I didn't have any supper."

A few minutes later I was finished. I sat back, lit a cigarette, and watched Ruth. When she finished, I offered her a cigarette, and we sat back on the couch comfortably. I looked around the room. It was furnished rather expensively. I saw to that because I paid for it, but it had never seemed like home until just now. Up to now it was just another place to hang my hat.

I reached over and drew her toward me. I put my arm around her waist; she seemed to fit in the crook of my arm. With my free hand I put out my cigarette and turned on the small radio next to the couch. Some band was playing sweet music. I generally go for rocky stuff, but this was just right.

She put out her cigarette and leaned back comfortably against me. A knock at the door—the waiter returned for the tray. When he had left, I put out the room lights and turned on the small lamps near the couch and sat down again. Her face was lovely in the dim ivory light. We kissed.

"Why did you run away from me in the hospital, Frankie?" she asked.

"I don't know," I answered slowly. "I wouldn't have run away if I had known."

"Things must have been pretty bad for you then," she said.

I didn't answer. I didn't want to think about them. Some things are better forgotten.

"Do you ever hear from your folks?" she asked.

"No," I answered. "I could never locate them."

"That's too bad. I know how they must feel. I almost gave up all hope of ever seeing you again."

"Would that have been so terrible?" I asked with a little smile.

She turned her head and looked at me. "You could never know just how terrible it might have been. I might have gone on waiting forever and turned into an old maid."

I smiled again. "Not you! There must have been other guys."

She nodded. "There were. But they weren't you, and you were what I wanted."

"I bet you say that to all the boys," I laughed.

She laughed with me, but her eyes remained serious. "Of course! It's part of the line."

"Feed me more, honey, I love it."

"You're fooling." A troubled look had come on her face.

"I'm not fooling, honey," I said. "I mean it. I love flattery. I'm a sucker for it."

She leaned her head against my shoulder, and we were quiet for a while. Then she looked up at me again. "Frankie, I'm worried. I'm afraid of losing you again."

"Don't worry, baby," I said quietly, "you couldn't lose me with a ten-ton truck."

"It's not that I'm afraid of." That troubled look had come back on her face. "It's the other things. Jerry—everyone's out to get you."

I laughed confidently. "They won't get me. They can't make a case no matter how hard they try. Everything's being done legit."

She moved away from me. "It's true what they say about you, isn't it?"

I shrugged my shoulder. "You know how people are: they love to talk just to hear the noise they're makin'."

"But it's not just noise, is it? It's true, you do run the gambling setup?" She was persistent.

"What if I do?" I asked. "Somebody has to."

She took one of my hands and looked at me earnestly. "You'll have to quit."

That was funny. I really laughed. A lot of people seemed to have that same idea lately.

"I mean it, Frankie," she said, still holding my hand. "If you don't, you'll only wind up in jail, or in some alley, riddled with bullets."

"I don't think so, baby," I said. "The law can't pin anything on me and most of the monkeys in town haven't the nerve to start anything on me because they know they'll never get around to finishing it."

"They will in time." Her jaw had set stubbornly.

I smiled. "Forget it. I'm not worried about it, and I don't want you to worry about it either."

"I wouldn't like it to happen," she said quietly. "It would be a terrible thing for me to wake up some morning and find you in jail."

"I'll be here tomorrow morning," I said pointedly.

"But how about all the other mornings after that?" There were tears in her eyes. "Can't you see, Frankie? We could never be married unless we were sure we'd be together—unless I was sure you were safe. There wouldn't be any happiness for us any other way."

I listened to her in amazement. Who said anything about getting married? But the more I looked at her, the better I liked the idea. She'd be nice to come home to. I laughed to myself. I got it bad, I thought—and quick!

"Why not?" I asked. "What has my work to do with our getting married? I make a lot of dough. If I didn't, we couldn't get married anyway. That's silly."

She shook her head. "No, it's not silly. You've got the idea that money can do everything. It can't! You can't buy pride and respect. The person commands them, not the price."

"I'm not ashamed of what I do." I was getting a little angry. "I had enough of crappin' around on measly little jobs and half starvin' to death, and I don't like it. And you don't have to be ashamed of me either. I worked damn hard getting a setup like this and I'm not going to throw it away because some stupid bluenoses say I louse up the air."

"You don't see what I'm trying to tell you, do you?" She was very still, her body almost rigid.

"No, I don't."

Her eyes had hardened, and her jaw had set into familiarly stubborn lines. "I didn't think you would," she said coldly. "I can see now there's no use in trying to make you understand." She walked toward her coat and picked it up.

I watched her. "What are you going to do?" I asked.

"Go home," she answered. Her shoulders sagged. Lines of weariness etched themselves around her mouth. "I was chasing a dream, I guess. There's nothing here for me."

I was angry now. "Nothing here for you?" I asked sarcastically. "If I played ball your way, what would be in it for me?"

Her head went up, her shoulders back, sparks shot from her eyes. "I'll tell you what's in it for you, if you don't know.

"It's a chance for you to come home, to become a human being. A chance for you to join society and live with people. A chance for you to hold up your head and belong to, instead of fighting against. A chance for you to come out of the jungle and stop snarling and scratching and torturing yourself into a frenzy of hate against the really important things around you. A chance for you to love and be loved, to share and be shared with, to give and be given.

"A chance to spend days without fear, without schemes, without mean little doubts to disturb your sleep. A chance for you to stop being lonely. A chance for you to live and be human and to have children—" Her eyes flooded over with tears, and her sobs struck in her throat. She couldn't speak. She just stood there looking at me, her heart in her eyes.

I didn't dare step near her. If I did, I would be lost. There was a tight, constricted feeling in my chest. I couldn't look into her eyes. I turned my head away. I had fought too long and too hard to relinquish what I had earned for anyone. I looked at the carpet. My voice was low and hard. "I'd rather have this," I said. "I know what this is."

She didn't answer. The tears stopped falling. She took a step toward me. Then her mouth set in a thin line, as if she were biting on her lips to keep from speaking, she turned and walked toward the door and went out silently.

My back was toward the door, and I heard the latch click gently. I sat down on the couch heavily. The perfume of her clung to my nostrils. I shut my eyes and could see her framed against my eyelids. Ruth! The name of the scent she had used suddenly popped into my mind. "Poor Fool!" They certainly named it right!

I certainly was!

Chapter Five

THE phone woke me up. I had had a bad night. For the first time in years I hadn't slept well. I turned and tossed, and, at last, in the early hours of the morning, I finally fell into a fitful sort of slumber. Cursing the phone, I reached for it, picked it up, and said: "What the hell do you want?"

"Frank," I recognized the voice. Alex Carson.

"Yeah, Alex, what's on your mind?"

"I've been trying to get you at the office all morning and you hadn't come in yet." I looked over at the clock—eleven thirty. I swung my feet over the edge of the bed and sat up. "They threw Luigerro in the can this morning," he continued.

"Well, get him out," I said. "You know what the hell to do; that's what you're gettin' paid for!"

"But, Frank," he protested, "he's in on a morals charge— Mann Act. He took a couple of high-school girls up to his place in Connecticut. The Feds have him, and the papers are raising hell. The kids' parents are making a stink all over town and the FBI picked him up this morning and won't let me get to him until their investigation is complete."

That was a kick in the teeth! Yesterday I told Allison out. Today they went to work—those babies didn't waste any time.

"Get to the kids' parents and buy them off." I didn't want Luigerro to open his yap.

"But that won't stop them," Carson said. "This is a Federal charge. The government presses it, not the kids' folks."

"Look," I said, "for Jesus' sake, use your head! Buy the folks off. Get a release from them saying they let the kids go with Louie. He was taking them up to visit a relative. I don't know how, but you get him out." I slammed the receiver savagely back on the hook and got out of bed and began to dress.

The goddam tail-crazy bastards. There wasn't enough legitimate tail around for them—they had to go and rob the cradle. I finished dressing and called downstairs to have my car brought out.

I got to the office about twelve and rang for Carson. He came quickly enough. He was sweating a little. "Well?" I asked.

"Give me a little time, Frank," he said, holding up his hands. "You can't do things like that in a minute."

"All right," I said, "but have him brought over here as soon as you spring him."

He hurried out.

I picked up the phone and told Miss Walsh to get me Allison at home.

A voice answered—his. "Hello."

"Allison," I said, without waiting for him to answer. "Kane. Can you get down here right away?" I was going to try to pump him for a line on Luigerro. He must know something about it.

"No, Mr. Kane, I can't," he replied. "I was through as of last night."

I didn't answer. I just hung up the phone. I spun my chair around and looked out the window and sat there for a moment, thinking. Then I turned back to my desk and called Joe Price and told him to get up here right away.

Price came in. He was a thin, sandy-haired man, with an ineffectual blond slip of a mustache struggling for existence under a fairly prominent nose. I waved him to a chair.

"What do you think of setting up a new outfit to handle the legitimate end of the business?" I threw at him.

He was no dope. He looked across the desk at me shrewdly. He could see what was in my mind, and hear the whistles blowing. But he was my man and he knew that too. "It's an idea," he said, a flicker of a smile crossing his face.

"Isn't it?" I smiled back.

"Yes," he said, "but what are you going to do with the rest of the setup?"

"Time will decide that for me." I shrugged. "In this business you never know what's going to happen next." If the government gets too close to me, I wanted to be ready to get out quick—but I wasn't going to do that unless I had to.

"But what about the dough the others have tied up in that end of the business?" he asked.

"Look," I said, crossing my feet, "they don't know about it now; why should they ever?" I lit a cigarette. "Screw 'em!"

He didn't say anything. I watched him think it over. I knew what he would do—what I told him to. He knew who put the gravy on his potatoes. I spoke. "Can you do it?"

"Maybe," he said, "but it will mean writing off almost a half a million for them."

"A mere detail!" I grinned broadly. "This is the time to start having some losses. They're blowing the racket apart in New York. What better excuse do we need?"

He thought a little while longer. Then he got up and held his hand out to me. "I'll do it."

I took his hand and shook it. "I knew you would," I said. "I'll write you in for a good deal."

He went out.

My share of grief wasn't used up for that day. Late in the afternoon, I got word that "Big Black" and "Slips" Madigan were tossed in the can by the D.A.'s office on a policy charge. Policy slips were one thing I didn't screw around with. It wasn't that I didn't care for a nickle-and-dime operation, but keeping track of it was too damn difficult. It was the one thing they ran on their own.

The pattern was shaping up fast. Lop off the fingers and you can't use the hand. And that's just what they were doing—one at a time so it would hurt. Meanwhile, the Mayor told the cops to go out and run the corner bookies off the street. The phone was busy all day with gees hollering for help.

Carson was busier than a one-armed bookie with two telephones. By the time the day came to a close, he was almost a total wreck. About six o'clock I called him. He came into my office, sweating bullets in spite of the cold weather.

I waved him to a chair, took out a bottle, and gave him a drink. If ever a guy needed one, he did. I grinned. "I hear you've been pretty busy today."

He took a quick swallow of his drink and looked at me, his mouth still open. Finally he managed to speak. "What in hell's the matter with you! You crazy? All hell is ready to bust open under you and you're grinning!"

I smiled at him again. "Take it easy, Alex," I said placatingly. "It's not too bad yet."

"Bad!" He got to his feet and yelled: "If I have another day like this I'll go nuts!"

I gave him another drink. When he had finished it and had calmed down a little, I asked him how he was making out with Luigerro. He told me he hadn't heard from the people he had sent out to see the girls' parents, but that he expected some word momentarily.

"What about Carvell and Madigan?" I asked.

He told me they would be admitted to bail tomorrow morning.

"That's good," I said. "And if we can get Luigerro out, we'll be O. K."

He got to his feet and started to leave. I called him back. "Take it easy, Alex," I told him, "and don't worry. This will blow over soon enough, and I can't afford to lose you."

He nodded and went out. I looked after him thoughtfully. He'd be a hard man to replace. I called Joe Price and asked him to come up. He came into my office with a sheaf of papers under his arm.

"Well," I asked, "have you given that matter we spoke about earlier in the day some thought?"

"Yes," he said. "As a matter of fact, I was just going to see you on it when you called. I put it down on paper to see how it looks." He held some sheets of paper toward me.

I took them and scanned them quickly. They were a survey of my interests in various businesses. They added up to an investment of about five hundred grand. "What kind of return can we expect from this?" I asked.

"I've got their last year's earnings on the second sheet," Joe told me.

I put the top sheet on the desk and looked at the earning sheet. After all salaries and expenses, they showed a net of about ninety-five thousand. Not bad! A guy could live on that! I looked up at Price. "Looks good to me." I smiled.

"I think so too," he said.

I lit a cigarette. "How did the pool go today?" I asked him.

"Bad," he said "We had too much trouble covering bets with all the excitement today. I think some of the boys are loading it into us while they have the chance. They're calling in late, and we dropped quite a bit."

"How much?"

"About twenty-one thousand," he said.

"That's good," I said. "Let them load it in and take advantage of the situation. At least they'll expect some losses that way." The bastards could try to screw me all they wanted. I was even going to help them do it. "Make that drop seventy-one thousand." I smiled. "And take fifty grand from the pool every day for the next ten days." That ought to cover the investment.

He opened his eyes a little. "If we break even during that time, it means the pool will go down to about a million."

"So what!" I laughed shortly. "What do you think they're trying to do? It's a question of who gets to the bank first, that's all."

He didn't say anything to that.

I continued. "Tomorrow, straighten out the legal end of it. Incorporate it in Delaware under the name of"—I thought a moment; I wanted a respectable-sounding name for it— "Standard Enterprises, Inc."

"O. K.," he said. "I'll take care of it." He stood up and went to the door. "I'll see Carson about it in the morning."

"Wait a minute," I said, keeping him from leaving the room. I didn't want Carson in on this; he was too close to the New York crowd. "You'd better see some legit lawyers on this—a respectable firm. I don't want any smell of this racket around it. Let me think a moment."

He came back into the room and sat down in a chair and watched me for a while. I turned my chair around and looked over at New York. The lights were flickering, and I could see the ferries moving back and forth across the river. I was trying to remember. When Jerry's old man retired, he joined some legal firm who wanted him for his connections. For a while he had been with them on a semiactive basis, but now while his name was still on the door, he was completely inactive. What in hell was their name? I was trying to remember. It would be a good gag if I could put it over. I didn't think that they would connect me with this. I laughed to myself—Jerry trying to put me in the clink, and his old man's firm, my legal business representatives! It wouldn't be a bad weapon to use if I had to. Suddenly the name came to me.

I turned back to Price. "I know an outfit. They're on Pine

Street. Driscoll, Cowan, Shaunnesy, and Cohen." I looked at him to see if the name registered.

It didn't. He wrote it down and put it in his pocket. He got to his feet. "I'll see them tomorrow."

"Good!" I said. "You know what to do. Use my name—Francis, not Frank—and set me down for eighty per cent of the stock and president. And yourself as vice-president and treasurer and twenty per cent of the stock."

His eyes were wide open now. They should be. I just gave him a hundred grand. But it was worth it; he'd pay that back a hundred times now that he was in on it. Owning something always gets more out of a man than just a job. "Frank," he gulped, "you're not kidding?"

"I never was more serious in my life." I smiled. "We're in business." I held out my hand.

Chapter Six

THE next morning Carson sprang Madigan and Carvell. Later in the afternoon the Federal court allowed Luigerro to post bail, and I sent word out for all the boys to be in my office at eight o'clock that night. Carson couldn't get to the kids' parents with my deal. That is, he couldn't get to one set of them. The other pair were willing to listen to reason and ten grand, but one wouldn't be any good without the other; so I told him to forget it.

It wasn't a bad day. The pool went up about thirty grand in spite of all the handicaps to keep it from operating, which resulted in a reported net loss of only twenty. Runners were still being picked up on the street and the Mayor was trying to get the telephone company to cut their service to the bookies' joints; but the way business operates, the company promised the Mayor co-operation, but the order was kicked around the place and finally lost somewhere.

Carson came in to see me toward evening and gave me a full

report on the day's activities at his end. Luigerro would have to face trial and there didn't seem to be a chance for him to beat the rap. Carvell and Madigan also would have to face trial but stood a fifty-fifty chance of beating it, and if they did lose they might cop a short stretch.

The papers were having a field day. They played up every move that Cowan made. His picture was splashed all over the front pages, and his political future began to look brighter than a new penny. They showed him entering the court, his hat raised to the camera, his trim mustache, Ronald Colman style, over his smiling parted lips. The kid certainly looked smooth— a lot like his old man too. I didn't notice it until just now, but he had baby-kissing lips just like his old man.

I saw Price, and he told me things were progressing nicely with the law firm I had sent him to, and that they had taken the matter under advisement and would let him know if they would handle it in a day or two. Things seemed to be going along a little better today.

I went out to dinner about seven and returned to the office a few minutes after eight. Most of the boys were there waiting for me. I shook hands with a few of them and invited them to sit down. I passed around some cigars and they helped themselves and lit up.

When they had settled themselves in their chairs and were puffing away comfortably at their cigars, I got to my feet and began to speak.

"You guys have been reading the papers," I said, "so there's no need for me to tell you what's goin' on. You know that.

"I called you over here for something else. We got a business to protect and war has been declared on us. If we want to beat it, we got to work closer together—closer together now than ever before.

"We got to be ready to take a few losses. What happened the last few days seems to indicate we're in some difficulties in that direction. Joe Price tells me you guys are calling in your stuff late and sometimes even after the race is run. I know you fellas are working under a terrific handicap, but without adequate provision and knowledge before the race is run, we can't do anything about controlling prices. Under normal conditions you know we don't take layoffs like that, but these ain't normal conditions.

"I want to turn down late bets and calls, but in view of the situation, I decided to put the question up to you guys. The pool has had a couple of bad days operating this way, and if you want to run it that way, it's your dough and I'll do what you say."

I stopped and looked around at them.

Moscowits lumbered to his feet. "I think Frank is right, boys. We must not take bets that way or soon we'll be broke."

Fennelli spoke from his chair. As usual he spoke quietly, carefully. "I know it's tough, but what else can we do? If we disappoint our customers now, soon we won't have any business at all. I think the sensible thing to do would be to take our losses for a while—we'll make it up soon enough."

Most of the others seemed to agree with Fennelli. I was right. The bastards were so busy grabbing they didn't care what happened to the pot as long as they thought they were getting theirs. I smiled to myself. "O. K., gents," I said, "have it your way. If that's what you want, I'll do it." I had figured them correctly. I knew if I put it up to them they'd do what they did, and at the same time it made it easier for me to do what I wanted.

"Now that that's over, I'm going to put some things on the line. You know Louie, 'Black' and 'Slips' were nailed. I don't know what they're going to get away with, but the rest had better not be caught." I looked at the three I had named. They were as embarrassed as a couple of kids caught in the cookie jar. I spoke to Luigerro first.

"Carson tells me you got a tough rap to beat and you don't have much of a chance to beat it. You'll be lucky with five years in the can and two off if you're a good boy."

Louie was sore. His face darkened, and he got out of his chair and walked over to me. "Your goddam lawyer is full of crap!" he shouted. "I can beat it. I got ways."

I was waiting for him to get sore. I walked around in front of my desk and faced him. "Listen, Louie," I said flatly, "you haven't the chance of a snowball in hell of beating that rap, and you know it! If you're thinkin' any ways else, you'd better forget it.

"If you're thinkin' of cookin' up a deal with the Feds and rattin' on us, we won't give you a chance to get to the can to serve your sentence. So play it smart." I turned my back on him and faced the others. "And that goes for the rest of you guys who were hooked. Play it straight and we'll protect your business for you. Play it dirty and you'll shovel coal.

"We're gonna hang together, remember that—hang together."

They were silent, so I went back behind my desk and sat down and watched them for a minute or two. Then I began to speak again. I spoke more quietly and easily. "What's done is done and we can't do anything about it. But those of you that haven't been touched had better be careful.

"If you guys are married, go home to your wives every night. Stay out of crap games and card games and any gamblin' joints you're interested in. I don't want any of you guys pinched for anything—not even disturbin' the peace.

"If you got any tail you're keepin' on the side, get rid of it. Send the broads to Florida for their health. You don't want to keep anyone around who might give the coppers a line on you." I looked over at Schutz. He was keeping two frails in the same building on Park Avenue in different apartments. Neither knew of the other, and if his wife knew of either there would be hell to pay. I turned to Jensen. "If you're smokin' around with any hot stuff, take my advice and keep away from it." Jensen knew what I meant. His passion for stolen gimmicks like jewels and hot cars was fairly well known. All you had to do to sell him anything was to tell him it was hot. He would smell a bargain and run after it until he was suckered in. I looked at the others. "If you got investments in any cat houses, get rid of them. It may cost you a little cabbage now, but better a little now than everything later.

"Remember this: for every one of you that gets clipped, it gets tougher for the rest of us to operate. If they get enough of you, the rest of us will be out of business."

I paused a moment and lit a cigarette. "If any of you guys don't get what I'm sayin', it's gonna be tough on yuh. You've never had things so soft in your whole life. Don't kill it now."

I stood up. "Any questions?"

Fennelli got up and walked up to the desk. He stood there, slim, suave and cool, his customary black Homburg perched delicately on his head. "What do we do if they nail you?"

That was a question I had been waiting for. I faced him. "If they nail me—which I don't think is gonna happen—my advice to you guys is to pack up and go. Without me around to look after you guys, they're gonna pick you off like flies."

He smiled. He thought he had me there. "We got along before you came in."

"You did?" It was my turn to smile. "You mean you were lucky to get along before I came in. You were lucky to live till then with the amount of lead you caught. If you want to go back to that, you're welcome to it." I looked past him to the others. "You guys depend on me as much as I depend on you. If I go down, you'll all go down. If you go down, so will I."

I stopped for a moment. "And just one more thing. Don't any of you guys get trigger happy. If you start shootin' with the cops, we're cooked. If we play it safe and quiet, it will all blow over. If we don't, they'll blow us over."

"Any more questions?" I stood there waiting.

There weren't any and the meeting was over. I watched them file out talking. I wasn't kidding myself; these babies weren't going to do anything for me. They had to be made to realize that if they sold me short, they would lose their shirts.

But I knew what they had in the back of their minds, and they'd do it if they thought they could get away with it.

Chapter Seven

I LET myself into my apartment about eleven o'clock. Two days had passed since Ruth had been here, but I could still feel the imprint of her presence in the place. I swore to myself. I was getting soft when a dame could do this to me. I had never let any broad get close to me since Marianne, and I didn't want to now.

I turned up the radio and listened to it for a while. Then the telephone rang. It was the desk clerk. "A Mr. Allison is here to see you."

"O. K.," I said, "send him up." Maybe he had changed his mind.

A few minutes later there was a knock at the door and I let him in. "Hello, Allison," I said, "what's on your mind?"

"This is official business, Mr. Kane," he said as he entered the room.

I crossed to the couch, pointed a chair for him, and offered him a drink. He refused. I helped myself. "What do you want to know?" I asked quietly.

He watched me intently for a minute before he spoke. Then he chose his words carefully. "I've worked for you about eight months," he said slowly.

I nodded but didn't answer.

He went on, still speaking slowly. "I know as well as anyone just what your business is, but there are a few things I would like to know for my own satisfaction. Not only for mine, but what you may tell me may be to your benefit."

"Shoot!" I said. "I'll answer them if I can." I lifted my glass to my lips and took a swallow of the highball and wondered what was coming.

He leaned forward, rested his elbows on his knees, and crossed the fingers of one hand with the other. "Have you any connection with the shylocks in New York?"

"No," I answered. I didn't. The shylocks were one of the by-products of the business, and I didn't bother with them.

"The opinion generally assumed differs with yours," he pointed out.

"I'm aware of that," I replied, "but I can't help what people say. My business is peculiar in that respect. I can't sue anyone for slander."

"How about organized vice?" he asked.

"If you mean women, dope and that sort of thing," I said, "you can count me out. I'm broad-minded but I'm no pimp."

"Then your only interests are in gambling?" he continued.

"My main interests," I admitted. He knew that anyway. "Principally bookmaking, but I have several others."

He leaned back and thought for a moment. "I think I will take that drink if the offer still holds," he said, smiling a little.

I poured the drink for him without comment. He still hadn't told me why he had come. We sat there silently for a while watching each other. He looked around the apartment. I let him look. He would talk some more when he was ready, and I could wait until he did.

"How long have you known Ruth Cabell?"

The question surprised me. I stalled. "For some time," I answered.

"She seems to think a great deal of you," he said.

"You spoke to her?" I asked. I wondered just how much she had told him.

"Yesterday," he said. "Why did she come to see you under an assumed name?"

"She's a social worker," I said. "I suppose she thought if she gave her true name I wouldn't see her. You know how they are. She was interested in reforming me." I laughed easily.

"I see," he said slowly. He wasn't through yet. "How did you happen to meet her?"

You got to take a chance sometimes. "At Bellevue Hospital about six years ago." I lit a cigarette. "I was sick. I had passed out on the street and was taken to the hospital—malnutrition. I hadn't eaten for quite a while, had been out of work, sleeping in hallways, subways and public toilets for several months, and I suppose she felt sorry for me."

He nodded. "I could guess as much from what she told me. You must have had a fairly rugged time of it."

I was right. She didn't spill. I smiled and borrowed his phrase. "It was rugged," I admitted.

He finished his drink, put the empty glass down, and stood up. "I guess that's all I had to ask."

I stood up with him. "There's no need to rush off," I said. "Why don't you stick around awhile?"

"I've got to get back to New York," he said, walking toward the door.

I walked with him. At the door he picked up his coat and threw it over his arm. Once more he looked around the room. Suddenly he turned to me and smiled. "You know, Mr. Kane," he said, "you could do just as well as this in almost any other line of business."

I smiled. "Maybe. But this one gave me a chance. The others didn't."

"You can still try," he said.

I knew what he meant. If I got out now before they could touch me, I'd probably be all right. "I'll play my hand out," I said. "I'd be a fool to quit with the cards I've got."

"Sometimes your cards aren't as good as you think they are. Then you go to the cleaners."

I shrugged my shoulders. "You can't win all the time," I said. "I know that much."

"O. K.," he said, turning to leave. "It's your funeral."

I didn't answer.

"Thanks for seeing me," he said.

I smiled at that. He was polite anyway. That was more than you got from the local coppers; there was something to be said for the Feds taking college men. "It's all right, drop in any time." I smiled, closing the door on him.

I turned and went back into the room. I hesitated for a moment, then went to the telephone and called Ruth. A man's voice answered the phone. "Dr. Cabell."

"Is Miss Cabell in?" I asked.

"Not at the moment," Marty answered. "Can I take a message?"

I thought for a second, then said: "No, thanks. I'll call back."

"Wait a minute," Marty said quickly, "is this Frank?"

I was surprised for the second time that night. What the hell! Did the whole town know she saw me? After I thought about it, I realized she would tell her brother anyway. "Yes," I answered.

His voice became excited. "Frank," he said, "this is Marty. How are you, boy?"

I kept my voice level and cool. "I know who it is."

He paid no attention to the sound in my voice, but went on, still excited: "Jesus, fella, I'd like to see you!"

I couldn't resist the contagion in his voice. "That's nice of yuh, kid," I said, my tone softening, "but it isn't very good for yuh to do that just now. It may lead to too many things."

"You mean Jerry?" he asked. "The hell with what he thinks! After all, we were friends."

"I don't mean Jerry," I said. "I mean me."

"Oh!" Disappointment was evident in his voice. "Can't we meet somewhere on the quiet and talk? No one would know about it. Ruth told me she saw you. Nothing came of that."

He was right about that but in the wrong way. "That's what I called to speak to Ruth about. A Federal agent was just in to see me. He had already spoken to her, and I wanted to find out what she had told him."

"I didn't know that," he said. "She didn't tell me."

"Maybe she didn't have time," I offered as an excuse for her. "Maybe he just saw her today. I'm sorry, kid, but I don't think we can do it."

"I see," he said quietly. "Shall I tell Ruth to call you when she comes in?"

"Please," I said and gave him the number.

"I'll tell her as soon as she comes in," Marty said.

"Thanks," I said. "So long."

"Good luck, fella," he said. "Remember me if you need a pal. I'm all for you."

"Thanks again," I felt sort of funny. I wasn't used to people being nice to me for nothing.

"So long," he said and hung up.

I put the receiver back on the hook and sat down and began to read a paper. About a half hour later the phone rang. I picked it up. "Kane talking."

It was Ruth. Her voice was cool and distant. "I understand you called me."

My voice matched hers. "Yes," I replied. "I understand Allison of the FBI spoke to you. I was wondering what he wanted."

"You mean you were wondering what I told him."

"You can put it that way."

"You don't trust anyone, do you?" she asked.

"That isn't my business. I can't afford to."

"If it will make you feel better," she said coldly, "I didn't tell him anything about us. Only that I met you at the hospital and was interested in your case."

"That's good," I said. "He saw me this evening and I told him the same."

"Is that all you called to find out?" A strange note crept into her voice.

I was casual. "That's all, baby," I replied. "I'll send you an orchid for knowing how to keep your mouth shut." I could fool her but I wasn't fooling myself. I didn't have to call her. I had learned all I needed to know from Allison.

"Keep them," she said, her voice cold again. "You don't have to bribe me." She hung up.

I smiled a little as I put the telephone down. When I got this business under control and out of the way, I'd put in a little work on her.

She'd come around.

Chapter Eight

IT WAS the day before Christmas, Tuesday, December 24th, 1940. I sat back in my chair and listened to the music coming from the floor below. Like many other offices, we had a Christmas party going full blast. Soon it would be time for me to put in an appearance there. It was expected, a sort of annual reminder to the employees that I was real, not a fiction of their minds. Throughout most of the year the average employee didn't see me, as I came in and left the office by a private entrance. The management of the various departments I left to the department head. From them filtered back the various reports to the few executives I saw, who would in their turn pass the information on to me.

Miss Walsh came in. She was wearing a new dress. I noticed that the women always put their best foot forward at these little affairs: flowers in their hair, new dresses, beauty treatments, bright smiles. "If you won't need me for the balance of the day," she said, smiling, "I think I'll go downstairs."

I smiled back at her. "You can go, Miss Walsh, it'll be all right." I took out the present I had bought for her a few days before. Usually I gave her a bottle of perfume or a box of candy, but this year I bought her a small wrist watch. She deserved it; she had been working rather hard since Allison had left, and many were the nights she had stayed late to help me out. "Merry Christmas!"

She took the closed package and held it in her hand. I could see she wanted to open it but didn't dare in front of me because I might think it rude. "Thank you, Mr. Kane," she said, smiling, "and a very merry Christmas to you!" She turned and went out.

I sat there for a little while longer and then went down to the party. It was going full blast. There were the usual number of slightly drunk, and everyone was in various stages of Christmas joy. As usual the conversation fell away as I entered the room.

For a few seconds there would be a little silence, broken by whispers as new employees would be told who I was, and then gradually the party would begin to warm up again. I would stand around for a while, smile and nod politely at whoever spoke to me, and then leave quietly.

This time I felt sort of blue. Usually I came away from these things with an inner feeling of strength and power, but this time I just felt empty. I watched the couples dancing around and wisecracking, and felt sort of left out of things. I might be paying for the whole shebang, but it was their party.

I shouldn't have had anything to worry about. Things had been rather quiet since Luigerro and the others had been pinched. The boys seemed to be behaving themselves, and the whole affair seemed to be dying a natural slow death. Day by day the news of me crept farther and farther into the inner pages of the newspapers, being pushed back by newer and more sensational copy. Yet I couldn't escape the sense of impending doom that seemed to envelop me like a dark cloud over the sun. I turned to leave.

"Mr. Kane?" the voice was soft and young and had a question in its tone.

I turned back. A girl was standing near me. She looked like her voice. Youth was scrubbed into her face, but her eyes were wide and a little overcome with her daring. "Yes?" I said softly.

A look of relief flooded over her features. I imagine if I spoke coldly she would have run away. "Would you care to dance?" Her face looked down and her hand made a gesture toward the floor.

I smiled reassuringly. "I'd be very glad to."

Her face looked up at mine at that. She sort of brightened up a little. I held my arms toward her and we began to dance. People stared at us. Let them stare, I thought. I have a right to dance here if I want to: it's my party. This was the first time I had ever danced at any of the parties.

She danced well—young and light on her feet. The music was gay and a little on the fast side. She fitted snugly into my arms and I could feel the pressure of her youth against me. She looked up at me as we danced; her eyes seemed to be studying my face. I looked down at her, and she half closed her eyes so I couldn't look too deeply into them. She half turned her face away. "You're a very good dancer, Mr. Kane," she whispered timidly.

I smiled back at her. "You mean you are. I wouldn't do half as well with anyone else, Miss—?"

She colored a little. "Muriel—Muriel Bonham," she said. And then as if the words had burst out of her. "I hope you don't think I'm fresh—I mean about asking you to dance."

I shook my head slightly. "I don't; in fact I'm glad you did."

She gained a little confidence at that remark. "It's just that I thought you looked sort of lonely standing there by yourself—not talking to anyone, I mean."

I looked at the girl again. I must be in a bad way if a kid could see it. "What made you think that, Muriel?" I asked lightly.

"The way you stood there watching the dancers, it was as if, well, as if you wanted to dance too." She was smiling now.

"I see," I said slowly. The music was drawing to a close. I turned at a corner and the music stopped. We stood there applauding. Her face was bright and shiny, her mouth gay and laughing.

There was something about her that seemed too young to be involved in this sort of business. I made a mental note to tell Miss Walsh to find out in what department she worked and have her fired. She would be better off out of this.

The music started again. I looked at her; she nodded and we danced another dance. When the music stopped I thanked her and went back to my office. I mixed a drink for myself and sat there until I could hear the music had stopped. The girl was right. I was alone. But you got to make up your own mind as to what you want. I had made up mine a long time ago.

I looked over at the telephone. It would be easy to call Ruth and wish her a merry Christmas. It was as good an excuse as any. Every day since the last time I had spoken to her, a florist delivered an orchid to her for me. She had never acknowledged it, but neither had she refused them. It would be nice to talk to her. I reached for the phone.

When my hand was halfway toward it, I stopped. I noticed the door was opening slowly. I opened the left-hand desk drawer and put my hand in it as I watched the door. My hand touched the cold metal of the automatic I kept there, and my fingers closed around it reassuringly.

A girl's head peeked in through the half open door. The hair, a pale gold color, shimmered in the dimming light of the room. She saw me sitting there, and opened the door wide and came into the room. "Were you here all the while, Mr. Kane?" Muriel asked.

I shut the desk drawer. "Yes," I said. "Why did you come?"

She was in front of my desk. "I don't know," she said simply. "I just had to." Her eyes were vaguely puzzled. There seemed to be something she didn't understand about herself.

I got out of my seat and walked around the desk toward her silently. Something inside of me was haywire. I was nervously taut and tense; my mouth was set in a queer hard line.

"Mr. Kane." She was a little frightened. "Mr. Kane, what are you going to do?" Her voice went a little thin and she seemed to shrink back from me.

I didn't answer. I put my arms around her shoulders and pulled her roughly toward me. Her hands pushed against my chest ineffectually. I held her against me with one arm; with the other hand I gripped her face under the chin and turned it up to me and put my mouth on hers and kissed her.

Her hands opened and closed themselves against my jacket and then clutched my pocket and held. It was a long, hard, brutal kiss. When I let her go, her eyes were half closed. She hung limply against me. "Is this what you came here for?" I asked harshly.

She paid no attention to the sound of my voice. Her head was on my shoulder, her face turned away from me, her voice small. All she said was: "Oh, Mr. Kane!"

I looked down at her. The little bitch was just begging to be laid. Suddenly I felt old and tired. All the fever pent inside me seemed to disappear. I dropped my hands and backed away from her.

She looked at me. "Mr. Kane, what's the matter?"

"Nothing," I replied. "Go home, baby, before you're sorry." I lit a cigarette.

"Mr. Kane," she said in that tricky, small voice of hers, "I won't be sorry. Don't send me away."

"Beat it!" I said. "You're too young to be playing these kind of games. Go home to your mother."

"I'm twenty, Mr. Kane," she said, drawing up her head in a funny, proud sort of way, "and I'm old enough to play at any sort of games I choose."

I looked over at her. I didn't speak.

"Mr. Kane," she said, looking down at the floor again, "who are you going to have Christmas dinner with?"

The question knocked me for a loop. It was the last thing I had expected her to ask. "Why?" I asked.

"Would you like to have dinner with me?" she asked, still looking at the floor. "I don't want to spend Christmas alone again."

The word "again" intrigued me. "Why?" I asked.

"I live in a boarding house," she answered softly. "My parents are dead and I haven't anyone to spend Christmas with." She looked up at me. Her eyes were blue and swimming in tears. "All the others," she said huskily, "they have places to go—but us."

"How do you know I haven't?" I asked.

"I can see it in your face, Mr. Kane," she said, looking straight at me. "I can tell when someone is alone."

I watched her for a moment and then smiled slowly. She smiled with me. "O. K., Muriel," I said as sternly as I could, "I'll have dinner with you; but remember: no funny business."

"Mr. Kane," she said, smiling slightly, "I'm no virgin."

I laughed and sat down in my chair. "Miss Bonham," I said, "neither am I!" I kissed her and we went out to dinner.

We had dinner at the Oyster Bay. She was a nice kid all right, but I wasn't in the mood. Besides, I didn't think she was as old as she said she was. After dinner I took her home; she lived out in Teaneck. I pulled up in front of the house she pointed out, and walked her to the door.

The light was dim inside the hall. I said good night and turned to leave.

"Aren't you going to kiss me, Mr. Kane?" she asked plaintively.

I laughed to myself. I must be nuts to pass this up. "O. K., baby!" I said. "Just a kiss!"

She came toward me. In the light her face looked older, wiser. "Mr. Kane, I'm not a child."

I put my arms around her and kissed her. When I let go, I knew she wasn't kidding. If there was a trick to kissing, she had it. I went for it again.

She was close to me: I could feel the whole length of her against my body. Her mouth was warm and sweet, her hands cupped over my ears, holding my face down to hers.

The voice came from right behind me. It was a man's voice, rough and harsh. It spoke to her not to me. "O. K., Bonnie," the voice said. "You can let go now."

The girl dropped her hands from my face. She stepped back a little. Her face didn't have any expression of surprise, wasn't even startled. I took a quick look at her and started to turn around slowly. Pinwheels were going around in my head. By the time I had finished turning and saw the two men—one with a gat pointed at my belly—only one thought remained.

This was the kiss-off.

Chapter Nine

I DIDN'T speak. My stomach tightened up; for a moment I felt like being sick, but I swallowed my guts and stood there.

"Frisk 'im," the guy with the gun said to the other.

"You don't have to," Bonnie said, moving away from me. "He's light."

"Frisk 'im anyway," the first guy said. "We don't take chances with this baby."

I held up my elbows while the second man shook me down. Then as he moved away, I lowered them. The girl now stood next to the man with the gun. I looked at her; she was perfectly composed. I was trying to figure the deal, but no angles popped fast. My brain seemed to be a little foggy; it must have been or I wouldn't have picked up a hand like this.

"Turn around," the gunsel told me, "and go out to your car."

I did what he said—you don't argue with a gat! But it didn't make sense at all. If this was a bump, this place was the best spot for it. There weren't any houses near the one we were in. A thought jumped into my mind. The girl had said her parents were dead. Only two people might figure that I would be a sucker for that gag. Only two people who knew my history were also concerned with my future.

Jerry and Silk.

If it was Jerry, I couldn't figure it. If it was Silk, I should have been knocked off in the house. I got behind the wheel of the car still thinking.

"Over the bridge to New York," the gunsel said, sitting behind me. The girl climbed into the front seat next to me. "You're going to see the D.A.," the man continued.

I let a little sigh of relief escape me. At least it wasn't a curtain. But I still couldn't understand how Jerry had come to do it this way. It wasn't the way I'd thought he operated. I spoke to the girl next to me. "You took me, kid."

"It wasn't hard," she answered unflatteringly.

She was right: I did it all. She just had to play along.

"How long have you been down at my place?" I asked.

"I wasn't," she replied. "I just walked in on the party and waited for you."

I started to say something else, but the guy in the back seat poked me between the shoulders. "Shut up!" he said.

I clammed up.

We got over the bridge and I started downtown. The guy tapped me on the shoulder. "Go to the Dauphin Hotel," he told me.

I knew the place. It was on upper Broadway in the Seventies. The deal began to smell up again. Something was cooking. I didn't know what it was, but I could smell it burning.

I parked the car on Broadway and we walked into the lobby of the hotel. The man looked at his watch. "We're early," he said. "Go into the bar and we'll have a drink. And don't screw around!"

Silently the four of us entered the bar. There was a booth empty and we sat down. The waiter came up and we ordered. I had a Scotch-and-water. I paid the tab. We sat there a few minutes. Then the girl got up and went to the telephone. She came back when she had made her call. I saw the gunsel nod to her.

He got up. "Finish your drink," he ordered.

I swallowed it.

"O. K.," he said. "Come on."

I followed him to the desk. He stopped there and said to the clerk: "Two rooms and bath for my friend here." He pointed to me.

The clerk held the registration book to me. "Sign," the gunsel ordered.

I wrote my name on the book: "Frank Kane." This was beginning to shape up. It had all the elements of a frame. Only I didn't know who was pulling it. And I couldn't figure the frame.

We were shown to some rooms on the fourth floor. I tossed a buck to the bellboy and he left. "Make yourself comfortable," the gunsel said.

I sat down in a chair near the window. The first gunsel crossed to the telephone and dialed a number; he had his gun out and was covering me. A voice answered the phone. "Mr. Cowan?" he asked.

The voice made a reply. The gunsel waited a few seconds and then spoke again. "Mr. Cowan," he said. "Kane is here in New York to speak to you."

The voice spoke a few seconds. Then the gunsel said, "He wants to speak to you alone." He listened to Cowan for a moment, then spoke again. "All right, he'll see you at the Dauphin Hotel on Broadway—suite four twelve." Cowan spoke again and the gunsel hung up.

The frame was set. The picture fell into shape in my mind like a jigsaw puzzle beginning to make sense.

The gunsel walked over to the girl. "It's all set, Bonnie. You can tell the boss the D.A. will be here in a half-hour."

She got up and started to walk out. I spoke up. "Good luck, baby!"

She turned to me and smiled. "Save it, big shot! You need it more than I do."

"Go on, Bonnie," the gunsel said. "Beat it!"

She left the room. The gunsel turned to the other guy. "Go down in the lobby and call me when he shows up."

The other guy went out.

The gunsel moved me to a seat between the door and himself. He sat down near the telephone. We stared at each other.

"Detroit?" I asked.

He didn't answer.

"What are you getting for this deal?" I asked.

He didn't answer.

"I'll pay yuh double what youh're gettin'," I said.

"Shut up!" he told me.

I fell silent. The frame was simple: knock off Cowan as he came in the door, rock me to sleep, plant the gat on me, and the case was clear.

No one would go for my story, and the guy that wired it

would gain both ways. He would have the D.A. out of the way and me on ice, and he could take over. It was Fennelli I was sure of that. He was the only one smart enough to figure out a frame like this. Simple, but good! Establish my presence—they did that at the bar and at the desk. Up comes the D.A. on a hot tip. Bang and I was fried. I began to sweat a little.

But we sat there staring at each other as the minutes went by, and it didn't look as if there were any way out.

I looked at my watch; there wasn't much time left. I took out my handkerchief and wiped my forehead. If any breaks were going to come my way, they'd better start coming—fast.

The phone rang. He picked up the receiver and held it to his ear. He listened a moment, then hung up. He got out of his chair and moved toward me. He pointed toward the chair he had vacated. "Sit there," he told me.

I sat where he told me. A faint hammering was beginning to go on in my head. My throat was tightening.

He moved to the right of the door and stood there where its opening would hide him. He pointed his gun at me and said: "Keep quiet and keep living!"

I spoke again—desperately. "You can't get away with it! A frame like this won't go. I'll pay whatever you say."

He looked at me. I could see a sort of contempt creep over his sullen face. "You're all alike: big stuff until someone cuts you down to size, then you begin crying!" He made a savage gesture with a gun. "Shut up!"

A second later there was a knock at the door. The phone began to ring. I didn't know where to look first. Automatically I picked up the phone and held it to my ear, and said: "Come in."

The door began to open and a voice started to yap in my ear. "Flix," the voice was saying, "the place is lousy with cops!" I slammed the receiver down without answering, and jumped to my feet. For once I was glad someone didn't trust me. Jerry had sense enough to bring the coppers along. He didn't trust me. I spoke quickly to the man at the door who was staring at me.

"There's cops all over the place!" I spoke in a low tone. "Stash it, I'll cover yuh!"

He looked at me indecisively. His hands were white around the gun; he half lifted it.

I took a step toward him. The gun kept going up. Jerry

stepped into the room between us. He didn't see the gunsel behind him. There were other men in the hall, looking at me curiously.

"I'm glad you called," Jerry said. "It's about time you got some sense."

Chapter Ten

A FLASHLIGHT bulb went off, and for a second I couldn't see. When my vision cleared, the guy behind the door had stashed his gat and was walking toward me. I remembered thinking with a foolish sense of annoyance that the next day my picture would be in all the papers. Then I laughed. "Come in," I said. "I'm glad to see you."

Men crowded into the room behind Jerry. "Is this a pinch?" I asked.

"Not yet," he answered. "You said you wanted to talk to me."

"I didn't," I said. "It was his idea." I pointed to the gunsel. "He arranged the meeting with a gun. It was going to be a double frame."

The gunsel swore and his hand streaked toward his pocket. One of the detectives clipped him, and the gunsel fell. I continued to speak as if nothing had happened. "As far as I'm concerned, I'd be just as well off if I never saw you."

The detective had the gunsel's gun in his hand; with the other he hauled the gunsel to his feet. The gee was a little dizzy. He shook his head trying to speak. "Kane arranged it. The son-of-a-bitch! When he saw it wouldn't take, he threw me to you."

I laughed derisively.

Jerry turned and spoke to the cops. "Take him downtown and clear out."

One of the detectives spoke up. "Maybe Kane's got a gun." He didn't want to leave.

Jerry looked at me. I shook my head, not speaking. He

turned back to the cops. "No, he hasn't." He spoke quietly. "Wait downstairs for us."

They cleared the room and left the two of us alone. I sat down in a chair. Jerry took off his coat and sat down and looked at me. "Did you tell the truth?"

I nodded. "It was a frame all right. They were going to knock you off and hang it on me. It couldn't miss." I took out a cigarette and offered him one.

He refused, took a cigar out of his inside coat pocket, and lit it. I lit my cigarette and we looked at each other. "Got any idea who is behind it?" he asked casually.

I smiled. Kid stuff! "If I had," I answered, "it wouldn't have come off."

We were quiet again. I studied him. He had grown heavier. His face had filled out. His hair was a soft reddish brown and had a little wave in it. He had a thin mustache and full red cheeks. He was developing a little stomach. There was a sort of complacent look on his face, a sort of smugness. His lips were full.

He was doing the same for me. He leaned forward. "Christ, you've grown old!" The exclamation seemed to burst from inside him.

I smiled again but didn't answer.

"I never dreamed we'd meet this way," he said.

I didn't speak.

He watched me a second. Then his voice became plain and businesslike. "You know how things are between us. I'd like to help you but I have a job to do."

"The old crap!" I thought. Aloud I said: "I understand."

"I have a few questions to ask you." He took a sheet of paper from his pocket, looked at it, then put it back in his pocket. He looked over at me. "Did you ever meet a man named 'Fats' Crown?"

I nodded.

"Where?"

"Around town," I answered. "I didn't know him very well and never bothered much with him."

"Yet, when he opposed your organizing the gamblers into one pool, you had him killed?"

I smiled. "I had nothing to do with his killing. I had nothing to do with organizing a gambling pool. I'm a legitimate businessman." I took a drag at my cigarette. "If this is what you intend asking me, stop wasting your time. I couldn't tell you anything even if I did know what you were talking about."

He froze up. "That's how you want to play the game?"

He was crazy if he thought there was any other way to play it. If he thought I would spill just because he was a childhood friend of mine, he should have known better. I wasn't going to give him anything that would cost me.

"Never tell 'em your right name!" I smiled.

"O.K.!" He got to his feet; he was angry. "I'm beginning to believe what that guy said—this was your frame."

"You think what you like," I said.

"Look," he said, "I'm trying to give you a break you don't deserve because I knew you. I told you months ago, when I started, to get out, and you didn't listen. Now I tell you I'm going to nail you. I purposely went easy on you, but from now on I'm out for blood."

He was a lot of crap! If I could have been had, he would have had me. He wasn't doing anything for me and wasn't doing anything to me because he couldn't. I stood up. "It's your party," I said, facing him.

"It's going to be your funeral," he shouted.

"Quiet!" I said. "The neighbors!"

His face turned a mottled red; the cords stood out on his neck. "You lousy bastard!" he shouted.

That took twenty years to come out from where he had kept it. I looked at him coolly. "You're not so bad yourself," I said, half smiling.

He sat down again. For the first time he used my name. "Frank," he spoke apologetically, "I didn't mean that. I'm sorry. I was excited. I don't like this job any more than you do, but I have to do it."

"Forget it, kid!" I said. "I know how you feel."

We fell silent for a while, each with our own thoughts. "Why don't you get out of this, Frankie?" he asked.

I didn't answer. An explanation would be a confirmation of his thoughts. I wasn't going to confirm anything for him no matter how he felt about me.

When he saw I had no answer he continued. "It would be easy to frame you for an attempt on my life."

I agreed with him. "Very easy!" But was that what he wanted?

"In the long run," he continued, "it might be giving you a

break. A term not too long, not too short, would take you out of this and put you safely out of harm's way."

I smiled and threw the book at him. "Are you trying to protect me or the people of your city?"

He looked up at me; a new light seemed to come into his eyes. "You speak plainly."

"Why not?" I asked. "You were given a job. Do it if you can. You owe me nothing."

He stood up. "We could be friends." He held out his hand.

I took it. "We are," I said. "But that's between us. Business is something else."

He still held my hand. "I'm going to bust up your racket," he said, smiling, "put you out of business."

I smiled back at him. "That's your job. You can try."

He let go of my hand. "You don't think I can?"

"I don't think you can," I answered.

"Will you come down to my office Monday if I let you go now?" he asked.

He was giving me a break. I nodded. It would give me a chance to bring Carson along with me. He turned toward the door. "Be there at ten o'clock," he said.

"I'll be there."

He turned and looked at me. For a moment his old smile flashed across his face. "Merry Christmas!"

"Merry Christmas to you!" I said. I watched him walk out.

I looked down at my wrist watch. It was after twelve. I went out into the hall and down to the lobby. The room had cost me fifteen bucks. I was glad to be able to pay for it. I went outside. My car was still parked where I had left it. A parking ticket hung from the steering wheel. I laughed to myself as I sat down behind the wheel.

I drove but a few blocks when a voice spoke from the back seat. "Hello, Frankie."

I didn't believe my ears. It was Ruth's voice. I half turned around in the seat and pulled over to the curb. "How did you get here?" I asked.

She got out of the car and climbed into the front seat with me before she answered. "Jerry was at our house when you called him."

"I didn't call him," I said. "It was a frame." I told her what had happened, leaving out mention of the dame.

Her face was tense while I told my story. When I had finished she spoke. "I had hoped you were beginning to see reason." Her voice was disappointed.

I reached over and took her hand. "Give me time," I said. "Someday maybe."

"But not today?" she asked.

"Today I got things to do," I answered. I tried to change the subject. "How did you find the car?"

"I followed Jerry," she replied automatically. She was thinking of something else. "When I saw your car I got into it and waited for you. I knew you'd be out sooner or later."

She knew more than I did a few hours ago. I wouldn't give a plugged nickel for my chances then. I stopped the car in front of Fennelli's place.

"Wait here," I said, getting out. "I got to see a guy. I'll be back in a few minutes."

She didn't answer. I went upstairs and rang Fennelli's bell. If he set the frame he would be at home with a few friends. I was right. Laurens opened the door. I walked past him without speaking.

Fennelli was kibitzing a card game, a glass in his hand. He looked at me, surprised. "What are you doing here, Frank?" he asked.

I laughed, coldly, derisively.

"In New York, I mean," he added.

That was the clincher. He didn't have to add that if he was clean. I walked past him toward the bedroom ignoring the other players. I held the door open. "Come in here, Silk," I said quietly. "I want to talk to you."

Maybe it was the lights but I thought he looked a little pale. I shut the door behind us and faced him.

"What's up?" he asked.

"Someone tried to knock off the D.A. tonight and set me up for it," I said.

"Who?" he asked.

"I don't know," I said. "Maybe you do?"

"This is the first I hear of it," he protested. There was sweat on his upper lip. "How did it happen?"

I told him succinctly. When I had finished he raised his hand to his face. "Whew, that was close!"

"Too close!" I said.

"And all you saw was those three?" he asked.

I nodded. "I don't know what happened to the other two, but the cops took the gunsel down to headquarters."

"I'll keep my eyes peeled, and if I get a line on it I'll let you know," he said. He had composed himself quickly.

"Keep an eye peeled for those three especially," I said. "I got plans for them."

"I will, Frank," he said, "I will."

I turned and walked out and downstairs. Fennelli couldn't afford to let them get where I could talk to them. I had just signed a kiss-off for them. That was O.K. with me. Fennelli wouldn't take another chance for a while—at least not until he stood a better chance than he did at this time.

I opened the door, "O.K. baby!" I said with a laugh, "I wasn't too long, was I?" There wasn't any answer. I stuck my head inside the car.

She was gone.

Chapter Eleven

MY MEETING with Jerry at his office turned out to be a farce. Carson was with me, and every time Cowan asked a question he advised me not to answer. I spent an hour and a half keeping my mouth shut, and when I left I knew Jerry didn't have anything to go on. He was just fishing. All they got was my picture.

The evening papers had it splashed all over the front pages. "This is the man," they said in the caption under my photo, "that the government of your city and state calls their Number One Public Enemy."

There was another item in the paper too. A man and a woman had been found shot to death in a field along the Boston Post Road. The description of the woman fitted the girl who had been part of the plan to frame me. Silk hadn't lost any time at plugging the holes in his raft. The other guy was still in the can, but I was certain that Silk would take care of him at the first opportunity.

At least one thing had cleared itself up. I could come and go as I pleased. I had promised Jerry I would appear any time he sent for me. I called Ruth that night.

"What are you doing New Year's Eve?" I asked.

Her voice was cool. "I have an appointment."

"Break it!" I said. "We'll do the town."

She hung up on me. I smiled when I put back the receiver. Things weren't just right yet, but in a little while—.

January went by and February came. Nothing unusual had happened, but I knew the beavers were still gnawing in the dark. The new organization I had formed was all set, and the next move was to send Joe Price out and have him set up an office for it. I was waiting to do that only when it became necessary. The boys had behaved themselves and business had come back to normal.

The lull ended near the end of February. The first kicker came when I got a call from Carson.

"Frank," his voice was nervous, "I've been suspended."

"What do you mean?" I asked.

"The Bar Association has instituted disbarment proceedings against me," he said, his voice trembling.

"That means you can't practice until your case comes up?"

"Yes," he said.

"Have they got a case?" I asked.

"Not much," he answered, "but they're going to string it out as long as they can, hoping for something to break." He laughed a little bitterly.

That something was me. "Well," I said, "come over here and we'll talk about it."

I hung up. I lit a cigarette and looked across the river. This was the real beginning of the end. They knew I couldn't break in another shyster at this stage of the game. The next step would be to knock off the boys. I turned back to the desk and called Joe Price and told him to come upstairs.

Two days later they went to work in earnest. Jensen was picked up as a receiver of stolen goods; they traced a hot diamond necklace to him. He was out on twenty-five grand bail, but I could get ready to write him off. I had to pass the word around to the boys that the legal department was temporarily out of business. They didn't like that. I didn't think they would; but then, neither did I.

The next blast came when someone tipped Schutz's wife off to the two dames on Park Avenue. She went over to the place, caught him playing sixty-forty with one of the two broads, and shot them both up. She didn't kill either of them, but the cops had her down in the can and she was singing away to high heaven about his territory. I could imagine the coppers taking down every word she spoke and making pictures with it.

At the end of the week I got Joe Price out of town. I turned the operation of his department over to a guy that had been his assistant. From the way things looked, the game didn't have long to go.

The last Sunday in February was the clincher. After that I knew the party was over. I had split Schutz's territory up between Carvell and Kelly and Fennelli. Somewhere along the line—I had an idea where—the word was crossed, and a couple of Fennelli's boys shot up Kelly as he left his home one morning.

It was Fennelli who called me. "Frank," he said quietly, " 'Piggy' Laurens just knocked off 'Iron Mike.' "

For a moment I was tongue-tied. We still would have had a chance if the boys had played it my way, but this would only turn public support more solidly behind the government's stand. I spoke quietly. "Who told him to?"

"I didn't have a thing to do with it, Frank," he said. I could detect a faintly mocking note in his voice. A sort of I-dare-you-to-do-anything-about-it tone.

"Then who did?" I shouted. "A guncrazy son-of-a-bitch like that doesn't go around doing anything he hasn't been told to!"

"He says he had a call from you." The voice came quietly through the phone.

I saw what the gag was. I spoke quietly again. "Since when does he do anything for me? He works for you."

"He said you called him and told him to take care of Kelly and that you would take care of him."

"You can tell him to go fry in hell as far as I am concerned!" I said flatly.

"But what if the cops get him?" Fennelli asked. "He'll sing and throw it on you."

That name "Silk" was right; this baby was smooth. "It's up to you to see that he isn't picked up," I said. "It may be pointed out that he works for you."

I put the receiver back on the hook for a moment, and then picked up the phone and called Jake Rance. Rance was the guy who took care of whatever publicity we needed. He planted information on winnings of bettors and stuff like that in the papers for me. "Hello," his voice answered.

"Jake," I said "Frank Kane. Got a story I want you to plant in Wetzel's column for me."

"What is it?" he asked.

"A certain smooth midtown operator knows more about the murder of 'Iron Mike' Kelly than he wants to talk about."

Jake whistled. "That's hot, Frank. I don't know if I could get it in."

"There's a grand in it for you if you do," I said.

"It's in!" he said. "What's up, Frank?"

"The rats are beginning to run," I said, and put the phone down again. Let Fennelli sweat that one out.

The item made the Monday column. "Piggy" was a dead pigeon two hours after the first edition hit the street. It seems he ran into an automobile.

Chapter Twelve

I WAS standing in front of the mirror shaving. I felt good. A faint touch of spring was beginning to creep into the April air. The sun was pouring in the window and I, like a damn fool, was humming. I put down the razor and splashed some aftershaving lotion on my face. Its cool menthol sting made my skin tingle. I combed my hair and left the bathroom, putting on my shirt.

I picked up the phone. A nice Sunday breakfast was in order and I felt hungry as hell. The operator came on. "This is Kane," I said. "Have room service send up something to eat." They would know what I wanted.

"Yes, Mr. Kane," the girl replied. "By the way, Mr. Kane, someone is here to see you. Dr. Cabell and his sister."

"Send them up," I told her, "and you better make that breakfast for three." I put down the phone.

A few minutes later there was a knock at my door. I walked over and opened it. Marty and Ruth were standing in the hall. I smiled at them and held out my hand to Marty. "Come in, boy," I said, "I'm glad to see yuh."

He shook my hand strongly. "Frankie," he said looking at me.

They followed me into the room. "You're just in time for breakfast," I told them, "and I won't take no for an answer."

We sat down and I lit a cigarette. The room was upset, as Sunday was the one day the maid didn't come in. "Don't mind how the joint looks," I said, waving my hand at the room. "Bachelor quarters."

Marty grinned. "Frankie, you look good."

"You look good, kid," I said, "and from what I've heard, you're going to do even better."

He flushed a little. "That's nothing," he said deprecatingly, "I like the work and I try."

Breakfast came up. We sat down and began to eat. Ruth was quiet. We didn't have very much to talk about. I smiled at them. "Do you ever hear anything of Mrs. Scott?" I asked.

"She's dead," Marty told me.

"That's too bad," I murmured.

"Yeah," Marty said. "She was the first one to give me an idea as to what I wanted. If it weren't for her, I'd never have gone in for this."

"Great gal!" I put in.

"She thought a great deal of you," Marty said. "In a way you were her favorite. She expected a great deal from you." He stopped, a little embarrassed.

I laughed and turned to Ruth. "What do you think?"

Her eyes were serious. "She was the first person to ever understand you, Frankie."

I thought that over. Maybe. Anyway things never go as planned. I shrugged my shoulders. "It's a long way back."

I was finished with my eggs and was starting on my second cup of coffee. Ruth leaned over and poured the coffee for me. My hand touched hers as I had started for it, and we looked up at each other, startled by the accidental touching. Her eyes were blue and deep. Then I looked down at my cup.

Marty started to say something but didn't say it. We just sat there quietly for a few minutes. Then I said: "It's damn nice of you two to come over!"

"It was my idea." Marty said, "I wanted to see you. It's been so long and I've been curious, and Ruth. . . ."

"What about Ruth?" I asked.

Ruth spoke up. "I wanted him to talk to you. He's your friend. He's got nothing to lose or gain by what he tells you."

I got up and walked over to the window. "I want friends," I said, "but no advice."

Ruth followed me to the window. She took my hand. "Friends are more than just people who will listen to what you have to say and agree with you. Sometimes they have to tell you things you don't want to hear for your own sake. Please listen to what we have to say."

I turned to her. I didn't care if Marty was in the room. I put my arms around her. "Baby," I said, "if you love me, why don't you let it go at that? Why keep knocking yourself out trying to tell me to do what I don't want?"

She leaned against me for a moment. "It's just that, Frankie," she said softly. "If I didn't love you, I wouldn't care what happened to you."

Marty looked over at us. His eyes were serious. "You really meant what you told me," he said to Ruth.

She looked back at him. "Yes," she said simply.

He grinned at me. "You might as well throw in the towel now, Frank. The little lady's mind was made up a long time ago, and you can't win."

I looked from one to the other. They were both smiling at the thought they shared. "What the devil are you talking about?" I asked.

"Should I tell him?" Marty asked Ruth, still grinning.

"No," she said, suddenly serious again, "that's one thing he'll have to find out for himself." She drew me back into the room. We sat down on the couch, my arm around her shoulders. She leaned her head comfortably against me and looked up at my face. She spoke to me. "Marty was in Europe a few years ago. He saw something there. I want him to tell you about it."

I looked at him curiously. "What?" I asked.

He cleared his throat. "It's kind of a long story."

"I got all day," I said, tightening my arm around Ruth. Like this, he could sell me the Brooklyn Bridge.

"I was in Germany in 1935," he began seriously. "I saw what happened there—what happens to a country when gangsters take over."

"Are you talking about Hitler?" I asked. "What's he got to do with me?" I fished for a cigarette. I remembered what had happened last June when France fell. People walked around in the streets talking in subdued voices, looking bad. There was a great deal of muttering about going to war with Germany. Business fell off a few days but jumped back to normal quickly enough. I think it even picked up a little. But we didn't go to war and I didn't think we would—especially if we kept on minding our own business.

Marty continued to speak, ignoring my question. "In 1935, Hitler was organizing his country. Ruthlessly he put down anyone who dared voice opposition to him. At that time he said: 'Today Germany, tomorrow the world.'

"Well, this is tomorrow. The tomorrow that he promised Germany. He's already delivered the continent of Europe as he promised and all that remains there is Russia and England. Then he will turn his eyes across the ocean to us."

He stopped for a moment and reached for a cigarette. I still didn't get what he was driving at. He put his cigarette in his mouth without lighting it and began to speak again. "When he first started, people said he wouldn't last. I said that too. But I pointed out that he would last as long as people refused to recognize him for the menace that he was.

"When the world does recognize him for what he is, he will be stopped. They're beginning to do that now and he is slowly being stopped. England is holding out, Russia is holding out. The man in the street is stopping him. They're stopping him with bridges made of their bodies, of their determination.

"When the man in the street decides you're no good for him, he'll stop you. No matter what you do to prevent him from doing it, he will find a way. You can't be strong enough or smart enough to beat the man in the street."

I held up my hand. "All right, so they're goin' to stop this bitch on wheels! I still don't see what it's got to do with me."

"You should, Frankie." Marty stepped in front of me and stood looking down at me. "The man in the street is against you. And if he says you gotta go, brother, you gotta go!"

I laughed at that. Everywhere I went, people kissed my ass. If they were so against me, why didn't it show? I told Marty what I thought.

"That's just it, Frankie," he replied. "That's just what I'm pointing out. When Hitler goes out, people kiss the ground before him. But they do it from fear—because they're afraid of what will happen to them if they don't.

"That's why people bow down to you. They're afraid of you. Your name has become a symbol of terror, of murder and thievery. They're afraid of your reputation, of the things people whisper that you did. Whether you did them or didn't do them is not important anymore. The fact remains that they believe you did them. And they're going to destroy you, just as some day they will destroy Hitler."

I laughed. "It doesn't make sense to me. I just want to be left alone. If no one bothers me I don't bother them."

He shook his head, "It's become a case of cry wolf."

"I can't help that," I said.

Ruth looked up at me. "You can quit before it's too late."

I looked down at her. "I've listened to your side, now listen to mine." I put out one cigarette in the ash tray and lit another. "For years I've tried to eke out an existence in what they call the right way. I worked hard for little money and little security and to what end?

"I wound up in a hospital because I was hungry and didn't have enough to eat; because I couldn't get a job that paid enough to give some sort of security; because all that Horatio Alger stuff is a lot of crap; because no matter how hard the Alger hero would work, no matter how honest he was, no matter how difficult his struggle, he never got anywhere until he either saved or married the boss's daughter. I couldn't find a boss's daughter.

"All I could find everywhere I turned was people like myself —hungry and poor and miserable, living off relief, off charity, or some job that barely gave them an existence and one which the fear of losing hung continually over their heads like a sword on a thread.

"I'd be a damn fool to try to live that sort of life, where a boss could fire you if you were sick on a job, where a man could tell you all you get is ten bucks a week when you need fifteen to live, or twenty when you need thirty, or thirty when you need fifty.

"Hell, no, I wasn't that crazy! I wanted to enjoy life, to have things: money in my pocket, a car, a nice place to live, the things that count—the things you can hold in your hand and feel and eat.

"This was the one way I knew to get them—the only way left open for me. So I got what I wanted."

"But, Frankie," Marty said patiently, "don't you see? It's partly your fault too."

"Maybe," I admitted, "but I didn't ask for it. I gave it a fair shake and it didn't work."

Ruth sat up and faced me. "Frankie, you should have lived a long time ago. But the days of piracy are over. You can't bully and swagger your way through life any more. You can't just take what you want and say the devil with the next man. You've got to live with people and share with them. You can't just crawl into a corner and ignore what goes on around you."

I thought of Marianne. That's what she wanted me to do: crawl into a corner and ignore the world. I had left her because I didn't want to do that. Or had I left one corner for another?

But Gerro had believed as Ruth did. He thought and acted according to his ideals, and what did he gain by them? I knew better than any of them what I wanted. And I was going to get it—everything I wanted—my way.

I stood up. I walked a little distance away from them and then faced the two of them. "I don't see your way any more than you see mine," I said quietly.

Ruth sprang from the couch and came close to me. "Darling," she said earnestly, her eyes looking straight into mine, "but we do see what you tell us. We do understand what you say, but it just won't work out that way."

I didn't speak.

She turned to Marty with a gesture of despair, "Marty," she pleaded, "please make him understand."

Marty looked at both of us. Suddenly he started for the door. "I'm going downstairs for a moment. This seems to be something for the two of you to work out," he said, his hand on the doorknob. "It isn't a question any more of who is right or who is wrong. It's a question now of who loves the most and who is willing to give the most." He went out.

She turned and stared at me. I took a step toward her and took her in my arms and kissed her. She was cold under my kiss. I kissed her eyes, her hair, her cheek, her neck and her lips. I brought her down to the couch next to me and kept kissing her, savagely, brutally. My kisses left marks on her skin.

Suddenly she turned and kissed me. I looked down on her face. Her eyes were half closed, her mouth tremulous. I held her close to me and could feel the longing in her in the way her body pressed to mine. "I love you," I whispered. Her eyes closed completely and she kissed me again.

"I want you," I whispered, "I need you. Don't let anything come between us." I kept kissing her as I spoke.

Her breath came quickly between her parted lips. I could feel her small white teeth bite into my underlip as she kissed me. Her hands held my face to her. Her hands guided my face to her breast and held it there.

My arms were under her and held her close to me. I turned my head into the cleft of her bosom and looked up at her. Her eyes were moist and her lips were parted. I could feel her trembling in my arms. "Ruth!"

Her eyes looked down into mine; tears came from the corners like tiny twinkling diamonds. There was love in them, and compassion and understanding and desire. Almost imperceptibly she shook her head. "No, darling," she whispered softly, "not this way."

I buried my face in the sweet smell of her body. "I want you," I repeated, my lips against her skin.

She crushed my face against her. "I want you," she said simply, "but not in this way only. I want you for keeps, not for minutes." She drew my face up to hers. She held my face in her two hands. I could feel her lips moving under mine. We kissed again and she held my face away from her. Her eyes searched mine. "Understand, darling?" she asked.

I looked at her for a moment, then I got to my feet. My hands searched automatically in my pocket for a cigarette. I understood all right.

It was either play the game her way or not at all.

Chapter Thirteen

HER eyes were fastened on my face as I lit my cigarette. I think she read my thoughts for she got up and came toward me. "You don't understand, do you?" she asked gently.

I shook my head. "No, I don't," I said, almost bitterly, "I can't see what difference it should make to you if you care enough. Would it be any better for us if I were a street cleaner?"

Her eyes were cloudy and unhappy. "It would help. It's not what you are, Frankie, it's what you do. You have to do hard things, mean things. You have to be cruel and ruthless. You can't just do these things during the day and be another sort of person at night. Eventually the two will fuse and you will become what you do."

I started to answer her, to tell her she was cockeyed wrong, but there was a knock at the door. Marty had come back. I let him in.

He looked at Ruth and then at me. His question was unasked but answered by our actions. He didn't offer any further advice; he knew when to keep his mouth shut. A few minutes later they left, and I was alone in the apartment.

I thought about what Ruth had said and how she felt about me. She should know that you just can't drop a good thing like this as easily as you can put down a book. Too much depended on it. I had worked too hard for it. And I wasn't going to throw it away for no dame—not even Ruth!

But the day was shot as far as I was concerned. The spring had gone out of it.

The next few months were surprisingly good for me. The boys were watching their steps, and Fennelli was behaving himself. Business was pretty good and I stashed the dough away while I could. I wasn't kidding myself. This wasn't going to last forever, but I was going to get as much of it as I could.

It was late in May before anything unusual happened. And then it came in a manner I had never expected. It was near four o'clock in the afternoon. The day had been a rather hectic one and I was pretty tired. The interoffice phone buzzed. I flipped the switch. "Yes?"

"Mr. Moscowits to see you," Miss Walsh's voice came through.

"Send him in," I said, flipping back the switch. I wondered what he wanted.

He came in, lumbering in his usual manner. I stood up and smiled at him. We shook hands and sat down.

"What's on your mind, Moishe?" I asked, still smiling.

He came right to the point. That was one thing I liked about him. He was of the old line of gamblers, one of those guys whose word was his bond, and who played it straight as he saw it. Nothing phony about him. "Frankie," he said, his voice, rough but quiet, "I want to quit."

I didn't answer, just sat back and looked at him quietly for a few moments. Then I lit a cigarette and asked: "Why?"

He was a little uncomfortable. "It isn't because I'm afraid. It's nothing like that, only—" He hesitated a moment before he continued. "I'm getting too old for this business. It's too much of a strain for me. I would like to go somewheres with my wife and enjoy a few years without *tsooriss*."

I sat there still watching him and wondered what to do. This wasn't the time for me to let anyone quit. It wouldn't look good to the others if I let him go. They would think I was going soft. But then, it was the guy's right to do what he wanted, and I knew he would play it straight and keep his mouth shut about us. Silently I pushed a box of cigars toward him.

He took one and lit it and watched me. We sat there quietly for a while. Then I said: "You know how the boys'll feel about it."

He nodded his head.

I continued. "They'll think you're yelluh and you're goin' tuh squeal."

He waved his hand toward me gently, almost paternally, "You know me better than that, Frank. Moses Moscowits never squealed on nobody in his whole life, and he ain't going to start at the age of sixty-two."

I hadn't realized he was that old. We fell silent again. I

turned my chair around toward the window. "What about your territory?" I asked, my back toward him.

I could hear his voice behind me. "The boys can have it."

"And your share of the pool?"

"You can keep that too if you need it." Moishe wasn't above a little bribery to get what he wanted. I calculated swiftly. His share amounted to about a hundred grand.

"Where yuh gonna go?" I asked. I knew he owned a little property out in California, and wondered if he would level about it.

He leveled. "I got a farm in California. I can live there nice and quiet, like my wife wants I should."

I swung the chair around and faced him. "When do you intend to go?"

"When it's O.K. with you," he answered.

I thought again for a moment.

He spoke. "Frank, money you can't enjoy is no good to a man. I got enough money and here I can't enjoy it. All the times it's problems and troubles and headaches. I want a little peace with my years."

I made up my mind. He was entitled to a little peace with his years and he should have it.

"O.K." I said, "you can quit, Moishe."

I'd swear tears jumped to his eyes, but he controlled himself beautifully. Just his voice, bubbling over with a sort of restrained happiness, said: "Thanks."

"You leave town by the end of the week," I said. "Don't say anything to anybody. I don't want any of the boys to know about this until I tell them, and I'll tell them after you're gone."

I dialed Mackson. He was the fellow that had replaced Price. "How does the pool stand now?"

"One million, one ten, Mr. Kane," he answered.

That made it easy. "Draw a check payable to Moses Moscowits for one hundred and ten thousand dollars and send it up here right away," I said, and put down the phone.

Moishe's eyes were shining. "If you need the money, Frank, I can wait," he said.

I shook my head. "You always paid your share; you're entitled to take it out."

Mack came up with the check. I took it from him and he left. I signed it and held it out to Moishe. He took it and put it in his pocket, thanking me as he did so. I gave him one last word of advice before he left. "Moishe, don't talk about this to anyone. Leave your apartment as it is. Don't try to sell anything or take too much with you. Get into your car with a couple of bags packed as if you were going to the mountains for a weekend. I want you to disappear and leave everything else to me to handle."

We shook hands and walked toward the door. He took a last look around the office before he left. "Frankie, my boy," he said, "take some advice from an old man. Get out of this while you can. You're a good boy and a smart one too. I lived a lot longer than you and I know. Not many of us get the chance to quit when we want to. We generally go while we're young—sudden.

"And the longer we last the harder it becomes for us to quit. We get mokey and greedy, and we usually settle for a bullet. If it was anyone else but you, I wouldn't be able to do what I'm doing. Don't let anyone stop you from quitting and pay you off with lead."

I cut him short with a laugh. "Don't worry about me, Moishe; just do what I told yuh."

"I will, Frank," he promised and went out.

I went back to my desk and sat down. It wasn't going to be easy to convince the others I had done right. But the hell with them!

A man was entitled to a little peace with his years.

Chapter Fourteen

A FEW days later Silk dropped into the office. He parked himself in the chair opposite my desk. He came to the point. "There's some talk around town that Moscowits is taking a powder."

"So I hear," I said noncommittally. If he wanted my interest he wasn't taking it.

He followed up. "As a matter of fact, Frank, some of the

boys are saying that you're behind him and he's working with your O.K."

"You all work with my O.K.," I told him.

He continued blandly. "They don't like it, Frank. They say you're beginning to slip."

I laughed. "What do you say to that, Silk?"

He ought to know. He tried to hang me twice, and he still was a long way from home. He didn't answer.

We sat there silently for a few minutes while I fiddled around with some papers on my desk. Then I looked up at him. "If that's all that's on your mind, Silk, you can blow."

I didn't even give him the satisfaction of saying I was busy.

He stood up and leaned over the desk to me. "I thought you ought to know what they're saying, Frank. If it's true they don't like it."

I looked up at him. "I know what they're saying, Silk. I know it long before you hear it. I also know who's saying it, and if I were you I'd put a zipper where you wear your mouth or one day you'll wake up and find it sewed up for yuh—with needle and thread."

For just the tiniest moment he gave himself the pleasure of letting his hatred for me jump into his eyes. But only for a second. It was too expensive a thing to overindulge. His eyelids dropped and he was back to normal. He waved his hand jauntily and walked toward the door. "O.K., pal," he said from there, "I told you," and went out.

I jumped on the phone and asked the girl to get Moscowits for me. He wasn't at his club. I told the girl to try his home.

A woman's voice answered the phone. She had a slightly Jewish accent. "Hello."

"Mr. Moscowits there?" I asked.

"No, he's not," said the voice.

"This is Frank Kane," I said. "Do you know where I can get him?"

"I don't, Mr. Kane," said the voice. "I'm worried; he didn't come home last night."

"Is this Mrs. Moscowits?" I asked.

"Yes," said the voice. "I'm worried, Mr. Kane. Moishe always calls up when business keeps him out."

"Where was he goin' when you heard from him last?" I asked her.

"He said he was going downtown to meet a couple of the boys. That was yesterday afternoon."

I thought a moment. Silk must have had Moscowits on ice or he wouldn't have come over here. "Well," I said, "don't worry. He's probably tied up in some deal and couldn't call you. I'll locate him and have him call you."

"Thank you, Mr. Kane," she said.

"That's all right. Good-by." I hung up and spun my chair to the window. It was a nice clear day, and you could see the cars driving along on the other side of the Hudson.

Sweet mother of murder! Silk had set me up again, and it was going to take more than a couple of breaks for me to look good after this. If they got rid of Moishe and I didn't stop it, my control over them would be shot to hell. And Silk knew that.

The phone buzzed. I turned back to the desk. "Mr. Price is on the wire," Miss Walsh told me.

"Put him on."

"Hello, Frank?" Joe's voice came over the wire.

"Yeah," I said. "How are yuh, Joe?"

"O.K.," he said.

"How are things goin'?" I asked.

"That's what I called about," he said. "This juke plant out here is going to be a gold mine. A government inspector and a couple of Army men just finished an inspection out here, and they want us to take on a government contract for radio-and-signal-corps equipment."

"That'll take dough," I said.

"No it won't," Joe's voice came back. "The government'll finance the whole thing. It's part of the national defense program. They put up the dough for conversion; we turn out the stuff and make profit on it."

I had other things on my mind. I wasn't going to worry about that crap too. "Look, Joe," I said, "I'm as jammed up as all hell here. You do what you think is right out there, an' I'll speak to you later about it."

"It looks good to me, Frank," he said. "I think there's a war coming on, and if we take it up we'll be six jumps ahead of the field."

"O.K., O.K.," I said, "you do it!" I hung up. What did I give a damn about war coming when I had a private war of my own to run?

I pressed the buzzer. Miss Walsh came in. "I'm not in to anyone for the rest of the day, understand?"

She nodded and went out.

I got busy on the phone. I had to find out where they took Moscowits before they got around to knocking him off. And if they knocked him off I wanted to get that check off him before they got around to it. I didn't think he'd deposit it until he got out to California, and I wasn't taking any chances.

By four o'clock I knew where they had him. He was in a garage on Twelfth Avenue. Fennelli was going to bring some of the boys over to see him at ten o'clock. I would have to get there first.

I called down and ordered the car out. About six o'clock I went downstairs and had supper, then drove over to New York. I had some time to kill until about eight-thirty and on impulse I drove over to Ruth's place.

The elevator took me upstairs. I walked over to her door and rang the bell. She opened the door.

For a moment she stood there in the doorway looking at me.

I couldn't speak. There was something on the tip of my tongue, like "Where's Marty?"—a stall maybe—but no dice! All I had to do was look at her and bang!—that old feeling!

She stepped back from the door; she still hadn't spoken.

I entered the apartment. As soon as the door had closed behind me, I kissed her.

"Hello, Ruth," I whispered.

She stepped back a little. "Why did you come?"

"To see you," I answered. I didn't know how much I meant that until I said it; then I knew.

She turned and walked toward the parlor. I threw my hat and coat into a chair and followed her. She took a cigarette from a case on one of the end tables and lit it slowly, deliberately. She knew she had me crawling and was going to play it out.

I walked over and took the cigarette out of her hand, squashed it out on a tray, and took her in my arms. She was cool to my touch. I kissed her. "Hello, Ruth."

Her hand had crept up and stroked my cheek; her head dropped to my shoulder. "Frank," she whispered.

"Change your mind, darling," I whispered. "We can't go—"

Her lips stopped my words. I held her close to me and could feel the pounding of her heart under my hand. She kissed me again. "No, my sweet," she whispered against my lips.

I drew her down to the couch. We kissed again. I could feel the pressures working in her. Her lips were cool to the taste but fiery with the promise. The room began to spin around. Suddenly she was crying against my shoulder. Her voice came heavy through her sobs. "Frank, Frank, you've got to stop. We've been through this before."

The room stopped its mad whirling around. I stood up and reached for a cigarette with trembling fingers. I looked down at her. She was sitting up, looking at me through eyes wide and filled with tears. I sat down and put my arm around her. I was all right now. I drew her head to my shoulder.

"Ruth will you marry me—now—later tonight?" I didn't recognize the voice as mine. It had a quality of pleading and longing in it that I had never heard before.

She didn't answer right away. For a few minutes she fought to control her sobs, then: "I want you so, darling."

"Will you marry me?" I repeated.

She looked deep into my eyes. "I can't."

I interrupted her. "You just said—"

"But, Frankie, I want you for always."

I looked at her. The room was dark and her face was a white cameo in the dimness. I reached out and put one hand on each side of it and drew it toward me. Her skin was warm and smooth and soft.

I made her a promise—the first I ever made. "I love you," I said, my voice shaking a little. "You won't have to wait much longer for what you want. You're going to be a June bride."

Her eyes searched my face. "You wouldn't lie to me, Frank?"

I shook my head. "Not to you, baby!"

She closed her eyes for a moment, her lips moved silently, then her eyes opened. "I still can't believe it's true."

I kissed her. "You can believe that, baby!" I said.

I left her at exactly eight-thirty.

Chapter Fifteen

I PARKED the car about two blocks away from the garage and walked the rest of the way. This was a neighborhood I knew well. I was brought up in it. This was part of the territory I first had covered for Keough. At night the section was deserted.

The garage was about a half-a-block long going down toward the river, and about a quarter of a block facing along the avenue. There was a big center door on the building, which was rolled down tight, and another entrance from a long alleyway on the side of the building.

I put my hands in my pockets. One hand closed comfortingly around the automatic I had put in there when I left the office, the other around a small pocket flashlight I had taken from my car. I walked once past the garage. There wasn't a sign of life in it. On the way back I turned up the alley. It was dark—really dark: I couldn't see a foot ahead of me. I put one hand on the side of the building and walked up toward the back of the alley. I didn't dare use the flash for fear I would tip myself off to whoever was in the building. I tried to walk quietly, but my footsteps sounded unnecessarily loud to my ears. My heart began to pound a little. My breath was coming in short gasps and sweat stood out on my forehead though it wasn't any too warm.

My hand hit a break in the wall. It was a door. The slightest touch told me it was locked. I kept going up the alley, hand along the wall, and came to a stop against a wooden wall. It was a cloudy night and everything was murky and dim, but I reached as high as I could and still the top of it was out of my reach. I felt along the wall for a break in it, but it was smooth and ran right to the building on the other side of the alley. I turned and walked down the alley, now on the opposite side, hand against the building. About halfway back toward the street there was a door. My eyes were used to the darkness by now, and I could see a little better.

I tried the door. It was locked. I looked at the keyhole. It looked as if an old-fashioned key would open it. I had one on my key ring. I took it out, fitted it into the lock, and turned. It squeaked a little but turned all the way around and the door was open.

I stepped into the darkness of the building and shut the door behind me and locked it. Then I took out my flash and turned it on. I was in some sort of a warehouse; there were big wooden packing cases all around me. I kept the flash pointed down toward the floor so that no light would show outside through any of the windows—if there were any windows. I walked toward the back of the building. There was a door there, and I let myself out and was on some sort of a loading platform next to a railroad siding. There were a couple of freight cars on the siding.

I looked over toward the garage. The siding went past the garage on the other side of a fence. The freight cars were right next to the fence. I clambered up the side of the one next to the landing, walked across the top of it until I was right behind the garage, then about one quarter the way down the rungs until I was on top of the fence. I turned and looked at the garage again, still holding onto the rungs on the side of the freight.

The garage had two windows that had been painted black, but some light crept through the scratches in them. There was also a door. I let go of the rungs and dropped off the fence. I let myself fall limply, softly to the ground, then straightened up and walked toward the door. There were some huge oil drums left outside the back of the garage. I stepped around them and put one hand on the door and pushed softly. It opened.

It was dark inside the door, but a light came from somewhere on the left. I turned toward the light and walked softly. There were several big Fruehauf trailers in there, and until I passed them I couldn't see where the light was coming from. Then I saw it.

It came from a little office at the corner of the garage. There were three men in there, seated at a table, playing cards. I recognized one of them as Moishe. I couldn't recognize the others because they were sitting with their backs partly toward me. I looked across the clear space between the office and me.

If I walked directly toward it they might hear me and turn, or maybe Moishe would see me and tip them off by looking up.

I faded back along the trailers to the wall, then moved up toward the office along the wall. That would give me only a few feet of open space to cross to get to the office. That was the only chance I had to take, and I had to take it.

Moishe was the first to see me. He didn't blink an eyelash, just threw three cards down on the table and said: "I'll take three."

One of the others said: "Can you beat that guy's luck? He calls for the limit each time and wins. I'm almost broke."

"What difference does that make?" growled the other. "Where he's goin' he won't need the dough. We'll get it anyway."

The first man laughed. "That's right, Flix. I didn't think of that."

Moishe picked up his three cards and looked at them. By that time I was in the doorway.

I spoke softly, hands in my coat pockets. "I'll finish your hand for yuh, Moishe."

Moishe looked up and smiled. The two men turned suddenly for the doorway. I recognized one: the man called Flix. He was the guy that had brought me into town that time for Silk. He was moving fast, his hand toward his gun on the table.

Moishe was faster. He picked up the gun.

I looked steadily at Flix. My voice was still soft. I took my hands out of my coat pockets empty. "Give him back his rod, Moishe," I said. "This baby thinks he's a powerhouse!"

Moishe looked at me as if he thought I was crazy. Then he held the gun toward Flix, who had frozen into a sort of semirigid statue goggling at me.

"Take it, Flix," I urged softly. "Take it, don't be bashful."

He tore his eyes from my face. He pulled his hands close to him, away from the gun in Moishe's outstretched hand. My hands were still empty. I walked over toward Flix. He was still seated, bent over in a sort of half-crouch. I leaned over him.

"Well, steamboat," I said to him, "you're not so tough without a rod, are yuh?"

He didn't answer.

I reached down and grabbed him by his lapels and hauled him to his feet. He stood there in front of me still half bent over. I brought my knee up under his crotch and he snapped forward still further. Then I hit him with the other hand on the side of the face. He went down in a heap on the floor. I kicked him in the side. He didn't move.

I turned to the other guy. "Pick him up and put him in a chair," I said.

The man looked at me. His face had gone white in the light. He seemed incapable of movement.

"You heard me!" I snarled suddenly.

The man jumped to do as he was told. When he had put Flix back in the chair, he turned to me. Flix was half in the chair, half slumped across the table. He wasn't out cold but he couldn't move.

Moishe was watching me. He didn't speak until now. "At first I thought it was you, Frank."

"I know what you thought," I said quietly, "but I gave you my word."

He finished. "But now I know different."

"O.K., Moishe," I said. "It's over anyway and doesn't matter. Beat it home; your wife is worried about you. As soon as you see her, get on your way."

I moved toward a chair and sat down.

"What are you going to do?" he asked.

"Finish your hand." I picked it up—not a bad hand either: Straight flush in spades.

Chapter Sixteen

I WATCHED Moishe walk toward the exit. At the door he turned and half waved his hand to me in a sort of farewell. I watched him a moment, then nodded. He turned and walked out.

I looked at the two hoods. Flix was beginning to show a little interest in things. He picked up his head.

I looked at him. "How long you been with Fennelli?" I asked.

"I don't know the guy," was his answer.

"Who told you to pick up Moscowits then?"

"A guy slipped me five C's on a street corner and fingered him for me."

I scoffed at that. "Don't give me that crap! A geister like you don't work without a cover."

He didn't answer.

"Who got you out on that gun charge?"

"My lawyer," he answered.

We sat there silently for a while, just staring at one another. Flix was stewing something over in his mind. I knew by watching him that it wouldn't take long in breaking out. All I had to do was wait for it.

It came sooner than I thought.

A flame seemed to burn bright in his eyes. "Why'd yuh knock off my sister?" he asked.

I smiled and could see he didn't like that. I smiled anyway. "I didn't knock her off. I didn't know she was your sister. And if she was your sister, why did you drag her into that racket?"

He didn't answer.

"I didn't knock off your sister," I continued, "but I know who did. Maybe we can swap some dope?"

He knew what I meant. He thought about that a few minutes. "Maybe we can," he finally answered.

I leaned forward. This was beginning to look promising. "Well?" I asked, "start talking."

He opened his mouth, but a creak from the front door stopped him. He turned his head on one side and listened.

I was listening too. I heard voices from the door. I stepped back from the light and drew my gun. The gun was nice and warm and cosy in my hand. I held my finger to my lips. The voices came closer.

I saw who it was: Fennelli, Riordan and Taylor. All they needed was a few more men and they would have a quorum. They were talking as they came up. They entered the room.

Flix had turned to face them; the other guy still sat in the chair. He didn't know what the hell to do he was so scared.

Fennelli still didn't see me; I was well behind the light. "Moishe," he said.

I stepped around the light in front of him. I still held the gun in my hand. "Moishe had to go out of town." I said. "I'm sitting in for him."

Silk didn't bat an eyelash. "Geeze, Frank, I'm glad to see you! I've been trying to locate you all afternoon. Moishe was trying to give us the slip."

I smiled. It was almost funny. "So you were going to stop him for me?" My voice was cold.

"Yeah," he answered.

"And you brought a couple of the boys over to see him when you couldn't get ahold of me?"

"That's right, Frank."

That was malarkey from away back! He had the guy since last night, and I saw him just this morning. If he wanted to level he had plenty of time to do it. I stood there silently.

He began to shift a little. His eyes wandered around the room.

I just kept looking at him. Suddenly I did something I had wanted to do for weeks. I reversed the gat in my hands and swiped him across the face with it. He went down to his hands and knees, his hands fumbling in the armpits of his coat.

I waited until he got his gun in his hand before I kicked it out. He was looking up at me, his face white. I ignored him and walked over and picked up his gun and dropped it in my pocket.

I walked around the table and sat down in the chair and looked over at Taylor and Riordan. "How do you two figure on this?"

Taylor answered. "We don't know anything about it, Frank. Silk just told us he had something for us to see."

I looked at them. They seemed to be straight enough. "Sit down," I said, waving my gun at them. "We got things to talk about."

They sat down. I looked down at Silk. He was still on the floor. "You too!" I said.

He got off the floor and sat down in a chair.

Flix was standing behind Fennelli. I looked at the two of them. "Flix was going to tell me something when you boys came in."

Flix didn't talk.

I leaned forward and stared at him. "I told you I knew who knocked off your kid sister. Only one other person besides you and myself knew about what happened that night you set me up for the frame. That was Fennelli. I went to his place right after it happened and told him the story. He promised to keep an eye open for the gees that did it." I paused for a moment. "I don't have to tell any more, do I?"

Flix stared at me savagely. His eyes were smoldering yellowishly in the light. Suddenly he reached down and placed his hands around Fennelli's neck and began to choke him.

Silk's hands struggled vainly trying to pry Flix's fingers from his throat. I sat there quietly watching. Silk's face turned red, and as his struggles lessened, his face began to turn blue.

I decided Flix had gone far enough. I didn't want him to kill the guy, just educate him a little. "O.K., Flix," I said, "that's enough."

Flix kept right on with his job.

I raised the gun and pointed it at Flix's face. "I said enough, Flix." I spoke gently.

Flix dropped his hands and stood there tensely. Silk slumped forward on the table: he was out cold.

I spoke to Taylor. "Get Silk some water."

Taylor got up and went around to a water cooler, took a little paper cup from the rack and brought it over to Silk. He stood there looking foolishly at me.

I looked at Taylor and grinned. I got out of my seat and went over to the cooler. I hoisted the whole water bottle out of the cabinet and went over to Silk and dumped half of it on him.

He came to when the water hit him. He made some unintelligible noises with his mouth, but his throat was too sore for him to speak. His clothes were dripping wet but he was sitting up.

I put the water bottle on the floor beside me and spoke quietly. "I want you boys to listen carefully. I gave Moishe the O.K. to quit. When you guys reach his age, which you won't if you don't play it straight with me, you can quit too. It'll be your privilege then. Until that time just remember who's boss."

I looked at them. They didn't answer. I spoke again. "Now beat it and take Silk with yuh and get him to a doctor. I don't want him catchin' cold or anything."

The punk that had been with Flix was the first out the door. The others followed a few seconds later—that is, all except Flix.

He stood there watching me.

"What do you want?" I asked.

He smiled suddenly. There wasn't much warmth in it, but there was respect.

"You're a hard guy," he said.

"Hard guys come a dime a dozen," I answered.

"Not the way you come," he said.

I looked at him. He was fishing for something—I wondered what. I didn't answer. If he wanted something let him ask.

He did. "I'm lookin' for opportunity," he said.

I tossed his gun across the table to him. He caught it and slipped it into his pocket and watched me.

I was thinking rapidly. The time had come for me to put a guy like that to good use. There were too many things going on to be smart about. I spoke slowly. "I need a guy who doesn't blow his topper in a corner, who doesn't let personal things affect his action."

"I'm a worker," he said, "not a hophead. I do what I'm told; that's my stock in trade."

I began to smile. This would give Silk something to think about. "You got a job," I said.

For two centuries a week I had me a bodyguard.

Chapter Seventeen

THE next morning I called Joe Price. When he answered the phone I began talking. "Look, Joe," I said, "I was all snarled up when you called yesterday, and want you to go over that deal you were telling me about."

He repeated the proposition.

I listened carefully. It sounded all right to me. "Do you have to be around there for a while?" I asked.

"I should be," he answered. "Why, is anything wrong?"

"No," I said, "but there's something I want you to do, and I'd like you to get back here right away."

"I'll be in on Sunday," he answered. Good boy! He didn't ask questions.

"O.K.," I told him. "Come up to the hotel as soon as you get in." I put the phone down and pressed the buzzer.

Miss Walsh answered.

"Send Powell in," I said.

Flix came in the door. It was the first time he had ever been in the office. He looked around, and I could see he was impressed with the layout. I told him to sit down.

I grinned at him, "How'r yuh feelin'?"

His face was a little swollen, but he smiled back at me. "Not too bad."

He sat back quietly while I told him what I wanted. From now on everyone that was going to see me would have to see him first, at the office and at the house. I arranged with the hotel to give him the room next to my apartment and to send everyone up to him first, even after checking with me. At the office he would sit at a desk in Miss Walsh's office, which was right outside my door.

When I finished I asked him if he had any questions. He had none so I sent him out. I leaned back in my chair for a moment thinking. If I knew Silk his next try would be to knock me off. There wouldn't be anything half-assed about it either. The only way for me to keep alive was to be one step ahead of him—or have him bumped. And I didn't want to do that. I had much better plans for the son-of-a-bitch.

I leaned forward and dialed Ruth's number on the private phone.

She answered: "Hello."

"Hello, darling," I replied.

"I had to call you," I said quickly. "I wanted to hear your voice."

Her laugh came rippling over the phone, "I wanted to speak to you too. I wanted you to repeat what you said last night. I just can't believe you mean it."

"I mean it, baby," I said. "I love you. Did you get my flowers?" I had sent her a corsage of orchids that morning.

"Yes," she answered. "They were lovely."

A few more words and we hung up. I felt good and pitched into the work on my desk, humming.

That evening I went over to see her. I imagine Flix got pretty cold waiting downstairs in the car for me until two o'clock in the morning, but he didn't say anything when I finally showed up.

Sunday morning at eleven Joe Price showed up. He looked at me questioningly when he first saw Flix. I told Flix I didn't need him, and when he left the room I brought Price up to date on what had happened.

He whistled. "I see what you meant when you said you were all tied up. What do you want me to do?"

I let him have both barrels. "I want to pull out. This isn't going to last much longer, and I have other plans. Do you think you could rig the books and records so that my name comes off everything except the door?"

He thought for a moment, then he nodded.

"How long would it take?"

"A few weeks of night and day work," he answered. "But we'd have to set somebody else's name up on it or it wouldn't look kosher."

"I got that all figured," I said. "We'll use Fennelli."

"I don't get it." He was puzzled. "How does Fennelli figure in on this? I thought he was out to get you."

"He still is." I smiled. "But he wants the business too. Well, I'm going to give it to him. Only he doesn't know it yet."

"O.K.," he said. "It's a little too much for me to follow, but I'll do it. When do you want me to start?"

"Today," I said, "after we eat breakfast."

I dropped Joe Price off at the office to give him a chance to look things over. Then I drove over to Ruth's place and picked her up.

"How about a drive in the country?" I suggested.

She nodded and went for her hat and coat. I wondered what she would say when she saw Flix. I would have to explain that to her without worrying her too much. But we spent a swell day anyway.

We drove up to Bear Mountain and had dinner at the inn, strolled around the place, then drove leisurely back to town.

It was June 10th before Joe came into my office rubbing his hands with obvious satisfaction. I looked up at him. "Well," I asked, "how's it going?"

He smiled down at me. "It's finished, all done."

"Good!" I said. "Now hop a plane out to the plant and get busy out there. I want you to buy a house for me and have it furnished by the beginning of next month. I'm going to move in then."

"Christ, Frankie," he said, "a thing like that takes more time than doctoring a set of books!"

"Get the best interior decorator in the section on the job. The house doesn't have to be too large; about six rooms will be enough. Pay whatever you think necessary to have it done. Get someone out there on the job and be back here by the day after tomorrow. I'll need you."

"O.K., Frank," he said, starting for the door. "But don't you want to look at the books before I go?"

I got out of my seat and walked around toward him. "Do I have to?" I asked. "The less I know about them the better right now. Besides I don't know a damn thing about them, if you say they're O.K., they're O.K."

"I did what you wanted," he said.

"That's good enough for me." I smiled. "No—on your way, pal! There's no time to lose. I got to get busy."

I turned and went back to the desk. Joe was at the door now and I looked over at him. "Thanks, Joe," I said.

He smiled and went out.

I picked up the phone and called Jerry Cowan.

Chapter Eighteen

AFTER my call went through about two secretaries, Jerry finally got on the phone.

"Jerry," I said, "this is Frank Kane. Are you free this afternoon? I want to see you."

"Come over here," he answered.

"I can't go to your office, but this is important and I want to see you alone."

"Where can we meet?" he asked.

"I'll pick you up on the Jersey side of the George Washington Bridge at four o'clock this afternoon. Plan to have dinner with me because what I've got to say will take a little time."

He was silent for a moment, then: "O.K., four o'clock."

I left the office at three. I told Flix to go back to the apartment and wait there for me. Then I drove up to meet Jerry.

I was there a few minutes before four, and I waited around.

At four o'clock promptly I saw Jerry. He was driving a blue
Buick sedan. I watched him park the car and look around for
me. He didn't see me. I honked the horn to attract his attention.

He looked over at me and smiled and waved his hand. I
made a gesture with my hand that meant: "Come on." I started
off, glancing into the rear mirror to make sure he was following
me. He was.

About a mile down the highway I turned off onto a small road
that ran down to Teaneck. I stopped in front of a parking lot.
Jerry's car stopped behind me, and I got out of my car and
walked over to him.

We shook hands. I smiled. "How are you?"

"Fine," he said.

"And Janet?" I asked.

"She's O.K. now," he replied, "but it was tough on the girl
losing the baby and then the doctor telling her she couldn't
have any more."

This was news to me. I hadn't known anything about that.
"I'm sorry," I said. "I didn't know."

"Well, it's over now," he said. "What's on your mind?"

I smiled. He was in a hurry but he was going to have to wait.
I would talk to him in my own time and in my own way. "Park
your car here," I told him, "and get in mine. We'll go somewhere where we can eat and talk."

An hour later we were at a small inn on Route 9 in a small
private dining room. We had Scotch old-fashioneds in front of
us, and I lit a cigarette. I looked over at him. "I suppose you're
wondering why the sudden rush act."

He nodded, not talking.

I went on. "Just how bad do you want me?" I asked.

"Getting you is my job," he answered simply.

Good! That was what I expected to hear. "If you busted up
the racket wouldn't that be enough?" I smiled. "Getting me
personally won't stop the organization, but I might make a deal
with you. I'll set up the racket so that you can break it up when
I go. I'll even give you a patsy: one with a record, one that
you've been after longer than you've been after me."

He lifted his drink to his lips and sipped it slowly. He squared
right off. "What do you want to pull out for? You know I
haven't anything on you—yet."

I squared with him. "I'm going to get married," I told him, "and my future wife doesn't approve."

He laughed at that. "Don't tell me a woman is going to do what all the city, state and Federal governments can't!"

I nodded ruefully. "It looks that way."

He was grinning now. "More power to her!" he said, shaking his head a little. "Anyone I know?"

I looked him right in the eye. "It's Ruth," I said simply.

He almost fell out of his chair. "Ruth!" he said surprisedly. "How long has this been going on?"

"Long time now." I smiled.

The waiter came in with the appetizer. We were silent until he left the room. Then Jerry spoke again. "I'd like to do something for you, more for Ruth than anyone else, but I don't see how I can accede. After all, I still have a job to do."

"Suit yourself," I said, "but there are more things to this that have to be clarified." I speared a clam on my fork and waved it at him. "You see, if you nail me you'll nail your old man at the same time. His law firm is handling several important matters for me."

Jerry put down his clam fork and looked at me. He was getting a little angry at that crack. "I don't believe it," he stated flatly.

"Believe it or not," I replied. "I know what I'm talking about."

"Dad would never take on a case from you."

"I didn't say he would," I retorted, "but he has, or rather his firm has. And that wouldn't look too good on the front pages of the papers, would it?"

Jerry didn't answer that. I could see him thinking it over.

I threw another few logs on the fire. "Look, Jerry, let's not be kids about this. We're grown-up now, and this is business—serious business. Just supposing there comes a time that you finally get enough on me to make a case out of. Supposing when that time comes somebody drags your old man's name into it. Supposing somebody says maybe that's the reason you didn't get me a long time ago: because I was paying off to your old man. You don't know the things people will say—or think."

He got out of his chair and walked around the table toward me. He grabbed me by the collar and held me. "If you have any intention of throwing mud at my father and covering him with your filthy slime, I'll kill you with my bare hands."

I sat there quietly looking up at him. Then I raised my hands and disengaged his from my lapel. "Homicide's as much against the law here in Jersey as it is in New York."

He looked at me for a moment without speaking.

I didn't give him a chance to talk anyway. "Look, Jerry, I'm not threatening your father. I'm trying to point out all the things that people might say. And there's no way of stopping them. I know. They say a lot about me that's so much bull, and yet I can't do anything about it." I smiled at him. "Go back and sit down, finish your dinner. When you hear the rest of my plan—who knows?—maybe you'll agree."

He went heavily back to his chair and sat down. He was quiet all through dinner. He didn't have much of an appetite: just picked at his food and listened. But when we went back for his car he had agreed to do what I asked.

I got out of my car and walked over to his and put one foot on the running board. I gave him a chance to save a little face.

He clambered in behind the wheel and sat there, his mouth set grimly.

"After all, Jerry," I said in a low earnest tone, "you are doing the job they gave you. You are busting up the racket. Even if it ain't according to Hoyle, the important thing is that you are doing it."

He looked over at me and smiled wanly. He was too discouraged even to pick up the lead. His voice was heavy and dull. "I guess so."

"You don't have to guess," I said positively. "You know it. You yourself once suggested the same thing. And it's results that count."

He stepped on the starter, the motor burst into life. He was about to start off when suddenly he turned and looked at me. "Frank," he said.

"Yes, Jerry?"

"You haven't changed a bit since you were a kid. But don't think you can get away with it all the time. Life has a funny way of catching up and paying off."

I took my foot off the running board and shrugged my shoulders. "Who knows?" I asked. His car started to roll slowly. I walked along with it. "Maybe I'll be lucky," I said.

He stepped on the gas and drove off. I walked over to my car slowly. When I got in I laughed a little to myself. Maybe I'll be lucky, I had said. But that wasn't all there was to it—you had to be smart too.

Chapter Nineteen

ABOUT eleven o'clock the next morning I got a phone call from Alex Carson. His voice sounded good for the first time in weeks. "Frank," he said, "the Bar Association dropped its charges against me this morning."

That was in order. It was one of the things I had arranged with Jerry. I acted surprised. "That's swell!" I said. "Get down here and we'll have a drink on it."

I hung up the phone and called Flix into the office. The next thing I wanted to do was to get Fennelli over here. And I knew he wouldn't come merely by invitation; so I sent Flix after him.

Alex came into the office a half hour after he had called. I got up and shook hands with him. "Congratulations!" I said. "I knew you'd make out all right."

He grinned. "They had me worried there for a while, I still don't understand why they dropped it."

"Sit down," I said. "I'll tell you why."

We sat down and I explained the whole setup to him. When I had finished he let out a long, low whistle. "Do you think you can get away with it, Frank?" he asked.

I nodded my head. "With your help I can."

He stood up. "You can count on me."

"Swell!" I said. "Stick around, I want you here when Silk shows up."

Flix brought Silk in about three o'clock. Silk walked over to my desk and threw his hat down on it. "You didn't have to send that lug over for me, Frank," he said evenly. He even managed to get a slightly reproachful note in his voice. "All you had to do was call me."

I smiled at him. "You know how it is, Silk. I didn't want to do you any less honor than you did me."

He skipped right over that crack and came right to the point. "Well, what do you want?"

I looked up at him a moment. This was important. If he didn't bite right I was a cooked goose. "You know my idea when we started this thing. The agreement was made to keep the industry in order. Of late you seemed to have other ideas—your own ideas on running the business. It would be very simple for me to have you knocked off—maybe a lot simpler than having Flix bring you out here, but that's not the way I do business. I run this as a regular business and I don't want any trouble. So I've decided to buy you out."

He drew his lips back slightly over his white even teeth, "Just what does that mean?"

"That means you give up your territory to me and get out of the business," I answered quietly.

"And how much are you offering?" he asked.

"One hundred grand," I replied.

He leaned forward against the desk. "That's only my share of what's in the pool," he said coldly. "I take a quarter of a million a year out of my territory alone."

"I know that," I said.

"And the pool pays about two hundred grand a year," he continued.

"I know that too," I said.

He was quiet a minute, then he spoke again. "And what if I don't sell?"

I shrugged my shoulders and didn't answer.

He sat down in a chair quietly and I watched him. Let him take his time, let him think about it. He'll come to the right answer. A few minutes passed by. His face remained impassive, unreadable; just his hands opened and closed.

At last he spoke. "What if I offered to buy you out?"

The fish was on the hook. "Not interested," I answered noncommittally. He stood up and walked around the desk to me. I looked up at him. "I mean for real dough," he said, "a quarter of a million."

I let his offer slide off. "I'm buying you out," I reminded him. "I'm not interested in selling."

He walked back to his seat and sat down. He took a cigar out of his pocket and lit it nervously. "Three hundred grand and a share of the profits," he offered.

I looked at him. "You interest me strangely," I said. "How much of a share?"

"A half share, payable monthly."

I switched my line. "I got to think about it. This is too sweet to give up."

He was pushing now. This was something he had wanted for a hell of a long time. Only he didn't know he was going to get it. "Frank," he urged, "it would be just the thing for you. No work—you can do anything you want outside this racket. Why, you could live on the fat of the land. Travel—women— anything you want."

It was my turn to stand up and play dummy. "It sounds good to me," I said, "but how do I know you'll play ball?"

"Certified checks in the morning sound convincing enough?" he asked.

I stalled a few seconds more, then gave in. "O.K., Silk, it's yours."

He stood up and held out his hand. "You won't be sorry, kid," he said. "Remember what I told you when you first came to me. I said you'd make a lot of money then, and I wasn't wrong, was I?"

I smiled at him. "You weren't."

We shook hands on the deal.

The next morning at eleven o'clock Silk came into the office. Carson and I were there already.

"Got the checks ready?" I asked.

He nodded and took them out and put them on the desk. "Made out just like you said: to Alexander Carson for services rendered."

I looked at them. He was right. I gave them to Alex. Alex endorsed them and handed them back to me. I pressed the buzzer for Miss Walsh. She came in with the envelope I had told her to have ready. I put the checks in the envelope, and she left the room while I was putting the envelope into my jacket pocket.

I looked up at the two of them. "This calls for a drink," I said, and brought out the old bottle.

When we had had our drinks I told Alex to take Silk out and show him around the place. They left the room together.

I called for Mackson, and he brought up the checks I had

ordered him to draw up. I looked at them. They were all there: the pool split up into component parts as of this date. I signed them and gave them to Miss Walsh to send out. I had everyone paid off, even Silk. Then I left the office by the private elevator and went over to the hotel.

Joe Price was waiting in my apartment. I gave him the envelope containing the checks Silk had given me. "You know what to do with this," I said.

He nodded. That was figured out too. An account had been opened in each of the banks where Silk had accounts. They were in the name of my new company. The checks would be properly deposited in each account. I left him and went back to the office.

An hour later Joe called me. "Everything's O.K., Frank," he said.

I hung up the phone. For a moment I hesitated; then I drew a deep breath and dialed a private number.

For a few seconds the phone at the other end buzzed, then I heard Jerry's voice: "Cowan."

"Frank," I replied. "It's your party!" and put the phone down.

A few minutes later Fennelli and Carson came back to the office. Silk was pleased. He had a broad smile on his face. "What a setup! Frank," he said. "I knew it was big, but I didn't know how big it really was."

I stood up. "It's not half bad!" I smiled. "How about another drink? We'll get into the operations tomorrow."

He followed me over to the liquor cabinet. I took out a bottle, filled three glasses, and handed one to each of them. "Here's luck!" I said, and tossed mine off.

Alex downed his, saying the same thing: "Here's luck!"

Silk just smiled and swallowed his drink. He was looking at me expansively. Suddenly he walked around the desk and sat down in my chair and put his feet up on the desk. He waved his hand. "Take a seat."

I smiled to myself. He didn't know just how hot that seat could get, but he'd find out fast enough. I sat down in a chair in front of my desk and looked at Silk. He smiled back at me.

Suddenly the door behind me opened. I didn't turn around. I knew who it was.

Chapter Twenty

SILK jumped to his feet. "What the hell is coming off here!" he shouted.

I stood up and turned around slowly. There were four men in my office. Flix had been shoved to one side, and one of the men had a gun pointed at his belly.

One of the men walked over to me. "Frank Kane?" he asked.

I nodded.

"We have a warrant for your arrest on a charge of conspiracy and bribing of public officials of the State of New York. We have a further warrant and subpoena pertaining to the examination of the books of Frank Kane Enterprises."

Carson stepped forward. "Have you a writ of extradition?"

The man nodded.

"Let me see it," Carson demanded.

The man gave some papers to Carson. Carson examined them carefully, then handed them back to the man. He turned to me. "It looks as if they've got everything figured out, Frank. You'll have to go with them."

I stepped forward silently.

The man walked past me to Silk. "Giuseppe Fennelli?" he asked.

The trial was completed the last day in June. On that morning Jerry got up in court and threw in the bombshell. He walked past where Fennelli and I were sitting. I looked up at him gravely. He didn't look at us. His face was white and grim as he turned toward the jury box.

"Gentlemen of the jury," he began, "this morning we received from the accountants the results of the detailed examination of the books and records of Frank Kane Enterprises. The examination had been conducted jointly and by agreement with the governments of the States of New York and New Jersey and with the co-operation of the Treasury Department of the United States. I wish to enter as evidence their joint report of the examination."

He held up a sheaf of papers. He looked at them a moment, then turned the first page and read from it. The first few lines were certificates from the various examiners. Then he read: "We the examiners find Frank Kane Enterprises, as originally conceived by the defendant Frank Kane, to be a legitimate and honest business insomuch as the defendant Frank Kane is concerned. We find that the financing of said business was arranged by one Giuseppe Fennelli, and that the intention of Mr. Kane was at no time to engage in the principal business of his financier. Toward that end Mr. Kane directed his efforts.

"He engaged in the purchase and sale of various businesses and securities such as he deemed necessary to the welfare of his business. During such time as Mr. Kane was conducting his business properly, his financier, Mr. Fennelli, was running a business within a business. Or more properly, Mr. Fennelli was engaging in his business of gambling and bookmaking, using Frank Kane Enterprises as a cloak for his enterprise.

"We are convinced that Mr. Kane at no time suspected that such uses were being made of his organization until very recently. Upon being convinced of such malpractices, Mr. Kane immediately took steps to dissolve his organization and returned to other investors in his company, including Mr. Fennelli, the amount of their respective interests with a letter explaining the reasons therefore."

Jerry turned and walked back from the jury box and placed the papers on his desk. Then he walked back to the jury box. He stood there quietly a moment. Then he began to speak again.

"Gentlemen, in view of the evidence I have just introduced, I have been convinced that a great wrong and injustice is being done to Mr. Kane. His entire attitude during this investigation has been one of patience and co-operation."

He turned and looked at me, his face was pale and his eyes were bleak.

"Gentlemen of the jury, the prosecution asks that a verdict of not guilty be returned for Mr. Kane—"

The words were no sooner out of his mouth than pandemonium broke loose in the court.

Silk jumped to his feet and grabbed me by the back of the collar and pulled me out of my chair. I turned and tried to get his hands loose from my clothing. Flash bulbs went off, and the crowd in the court surged forward trying to see what was happening. A court attendant pried Silk from me. I stood up and tried to straighten my clothing.

The judge banged his gavel down hard. An attendant cried: "Order in the court!" The noise didn't subside, and the judge ordered the court cleared. Police went down the aisles emptying the court, and in a few moments all was quiet.

An hour later the jury retired to consider the evidence and reach a verdict. They returned to the court at four-thirty. Fennelli and I were instructed to stand up and face the jury. We did.

I looked over at Jerry. He sat at his desk glumly, not glancing in my direction. The court was empty except for the press. Suddenly my throat went dry. What if something had gone wrong? What if I had come this far only to lose? A pulse began beating in my forehead. I could feel the color draining from my face, and I was angry with myself. I wanted to appear calm, contained. But my hand shook a little.

The judge looked at the jury. "Gentlemen of the jury, have you reached a verdict?"

The foreman replied: "We have, Your Honor." He cleared his throat and looked down at a sheaf of paper he held in his hand. He began to read from it.

"We the jury find the defendant Giuseppe Fennelli guilty as charged."

Fennelli suddenly slumped into his chair, his face ashen. A court attendant came forward with a glass of water, but Fennelli waved him away.

I remained standing as I was, still facing the jury. The pulse in my forehead was really jamming now.

The foreman of the jury continued: "We the jury find the defendant Frank Kane"—he paused for a moment, consciously dramatic—"not guilty."

Carson turned to me and grabbed my hand and began shaking it. He spoke low; only I could hear his words. "You did it, Frank, you did it!"

I turned and looked past him at Fennelli. Fennelli was staring at me, his hands clenched in front of him, his eyes burning into mine. Slowly I walked around the table past him. I could feel Silk's hand brush against my coat as I walked by. I paid no attention to it but continued walking—to the court grille, into the aisle, up to the door, out the door into the hall, down the hall to the street. And all the way I could feel his eyes burning hate into the back of my head.

Carson came running up to me. "Where are you going?" he asked.

I looked up at the sun. Its white, blinding light burned into my eyes and made me feel warm where before I had been cold inside. I lifted my hands to my eyes, shading them from the sun. "For a drink," I said, my voice shaking a little. "I need one bad."

I left him standing on the steps looking after me. I went around the corner. There was a saloon there. I pushed my way through the old-fashioned swinging doors and went into the bar.

"Double whisky," I said to the barkeep. He placed the drink in front of me, and I ordered another. I stood there for a few moments looking at it, then began to raise it to my lips. Someone touched me on the shoulder.

I turned slowly. It was Flix. His face was impassive. "You made it?"

"I made it."

"What about him?" Flix asked, jerking his finger toward the door.

I knew who he meant. "He didn't make it," I said, swallowing my drink and ordering another. "Have one, Flix?"

Flix ordered the same. We stood there side by side. The bar was fairly crowded and we were pressed closely against each other. I could feel a gun in his pocket. Flix lifted his drink. "How much time do you think he'll get?" he asked, his voice flat and quiet.

"About ten years—with time off."

Flix swallowed his drink. His voice was still low and quiet. "He's not going to let you get away with it."

I turned to Flix. I was beginning to come out of the fog. "How do you know?"

Flix shrugged his shoulders. "It figures."

Suddenly I was alive again. Flix was right. Jail wasn't enough to stop a guy like Silk. He could pull wires from inside. I stuck my hand inside my jacket pocket for money to pay for the drinks. My hands closed about a bit of paper in there. I took it out and spread it flat on the bar to read.

"I'll get you for this," it said. That was all. No signature—it didn't need any.

I looked at Flix. His face was impassive. I ordered two more drinks. The barkeep set them down in front of us. I picked mine up and turned to Flix. "Here's to your sister!" I said.

He was fast. He lifted his glass and we drank.

I half finished my drink then spoke again. "Here's to ten grand!"

We finished the drinks and the barkeep brought two more.

"How do you pay?" Flix asked.

"Usual terms," I answered. "Fifty per cent down, balance upon delivery."

We downed our drinks and I threw a five-dollar bill on the counter to pay for the drinks and we walked out.

We stood in the street a moment. I looked at him. "Carson will give you the dough. Contact him tomorrow."

He nodded.

I flagged a passing cab. It screeched to a stop in front of me. I got into the cab. "So long, Flix," I said.

His face was calm. "So long—hard guy!"

I sat back against the cushion as the cab drove off. This was bad. Some day I would have to deal with Flix—but that would be later. I was snapped out of my reverie by the cab driver.

"I can drive all day, boss," he said, "but don't you want to go somewhere?"

Chapter Twenty-One

I WENT back to my apartment and changed my clothes. Then I ordered the car out and drove back to New York.

On the other side of the bridge I pulled over to a newsstand and bought the *Evening Journal*. There was a big red scare-streamer headline across the top of the page: "KANE FREED—FENNELLI GUILTY." Below it was a black lead line: "Cowan Smashes Rackets." There was a picture of Jerry leaving court after the trial. The caption below it read: "Jerome Cowan, Racket Buster." He was smiling into the camera.

I laughed softly to myself. Leave it to the papers! The next thing you know they'd have him running for Governor. I threw the paper out the window and drove on.

I pulled to the curb in front of Ruth's house, got out of the car, and went in. The same funny elevator boy that had first taken me up was on again. He kept staring at me curiously all the way up. I got out at her floor and walked to her door. I pressed the bell button.

I could hear the chimes all the way back in the apartment. I waited. It seemed like an hour. At last the door opened. Ruth stood there.

I just stood there and looked at her and she looked at me. It was almost as if we were strangers—as if we had never seen each other before.

"Ruth," I said, standing there in the hallway, not daring to move.

Suddenly she was in my arms, crying: "Frankie, Frankie!"

The door closed behind us. The hall was dim. Her head was against my chest and the sobs racked her throat. I stroked her head, softly, gently. "Ruth, Ruth, it's all over! Don't cry, darling."

"Frankie, I thought you weren't coming back."

"I promised, Ruth, I promised."

She looked at me. Her head was up, her eyes strangely luminous. I kissed her. I could feel her lips quivering and trembling.

"Darling, darling!"

"I was afraid you'd change your mind, Ruth. I was so afraid."

She covered my lips with hers.

Arm in arm we walked into the living-room. We sat down on the large sofa. She turned to me. "It's the last day in June, Frankie."

"That's why I came," I whispered. "I said you'd be a June bride. Get some things packed. We're going up to Meriden to be married."

She moved away from me, toward the other end of the sofa where the cigarettes were kept in a small china tray. A look of studied calm came over her face as she took one. I lit it for her, watching her face as I did so. She looked back at me, her eyes unblinking.

I waited for her to speak. At last, after a few deep puffs on the cigarette, she did.

Her voice was calm. "No, Frankie, we're not getting married."

It was my turn to act calm. I lit a cigarette before I spoke. Then I asked simply: "Why?"

"Because you don't love me." She held up her hand to keep me from speaking. "Not really, you don't. It's all part of the plan you have—just like the deal you made with Jerry. To step from one phase of your life to another, you're only marrying me to complete the transition. The perfect touch! You're ready to don the mantle of respectability, and you only want me to furnish the finishing touch to the costume.

"You haven't really learned anything. You really don't believe in what you're doing. You're only doing it because you know you're through and you're making the best of a bad bargain. Jerry told us what you've made him do, and it didn't take me very long to sit back and think things out. You've got to learn some time: you can't just bargain with people's lives."

I cut in. My voice was still quiet. "Do you love me?" I asked.

She looked at me. Her face had grown very pale. "Love you?" she asked. "I've loved you so much ever since we were children that at night I couldn't sleep for the wanting of you, that when we didn't know where you were I would dream about you, that all these last months I was longing for you to take me—I wanted your child inside me under my heart." Her voice was strained and shaking with emotion, "That's why I won't bargain with you, Frankie. That's why I'm not going to marry you."

I crushed my cigarette out in the tray beside me and took her by the shoulders roughly, squeezing my fingers into her arm. She made no sound, just looked up into my face.

"You stupid, little fool!" I was raging mad. I could feel the pulse pounding in my forehead. "Maybe that's the way it started, but can't you see what I've done is for you—that what I've thrown away has been for you? Don't think I couldn't have cleaned up this mess if I didn't want to. I had a dozen places in the United States I could have gone to and operated from, and they never would have been able to touch me. I didn't have to quit. I quit because of you. If it weren't for the way I felt about you, I would have beat this the same way I beat everything else that got in my way; I'd have ruined Jerry's career as I could have.

"You were the only reason I threw in the towel—because I fell for the line you gave me. Maybe I always knew deep inside you were right, but it was for you that I did it.

"I didn't make any bargain with you. I've turned my life inside out for you, I've traded a fortune for you, I've traded a loaf of bread for a pie in the sky, steak and potatoes for an ideal. And if you still think I don't love you, baby, you can go to hell!"

I let her go. She sank back on the couch, and I started out of the room.

"Frank," she called after me in a still, small voice.

I turned around. She was standing there, "Frankie," she said in the same small voice, filled with wonder, "you're crying!"

Ruth and I were married at Justice of the Peace Smith's in Meriden, Connecticut, on Monday, the last day of June 1941.

The justice's voice was deep and strong.

"Do you, Francis, take this woman, Ruth, to be your lawful wedded wife, and promise to love, honor and cherish her, in sickness and health as long as you both shall live?"

"I do."

"Do you Ruth, take this man, Francis, to be your lawful wedded husband, and promise to love, honor and cherish him, in sickness and in health, for richer or for poorer, as long as you both shall live?"

Ruth looked up at him then at me. Her eyes were the deepest blue I had ever seen. Her voice was warm and soft and rich. "I do."

The judge made a gesture. I placed the ring on her finger.

He held up his hands. "By the powers vested in me by the state of Connecticut, I pronounce you man and wife." He drew a deep breath. "You may now kiss the bride."

I turned to kiss her. Her lips pressed against mine lightly then drew away. I looked at the judge.

He smiled at me. "Congratulations, young man! Two dollars, please."

I gave him five for luck.

We got back to my apartment about eleven o'clock. I carried her over the threshold and kissed her.

"Hello, Mr. Kane!"

"Hello, Mrs. Kane!"

I put her down and went over to the phone and got room service. I ordered four bottles of champagne and they came up in a jiffy.

I waited outside the door while she made ready for bed. Nervously I drank from the glass in my hand. I walked over to the window and looked out. New York was bright across the river.

I smiled at my reflection in the window pane. Suddenly I lifted a glass to New York. "Here's to you!" I said.

My reflection in the window lifted its glass and drank to me.

"Frank."

Her voice was so soft I almost didn't hear it. I turned from the window and went to the door. "Yes, Ruth."

There wasn't any answer. I put the glass down, flicked off the wall lights, and opened the bedroom door. There was a soft lamp glowing near the bed. I crossed the room.

Ruth was standing near the window. She held her hand toward me. "Frank, come here a moment and look."

I stood beside her, but all I could see in the glow of the light was Ruth.

"Frank," she said, her voice strange and full of mystery, "look out of the window. Did you ever look out and see the whole world before you? A world, large and beautiful, waiting for you?"

I didn't answer. The moonlight fell across her face. She was beautiful.

She turned toward me. "Frank, what do you think our son will be like?"

I kissed her lightly on the cheek. She moved closer into my arms.

"I don't know," I said softly. "I never thought about children; I never wanted any."

She moved still closer to me. "Do you think he'll be like you—wild and strange and wicked and handsome?"

I tightened my arms around her. "If he's anything like me, we'd better not have him."

My lips were against her throat. Her voice was whispering in my ear: "Frank, our son will be beautiful." I moved my lips along her neck to her shoulder. "Frank, do you know you're beautiful?" I laughed and moved my lips along the swell of her breast.

Her hands suddenly caught my head and held it close to her. She bent and kissed the top of my head.

I lifted my lips to hers. They were aflame. "Do you know you're beautiful?" I whispered.

She reached out one hand and turned out the light.

It was later—much later. I had lain there quietly a long time watching her sleep. There were little tears in the corners of her eyes. I reached over and brushed them away. Suddenly I wanted a cigarette.

I fished with one hand on the side of the bed. No cigarettes! I moved slowly, carefully: I didn't want to wake her.

I could still hear her voice: "Frank, are you happy? Am I all you wanted me to be?"

I went into the other room. I closed the door quietly and flicked on one of the table lamps.

She was all I ever wanted.

There were cigarettes on the end table. I went over and picked up the pack and took one and lit it. I drew a deep breath of smoke and let it come out my nose. It smarted a little and felt good.

I looked down at the table. There were some letters there that had been delivered while I was away in New York. Idly I picked my way through them: some bills, some advertisements.

I was at the bottom of the pile when I came across the post card. It was a penny government card. On the back of it was something that looked like a printed form. I read it.

Local Board No. 217
Selective Service.
    Notice of Classification
Registrant . . . Francis Kane   Order No. 549 has been classified in Class . . . 1A   Until. . . . . . by x Local Board.
June 25, 1941

My cigarette was almost finished. I put it out in a tray and walked toward the bedroom. It wasn't until I reached over to put out the light that I realized I still held the card in my hand.

I flicked off the light and scaled the card across the room. The hell with it! I'd call Carson in the morning and get him to fix it up.

What Came After

MARTIN suddenly felt weak. He sank into a chair and stared at Janet. "What do you mean?" he asked, his voice trembling.

Jerry too looked at his wife. This was what he wanted to know. He already knew part of the story but now he was to hear the rest of it. Some of the tension left his face and he leaned back in his chair.

"We all knew Ruth was going to have a baby," she began, seating herself so that she faced the two of them, "and when we received the terse telegram from Frank that Ruth had died in childbirth, containing no allusion to the child, we assumed that the child had perished with her. We were wrong.

"You, Martin, were already overseas, and all we could do was to write and tell you what had happened. A month later Jerry went over, and for a while life just seemed to stop.

"A few weeks before Jerry came back, a visitor came in to see me. He was a chaplain—a captain in the outfit Frank was in—and had seen him die. We already knew that Frank was dead. I received word from the War Department about him on April 16th. But Captain Richards brought a message: a letter from Frank that he had entrusted to the chaplain to deliver personally."

The chaplain was tired. It seemed like years since he had last slept. A man lived a thousand years from morning to night every day. And a thousand years a day was too long a time to live.

The sound of the guns had fallen away to a dull boom he scarcely heard. Yesterday this had been a field hospital; today it was a base hospital—the front had moved thirty miles away in one day. And still the wounded kept coming in. The doctors worked frantically, ceaselessly, tirelessly, but still the wounded piled up in front of the door of the operating-room.

He stepped out of the small building that served as the hospital. On the ground as far as a block away the wounded were lying on stretchers, awaiting their turns in the operating-room or transportation to the rear. It was almost night. The first star flicked incongruously in the sky. Slowly he picked his way past them to his tent. He had to get some sleep. He couldn't stay awake any longer, even if in his sleep he would see them, their faces white with pain, and hear their voices heavy with their suffering.

Slowly he walked toward his tent, his head bowed, his feet dragged, his heart heavy in his anguish.

"Captain Richards."

The chaplain heard the voice. He felt it rather than heard it. Its impact was more mental than physical. As a sound it was almost nothing in the intensity of pain that surrounded it. He stopped.

"Captain Richards, over here." The voice was weak but steady.

The chaplain walked around a stretcher to the sound and looked down at the man who had called him. The man was one with the others. He was anonymous: another man wrapped in a blanket up to his neck, only his white face staring up at him. He didn't know the man and got to one knee to better see him.

"Captain," the man said, "don't you remember me?"

The chaplain shook his head. There were so many men. "I'm Kane, remember?" the man asked.

With a feeling of shock the chaplain remembered. He remembered the first time he had seen the man. He had just come into the army then, and Kane was a sergeant. He had asked Kane to attend some services. Kane had laughed. What was it he had said? It was hard to remember, it was so long ago. Oh yes, Kane had laughed. "Going to services now won't help me much, Padre," he had said. And the chaplain had answered: "Going to services will always help. It's never too late to turn to God." And the man had laughed again and answered: "If it

ever comes to that, Padre, I hope to do my turning in person,"
and had walked off. The chaplain had watched Kane for a
while after that. He thought Kane was rather old for so strenuous a fighting job, and was surprised to learn that despite his
almost white hair Kane was still in his early thirties.

"Yes, Kane, I remember now," the chaplain said. He pulled
his coat tight beneath him and sat down on the cold ground. He
sat on a small rock and shifted his position a little until he was
comfortable. He could see the red first-aid markings on Kane's
forehead now. The moon was coming up.

"I'm going to die," the man said simply. There was no fear in
his voice—he was only stating a fact.

"Come now," the chaplain said, trying to get some cheer into
his voice—but it didn't sound right even to his own ears—
"don't talk like that!"

"Don't kid me, Father!" the man said. He tried to laugh, but
his laugh was only a windless, choking sound. "They don't live
with what I've got. I've seen too many of them."

The chaplain tried to speak but the man cut off.

"Oh, it doesn't hurt, Padre. That's not it. I'm so full of
morphine I don't even know if I have a body—that is, if I have
one." The man's eyes turned toward the chaplain. "Besides,
they put me on the wrong side of the hospital door."

Startled, the chaplain looked around him. The man was
right. Those that could not hope to live were placed on this
side; those that could were on the other side of the door.

"I've been watching them walk past me for the last two
hours," the man said. "Every now and then one of the first-aid
men would give me another shot of dope and chalk up the score
on my forehead." He chuckled again, the same windless,
soundless laughter. "I don't blame them. It's better to help those
that have a chance."

The chaplain found his voice. "Look, you're going to be all
right, I tell you."

"O.K., Father," said the man in an oddly comforting voice.
It was as if he were whole in body and the chaplain were in his
place. "If you say so. But there's something I want you to do for
me just in case I do go."

"What is it, Kane?" the chaplain asked. The rite of absolu-
tion came into his mind. They all came to God sooner or later.

He was a little disappointed in the answer. "I have a letter I want you to deliver for me, Father," the man said quietly. "Deliver—not mail. It's in my pocket. Get it."

The chaplain bent forward, put his hand under the blanket, felt for the letter, found it, and took it out.

"That's it, Father," said the man. "It's to a woman." He saw the look on the chaplain's face. "It's not to my mother, wife, or sweetheart, Father. They have gone before me. It's to a friend and her husband and their friend and I don't want them to get it until the war is over and they're all together." He fell silent. Thoughts were flickering through his mind.

The chaplain watched him for a few moments silently. Tiny drops of blood were falling from the man's ears, forming a large dark blob on the stretcher that kept steadily growing larger. "Don't worry about the letter, son. I'll deliver it. Is there anything else I can do?"

Only the man's eyes seemed to move. The chaplain had the impression they were laughing at him, that they read his mind and intention. "Yes, Father," said the man. "Give me a cigarette."

The chaplain stuck a cigarette in the man's mouth. The man's lips were cold and thin. He could feel them move under his fingers, say a thank you that was almost like a kiss.

He turned around to get a match from his back pocket. When he turned back the man was dead.

He had slipped from this world into the next without sound or motion. Only his eyes were open. They seemed alive with expression. The chaplain looked at them a moment. They were softer now than he had ever seen them. They were warmer now than he had ever remembered them in the living man. A veil had dropped from them.

They looked grateful.

"This chaplain had promised Frank he would deliver the letter himself. He kept his promise. He told me of Frank's wish to have you all see it when we could get together." Janet looked at her husband.

"Then that's why you didn't tell me before," Jerry said, "why you didn't tell me where you got the idea, why you only told me that the chaplain had told you of the child."

"Yes," Janet answered simply. "I wanted you both to hear it together." She went to a small cabinet in the corner of the room and took the letter from it. She came back to the center of the room and began to read from it. She spoke quietly, plainly, with a tangible expression of feeling and warmth.

"The letter is dated December 5th, 1944."

Dear Janet,

I am writing a letter I hope you will never get. It is strange to write something you know may never be delivered but it is stranger still to imagine it will be. If you get this letter I will be dead. It isn't because I have any premonition of death that I take my pen in hand but it is just because, after all, there is the possibility that I may die rather suddenly.

It seems that many years have passed since we hit the beach on D-day, but it was just last July. Since that time a lot of things began to add up in my mind and make sense. Many things have happened and there is much I want you to know and much I have to ask of you.

A long time ago Marty once compared me to Hitler. I laughed then for I didn't understand what he meant. Now I know. I learned it from living with Ruth and I learned from these last five months in Europe. I learned that you cannot live without regard for society and the so-called common man. For to live so, is to live without regard for yourself.

And I began to wonder, what it was that made me what I became. Then I realized for the first time it was from living alone. A man can live alone if he shares his rooms with twenty other humans and shares his heart with none. That was the way I had lived for the most of my life until I married Ruth.

As you know, Ruth died in childbirth. I don't think you know that the child lived. We had a son.

I hadn't thought about having children. I didn't want any. But she said, "I want your son. I want him for many reasons. Because he will be you again. And I can keep you close to me, even when you're far away. And I can give him, so giving you, all the love and care and dreams you never received.

"Give me your child, my darling, so that I can make you whole again, make you live again." All this she told me.

And when our son was born and she knew she would not live to make him whole, she whispered to me, "Don't let him down, Frankie. Give him his childhood and his dreams, let him taste the pleasures of his youth and grow into the man he could be. Give him all the things I wanted to give him."

I promised her I would.

But first I had to come home from the Army. And then when I thought that there was a chance I might not come home, I worried about keeping my promise to her, and so I ask of you to help me keep it. Take our son into your heart and home and give him your name and all the things I know you can give.

I am a fairly wealthy man. He will never lack for money. But what he will lack are things that money can't secure. These are the things that you can give him.

Don't let him grow up as I did. Sheltered and clothed and fed and cared for, and yet poorer in human qualities than the poorest of men. A man needs more than food and clothes and money to make him human. He needs love and kindness and affection.

He needs people, a family, to give him an anchor, to give him roots in the earth, in society, to teach him the true values in the world. The values that I learned from Ruth.

I took my son to the Orphanage of St. Therese and gave him into the care of Brother Bernhard. I have had letters from the good Brother that tell me little Francis is very much like me. And I am proud. Not only because he is like me, but because in him I see his mother. She looks out of his eyes, which are blue like hers. He smiles with her smile, and yet he is like me.

As you can see I have learned a great deal from Ruth. I have learned to love and that love meant giving, not taking. And I have learned that you can't give if you haven't anything to give. You have much to give. I know that, for I can remember.

Read this to Jerry and Marty when they're together, if you can. Tell them both that their friendship always was one of the brightest parts of my life. That nothing that happened has ever dimmed or caused me to lose my feeling for them. Tell them both, that I want them too, to take our son into their hearts and give him all the things I know they can give him.

Humbly I beg all of you to take my son into your home.

Help me keep my promise to Ruth.

With affection,

Frank

From eyes that were proud, Janet looked at them. A moment passed while they all were silent and looked at each other. Suddenly they smiled and magic came back into the room. It was filled with hidden charm and warmth.

Tears came into Janet's eyes as she looked at Jerry and Marty. Unconsciously she held her hands toward them. There was no need for questions.

They all knew the answer.

Harold Robbins

The World's Best Storyteller

When you enter the world of Harold Robbins, you enter a world of passion and struggle, of poverty and power, of wealth and glamour . . .

A world that spans the six continents and the inner secrets, desires and fantasies of the human mind and heart.

Every Harold Robbins bestseller is available to you from Pocket Books.

____THE ADVENTURERS 47159/$4.50
____THE BETSY 44586/$3.95
____THE CARPETBAGGERS 47984/$4.50
____THE DREAM MERCHANTS 82307/$4.50
____DREAMS DIE FIRST 44589/$3.95
____GOODBYE, JANETTE 82481/$3.95
____THE INHERITORS 44590/$3.95
____THE LONELY LADY 46475/$3.95
____MEMORIES OF ANOTHER DAY 50923/$4.50
____NEVER LOVE A STRANGER 44596/$3.95
____THE PIRATE 44592/$3.95
____79 PARK AVENUE 44593/$3.95
____SPELLBINDER 41636/$3.95
____A STONE FOR DANNY FISHER 44594/$3.95
____WHERE LOVE HAS GONE 44595/$3.95